also by vanessa zian

Dog Tags & Lace Series

Midnight to December

Ruby in July

Mine after October

March becomes Dawn

Standalone

The Lifecycle of a Crush

midnight to december

vanessa zian

Cover Design - Lori Jackson Designs
Design Concept - Willow Winters
Editing - Jacqui Muller
Proofreading - Catherine Elaine

To my clients.

Past and present, official and unofficial, in offices and front porches alike—this book is for you.

You all show me more about what it means to be beautifully human than any podcast, textbook, theory, or poem ever could. It is a privilege and honor to share a space with you, and hear you bravely share your stories.

No matter the hardship or tragedy, you are here. You survived. Know that your story is yours, and it's beautiful. You hold the power to make it so.

And to Matthew. You know why.

content notice

My books weave in subplots of trauma and may be triggering to some, but there's good reason for it. I'm all about the happily ever after, so you will absolutely get that. But my aim is to leave the reader with the ultimate narrative full of truths, no matter what the trauma. We all have experienced some at some point, whether it be "small t" or the "Big T" kind.

We learn by sharing stories. We heal by tweaking the narrative. And we soar when we can join forces and journey together. It's what I'm here for, and I'm so glad you are too.

december

· · ·

And so with December we seek to learn and reflect
Consider the passing of the months
Look into the wells and brave all that is hidden
Hidden beneath
Hidden within
December reveals if we dare let it
Preparing us to start anew...

~Raina G. Blake

prologue

. . .

Twenty-six years ago

H AD SHE KNOWN what she would endure in mere minutes, how her life would forever change, then she wouldn't have enjoyed that last car ride with her family.

Which is funny, really. We often wish we had a crystal ball. A simple spherical structure to display the images of our future with one quick command. Just imagine it...no more crippling uncertainty, no more worry of the unknown, because a preview of our future would be within our power. Anxiety is the handiwork of uncertainty, and glimpses into our future would eliminate anxiety's power.

And yet, we don't realize that every now and then, ignorance is bliss. Her bliss meant she had no idea of the events that were about to unfold, the literal turning upside down of her world.

So in that way, she was fortunate. She had no crystal ball. Instead, she had a hexagon box. And inside that hexagon box were two treasures.

She held that box to her nose and inhaled with appreciation the remnants of cinnamon and clove. It smelled just as it should, this keeper of sentiment and tenderness. James had indulged her with the purchase. Always the frugal one, he took convincing, but she knew he'd appreciate the crystals once he saw them glittering on their tree. Keepsakes. Forever to be cherished.

They drove through the tree-lined back roads with their bare remains of leaves, undressed in the aftermath of fall. The sun was low and glimmering through sporadically, a flashlight morse code popping out nonsensical messages. She closed her eyes and could still feel the sun's pulsing call through the limbs.

It was her favorite time of year, the most wonderful time indeed! And finally, finally she had something luxurious to commemorate the season. Something to show off. Little trinkets, a symbol to show her mom and all who doubted them just what she and James had accomplished.

She could hear their naysaying voices now, the scolding she was given a couple years back. *"You're not even twenty! Too young to know what love is, Lori,"* she'd heard more than once. *"You want to be tied to James forever? You don't have to go through with this pregnancy."* It would make her skin crawl, the squeeze of rage deep in her chest.

They just didn't understand the love that she and James had.

Those reservations and criticisms were buried in the past now, she reminded herself. She and James had saved for so long to be able to afford luxuries like these ornaments. The rare dinner out.

Their home.

They pinched pennies, cut coupons, looked longingly at anything deemed an unnecessary expense. Her credit card would have been her go-to, but James insisted they put it aside and save instead. Reluctantly, she did, and now she was glad her husband had the good sense to focus on the future.

Because with James's relentless financial planning, here they were now, finally able to splurge a little this Christmas. It was the first in their new home. All those longed-for clothes and shoes, lost in the matrix of budgeting, now a distant past as Lori realized she had so much more. Now they would be able to see the illumination of a fresh seven-foot Christmas tree in their living room. A matching fireplace garland adorned with silver and white and sparkle and warmth. They'd set neatly wrapped presents under the tree, with the wrapping paper in carefully selected variations of red and silver (they *had* to be all red and silver!). It was her wish, and James happily obliged.

A bump in the road jostled her out of her daydream and Lori returned her attention to the precious cargo of the small box she was holding. The ornaments felt slightly heavy in her hand, these two delicate keepsakes, one for each of their children. The crystal snowflakes had a surprising power to make Lori feel like all was right, all was complete. With the box nestled safely in the confines of her coat, she reached over and squeezed her husband's free hand. She and James had everything they ever wanted, finally. A tiny-but-perfect house, his impressive new job at an influential bank, perfect boy and girl twins (how had they gotten so lucky?!)—their little love babies, now three years old. James Junior and Raina Georgia— JJ and Reggie.

So while Lori had no crystal ball, she did have crystal snowflakes, and because of that, she believed all was right with the world.

***

Present Day
Reggie
NERVES ARE A HELL OF a thing, aren't they? In my twenty-nine years I've never been one to let myself get overly emotional, but these days that just doesn't seem to be the case. And dare I admit, I think it's a good thing.

I'm standing here, shivering and pulling my jacket tighter and I'll tell you what, I have butterflies in my stomach. It's true. I look up at the sturdy brick house, glistening with the morning's flurries and emanating December's enchantment. I hope to add a little more magic in just a few moments once I step foot upon the brilliant black and white marble floors of the house. It's been dark for far too long and we could all use a little more light.

Perhaps I'm being too harsh though, because that shadowy journey has in fact led to this moment here, led to the gift I'm about to give. A gift that has long been separated from its recipient, unjustly estranged from its rightful owner. And life is nothing if not a series of journeys, right? Some journeys are sparkly and shiny like a new piece of jewelry, and some journeys less so. I, like most, have always had a preference for the former—sparkles and sugar and spice and all that, and certainly there's nothing inherently wrong with that desire. But, my friends, we need to be honest with ourselves first. And sometimes that means facing the monsters, scary as they may be. When you face them, you can chisel away at them and suddenly the monsters become mere sweet little things, not so scary at all.

And that's when you know you've really healed.

But for now, I need to explain to you just why what I'm about to do right here, right now, why this gift is so very incredible. While I can't share the story of the other players in this journey, I can share my own. And for me, I suppose it starts in kindergarten.

You see, my first kiss was in kindergarten, on the bus ride on the way to kindergarten, to be precise. Now calm yourself, I know what you're thinking, and I assure you, it was all very darling and sweet and innocent. Really. He's always been a dear, that Joey. At the time of this kiss, he was in kindergarten too. Joey lived just a few doors down from me and I always loved playing with him. But my gosh, that kiss of his (on the cheek, because it *was* kindergarten after all), well, it caught me by surprise. I instantly jolted back, wishing with all my might I could be anywhere in the world but on that stinky bus, older kids laughing at the bold move they just witnessed at my expense.

And me? I stared at those brown seats, losing myself in the texture of the plastic-y material, the grooves a chaotic pattern mimicking the chaos of my feelings in that moment.

Now this story isn't actually about Joey entirely, because while Joey isn't the eventual love of my life, he is a guest star in many of my future awakenings. Awakenings that delighted and confused me, and taught me more than I perhaps deserved about what it means to be loved with steadfast loyalty.

But ah, what a kiss from one charmer of a boy that day on the bus.

I RECALL ONCE MY MOTHER asking me who I thought my first kiss would be (*true* first kiss, bus-ride cheek kisses aside). I was nine at the time, awkwardly aware of things like periods and bras, but feeling like a ticking time bomb wondering if, when, or how those things would happen to me. We were floating in our pool one exceptionally hot afternoon when my mother suspected that I wanted to talk.

She's always been a beauty, my mother. I can still see her there now, exquisitely glamorous in a black halter one-piece, burgundy hair tucked under a large-brimmed hat, long limbs draped over her pool float like a model on a resort ad. I was strangely quiet at that moment, and I imagine my mother knew I had something on my mind. She started off casually.

"Reggie, love." (My nickname, you should know. Short for Raina Georgia. Apparently my mother and my late father conceived my brother and me while on a road trip to the Peach State. Now how's that for creativity? But they were quite young when their love accidentally created us, bless their little hearts.) "What's good about your summer so far?" she continued.

It was August and we were already planning on back-to-school shopping soon. I remember thinking her question was odd as summer seemed to be nearing its end. But that's mom for ya, always a little quirky and just a hint off the mark.

"Hmm?" I looked at her as if I didn't hear. Not that I was being mischievous, I just heard her more outside of my mind, like a faraway voice, and needed a moment to bring myself back to the present.

"Your summer? Delightfully fabulous so far?" She's always been incredibly optimistic. The very idea that my summer could be anything but good was simply unheard of.

"Yep. Good so far," was all I could offer. I knew she wanted more from me, but I just didn't want to give it. I liked this small semblance of power I held in the presence of my whimsical mother, silly as it may be.

"Fourth grade! Your next step. Exciting you know, because you're no longer a little kid in fourth grade. It's the fourth and fifth graders that rule the school, the big kids." Oh, the glint in my mother's eyes, I could see it even through the shadow cast upon them by her sun hat. "How exciting," she said, almost to herself. I could see her slipping to being lost in thought already. I had gotten used to that about my mom by then.

I remember looking at her, my eyes and nose just above the water. Shoulders, body, chin all safely beneath the surface. Cool and fresh and weightless. I popped up just enough to respond.

"Big kid?" I asked. I remember being annoyed by that suggestion of hers, though I couldn't say why.

My mother's eyes blinked rapidly, her reverie fluttering away as she returned her attention to me. "Well, yeah, big kid. Getting crushes, having admirers, though you already have acquired a few." She smiled cheekily at this, and I couldn't help but feel a tiny blossom of pride at my young conquests. My mother knew of them all—Joey from the bus, sweet Ian who would share his candies, Caleb my betrothed (he asked! I said yes, though depending on who was nicest to me on the playground, that promise could change from day to day). I was a bit of a vixen, though I didn't know the word for it just then. To me I was just a friend to all.

I smiled and bounced a little out of the water, allowing the contrast of the cool breeze on my wet skin to meet the enveloping warmth of the sun. A combination I still love to this day.

"Yeah. I guess so," I replied, meeting her eyes and her smile. It was like we shared a little secret, she and I. A lot of my relationship with my mother had always been like that, little side glances and conspiring smirks. Mom has always had a gift for making those within her orbit feel as though they were in on something exciting together.

But as much as I liked to think my capacity for love was mine alone, I had a guess from which parent I likely acquired it. My mother had had more than one great love, after all.

"Who do you think your first kiss will be?" she asked. And there it was, my mother the romantic in full force, her agenda now clear. I went so many years seeing her as just that—a queen of hearts with an innate capacity to find love in her life. It seemed inspirational yet cryptic to me.

Despite my confusion about my mother's interest in who was kissing me, I didn't see the need to question her motives. To me it was all in good fun. I eagerly drank what she would pour into my cup. I was young with a craving to grow up and was thrilled with the idea of my first on-the-lips-kiss being on the horizon.

I answered with serious wisdom. "Well, Joey probably. If he was confident enough in kindergarten, then he would probably be confident to kiss me again."

And I was right. Kiss me again he did—if only it were as simple as that childhood love.

I digress though. Patience my friends. Ultimately my intention here is not to tell you of the innocent(-esque) pleasures of our dear Joey—oh no. What I am here to share, what you need to know about, is the roller coaster that ensued in the later days of my relationship with Joey. And how that relationship all came to a breaking point just over two years ago.

Joey had my heart, it's true. And in some ways, he always will. But my soul, my very essence of being, my flesh, my everything, well, it reluctantly belongs not to Joey, but to...hmmmmm—I'm not even sure I can say it yet. Not sure I've earned your trust yet. A girl has her secrets, you know, and likely more needs to be explained before I share mine.

So for now, we shall call our mystery man "X."

Let's begin.

july

. . .

We longed for it
And it came alas one simmering day
We ached for its heat
Its passion
Something to remind us what we live for
Why we work
All so that in July we can play

~Raina G. Blake

chapter one

. . .

Two years ago

X

THE SMALL BOX in his palm has a peculiar shape, a hexagon. The fabric on the corners is faded and worn, an indication of its age and the turbulence it has seen. A perpetual salute to the mourning of its owner. It has a right to mourn.

He holds it tight, nostalgic over all that box and its contents have seen throughout its lifespan. More than most, without a doubt. This small hexagon made of cardboard, a subtle hunter green paisley pattern on the fabric of its lid and base, that box had traveled to countries and continents your average American wouldn't dare. It had seen fires, seen death, it had even saved life. It had lived many lives.

And so had he.

He switches off the ignition and returns his attention to the box in his hand. Curls his fingers around it with a quick squeeze before adjusting in his seat. His eyes dart around the parking lot as he searches for signs of any familiar faces. None yet. He places the box in his gym bag. Reaches for the towel sitting on top, dabs the slight sweat that had formed on his temples despite the blast of cold air from the AC. Was he nervous? It was a feeling he wasn't accustomed to; he had no reason to be. Yet he can't deny a certain tingling sensation in his arms and chest at the knowledge of the encounter he is about to have. The past that is about to make its way back into his present. Anticipation is more the fitting word.

He straightens up the collar of his shirt, makes microscopic adjustments to his rolled-up sleeves, his forearms swelling beneath the fabric. Broad shouldered and lean, he had opted to dress tonight in the slim-fitted button down as opposed to shorts and a tee, though by the sights of this pub he has a distinct feeling he'll be out of place. He smirks, hell, he knows he'll be out of place here with the sheltered local townsfolk likely to call this their watering hole.

It feels odd to him to be back in his hometown after so many years. Things are different, trees larger to the point of hiding the structures behind them. New shopping centers and altered roadways have him using GPS just to get around. It barely feels like his home anymore at all. He hopes in time that will change.

He prepares to reach for his door handle, ready to go in, when he catches sight of someone walking to the front door.

It's her, he thinks. He's certain. She's taller than he remembers. She's shed the straightness of her barely developed body in exchange for subtle curves accompanied by long and lean legs.

She's making her way across the parking lot and the waves of her reddish-blonde hair confirm it's definitely Raina Blake, he knows it as he watches. He notes her elegant strides, the fabric of her slim black jeans clinging to her long legs like a union meant to be. Time stills and she moves like slow motion in his mind. He takes note of her curves, the way her stride of each step creates a shift in her ass, a delicate rounded roll of sensuality, and he realizes with mild amusement certain extremities stirring responsively in his pants. He smiles to himself, caught off guard. He can't remember the last time the mere sight of a woman in heels aroused him quite so instantaneously. At thirty-nine he had long ago gained better self-control. But then again, she's no ordinary woman, is she?

He sighs, eagerness stirring in him. He watches as her red heels bounce up the couple steps into the bar. She reaches for the door and then pauses, glancing behind her to scan the parking lot.

And that's when he finally catches a full-on glimpse of her face.

It's been years since he's seen her, and he sharply inhales at the sight. She's wearing a sleeveless black blouse, unbuttoned low. A peek of a lacy nude bra teases with purpose. Pouty red lips complete her simple color palette. Her strawberry blonde hair falls to one side, wavy and a little wild. He can't tell from here, but he knows her eyes are green with hints of blue. For a moment his mind panics that she might see him watching her. But he catches himself, remembering that chances are that she'd probably struggle to recognize him without their upcoming reintroduction.

Because she had only been a girl of sixteen when she saw him last, over a decade ago.

He breathes in deeply, then exhales with intention to collect himself. He thinks about the box in his gym bag, though for what reason he brought it here tonight he can't say. He isn't quite ready to part with it, even if it is the right thing to do. There's a time and place, and this isn't either.

All he knows at this point is that Raina Blake is no longer a girl. This girl he has thought of countless times over the years, watched from afar with an intensity and curiosity that he did not understand, a protectiveness that was visceral—this girl is now a woman. A woman with grace and poise. Curves he is shamelessly admiring.

This woman, Raina Georgia Blake, is without a doubt, connected to him. And that realization thrills and intoxicates him, even if there's no sense to be made of it.

But could she ever forgive him if she knew the truth?

chapter two

. . .

reggie

I HAVE ALWAYS loved a good dive bar. You know, the kind that affectionately calls itself a restaurant, the kind where the beer pours endlessly, the crowd is locals, the energy is escapism, and the food is fried. This particular spot here on the main street of our little town serves as a hybrid of sorts. Part dive bar on some nights, part bohemian cafe on others. Artists spilling out from their day jobs to fulfill their fantasies of avant-garde living.

Tonight, on this balmy July evening, it's the latter, and I'm sitting here at the request of a girlfriend of mine, Sarah. More an acquaintance, you could say, as we play the game of old dear friends, and it works well for us. As the bartender here, she pours me generous drinks and I return the favor with generous tips. I have no clue of her last name, Miller or Martin or something like that, but, golly, to an outsider, sweet Sarah and I could be the best of friends.

Now I sit here because she had talked me into joining in on open mic night a couple months back. A way to help stir up the Moon Lounge night life—if open mic night can in fact do that.

Her brother owns the place and they had been toying around with the idea. A couple beers in and I had offered up my minuscule poetic talents to add to the roster, a pastime I continue now and again. A fun little antidote to the mundane day to day.

So here I am on a Wednesday evening, glass of wine in hand (so much more sophisticated for a poet to be drinking wine instead of my beloved lagers), paper in the other, mic and a partially listening crowd in front of me. The obligatory bar stool beneath me, a tiny perch for which to balance and rest my weight. I hook my red heels in the bottom rung of the stool and try to ignore the little stomach flip my belly is conjuring.

Generally speaking, my pop-up poetry routines here are more funny than anything. A quip about the latest pop news, an ode to everyone's favorite bar fly regular of the joint, that kind of thing. Easy crowd pleasers as we are all looking for a laugh to momentarily hide away from our daylight troubles.

But tonight, I have something different in mind. A little something more. Where it came from and why, why now, I'm not entirely sure, but I suppose there is something in this July air. Something taking over me, or brewing inside and these words had just bubbled up and out of me a few days ago. So I abandoned my planned comic routine and thought, what the hell? Let's see if anyone even notices.

I scan the crowd, take note with relief that most of them are clinging for life to their beers and drinks, lost in whatever is showcased on the large screens adorning the walls, or perhaps discussing the philosophies of quality culture currently up for debate. Quietly and for me, safely, chattering amongst themselves.

I clear my throat, tap the mic, 1...2...3.

Armed with my paper in hand, I open my mouth to deliver my title when I see him step inside as the door closes behind him.

X.

He's walking to the bar. I see him exchange words with Sarah, see her point over to my previously occupied table where my best friend Lucy and her fiancé Justin sit waiting for me. X smiles and nods at her, and I feel a little flutter in my chest at the sight of his smile. He pushes himself off of the bar and begins walking towards our table per Sarah's instruction.

His tall body creates strides that are long and panther-like. Purposeful. Hunting, it seems. He looks oddly out of place in a bar like this where people generally stumble more often than effortlessly glide. He's neither local townie nor hipster artist, but a breed of his own. I note with admiration the way he's dressed—charcoal slacks and a crisp white button-down. It's something I admit I'm a bit of a sucker for. The young men navigating their twenties along with me don't generally dress up, but, boy, as I sit here watching X, I sure wish they would.

For some reason, my breath catches in my throat. I recognized him instantly, of course. I've known him since I was a little girl, but it's been years since I've seen him. Instinctively I look for a wedding ring, though I can't tell you why. I feel relief upon seeing none. A beautifully bare and exposed fourth finger on his left hand.

An unexpected flush comes over me. I look to my left and out the window to briefly reset before glancing back at the crowd again.

I make direct eye contact with X.

I swear he can see right to the depths of my soul, and we haven't so much as exchanged a word. But he remembers me, all right. That much is clear based on the intensity in his eyes. He clenches his jaw and casually puts his hands in his pockets.

We hold one another's gaze for a moment before he breaks the tension with a terse smile and quick nod. I try my hardest to put on a megawatt smile in return, and I go back to my task at hand. In my peripheral vision I see him shake hands with Lucy and Justin before taking his seat.

"Yes, well. Let's dabble in some poetry now, shall we?" I say, hoping my nerves aren't seeping into my voice. X makes himself comfortable, eyes held steady on me.

"This little gem of mine is called 'A Hundred and More.'" I take a deep breath, attempting to slow my fluttering little heart. I mentally prepare myself for the slow execution of my reading.

And then I begin.

"I have lived one hundred thirty-seven lives."

I look up and back at Sarah, watch as she pours a beer from the tap, glancing at me with a little smile and encouraging nod. I look back down at my paper.

"Some of which were quite short." I take another nourishing breath in. This is feeling harder to do than I thought it would.

"And ah, I too have felt that hole in my heart
In a babe's untimely passing
As such is our spiraling circle of time
Rinse and repeat, if you will."

Another quick glance up. More people are paying attention now. Watching and waiting. I avoid looking at my table of friends and X. I'm not sure I want to watch their reactions as I imagine they're surprised to hear my seriousness. I continue.

"We hate that in the flesh
So simply
Our bodily souls often are.
The sweet spot in history
Brief
A beat, only
Or maybe painfully long.
We long and belong
And it's others that suffer along with us."

Someone coughs. I hear some murmurs of politely quiet conversation, but mostly the room is hushed and listening.

"We hold and cling and beg and sing.
I too have felt the anguish in still living
Too much oxygen
When there should be none
Not enough for some."

I shift my weight around on my stool. Cross one leg over the other, re-hook the heel of my foot in the bottom rung.

"My one hundred thirty-seven lives

A gift, they say.

Gifts cost

They charge

So I pause

In a hope to flip and switch

and find

a way to take charge."

The room is now eerily quiet. I look up and feel a shift in the energy. Some quiet murmurs, some stunned eyes peer back at me.

A woman cloaked in gauzy chiffon breaks the silence. "Is that it?" she asks, not unkindly. Confusion and slight awe mix within this stranger's tender, questioning eyes.

I nod with a nervous smile and respond into the mic, "That's it, yes!" and I breathe a sigh of relief and pride. The captivation of the audience is unexpected and rather addicting.

It's X who starts clapping first. His handsome face is serious as he rises out of his chair, a move which feels dramatic in our glorified dive bar. But I'm not sure a man clapping has ever looked so sexy. *Where did* that *thought come from?* I think to myself.

A few others notice him stand and follow suit, rising and clapping too. "Yeahhhhh! That was incredible," sing some kind enthusiasts from the crowd.

The rest of the crowd seems to sigh with a little tension relief. They clap and do that snap thing which I never did understand, but I'm grateful for, nonetheless. Some give a brief little half-rise out of their chair, nodding and clapping before sitting back down because this sure as hell isn't Broadway. But X continues to stand and clap and lead the way for others in noises of praise and spirited "Wa-hoos!" His face is stern and once again, I'm captivated by the intensity in his eyes. His body language is all encouragement, but that *look*. It's something else, something darker.

I unhook my heel, uncross my legs and stand as well, a little wobbly at first. I lean down to my mic. "I really thank you all. Sarah must be killing it with the drinks tonight because I'm not sure I deserved quite so much praise!"

"Yeah, you do, Reggie!" Sarah calls from behind the bar.

"Well, I really do appreciate you bearing with me in a mini poetry adventure. Thank you." I turn to my left where our next victim stands waiting. "And next up we have the dazzling vocals of Ruby on guitar! Bring your hands together for a warm Moon Lounge welcome." I step aside with relief at having Ruby take the limelight so I can safely step off stage. I'm thankful for the wine glass in hand and take a sip, willing my heart rate to slow down.

But of course, my next steps are to the table where a certain man is sitting there waiting for what I hope is me.

chapter three

. . .

X

THE POEM IS no coincidence. He knows too well what it means, and he half wonders if she had opened her mind to the subconscious that had created it. Or does she believe it's just a random sentiment, no real meaning behind it? He sips his beer and observes that their table companions don't seem to want to broach the topic of her poem, instead opting for the safe, "So good, Reggie," from Lucy if he remembers correctly, and "Wow, I don't know how you can step up there and do that, I'd have to be drunk!" from Lucy's fiancé, whose name he realizes he has already forgotten. Justin, maybe?

So there he sits, watching more than participating in the interaction, and he feels oddly disappointed at a lack of more monumental enthusiasm in what feels to him like a big night. But then again, other than his return to town, to this crowd, it really isn't much of a big night at all.

His phone buzzes and he looks at it discreetly. One thing he can't stand is a table of people all staring at their phones and avoiding actual conversation, but he's waiting for someone. And of course, the text comes in.

J: Sorry, not gonna make it tonight, no one to cover for me. You didn't head out to the bar already, did you?

X: I did but it's fine.

J: Oh no, shit dude I'm sorry. Tell the gang to keep you entertained, don't be all stiff and weird, have a little fun

X: No idea what you're talking about, I'm the life of the party.

J: So you can teach an old dog new tricks lol

gotta go, tell everyone hi

He clears his throat before interrupting the nachos attack happening in front of him. "Just got a text from Joey, I assume you all know him?" he says to Lucy and Justin. They nod in confirmation. "Said he's not going to make it tonight."

Lucy laughs, long thin arms crossed over her chest. "Figures, we can never seem to all get together. Sorry babe," she says, turning towards her fiancé. "But at least you have a backup guy here to keep you company," and she nods in X's direction.

"Please, I'm so used to being the third wheel. Though a guy could be in worse company than gorgeous babes like you two." Justin flashes a grin to them before raising his beer in X's direction. "But thanks anyhow. Cheers man, welcome to Garden Springs."

X begins to chime in and clarify when Reggie surprises him by beating him to it. "Actually, he's originally from here," she says. "Born and raised, like us."

He watches her with curiosity. They aren't strangers to one another, it's true, but X feels surprised to hear Reggie speak about him in this way. Like she has interest in him and his life. Is it possible she feels the same pull he does? And if so, what does that mean? He shakes the thought out of his head; of course she doesn't.

"Oh no shit, really?" Justin says.

"Mmm hmm," Reggie nods. "Though it's been what, about ten years since you were last in town?" She turns her attention back towards X, an emotionless look on her face. What is she thinking about? What's behind those eyes that give nothing away? He wants the woman that was on the mini stage moments ago, sharing her words and full of soul. As she sits here now, he gets the feeling she's behind a mask, and he wants to reveal what's beneath.

X nods his head. "Ten, closer to eleven years, yeah." He can't believe how thrilled he is to hear her talking about him as if they are old friends, not just the young teenaged girl she was and late-twenties guy X was when he last left town. When he left them all behind. Logically, he realizes Joey would have told Reggie something. Reminded her of X's recent military retirement in anticipation of knowing he'd be seeing them again tonight.

But for some reason he's had this feeling of distance from her that he now recognizes is more self-induced. Does she know the whole of it? No. But that doesn't mean she has no clue who he is, of course. He turns and arranges this new concept in his mind, this idea that Reggie Blake has the sense of some established relationship with him. Maybe even remembers their past interactions, brief and far between as they were.

"Yes, ten or *eleven* years ago, as precision is clearly important to some," Reggie clarifies, looking directly at him, eyebrow raised. Is she teasing him? He laughs at her small mock, swells with a little pride at the banter in her joke at his expense. No, she is not sixteen anymore, not the girl he used to feel he needed to protect.

"Precision can be life or death, you know," X counters.

"I'd say I understand that. Probably know it better than most," Reggie says. He's taken aback at first, but she goes on. "I actually considered naming my practice 'Precision Therapy and Fitness' for a minute, but ultimately went in another direction." Again, he can't help but feel overwhelming pride in her, in this seemingly ingenue who is in fact anything but. A practice owner at just twenty-seven. That had to be unusual.

Lucy cuts in. "I'm glad you did. 'Precision' felt unnecessarily cutting somehow. 'Warrior' is much better." She turns towards X. "Speaking of, you're in the military, aren't you?" she asks. And that's when X realizes he's met Lucy before too, also years ago, though with minimal interaction. It's all coming back to him. Strange how the memories in our minds can be reorganized and catalogued—adapting and rearranging according to current circumstances.

"I was, yes. For twenty-one years. I just retired," X replies.

"You look far too young to be able to use the word 'retire.' Must be bizarre to complete a career so early on," Lucy says.

Her fiancé chimes in. "What branch?"

"Army."

"Deployed at all?"

"A few times."

"Afghanistan?"

"Correct."

"Killed anyone?"

"Justin!" Lucy slaps his shoulder. "Jesus, you're sick."

"It's a fair question," Justin grumbles. X notes the dynamic between the two, Lucy and the fiancé. She's all poised charm, he's more playful immaturity. It works for them, from what X can tell.

"From what I hear," Reggie jumps in, "you did potentially take some lives but more importantly, save some of your men too, isn't that right?" She looks at X, her jade eyes direct and focused. Challenging, even. It takes him by surprise. She has a confidence he hadn't expected. He'd noticed it earlier in her easy stride when he caught sight of her walking in. There was a self-assurance in her steps, her mannerisms, and the way she's looking at him now as she asks him such a direct question. He can't help it; he finds her sexy as hell. He knows he shouldn't, but he does.

"That's one way of looking at it. Joey may have exaggerated the experience a bit," he responds. "I was just doing my job." He hesitates, unsure exactly how else to answer, how much to share. Plenty of men love to take glory in the gorier aspects of the job, but not X. Not his style, not his game. In social settings he's usually content to be on the sidelines of the war stories, letting one of his other comrades take center stage to share an incident or two. He'll offer up an added point of view for them now and then, or play off their set ups to enhance the story teller's punch line, perhaps. But that's about it.

Reggie seems to continue studying him, waiting for him to explain more. "I was a field medic," X adds, hoping that closes out the topic. The attention makes him uncomfortable, at least in this environment with an expanded audience. If it were just Reggie, he'd feel less on guard. But talking about his experiences here now feels like a wrecking ball threatening to pummel and destroy the mood. He never was the showman type with the gift of selling a war story to make it sound thrilling and exciting. Which is one of the many reasons he'd rather stay quiet.

"So a medic in combat?" Reggie confirms.

"Yes," he replies carefully. "Though maybe not the most appropriate happy hour conversation to be had."

Reggie smiles. "Aw, now. Timing is never perfect, is it? And besides, everyone loves a good hero story." She leans forward on the table, leans on her elbows, clasps her hands beneath her chin. Lacy bra in view. God, he loves the way she talks. No pleasantries, just to the point, cutting through the fluff. He wants to hear more from her, anything at all that she has to say. She has an unruffled serenity about her. The young Reggie Blake, she's clever and confident.

Justin signals for the waiter, quickly raises his glass and gestures for another round before returning his attention to the table. "I, for one, love a good hero story."

Lucy looks at Justin with a commanding fire in her dark eyes. "Quit bullying him to spill his guts right now. He just got back to town. Give it a day or two before you bombard him. It's invasive."

"It's alright," X offers with a low raise of his hand to wave off the perceived offense. "I have a good story or two, maybe not quite hero level, but some other time for sure. Happy to share." He's hoping that settles it and they forget to ever ask him again.

Reggie leans back in her chair. "Good then. We'll hold you to it."

"Sounds like a threat," X smiles.

"Does it, now?"

"A little. I don't mind though." *Not with you, anyway.*

"Oh good, the relief I feel. Wouldn't want to shake up the big, badass hero." Reggie mocks a gesture of wiping sweat off her brow. "But I need something more than these nachos, I'm thinking fries and a terribly greasy burger. You guys?"

"You eat like a linebacker, Reggie," Lucy murmurs absently.

"I work my ass off all day with barely time to scarf down half a banana, and I'm starved by the time the day is done." She sips her wine. "A salad just won't do right now, love," she says to Lucy with a warm smile. He's loving the way she moves, the lilt in her voice. There's an enchanting appeal about her. Maybe it's the reddish blonde hair; a fiery spirit seems to emanate off her.

The lace of her bra continues to make guest appearances and X struggles to keep his eyes up. He wants to run his fingers between her skin and that lace. He tries to squeeze the image from his head, but the vision of her naked is relentless in its violation of his mind.

His thoughts wander to how she might sound when she's touched. He can imagine her in his bed. Blindfolded and spread out before him. Waiting. He'd make her wait, as he has the sense that she's one used to immediacy. He'd use a feather perhaps, to softly skirt across her ribs. Move and swirl and kiss and tease. He can imagine her soft whimpers when eager and in need.

In particular, he wants to know what she would sound like when she is close to orgasm.

And he wants to be the one to give it to her. Slow and drawn out, until she trembles from the intensity of it, barely able to stand it any longer.

Silently he curses to himself, aware of how inappropriate his thoughts are. How is she doing this to him? What's happening? He has to get a grip, but there's no way in hell he can deny his draw to her.

It can't be all in his head.

Her poem. Tonight.

Did Joey give her a heads up that X would be here tonight? Did she know she would have X's audience? Or is he a fool to think she'd have any idea or even care? No matter what, he knows his lewd thoughts of her need to stop.

"And you, hun?" His thoughts are interrupted. X looks up to find the waitress looking at him, pen and pad in hand, ready for his order.

"Me, hun?" He smiles at her and points innocently to his chest, determined to regain control. He realizes with mild embarrassment and surprise that he'd barely registered the presence of the waitress as she took everyone's orders.

"Oh, you're something," taunts Reggie. "Yes, you, *hun*. We've all ordered, though clearly your mind was elsewhere."

If she only knew.

"Right. I'll have the same as Reggie over there. The burger and fries?" He looks at her for confirmation.

"Black and blue, medium rare?" the waitress confirms.

Fitting, he thinks, smiling to himself. Yes, he has to get to know this grown-up Reggie better.

"That's the one."

chapter four

. . .

reggie

BY SOME FATE of the car ride Gods, I find myself the sole passenger in X's car at the end of the night, after the Moon Lounge. I'm intrigued by him, I admit. There's something about his demeanor, slow, like he has all the time in the world, though I know he's been through hell. I remember hearing some stories from Joey, remember the worry from everyone. We were in high school when X deployed and I was probably a little too caught up with the turmoils of how my hair looked every day to pay good enough attention to anything else, but now I'm insanely curious.

I steal a glance to my left, take in the ridges of his profile and the casual drape of his arm on the door. His other hand gently guides the steering wheel and I think about the ease he exudes so naturally. A confidence that I myself fear I'm lacking in this moment, though I'm not sure why.

"What does the poem mean to you?" X asks, interrupting my thoughts.

I shift in my seat to turn towards him, allowing myself the

briefest moment to admire his broad shoulders. "My poem? From the bar?"

"Unless you told another one tonight, then yes," he nods. "The one from the bar."

"Nope, no other poem from tonight," I say, not sure I'm loving him probing like this.

"Right. So what does it mean to you?" He challenges me with the question. His baritone voice is undeniably sexy. It unsettles me.

"Well, what did it mean to *you*?" I counter. I can't read him and I'm not used to being asked about my poems. I'm cursing myself for going the serious route in tonight's instead of my usual nonsense silly. I'm not about to open my heart up to this man.

I look around at my surroundings, try and get my bearings in this unfamiliar setting. X drives a sturdy yet luxurious SUV of some sort, black and dust-free to the point of being clinical. It pisses me off for some reason. I think about my own little car and the crumpled receipts decorating my center console. But here's this military combat vet, driving me home from my grand ole stage appearance and he spares no time in cutting right to the core of meaning and insights in my silly little poem. I just want to get home. Pretend it didn't even happen. I hadn't expected someone to actually pay attention to it, or to care enough of its meaning.

I'm waiting for X to respond and take the spotlight, but he lets my question hang. His calm demeanor has such an essence of mystery and control. I'm not used to it from other guys. I'm used to gaining the upper hand with a little flirtation and humor, but I find myself stumbling and awkward in his presence.

"You're avoiding answering me," he says. I'm taken aback, though there's no judgment in his voice from what I can tell. I look to read the profile of his face. It's chiseled with a strong jawline, angular with the exception of soft lips appearing among the early days of a stubbly beard. I study with scrutiny, fixated on catching him somehow with judgment. I have this overwhelming will to prove myself right, that he really is out to get me with his forward question of what on earth my poem meant to me. The nerve.

I reflexively tuck my hair behind my ears, hating how he seems to put me on guard. Is it his age? He's older than me, twelve years or so, but there's something else about him that makes me squirm. Only a little though, only until I figure out this power imbalance. I take a deep breath.

I go for my usual charm and disarm approach. I smile coyly and raise an eyebrow. "Now, sweetheart, I bared my soul out there with a poem. Exposed my feelings and inner thoughts. It's your turn to open up." *Sweetheart*?? That was bold. I wave my hand towards him, inviting his response. "What. Did the poem. Mean. To you?" *Please just answer.*

"No." I hate that arrogant smile on his beautiful face.

"No? Well, dear me, I don't think 'no' works as a proper answer here." I resolve to keep my guard, but admittedly it's faltering.

"No, you did not 'bare your soul' as you say. You said a beautiful poem in a tiny open mic night. At a bar in a small town full of drunks and hippies that applauded politely because you're attractive." His eyes glance over to my chest, I'm pretty sure. "But they likely have no idea what the hell you were even talking about."

Alright, yes, I'm clinging to that whole 'you're attractive' bit a little too much. Wouldn't you?

I feign a look of stunned and appalled and try to hide the actual consternation of my reaction. "First off, those bar 'drunks' as you call them are lovely people, so leave your judgment aside. We're all just trying to live our best lives, and for some that looks like companionship in a setting fit for libations."

He smiles a little, shakes his head in amusement. "Is that so?"

"Yes," I nod.

"Fine. You're right. I apologize."

"Good." *Good*. I like feeling like I'm getting to him. Or at least I hope I am.

"Well, Raina?" He glances at me with a smirk.

"Well what?"

"Is there a second off?"

Oh. Right. I clear my throat. "Yes—second off, you don't have a right to pretend you know anything about me."

He contemplates this. His slow responses are methodical and infuriating. My mind, on the other hand, works like a ping-pong table, or maybe a squash court. Is that the one where the balls go in every which direction? Bounce off of walls and all? Whatever the sport, my mind bounces around like it, and I feel a little off-kilter with his soothing inflection and controlled cadence.

His baritone voice rattles around us as he attempts to explain. "I never said I know anything about you. You jumped to that on your own. All I did was share my perception of hiding in your performance, based on *your* avoidance in my prompt to have you explain what it was about. Which was a pretty simple question." He looks pointedly at me.

I pull my eyes away from his and think about this for a moment. He has no idea what he's talking about, I wasn't hiding. I shared a poem, a *real* poem for God's sake. Where's the hiding in that?

I turn back to him. "Well, go on, Mr. All-Knowing Combat Badass. Enlighten me, tell me more about your perception then." I watch as his hand slides down the steering wheel to rest on the console between us. I feel a surprising charge at the proximity of his arm next to mine.

"Perception of you?"

"Of me, yes," I say, pulse racing a bit with that arm of his so close to my bare skin.

He sighs, collecting his thoughts, I suppose. "You put on a good show, it's true. You have a quality about you. A magnetic appeal, and you know it, I believe. You want to share things. Want to be heard, but you veil it."

"I veil it?" I stare at him skeptically, singular eyebrow raised once again. I'm genuinely intrigued now, he's not wrong, but my stomach is doing flips and betraying my will to be cool.

"Yes, you veil it. You put a little out there, like in that poem, but there's a veil over it, making it slightly inaccessible and blurry."

"Blurry?"

"Yes. Blurry."

"Well, now, spoken like a true poet," I say. He tortures me with more silence. What is going on in that beautiful head of his? "Maybe you just didn't understand the poem," I shrug, turning my attention back out the window. A swirl of trees and bushes swoosh past me. In the distance is a water tower with our town name, Garden Springs, PA. Large and proud. A sturdy anchor point to the dizzying pass of lush, unruly greenery.

"Maybe you're just telling yourself that you don't want anyone to understand it," he says.

"My oh my. Fine, I'll play along. If that's the case, if I value a little, oh I don't know, keeping things to myself, is that so bad?"

"I don't think it's a matter of good or bad."

"Meaning?" I ask, my fascination building despite myself. We're stopped at a red light. A warning sign to quit while I'm ahead, perhaps, but I can't. I find myself eager to hear what he has to say, if only so I can prove him wrong.

"Nothing's that simple, Raina."

"Sure, it is—good, bad. Right and wrong. Seems rather straightforward to me."

"Maybe you like to see things as black and white. Good or bad, right or wrong." He glances over to me. "To share or not to share," he says before looking back to the now green traffic light.

"I thought you said you weren't going to pretend to know anything about me."

"Christ. You asked, didn't you?"

I roll my eyes. "Fine. Carry on."

"You sure you can handle it?"

"Don't underestimate me."

I watch as a smile forms on his lips. It stirs an irritation in me.

"I wouldn't dare underestimate you. But the fact remains, 'baring your soul' as you say is not exactly what happened back there. I'm in no way saying that's good or bad. I just think you could be more honest with yourself about it."

I press further. "And what, dare I ask, do you suppose I'm not being honest with myself about exactly?"

"That there's hurt and suffering, and that it's hard to share our hurt. Hard to admit it even exists, because it feels weak. So we default to black and white thinking. It simplifies the messiness."

"You're saying I do that," I confirm, skepticism oozing out in my tone.

"We all do to an extent. I have too, without a doubt. Everyone likes to safely see things through the narratives we build for ourselves, and that's that. Again, simplifies things," he says.

I hate how much sense he's making, and how much I want to hear more. "When have you been known to do that, build these simple and safe narratives?"

He's quiet for a moment. Lifts his arm and rubs the stubble of his beard before dropping it back down next to me. "Do you know anything about the branches of the military?" he asks.

"I think I understand the basics, yes," I say with a hint of sarcasm.

"Well, there's a running joke that the Air Force is really the Chair Force. Us Army guys like to look down on them as having it easy. They get the nice accommodations when we get the tents. Shorter deployments to our long ones, that kind of thing."

I pinch my brows in confusion, not sure where he's going with this. "Okay," I say tentatively.

"Usually, downrange we all travel to and from our destination in jump seats on C-130's or other large cargo aircraft packed in like sardines. Not exactly luxury traveling, right?"

I nod and picture the random film scenes I've seen. Uniform-clad bodies armed and ready to fight in the green and gray land-scape of a military aircraft.

"But on my last deployment, on our way back out of there, we were picked up in Turkey by a chartered commercial airline. A group of Air Force guys, ammo troops, had already been on the aircraft when we boarded. They had been picked up earlier in Kyrgyzstan. And these guys were all in the first and business class seats, having been first on the plane.

"We're all thinking 'typical Chair Force,' right? Some of my guys were pissed, but I was trying to tell them it's all good, first come, first served. That we're all fighting the same fight, even if not everyone's out there kicking in doors. I didn't necessarily believe that though. Just trying to keep my guys in the right head space."

I bite my tongue from saying something smart like, "How noble of you," but I can't help that that's where my head went.

X continues on. "So we're piling into our coach seats, and this one Air Force guy gets up. Nudges the guy next to him and nods his head in our direction. Says he's going to the back."

"The back of the plane? Like to give you the first-class seat?"

X nods. "Yeah. Guess my guys and I looked like hell. Air Force kid saw that."

"Then what?" I ask, my interest growing. "Did you take his seat?"

"Not just his. All the Air Force guys got up and moved to the back for us. Cleared out all of first and business class, and we took over. And as much as I wanted to see them as the bad guys, the spoiled ones who did nothing, I couldn't. I knew that they too were tired and missing home and happy to be getting the hell out of there. We were all in the same fight in our own way. Maybe we didn't see the same things, but their experiences were still valid. It was harder to ignore that when someone so clearly recognized it in seeing us, make sense?"

"The pain holds the same value, it's just different."

"Exactly. My previous narrative was obliterated. It wasn't us versus them. Not one that's good, one that's bad. Not black and white. Always shades of gray in between, and more to the story." He glances back over to me. "You not wanting to share too much isn't a good or bad thing. It's just a matter of what you're ready for. Being honest about things that cause suffering can be hard; it's okay to admit that."

"Suffering," I repeat quietly. I'm not sure what to say to that. His use of the word has me feeling off, and I shift uncomfortably in my seat, the leather squeaking in a way that feels terribly amplified and unglamorous. "Suffering's a strong word," I say.

"Yeah. It is. Look, maybe I'm misreading things."

"You think?"

He raises a hand in defense. "Just making conversation here."

"Do you always dig deep when politely conversing?" I jab.

He shakes his head and smiles. "There's no winning with you, is there?" he says. I can't help but smile a little too.

"What can I say, I like to win," I say, thinking that will shut down the conversation. But X has one last point to make, apparently.

He sighs. "I can tell. It's an admirable part of your drive." I feel a squeeze of sorts in my chest at his compliment. "I just know what I've learned, and if we look at things in only one way, it's isolating. We put up our walls to protect ourselves, but it keeps people from getting in. Nothing's that simple, nothing's black and white. Those guys from the plane? The Air Force guys? Some of my closest friends now, even scattered across the world as we are. We didn't get there by snapping judgments on who had it worse; we got there by asking questions. Listening to the other person's experience. Making space for that suffering instead of framing it in a 'who's a bigger badass' pissing match."

All I can do is nod. I see what he's getting at—connection through facing our hurt—I just don't like it. It doesn't sit well with me somehow, though I can't pinpoint why. The rest of our drive continues in silence, with that last line of his sitting heavy in the cabin space of his car. *Making space for suffering.*

Eventually we pull onto my street, and I point to my driveway. "Right here, that's me."

X slows down the car as he nears my house. "Listen," he starts, and I brace myself. "I apologize if I offended you. That was not my intention," he says to my surprise. It's easier when I'm annoyed by him. This kindness thing feels a little too warm for my liking.

He parks the car and turns his wide shoulders towards me as best as he can within the confines of his seat, casually resting his elbow on the steering wheel. He's tall, over six feet, a contrast to my five-foot-five height, and his body seems possessing in this space. I glance down and note his muscular thighs, and his bulge under the charcoal fabric of his slacks. I look back up, see the throb of his pulse on his neck. Hear the soft hum of an unfamiliar song on the radio. He smells like fresh ocean and salt, his cologne distracting. My strange flutter of attraction to him is throwing me off guard, he makes a couple wise points and I'm suddenly putty around him.

I brave meeting his eyes, and to my surprise, I laugh out loud, just a little at first but soon big belly laughs are overtaking my body, and I struggle to stop. Don't you just hate that? Hate when emotion bubbles up in innocuous laughter to the point of being a little out of control? But there it is.

"What's so funny?" he says, rubbing his hand over his chin, a quizzical look in his amber eyes.

I wave a hand to dismiss him. "I don't even know. But I'm not easily offended, I can tell you that."

"Okay?"

"Especially by men I haven't seen in a hundred years..."

"A hundred years like the line in your poem," he adds with a smug smile. Damn, he's sexy.

"Yes! Yes, well done. Like my poem. That's right." My laughter continues, with a twinge of sadness.

My poem. He really listened to it, which scares me a little. Does he even know my story? I feel exposed and I'm not liking it. Too much grief to put out there, and for what? Despite his whole sharing-space-for-suffering and all that nonsense, I know that the past is over. No sense in dwelling on it. I internally attempt to shove down the threat of flashback images, my late twin brother JJ unwelcome in my mind at this moment. I work to push down the emotions or whatever this feeling is bubbling in my belly, my chest.

I have to get ahold of myself, this is not me. Not my thing, the drama of big and open feelings.

Apparently, it's evident to him that I'm feeling something strange in this bizarre moment of a simple car ride. "Are you alright?" He gently places his hand on my elbow, resting on the center console. I jolt back in surprise. He just as suddenly pulls his hand back. "Jesus, I'm sorry," his low voice says. "You just looked like you needed a..."

"A what?"

"I don't know, something." He swears softly again and turns forward, eyes held straight ahead.

"I can't...! Oh my God, I can't even." I continue to laugh, tears pricking my eyes. I feel absurdly on the verge of full-blown sobs. Hysterical laughter threatening to turn to hysterical tears. This is usually how it happens for me, the rare time I allow emotions to escape. Always out of the blue and too big to capture properly. I guess that had been one hell of a poem. I silently curse myself for using it for tonight's performance.

I have to get out of this car. I reach for the passenger door handle, feigning casual ambivalence while really trying desperately to get the hell out of the constriction evoked by his damn presence. I pull the contraption and use the action as a desperate momentary distraction from the well of emotions.

I take in a deep breath, hold it for a moment, and release. I nod once, willing composure into existence.

"Well. That was fun," I say brightly with a smile I imagine doesn't quite reach my eyes. "Thanks for the ride." I stare back again at the pulse on his neck and feel oddly turned on by the little stubble from his beard. He has some gray in there, but not much. Just enough to be interesting and distinguished. Worldly, even. The hair on his head mostly remains warm brown and impeccably effortless looking. He probably woke up, ran a hand through it and left the house, the prick. Why am I so angry with him? The wine is having the opposite effect on me tonight, I figure. I quickly calculate for the next full moon, hearing my mother's voice in my head as she attributes most any anomaly to the moon.

Lord, if this gentleman by my side had any idea of what happens in my whirlwind of a brain.

Then again, I get the feeling he does.

And then that impulsive nature in me takes over—I lean over and kiss his cheek. I don't know why; it's a forward move, too intimate given the setting, the person, the confines of his car. But it feels like the most natural thing in the world somehow. Is this a normal gesture? If this were, oh I don't know, somebody's Aunt Sally, would I lean over to give a kiss on the cheek?

No matter, here I am kissing it, and I'm satisfied by the feel of his stubble on my lips, charged and mildly electric. His cologne intensifies the experience. For an insane moment I have the urge to move my lips to his, wrap my arms around his neck, throw myself towards him as close as the center console could possibly let me, chest meeting chest.

Which would be incredibly wrong, obviously. I instead opt for just a little neck caress with my right hand. A little tease of a gesture, completely beyond my control.

I want him to want me.

Yes. The thought takes me by surprise, but it's true.

My lips rest a beat too long on his stubbly cheek, with my hand on his neck, thumb ever so slightly caressing the stubble on the other side of his face. And then I pull back. My chest and belly are tight with some incomprehensible need erupting from within. I want more.

"Thank you, Raina. For a beautiful poem." His voice is hoarse, I take note with mild satisfaction. If I'm not mistaken, I can see the desire in his eyes as he stares into mine. *God, I hate myself for this insanity.*

In mere moments, I went from desperately trying to get out of his car to feeling like I never want to leave this space with him. I place my hand on his chest, dare to look deeper into his eyes. His button-down shirt is surprisingly soft, a stark contrast to the hardness of his chest. Touching this man is a bad idea, I can see that now. It charges something between us, but it's too late.

I let my hand slowly slide down his chest, letting it come to rest just above his waist, going against my desire to continue. "Call me Reggie, *hun.*" I blink slowly and heavily. Seductively, with any luck, and add a little smile for full effect.

Reluctantly, I turn away and hop out. Close the car door and walk inside, thanking God he doesn't try and be a gentleman and walk me to my door. I'm not sure I could stop myself from actually kissing him if he did, and the shame of these thoughts doesn't seem to be enough to control my instinct, my need to touch him. *What the hell is happening to me?*

And fuck if that isn't so incredibly immoral, I think to myself as I hear the purr of his engine slowly quiet with increasing distance down the street. Immoral and wrong, given who he is.

RED OVEN MITT IN HIS left hand, Joey grasps the handle of the cast iron skillet as I look on from my seat at the small kitchen island. He stirs with flair with his right, the concoction of a stir fry at his carefree mercy. He grins at me, clearly pleased with the sizzle of the shrimp and veggies. The man creates a dance over the stove, and I watch with admiration, safely away from the fiesta. Beer in hand, I'm exactly where I love to be on any given evening.

I've resolved to get X out of my head and shake off the odd

experience of the other night. It was a fluke, that's all. He whirled into town, tried to make small talk about my poem as he kindly gave me a ride home, nothing more. Nothing.

My cheek kiss could have been considered normal, I tell myself. I kiss the cheeks of loved ones all the time in greeting. Sure, maybe that one was a little odd given its beat-too-long timing, but maybe he'll blame himself for that. Right? Right.

Surely X felt badly for probing. Surely he knew that the polite thing to do would be keep things neatly zipped up. Key locked away.

Surely I was imagining this thing between us and he doesn't actually care a thing about me, as I confusingly both want him to and don't want him to.

I return my attention to the actual man of mine in front of me. Shake off my thoughts of X. I admire Joey standing there in his navy joggers ("yoggers," as I often tease him) hung low on his hips, happy trail just above the surface. Bare chested with courage over the gas stove, claiming he's still hot from his workout. (Let's be honest though, we both know he's showing off for me.) I know pops of burning oil sear his exposed skin now and then, but he looks so at ease and unaware, grinning with pure joy. The boy can cook, there is no denying that. Joey, my sweet Joey, is a man of many talents, and cooking with a smile is one of them.

He can make damn near anything feel fun.

"So, my best gal," he turns to the mini kitchen island stool I occupy and offers me a spoonful of succulent shrimp. I greedily oblige, open my mouth and moan as the flavors join forces on my tongue. I can't help the moaning that continues to follow. "And? What do you think?" His dark lashes curl so perfectly over his dark eyes. I can see the pride in his dimples.

"I think I didn't know shrimp could have so much flavor, babe."

"Aw, well, shucks. You know just how to make a man feel good about himself." He turns back around to the stove and dips a finger in the sauce, sucks it with a critical and concentrated furrow of the brow, nods once in silent affirmation. "Yup, it's good. It's nothing special, really. Just the Thai peanut sauce I've done before, remember?"

"I remember," I murmur as my mind wanders back to the first time he used Thai sauce in a dish to surprise me. We stood at the stove and ate dinner right out of the pan that night.

"It's all about the fresh ginger and cilantro. Only fresh," he declares with authority as he turns back to the stove.

I love to watch Joey work in the kitchen, it's where he's most happy. Truth be told, Joey is happy almost anywhere, but the kitchen is where his real skills take center stage. Lucky for him he's naturally slim, or he'd be the size of his apartment. And lucky for me he lifts with the diligence of any gym rat, so that his shoulders nearly *are* the size of his apartment.

"Can I help with anything?" We both know the answer to my pointless question.

"I wouldn't let you if you tried," he teases. I watch his muscles ripple and roll as he works. His shoulders and back move rhythmically with his swaying hips. Like I said, a dance.

"How did it go the other night?" he asks.

"Hmm, other night?" I'm too busy admiring his bare back. With Armenian roots on his mother's side, and Italian on his father's, Joey Conti Jr. has a naturally bronzed body, his tan even more enhanced currently thanks to our recent beach excursions.

"Yeah, poetry night. My mom says she wants to go the next time you do one."

"She does? Oh, I love that woman," I gush, flattered at her interest and support. Joey's mom, Isabella, is one of those women that would probably be terrifying if I hadn't known her most of my life. She's a stunning woman even through middle-aged crinkles and the gray streaks that accompany her dark hair. Polar opposite to the whimsical nature of my own mother, Isabella has always had a no-nonsense approach that resonates with me. And an innate ability to be a kind of mentor to damn near everyone blessed to be in her circle.

"She loves you too," Joey says with a grin. He walks towards me and grabs my nearly empty beer bottle. "I'm sorry I couldn't make it though," he says, dumping the remaining contents of my beer into the sink. Without asking he grabs two more from the fridge, pops open the tops and settles mine in front of me.

"But how did it go?" He lifts his beer towards mine. "Cheers," he salutes. We clink and I use the sip time to contemplate my answer.

"Good," is all I can come up with, though I know he will want more.

"Good?" he asks predictably.

"Yes," I nod. "Good. Really good," I add, hoping he'll just be happy for me and let it go.

"The beer or the poetry night?" He leans toward me with his inquiry, a look on his face that's probing but playful.

"Both." Truth is I'm nervous to say more, scared I'll blurt out all my wicked thoughts of X.

"Gee, Redge, for a poet you don't have much to say about it," Joey winks at me.

I smile. And then instantly my mind betrays me once again and flashes to an image of me straddling X in the car, imagining what would have happened if I had given in to primal urge and instinct and grabbed his collar and took his mouth to mine. *What is wrong with me, where are these thoughts coming from?*

Thankfully Joey is back at his work, squatting slightly and spooning the contents of the stir fry onto his white square plates with care. He will no doubt be opening his own restaurant by the time he's thirty, if not sooner, and he takes dinner presentation very seriously. Probably one of the only things he takes seriously.

Other than me, of course.

"I take it you had a good reading then, right?"

"It was a good reading, yes." I sip my beer again, willing myself to stop the unfaithful thoughts of X and his car. His stubble. His stubble under my fingertips. The way he talks to me like he knows me. His ocean and salt smell. His chest. His chest under my hand. God, I'm shameful. Shameful and confused.

I mean here I am, sitting in this darling little apartment with my darling little boyfriend that has been begging for us to move in together. My Joey, my first love. My only love, really. He's easy and confident and sexy and can cook, for God's sake. What more could I want? I blame Disney. That has to be it. Disney has fucked me up and so the good and easy is just not enough for me, apparently. I want drama and magic carpet rides and who knows what else.

And of course, there is X.

God, the smoldering X. The silent and inaccessible X. He intrigues me and I haven't been able to get him out of my mind since Wednesday night. Am I just bored? Is that it, I have it too good? Have to self-sabotage? I loathe myself and my passions, but here they are.

I need something stronger than this beer.

As if on cue, I look up to find Joey staring at my cleavage, my breasts popping out with pillowed perfection in my square-necked beige top. He licks his lips and raises an eyebrow. I note his beautiful bare chest, his low sweatpants teasing what is just beneath, his bulge showing through. He tucks my hair behind my ear. Looks expectantly into my eyes.

"Cooking gets you all hot and bothered, doesn't it?" I look into his dark eyes as he studies me like he wants to devour me. I need to let him devour me. Maybe that's just the answer here. Work schedules have kept Joey and I apart for too long and I'm insanely frisky to the point of letting myself be turned on by the forbidden fruits of another man.

"I'm saying, fuck dinner. It can wait," he says with a wolfish grin, framed by those dimples of his.

"Oh my, you are proud of your work tonight," I tease. Good. This is what I need.

He leans down and with one swift move, brings his hand down my left breast under my shirt and bra, cupping the rounded form. My nipple springs free and he wastes no time leaning down and ravishing. His mouth is warm and enticing. I throw my head back and groan, gripping the hard edges of the bar stool. Forcing myself to be present in this moment with him, and not elsewhere on a certain other man.

Amber eyes and ocean and salt.

No!

Be here, Reggie, I tell myself. Joey. Joey. Joey's skin. Joey's shoulders. Joey's tongue.

Joey. Not X.

X and his gravelly voice.

"You smell so good, I've missed you all week." Joey's released my nipple and is kissing my neck, my jaw now.

I spring my eyes open and will myself to focus on the beautiful man here with me, showering me with all the love in the world.

I don't deserve him.

"I fucking worship you." See? He worships me. Me. Yes, my darling Joey. I love him, I really do. This is my man. This is what's real.

I open my legs to wrap around Joey's hips, and he uses his free hand to shift the barstool closer to him. It's one thing I have always loved about Joey. He knows what he wants and goes for it. Always. And I have a swollen ego as a result of how directly he has always wanted me.

I'm so unworthy.

He returns to my nipple and bites, rolling it between his teeth. Pain and pleasure snap me out of my intruding thoughts, and I grab the waist band of his pants. I can do this. I know this. He sucks and tugs, and moves to my other breast to free it next. His tongue circles and rounds my nipple, and I feel the pleasure rippling through me. I focus on it. Focus on the ache and need deep in my belly.

For this man right here.

Here.

"You're so fucking sexy, Redge." Joey pulls my hair and tugs my head back, greedily sucking on my neck, that sweet sensitive spot I love. I moan and push my hand down his pants. He wears no underwear, as is his style, and his cock springs free with ease. My cock. A cock I have known and loved for so many years. I stroke slowly and his dancing tongue continues on my neck. He groans, and I feel the wet tip of his dick under my thumb. Yes, this is what I want. Right here in the palm of my hand.

"Mmmm, I love it when you cook. It gets you going, doesn't it?"

He abandons my neck and growls at me with a grin. "Shhh, no more talking." He tugs on my shirt and yanks it down to my waist, allowing my already spilled out chest to be fully free. I will his cock closer to me, hot with the frustration of the fabric of my slacks in the way.

He grabs my ass and yanks me off his bar stool. Pushes my pants down, tugging with a careless aggression that I love. Joey likes it quick and rough, as do I. Quick and dirty and to the point, wasting no time. I like that. It's efficient.

More than efficient, it's hot.

He turns me around and pushes my shoulders down towards the bar stool. My ass lays bare and exposed to him, my pants only halfway down my legs. I steady myself with my forearms on the stool. Slowly he brings one hand down my spine, the only slow movement he's made so far. *What would it be like to slow things down?*

He drops and kisses each ass cheek gently, then bites the left side. I cry out, desperate for the contact again, desperate for his touch. Desperate to keep my spiraling mind in this moment.

Joey's touch.

Here. Now.

He reaches under my ass, between my legs, runs his fingers up and down. "I love when you're so fucking wet for me. I fucking can't stand it." He rubs and circles and dips a finger in and out.

"I thought you said no more talking?" I breathe.

"I did," he groans between kisses to my back.

"Proud of yourself, are we?" I'm going for coy, but it comes out more as a whisper.

"Are you ready for me?"

"Fuck yes, Joey." I barely can get the words out. I'm here now. Yes, Joey is what I want. "Now," I whimper.

He slams into me. I steady myself once again on the bar stool as pain and pleasure mix with the feel of him inside me. He grabs my hair, yanks my head back as he begins his thrusts. His hand moves around to stroke me from the front, and I move in rhythm, arching my back and loving the inescapable tug of my head pulled back, forcing my gaze toward the ceiling.

X behind me, filling me.

No! No, it's Joey.

But you want X, admit it.

X.

My pleasure is rising and rising, and I can't help but go with the thoughts accelerating it.

> *X...xxxxx*
> *xxxxxx*
> *xx*

My climax comes quickly and shamefully, thoughts of X winning their way. Joey follows suit in a shudder. He squeezes my hips with one last deep thrust in, and then slowly withdraws. I feel his lips, tender once again, to give the top of my ass one last kiss.

He grabs a napkin from the basket in the center of the island, and wipes down his cock briefly before effortlessly popping it back in his sweatpants. I stand up, a little dizzy. He hands me a napkin as well and I clean myself up. Lift my pants, tuck my breasts back in my bra and attempt to compose myself.

My thoughts are that of a cheater.

Joey grins at me. "Shall we eat?"

I've lost my appetite. Which would probably kill him to hear that more than it would my reckless little cheating thoughts. And I could never break Joey's heart, so I reply with the best response possible. "Well, yeah, I'm starving now." I'm rewarded with his wink.

As we eat, I force myself to be present, and decide once and for all that I will not, will *not* allow myself another thought of X.

chapter five

· · ·

Twenty-four years ago

lori

HER FEET ACHED, and she was sticky with sweat and cheap beer. Forcing herself to look anywhere but the swanky LED clock, she wiped down the bar for the thousandth time that night and scanned the faces of her customers.

This was never Lori's dream, standing here hustling and plastering on a smile, serving drinks and foolish pleasantries and whatever else the job demanded. However, the distraction was in fact a relief from the pain of her broken heart, she had to admit. And thankfully she knew how to use her looks to her advantage.

With her best mask on, Lori had shown up to the place last year, armed with a low-cut top and her million-dollar smile. Her mission was simple: if she was going to be serving drinks, it'd be some place where the tips were meant to brag, and the customers had egos she could stroke. Her plan worked, and she landed a job at an upscale restaurant/bar just outside the city, a choice spot for business meetings and happy hour high fives. It meant she could look forward to a decent cash takeaway at the end of the night. She needed the money and hated with all her might having to count on her mother.

But it's where she was now. A single mom, broken-hearted and all alone.

Sweltering and eager for cool weather as she was, Lori knew that summer would be over in a mere flash. The money would be better in the fall when the usual suspects returned from the beach getaways, tanned and glorious and hungry for their evening happy hours. They would share their tales with her and politely ask if she had done anything exciting this summer. Maybe she'd fabricate a getaway of her own—a mountain retreat in the most darling little cabin! Oh, you should see this tiny little piece of heaven, hidden away in the depths of the forest, waiting to enchant! Lori had a vivid imagination, and the fantasy lie was tempting to share.

More often than not though, when her customers did ask about her life, and when she was feeling particularly depressed and miserable, she would tell them the truth— *"No fun plans for me. I'm a widow with a kid."* The looks on their shocked faces would amuse her. *"How terrifying! A widow so young?"* they'd say. And she'd go on in her usual elevator speech to lifelessly explain the tragic car accident that happened year before last, when she lost her husband and three-year-old son, and the customers would feign genuine concern and offer up a big fat tip.

She hated that she felt like she deserved that tip. What a measly repair attempt to her broken heart.

But she'd take what she could get.

Every now and then she'd have someone recall the incident. Lori hated that more than anything, hated that strangers felt like they knew her, all from a sad little newspaper blurb and whispers around town. *"Right! Yes of course! Christmas time, a mystery cause, or an ice patch or something, wasn't it? Flipped the car right on its driver's side?"* She'd play along, leaning into this strange new role of hers as grieving widow and mother. And she'd grace them with a mournful nod as they continued on. *"My God, I remember that and remember thinking how terrible for that poor surviving young mother and her little girl, that was you?"* Lori would slip into the facade of this role as properly as she could. They wanted tragedy and grief? She'd give it to them for all it was worth.

Until her shoulders would tense up, a warning sign that she could chatter on not a second more. That's when she'd have to fight back vomit and the instantaneous flashback of being on the side of the road that day.

The cold pavement. The fuzzy blur as she slowly regained consciousness. Barely aware of the hysterical Reggie in her arms, ambulance cries off in the distance. Some stranger helping her. No idea what happened and the hell her world had just entered. No idea yet that her boys, the two men in her life were—

She couldn't even say it. Couldn't say the accurate words to summarize her life without them.

"No longer with us," was usually the best she would muster up, but Lori knew it was doing her boys a disservice to not say it like it was. Yet she just couldn't bear to get the words out.

How many nights had she spent crying in bed with Reggie? She knew she should be strong for her. Strong for her precious little girl, her only thing left to care about in this world.

But the depression was stronger. Much stronger. A lead blanket, thick and heavy, on top of her, suffocating her with its demons. Its threats, its blackness, daring her to even attempt any semblance of joy. Her tears were her good days. It was the numbness that was worse. And Lori's depression was threatening to kill her and her daughter.

Lori did what she knew she had to do—she had her mother come. It wasn't the best choice, different as Lori and Kathryn were, but it was the only way she was going to survive. Plus, she needed her mom's help for childcare. Having moved away from their home town for James's new job, Lori had only acquaintances nearby. Forced friendships at best, none of which she trusted, none of which could aid in her crippling loneliness. She still found herself reaching for James in bed at night, or calling for him to check on a mysterious scratch she'd find on Reggie, consumed with worry and eager for his opinion, only to realize with a stab to her heart that the man she had come to depend on for comfort and support was now reduced to a whisper of her past. A phantom she had started to wonder was ever even real to begin with, or a fairytale dream concocted in her over-imaginative mind.

Then there would be the dress she couldn't fully zip on her own, or the jar that proved to be beyond her strength. Moments later she'd find the jar mysteriously on the floor by her feet, a shattered mess with its gory contents smearing down the adjacent wall, no recollection at having been hurled by Lori's very own hands.

She was drowning in her tragedy and needed her mother's help. There was no other way.

Her mother tried to get Lori to take the pills, the "daily dose of forced optimism," as Lori liked to call them. But at that time Lori wanted to feel the pain. She craved the anguish. It was the only thing that felt right. For to survive without James and JJ, and to feel happiness—well, that seemed the most tragic thing of all.

The clattering sound of a dropped dish from the kitchen beyond brought Lori's attention back to her current reality. She looked at the clock—almost midnight and time to go home. She wished she could blink and have it be past December 11th already, as the pain in the months leading up to the anniversary of her hell was almost worse than the anniversary day itself. She learned that last year.

But then again, her little Reggie would start kindergarten in the fall, and she wanted to attempt to cling to these next few weeks she had left with her. Lori's mother warned her that when your baby starts kindergarten, time supercharges forward and takes your breath away.

Her heart ached right along with her feet at the thought.

"Incoming," her coworker Isaac warned. "That table over there, the suits getting ready to head out? They were eyeing you up and I think one of them is heading this way."

Lori dared a peek.

"Ooo yeah, he's a silver fox. Rich, too, from the likes of his Rolex," Isaac whistled.

Lori swatted his shoulder. "Then you take him."

"Nah, not my type. Too 'green flag' for me. I prefer the starving artists with the repressed childhood trauma and a painkiller addiction."

"You're sick."

"The heart wants what the heart wants," Isaac shrugged. "Now pull down that V-neck some. You're beautiful, take advantage for fuck's sake."

"Shhh, he's coming up," Lori mumbled out the side of her mouth. Her heart started unexpectedly galloping, a ticking bomb in her chest. Isaac scurried away to leave Lori on her own. She continued her tasks, scrubbing and cleaning and erasing the soils, willing the actions to erase the soils of her mind. She was sick of them.

"Is it too late for a drink, gorgeous?" Lori looked up to the mass of the man of Isaac's warning. Reasonably handsome, pale gray suit that had to be custom to stretch over his boulder of a chest. No tie, first couple buttons undone. He looked about mid to late forties. Definite air of arrogance that she found attractive. He made her heart flutter. Lori was surprised by her attraction to him, given he might possibly be twice her age.

"We close at midnight, so you're a little late," she said.

Gray Suit leaned casually on the bar. "Perfect then. Right on time, just under the wire." He grinned. He had a handsome smile that seemed to say, "I've got a secret." Lori kind of wanted to know what it was.

She attempted a smile in return. Gray Suit had something wickedly fun about him, like he hadn't a care in the world. Lori longed to not have a care in the world too. He certainly had a confidence to him that she wasn't used to. She tucked a loose strand of hair behind her ear. "I can't say that 'just under the wire' is right on time."

"Ah, you caught on to that, huh? Fair enough," he said, slapping his hand on the bar before pulling away. Lori's knee-jerk disappointment surprised her.

But then Gray Suit turned and leaned his forearms on the sleek mahogany again. "But you know what? Was hoping you'd maybe make an exception. Just finished a meeting and need a celebratory drink." Gray Suit leaned forward even further. "And you might be the perfect company to have while I do." He gave Lori a conspiratorial wink. She studied his face, clean-shaven with some fine wrinkles that added to his charm.

"Oh yeah? How's that?" she countered as she resumed her clean up. *Please tell me something sweet,* she thought. *Tell me I'm pretty, I'm lovely, I'm the moon and the stars and there's a dream for me.*

Tell me, tell me, tell me, tell me...

"Wish I knew how to describe it. There's something about you. Noticed it as soon as I walked in."

Tell me, tell me what it is.

Lori's words betrayed her thoughts, though, and she blurted out, "Exhaustion?" She dropped her rag and grabbed her water bottle, taking a long swig while meeting Gray Suit's gaze. She screwed the cap back on the bottle. "Delirium?" *Stop it!* she thought. *That's not sexy or cute.*

He leaned back. "Aw, now I feel bad. I'm bothering you." He gave her a genuine look of apology with hands up in the air in defeat. "Didn't mean to be a burden."

Lori sighed. She was being a bitch and that wasn't like her. It saddened her to realize it. The Lori pre-accident was all bubbles and sugar, a playful young woman who found joy in everything. Rarely said no even when she should, and certainly didn't let opportunities slip by.

She wanted that Lori back. "You're not bothering me," she said. "I'll get you a drink. What'll it be?"

"You sure?"

She dug deep to find her best smile. "Yes, yes, I'm sure."

"Good. One condition though." He held up a finger.

"Oh? Now there's a condition?" *You want to take me home with you? Please take me home with you.*

"Makes it more fun."

She raised an eyebrow. "Let me guess, you want to buy me a drink too?"

"No, but I'm guessing you get that a lot from other guys, huh?"

Lori laughed. "Oh yeah, they do try." Though up until now she had never cared to indulge them beyond the hours of her shift.

But she found that she was drawn to Gray Suit. He had style and wasn't nearly as obnoxious as the usual crowd here that tried to hit on her.

And he could distract from the pain. The torn-out pieces of her heart. JJ, her baby boy.

And her James...

Gray Suit rested his chin between his index finger and thumb. "Lori, can you really blame them?"

"How do you know my—"

"Name?" He pointed to her water bottle. "You have it written on there. I can read. Figured you wouldn't be drinking someone else's, little lady."

Embarrassed, she looked down at her dirty sneakers, covered her face with her hands. "Uggh, right. My water bottle, of course."

"Alright, alright. I can take a hint. You're thinking 'get this guy outta here.'"

"That's not what I'm thinking."

"No? What are you thinking then?"

That I'm nothing without my James and my JJ. "I'm thinking I want to know what this other condition is so that I can hurry up and get you your drink and then close up shop here." *What, no!*

"So I was right then, you are thinking about how to get me out of here," he challenged, making no attempt to hide the dejection from his handsome face.

She shrugged and adjusted her shoulders in an attempt to regain her posture. The push and pull in her brain were threatening to unravel her. She had a chance here. An older, suave and sexy gentleman that seemed to find something special in her.

Lori needed this.

It had been so long since she actually had the desire to flirt. She felt like she was riding a bike for the first time in years. But this was different. This was riding a bike up the side of a mountain, fighting gravity from yanking her back down with every push of the pedals. *Try. Just try, Lori.*

You can't be sad forever.

With Herculean effort she smiled again and met his eyes. "Forgive me, I'm just tired and unnecessarily cranky." She touched her chin to one shoulder in what she hoped was an adorable half shrug. "But I would love your company. What can I get you?"

"Tell you what, beautiful. Forget the drink and I'll get out of your hair, though here's my payment for your troubles since I know I slowed you down." He slipped over what appeared to be a twenty and a grenade to her infinitesimal moment of hope.

"That's really not necessary." They locked eyes. Lori noticed his were a startling ice blue.

"It's perfect, because a drink is too temporary." He continued to meet her gaze, unwavering.

"Too temporary?"

"Yeah. One drink with you I'm pretty sure would be a tease. I'd only want more time."

She felt her cheeks flush, flattered. A little swell of ego was making its way up to her head. Could she actually like this guy? Gray Suit businessman guy? He had to be at least fifteen, maybe twenty years older than she was. But there was something undeniably sexy about his easy charm. *You can do this,* she thought.

He continued, "My condition was going to be that you give me your number."

And there it was. Words she was hoping to hear.

She gave it to him.

SOMETIMES WHEN YOU KNOW, YOU know. And for Lori, that meant knowing that Richard Meyers (as Gray Suit's name turned out to be), was going to be her next husband.

On their first date, he took her to an upscale restaurant owned by a friend of his. They were given celebrity treatment, seemed to sample every item on the menu, tasted wines Lori pretended to know anything about. She felt like a movie star, red carpet rolled out for her.

Date two he whisked her away on a jet for a show in New York. The latest Broadway hit, with backstage passes where she acquired autographs on her playbill, feeling yet again like a star by proximity. An actress in her very own performance of a life unmarked by tragedy.

Date three was a weekend at Richard's beach house, (though they saw little of the actual beach). Lori diligently called her mother every night she was away, committed to checking in on her Reggie, and Richard would remark on the incredible mother Lori so clearly was. His own children were nearly grown, with little involvement in his life thanks to his ex-wife's attempts to alienate them from their father. He'd tell Lori she was healing his own broken heart, and Lori knew in her bones he was healing hers.

James would attempt to infiltrate her thoughts, it's true. Lori pushed down with force. Easier to do when the distraction was as intense as Richard.

Richard was high-octane fuel. His presence had an energy that swallowed her up with perfection. Everything he did had a lightning speed to it. If he had an idea, no matter how random or impulsive, he went with it. Always on the move, always onto the next adventure. Unstoppable in his vigor and power. She struggled to match his energy at first. But she quickly learned to let go and fly along with it.

By date number seven, Lori was pretty sure she was in love.

They were tangled in Richard's bed sheets. Lori was running her fingers through the sprinkle of hair on Richard's chest. She watched as his chest rose and fell beneath her hand, the essence of life steady under her palm. She noticed the little hook in his nose, more prominent now as she stared at him from his profile. She found it sexy as hell, a balance from his otherwise perfect everything.

"What are you thinking?" she had asked.

"I'm thinking that if you keep taking up all of my time, I'm going to lose my top accounts and go broke."

She slapped his chest playfully. "You will not."

"Careful with that wickedness. Might have to punish you." He grabbed her wrists, hurled himself on top of her as he rolled her on her back. She loved the power he possessed. Craved his dominance. A dopamine hit she couldn't get enough of. The antidote to her sadness. Lori was coming back to life, and Richard was the key.

"I won't mind," she said smiling up at him. His frame towered over her, his fingers wrapped tightly around her wrists as he held them up above her head. Her naked breasts lay spread along her ribcage, nipples swollen from previous possession by Richard's mouth. She felt raw and exposed to him and deliciously vulnerable. It thrilled her.

"Watch it with that attitude, little lady. You know what you do to me." He smiled with a mischievous glint in his eyes. Icy blue usually but deepening in color as he looked down at her.

Lori giggled up at him, and with lightning quickness, snatched her wrists from his grasp and crawled out from under him.

Richard played right along, chasing after her. "Oh, you better get back here, little lady." That had become his favorite phrase to use with her, and she ate it up like a waffle cone of vanilla on a hot summer's day.

She crawled her way to the side of the bed before tumbling over the edge and onto the floor, palms just barely catching her. Richard snatched at one of her ankles, still dangling on the bed. But she wriggled free from that grasp as well. "You gotta be faster than that," she called after him as she crawled away on the floor. The carpet scratched at her bruised knees, but the pain barely even registered for her. She was the mouse, Richard the cat, and this chase her new favorite form of escape.

She rose to a stand and ran across his bedroom and down the little hallway that led to the master bathroom. Her feet touched the cool tile of the marble floors as she quickly closed and locked the door behind her.

"You're gonna get it now, Lori. *Nobody* runs away from me." The sound of his voice booming on the other side of the door gave her the sweetest of thrills.

She leaned up against the door, feeling the wood grain on her naked back. She jolted at the banging behind her head.

"Open up," he said, his deep voice full of power and command, even through the muffle of the door.

With a smile, she said, "What's in it for me?"

"Oh, you think I can't give you what you want? I know what you want."

"And what's that?"

"Christ, you little cunt," he said with amusement. She'd never been called that before. The word landed hot and enticing in her belly. "You're gonna get it now."

She heard the click of the door lock and was thrown forward as he opened the door with a force. Richard's hand snatched her arm, and this time there was no escaping his grasp.

"I said, no one runs away from me." He yanked her body towards him, his chest a mountain of stone on her back. He grabbed her other arm and locked them both behind her in his grip.

She tried to wriggle free, but his hands only squeezed tighter on her arms. Her back arched. Her breasts met the cool wall as he pushed her up against it. Her right hip pressed firmly against the black granite vanity top. The feel of him behind her, encasing her, trapping her...it was exhilarating. Intoxicating. She could feel the hair around his cock scratching on her lower back. He was hard now, and she could feel her own body respond with the ache of desire.

With his mouth on her ear, he whispered, "You're going to pay for that, you know," and she couldn't stop her smile.

He pressed even harder against her back as he reached a hand up to cover her mouth. "Did I say you could smile?" She shook her head no. "You think it's funny to make me chase you, naughty little lady?" Again, she shook her head no. Her heart raced at the thrill of what he was going to do to her. They hadn't made love like this yet, with this kind of intensity. Nor had she experienced anything like that with James.

But with Richard, she felt something different. And she played into the role of submission with a natural ease that surprised her.

"What am I going to do with you?" he grumbled in her ear. She could feel his mouth move down her neck, her shoulder, down her back before finally landing with a hard bite on the flesh of her hip. She cried out in pain and felt the sting of a hard slap on her rear. "That's enough out of you."

Richard rose back up, spinning Lori around to face him. With one hand he kept hold of her wrists behind her back as he pressed his body against hers. With the other hand he wrapped his fingers around her neck. "You're mine," he said, "and you will do as I say. Is that clear?"

He kissed her mouth before she could respond. Tender at first. Slow and gentle, a contrast to the grip on her neck and wrists, still behind her back. Then he deepened the kiss, his tongue consuming her mouth. His hand squeezed tighter around her neck, and she felt herself struggling to get air.

She loved it.

Loved the feeling of powerlessness with Richard. Loved how he took charge over her. There was a euphoria rising in her at the relief of succumbing to Richard's will.

He pulled back from her, and she gasped for air. He released her neck and hands before dropping to insert a finger into her. He smiled wickedly at her. "You dirty little cunt. So wet for me." She closed her eyes and groaned as he dipped in and out, rubbed around her clit, back in again. With another hand he squeezed her breast, then dug his palm in and pressed her against the wall. The pain and pleasure mix made her dizzy, and she began to tremble as she neared her climax.

And then Richard stopped.

Lori popped open her eyes. She watched with wonder as he took two steps backward, a smirk on his face. He slowly shook his head from side to side, his smirk widening into a wicked grin. "That's for making me chase you, little lady. I don't chase anyone. You understand?"

She nodded her head, her pulse quickening at the question of what he was going to do next.

He stepped back towards her, placed his hand on her head and pushed her down. She dropped to her knees on the cold tile floor. He shoved his cock into her mouth, and she fought with all her might the gag reflex evoked by his cock, the delicious feeling of him deep in her throat. She sucked and heard his breath quicken with each movement of her mouth up and down his shaft. He thrust further into her, slamming her head against the wall behind her. Tears pricked at her eyes as she worked to take him in, over and over. Filling her head. Filling her so there was room for nothing else. It was ecstasy.

He pulled at her hair and came with a shudder. His hot liquid shot into her mouth, and she reflexively swallowed, again fighting the urge to gag. She wanted to do this right for him. She was frantic with the need to give Richard the maximum amount of pleasure, to do what he wanted in just the right way.

An obsession to please him had become blinding.

He released her hair and pulled back away from her. Patted her on the head and said, "I hope you know what you've started." Her belly flipped. She could only imagine what she started, and she knew she needed Richard with a force that was unstoppable. She was addicted.

He knelt down to her level, dragged his thumb across her lips, down her chin, her throat. Kissed her mouth chastely. Whispered, "Good girl," and rose to his feet. He walked out of the bathroom, leaving her alone.

Lori slowly sank down to lie on the floor. She stared up at the ceiling, a crystal chandelier dangling above her.

Her pulse beat a steady rhythm in her head. A low drum.

Buh-bum. Buh-bum.

It slowed.

And slowed.

After several minutes, her breath was finally calm as she fixated her gaze on the glittering chandelier. She blinked away a tear, feeling it roll down the hill of her cheekbone and lose itself in her chestnut hair.

A serenity swept over her, her body feeling like it was floating in a far-off place.

"I love you," she whispered.

But there was no one there to hear it.

august

. . .

So it rolls and boils, the frolic and delight
Our action and sparks addicting
To be still becomes a bore
We've tarnished our complexion, turned to desire
Bitten the apple, and been bitten in return
But must that be so wrong?
It's only our heat and need
Don't let it be wrong to need

~Raina G. Blake

chapter six

· · ·

Two years ago

reggie

I ONCE HAD a goldfish as a kid—you know, those little carnival prisoners? You win them for popping ping-pong balls into cups, a precursor for training the innocent to kick ass on the sticky basement floor of a frat house in a beer pong battle one day. I always wondered what they did with the extra fish at the end of the night. Did they ride along to the next carnival, depressed and captive?

Anyhow, I had won mine, and we had no idea he would last as long as he did, but I think we got something like six years out of that thing. Six years of staring in his tank, picking out new decor for him to swim in and out of. Hot pink and orange gravel rocks and gaping little mouth O's to be intrigued by. Six years of his loyal love.

I had named him Goldie. Feel free to laugh.

Though before you get too comfortable chuckling at my terrible cliche of a goldfish name, I should tell you that I had actually named him JJ at first—after my late twin brother—but my mother promptly had me change it.

"That name belongs to someone else, Reggie," Mom had said one afternoon. She was sitting at our kitchen table, and I watched as she gazed off into some indistinguishable sight beyond. She twirled her hair between her fingers and looped the strands into a small knot before abruptly giving one final tug, then dropping with an exasperated groan. I remember being confused by my mom's stern reaction. She was rarely one to be upset or sad or angry, usually. Anxious, maybe. But mad? Not as often.

Except for when she was at her limit, with minimal understanding on my end of why, exactly. That's when her anger would come full force, and I'd scurry like a scared little bunny, hiding in my room. A blow-up for her was a hurricane of pent-up rage that had long been seeking an outlet, but it didn't happen often.

"I know who the name belongs to," I had responded, wanting her to see my point, to see the beauty in the idea. "It's to remember him." My sweet little seven-year-old face looked at her with hope. Even back then, I think I knew I was losing my memories of JJ and my dad. JJ and I were only three at the time of the accident, and naming my goldfish after him seemed like a great way to hold onto a fading concept. To keep my brother and dad both from slipping right through the fingers of my mind.

Mom had sighed and rubbed her forehead. I had picked up on that signal of stress of hers by then. "Please, honey. Something else. Anything else." I knew that reflexive massaging of her temples and face meant she was battling something larger, and that my measly little needs should back pedal and retreat.

I peeled my eyes away from her and returned my disappointed gaze back to the goldfish and his bare glass bowl, a kitchen bowl we used for making cookies and brownies. A temporary home for him, though I think I liked the bowl better when it held the promise of baked goods.

"Fine. We'll name him Goldie," I said. I hoped my lack of creativity would wake her up to my frustration, but it was a failed attempt.

"Great! Goldie is perfect." She smiled robotically, and I knew her heart wasn't in it. "I tell you what, you and I can go shopping. I'll let Richard know that we'll be grabbing dinner out, just the two of us, and we'll get Goldie all the goodies he needs. New tank and food and a treasure chest and things to put in there, alright? Richard's probably working late, anyhow." Her words spilled out in a fast and excited rush. I watched her smile and get back to the magazine splayed out in front of her, the relief at having sufficiently moved on from that potential debacle clear on her face.

I think about that memory now as I sit here at work and stare at our office aquarium. Far beyond basic kitchen bowls, ours is a miniature sea, nestled in the wall of charcoal cabinets. A respite from the mundane office supplies storage to the left, and the shelves on the right lined with books on anatomy and the highly professional Evidence-Based Physical Therapy Practices (because someone based evidence on it, it must be good!). Our tank here is filled with more exciting creatures than the future generations of Goldie, and I enjoy the aquarium and find the fish a calming addition to an office I've always hoped to make feel tranquil. A place of healing. Recovery.

Though it wasn't always my dream to become a physical therapist—I just had a general interest in health sciences. This particular career seemed to make sense and have a clear path to follow. I liked that about it. I liked the direct route, and the potential to open my own practice had real appeal. My space, my rules. No dreaded interview questions of "Where do you see yourself in five years," requiring a fake and excited, yet contained response. My clinical interviews were enough for me.

Even better, I could provide a role for my mom. Lori Meyers, Office Manager. (Though truth be told, she's more office assistant than anything else, and my gracious business and marketing director assumes the bigger tasks for her. But you didn't hear that from me.) Always my cheerleader, offering Mom the job seemed like the right thing to do, as it provided her something she could feel proud of. She worked years ago as a bartender for about a half a minute, from my understanding. It's how she met my stepfather, and the rest is apparently history.

Up until he, too, made her a widow once again. A heart attack. I was fifteen at the time. For a short while, she went into a catatonic state of emotionless robotics, and I became the mom, then. Still am, really.

Richard and mom had been together for ten years.

But the real news of the day, ladies and gentlemen, is the patient on our schedule, in our midst at this very moment for his first physical therapy appointment. You guessed it—the man we've all come to hardly know, but absurdly love—the object of my forbidden desires.

X.

No doubt whoever put him on my schedule didn't know the conflict of interest there. Thankfully, I caught it and made the switch to one of my employees, Mary. As our resident Mama Bear physical therapist, Mary is wise and tender and in that stage of career where she should be retired, but she refuses to sit at home doing nothing. I chose Mary for X's care due to her experience, I assure you. Not because my other option is young and single, nope. It's Mary's experience I want for X.

But there he was. A giant red flag on my patient roster. And I had been doing so well (*lies*) not thinking about him these past few weeks.

He's scheduled for the last appointment of the day, and I can't help but wonder if that was on purpose. Is he hoping to close out the day with me?

I roll my eyes at myself, frustrated with the ridiculous thoughts running rampant through my mind. It's almost seven and I know he'll be finishing up soon. When he came in, I had been holed away in my back office catching up on the endless pile of chart notes.

Not hiding—no. Not avoiding him coming in and me having to greet him. Not rudely leaving it up to my mom and/or Mary to explain why he had been reassigned to work out that shoulder issue with her and not the practice owner who was too cowardly to face him, but who is now anxiously sitting back at the front desk pretending to look busy while actually willing the day to be done so I can see him. Nope.

"I'm heading out, sweetie, if that's okay," my mom interrupts my thoughts. She smiles and swings the strap of her purse over her shoulder.

"Yeah, sounds good. Drive safely." I lean back in my chair and dart my eyes toward the clock for the hundredth time.

"Mary should be just about finished with her patient," she adds, as if it's not at the forefront of my mind.

And then, like a cat with a sudden inhumane hearing, I perk up at the sound of soft chatter and footsteps coming down the hall. *It's him.*

X and Mary round the corner and my stomach does a flip. I scan his body and drink in his broad shoulders as he rotates his arm, stretching out the kinks. Mary points him to the front desk, to me and my mom, and my pulse quickens. I can't explain why I'm nervous; it's not as though X can read my mind and knows all the screen time he's received lately.

X steps further into the waiting area as Mary retreats back down the hall. "Have a good night," she says with a quick wave in our direction. This was a late day for her, I know she's eager to wrap up and head home.

"Good night," my mom and I call after her. X thanks her again, and then Mary exits out back, leaving the three of us. We hear the jingle of bells from the employee exit leading to the parking lot. The bells hit my nerves with a jolt, like an alarm indicating it's time for me to gather the courage to finally greet X.

I rise and try not to focus too much on how good he looks in his black t-shirt, muscles swollen from whatever treatment assessment Mary put him through. "Well, hey there," I say. "What brings you into my little spot here?" *God, I sound ridiculous.*

"'Little' might be an understatement," he says with the tilt of his head.

I tuck a strand of hair behind my ear. "How so?"

He slips his hands in the pockets of his dark jeans. "More like small but mighty, maybe. I'm impressed, Reggie. Much nicer than any other practice I've seen. Different vibe here."

"Really?" I squeak out, trying to push down the instant shot of dopamine I feel hearing his praise. "Thanks. I wanted to go for something that didn't feel too much like torture."

He laughs. "I see. I mean the discomfort was there," he says, raising his right shoulder in reference, "but all for a good cause." He nods towards the aquarium. "The fish are a nice addition."

In the corner of my eye, I see my mom gather her water bottle and phone from her desk station. She looks back up, scanning the sight of X and pauses, furrowing her brows.

X removes a hand from his pocket and steps forward to reach out to her. "Hey there, Reggie's mom, right?"

I see the light of recognition dawn across her face, and I realize she must not have been the one to check him in. *Shit*. Couldn't she have left already?

She extends a hand for him to shake. "Lori, that's me! Thought I knew that name on the schedule. It's been a while, I think we met a few times back in the day. Last I remember was at a—"

"A BBQ?" he interjects.

"Christmas party," she says, both saying their respective presumed social engagements at the same time.

She laughs. "One or the other!" Her voice is doing that high-pitched thing she does around men. I can see her looking at him with admiration and an embarrassing twinkle in her eye. Not that I can blame her—he's handsome, his smile can just about melt your heart, and I'm actively watching hers puddle around her like hot cocoa on a snowy day.

I attempt to think of what a normal way to join in on this conversation would be. What would a sane person who wasn't obsessing over a man she barely knew say at this moment? I clear my throat. "Yeah, Mom, I forgot to mention who was back in town. You remember—"

"I sure do," she says. "Welcome back! In town for a visit or to stay or what? Ohhh I hope it's to stay." She flashes her most dazzling grin. *Is she flirting?*

Mom remains a complete babe, you should know, and she's young for having a daughter of twenty-seven. But not that young. I quickly do the math, far *too* quickly, as I realize with disappointment there's only an eight-year age difference between my mom and X. She's forty-seven to his thirty-nine.

Fucking fantastic. I'm jealous of my mom. She's always had this bizarre air of innocence to her that men seem to love.

"You're in luck, then," he says. "I'm here to stay. Settle and grow some roots, maybe." X crosses his arms against his chest, causing his biceps to bulge even more. His eyes dart over in my direction.

Mom brings her hands together in a most enthusiastic clap. "How wonderful! Oh, good!" She runs a hand through her hair and I wonder if she's contemplating breaking out into cartwheels. Maybe erupt pompoms and perform a cheer dance for him. Or tap shoes and a jazz routine, sequins and top hat adorning her lovely hair as she circles the Shiny Mr. X with unwavering worship and affection.

She's all but done it before with past boys in my life. And I'd have to swoop in, save her from herself and the confused, but highly entertained teenage boy from the cougar charms of Reggie Blake's Eternally Broken-Hearted and Starved For Love Mom.

But wait, what have we here? X is turning his attention away from her, and toward me? "Reggie, I was hoping I could maybe walk you out? Mary said you'd probably be wrapping up soon." *Stop it.*

My mom steps out from behind the desk. "Perfect, I was just leaving myself. We can all walk out together!" Lori sings. I'm downgrading her from "Mom" to "Lori" for the time being. "Unless you're still working?" she asks me.

"Nope," I confirm far too quickly.

"Lori, I'm happy to walk you out," X looks at her with all the warmth in the world. Is it just me, or is it the look you'd give a child? "But I confess, I was hoping to have a word with Reggie alone."

I try and lift my jaw from the floor at the sound of his voice uttering out the words "Reggie" and "alone."

~~My mom~~, Lori seems unfazed. "Oh, alright. Well, no matter, I'd love your escort. Can't promise I'll return you back, though, handsome," she says, making her way to his side.

"Behave now, Mrs. Blake," X says. He offers her his arm and she leads them both down the hall and out toward the employee exit.

"Call me Lori," she says as I watch them disappear out of my line of vision. "Though it's Lori Meyers, actually, not Blake. I remarried not too long after Reggie's dad passed away."

"Oh, that's right." Their voices become more and more quiet as they make their way out.

"And fate seems to have it out for me as it took that love of mine too. You better watch out! I swear, I'm a bad luck charm." I inwardly groan.

"No you're not."

"Ohhh, but I am." And they mumble along, leaving me and my racing heart.

A muffled laugh.

Continued indistinct chatter.

The jingle of the door swinging open.

Swinging closed.

Lock.

Shit, I think, remembering that the door locks automatically. I wonder with mild panic how he's going to get back in. Will my mom give him the code? Do I go wait out back for him? No, I don't want to stand there awkwardly doing nothing.

I should have walked with them. Or is that too much?

I rub my temples, feeling like I'm losing it.

But I have to know why he wanted to talk to me. That's what he said, right? Talk to me? Or walk me out?

Does it really matter?

I feel so oddly at a loss in an office that I've spent so much time working to make feel warm and welcoming. I look up at the aquarium and see its occupants swim and stare at me with sidelong glances of judgment, maybe pity. *Poor lady*, they're saying, fins all a-flow, colorful and glorious. *Landlocked in the depths of her mangled up mind.*

I sigh heavily. I need a therapy session. It's been a few weeks and it's clear I need to work out some things. Conjuring up naughty images of other men is not my usual style, especially not a man like X.

Speaking of, where is he now, and is he really coming back in to talk to me?

And if so, why?

chapter seven

. . .

X

A WARM BREEZE picks up as he rounds the corner back to the front of the building, having safely deposited Lori to her vehicle. He feels some semblance of sympathy for the woman, though he knows pity is a homeless essence wandering aimlessly in one's mind. His pity won't do her any good; never helps anyone in the long run. But it's there, nonetheless. His instinct was to look Lori in the eyes, steady her frantic mind and tell her to just relax and be herself. Assure her that in authenticity, she'd find her way out of suffering. But what the hell does he know? He's just as guilty of running away too.

Or at least, he had been. But not anymore.

X gently knocks on the glass of the front door of the office, not wanting to barge in and startle Reggie. The sun is making its descent in the summer sky, and he glances down and notices his shadow stretching out long by his side, parallel to the building. He looks back up through the glass and catches sight of Reggie rummaging behind the front desk, smiling and giving him a quick wave to signal him in. He gently pushes the door open and steps forward into the waiting area, offering a smile to the woman before him.

She's professionally dressed in a simple black pants and shirt combo, her practice name embroidered on her chest. "Warrior PT." He couldn't have picked a better name and he wonders how she came up with it.

X notes with admiration Reggie's work-mode demeanor. It's different from the bar-variety of her, but still her. She moves with a quickness and efficiency like she's on a mission. He gets the sense that Reggie isn't one to sit still.

"I thought she might have kidnapped you," she says with a small smile. She leans down toward a computer, eyes focused on some task, and the glow from the screen illuminates her face.

He steps forward to the raised counter on the other side of the desk, directly across from her. "Did you call out a search party?"

"I did," she nods. "They're terribly slow, though. Good thing you seem to be faster."

He shakes his head with a laugh. "It was a battle."

"I can imagine. I was raised by her." Reggie stands and looks up at him, then gives a slight smile before moving around to the front of the desk, standing beside him. She leans an elbow on the ledge.

He leans back, resting against the counter and crossing one ankle over the other. "So I guess you'd know her better than anyone."

Reggies clasps her hands in front of her. "I like to think I do. But I suppose we all have a little mystery within us."

They hold one another's gaze in a momentary standoff, and he scans the depths of her green eyes, dotted with specks of blue. She relaxes her jaw, slightly parting her lips, and he clenches his fist in an attempt to distract himself. Neither one of them look away.

It's Reggie that breaks first as she drops her hands and steps away from the counter. She starts laughing and the sound effectively cuts the tension he can't sure was real or imagined. "Alright," she says. "Fun as this is, what can I do for you? *Hun?*"

X huffs out a laugh in return. "Hun, right." One hand in his pocket, he runs the other hand through his hair. "I'm not going to shake that, am I?"

"Oh please, you love it." She rolls her eyes and crosses her arms over her chest.

He drops his hand and mirrors her pose. "Actually, I think *you* love it."

"Only until something better comes up to tease you with," she dares, eyebrow raised.

X looks at her a moment—probably a moment too long—but he can't help it. She radiates something, and he loves her subtle humor. He needs to be careful with his surprising and inappropriate attraction to her.

He slowly shakes his head. "When did you get all grown up, Reggie?" he mystifies. "You're supposed to be sixteen and just a kid, still. Not this bantering minx."

Her eyes glance to his hair. "And you're not supposed to have that sprinkle of gray by your temples, yet here we are."

"Here we are," he nods in agreement.

Reggie's stomach chimes in with a growl that even the fish stop to turn toward in shocked response. She places her hand on her belly as if covering will quiet it.

"Did you eat today?" X asks, remembering what she had said on the poem night about barely eating all day while at work.

"A bite or two here and there." She shrugs. "When I'm in work-mode, I'm just on the go. I don't really stop to think about much else."

He nods toward the street beyond the front door. "Come on, let's get you fed."

"Right now?" she asks, as if he had offered up a steak at six o'clock in the morning.

"I don't think your stomach will wait."

She drops her gaze and runs her hands over her shirt, smoothing it out, seeming to contemplate his suggestion. Finally, she looks up at him. "No, I suppose it won't," she says, rounding the corner back behind the front desk. He watches as she shuts down the three computers, one by one.

He scans the room to see what he can help her with in closing down and finds the waiting room TV remote. He powers it off, followed by some scented oil contraption, then gathers the scattered magazines and places them in a nearby bin before scanning the room for anything else he can do. A brochure for the practice catches his eye and he picks it up and thumbs through, disbelief and awe in Reggie and her thriving business.

She turns off the final light and X looks at her as she tilts her head toward the front door. "You wanna check out Main Street?"

X replaces the brochure in its spot, resisting the urge to fold it up and take it with him. "Sounds good, yeah. You have the perfect location here, don't you?"

"Meaning?"

He motions toward the window. "Surrounding shops, yoga studio next door, restaurants."

Reggie smiles as she starts walking toward the back of the office. "True, and by design, without a doubt." She turns around, walking backwards and hooking her thumb behind her. "Let me just do a quick final sweep of the shop, here, and grab my things."

He nods and waits as she retreats, and he scans around the waiting room. It's clean and modern with charcoal cabinets and walls of sage green. A large, blown-up photo of palm fronds hangs prominently on one wall, the leaves almost unrecognizable in their zoomed-in capture. Black and white photos adorn the other walls, various images of bodies in motion. A dancer, a gymnast, a martial arts extraordinaire balanced on one hand, feet defying gravity mid-kick above him.

It's a complete contrast to the other clinics his shoulder injury has caused him to frequent. Here, there's soft recessed lighting, not cold fluorescents. There's an actual ambiance that he imagines was also by design, much like Reggie's chosen location. It's a space that's comfortable to be in. There's a sophistica-tion to it.

He thinks back to the Reggie he last saw, sixteen-years-old and introduced as Joey's girlfriend, an upgrade from "friend," as they had been since kids. Even then, X remembers thinking she had a maturity about her. At a party thrown in preparation for his second tour, she had asked him questions about his deployment with a kind of calm curiosity. They were different from others' questions that teetered on melodramatic. Reggie had taken him by surprise with her interest, her questions delicate and informed. She had even gone so far as to ask if he believed in his purpose there in Afghanistan, and then quickly retracted the question with an embarrassed flush. He can remember it like it was yesterday.

Today she wouldn't have reacted with that embarrassment. He believes with a hundred percent certainty that the Reggie of today would march straight ahead, full force with her line of questioning. A passionate mission on her mind.

He wonders if Reggie remembers that interaction with him.

"Alright, where to?" she asks as she reappears. "I texted Joey to see if he could meet us." She steps toward X, keys in hand, and he takes note of her change of clothes. Office attire switched out for a maroon sundress and sandals.

"You always have a change of clothes with you?" He wants to tell her that she looks gorgeous. Sexy. Tempting. That her dress hugs her in all the right places and makes him want to rip it off and see what's underneath.

But he knows better and refrains.

"I usually walk in here with my regular clothes, change into the work uniform for the day and then change back out. Helps me mentally separate work from personal time."

He nods with understanding. "Smart. Don't take your work home with you."

"Exactly. Though truth be told, it creeps in anyway, but it's the thought that counts, right?" She smiles brightly and X watches as she walks around the room to double check on everything. It's sexy as hell to observe her in her element, taking care of her space, the routine automatic. She finishes and returns to his side, and he allows his mind to briefly imagine reaching for her and pulling her body into his chest. He clenches his jaw, collecting himself.

"Ready?" she asks.

"Sure," he says, and they step outside with Reggie locking the door behind them.

"Well?" She looks up at X with question in her eyes. "Thoughts on where to go?"

"I'd say you know the area around here better. It's changed a lot since I lived here. What's good?"

"This way," she points her head west and they walk up the brick sidewalk, deeper into town. "There's a few options as we get closer to the town square."

He follows her and has the instinct to put his hand on the small of her back, but he knows touching her is something to steer clear of. He learned that the night he drove her home from the Moon Lounge. Instead, he keeps his hands to himself and his eyes firmly fixed in front of him. She's with someone, he reminds himself. "Not too out of the way for Joey if he's coming from the city?" he asks.

"He'll be a while anyways if he can even make it."

They walk in silence for a few steps, sun low, bright and hot to the point of stifling. He walks on the side closest to the street, the protective nature in him in effect even in this moment. A breeze kicks up and he catches the scent of vanilla as Reggie's hair momentarily lifts off her shoulder. An urge to pull her close and inhale overcomes him, and he attempts to distract himself with feigned interest in the surrounding buildings and shops.

"I'm always freezing in the office, but my God, it's hot out." Reggie grabs her hair and pulls it over her left shoulder. He looks down and sees a small cluster of three freckles on her skin where her neck and shoulder meet. A perfect target to softly kiss.

Frustrated with himself, he tries to keep the conversation in safe territory to clear his unwelcome thoughts. "When did you open your clinic?"

"Just two years ago. Basically as soon as I was licensed and able to practice on my own. I contemplated applying with some of the established spots around here, but knew that my ultimate goal was going to be my own practice, so I figured why wait."

"Makes sense. Take the plunge and go for it."

"Exactly. Plus student loans could be paid off faster if I wasn't giving such a high percentage of my salary away." She glances up at him and smiles, and he smiles and nods in return.

"Smart woman. Were you worried about getting enough patients in?"

"Oh yeah," she says, adjusting the strap of her purse. "And of course I had to pick a location, as you so well noticed, that is pretty high traffic, here in town."

"More costly."

"For sure. But I fell in love with it. I love the old-time charm and brick sidewalks here, and I had the opportunity to gut the space and start fresh. The space before it had been an old travel agency. And then I *really* lucked out when I applied for and won a women entrepreneur's small business grant."

Reggie comes to life as she talks, and X can feel his growing draw to her and her passion. It's as if she is someone that has always known exactly what she wants, and she goes for it. No hesitation, no second guessing.

He, on the other hand, has hesitated about most everything. And it's cost him.

"You amaze me, Reggie."

"Oh yeah?"

"Yeah. That takes guts."

"Says the man who has been to war."

"I think you give me too much credit."

"Who says I'm giving you credit?" She looks up at him with a smirk. "Teasing of course. You deserve a little credit."

He smiles, refraining from a response that would lean toward flirtatious, and they walk a few more steps before stopping in front of a small cafe. A cluster of chairs and umbrellas spill out onto the sidewalk. "You like Italian?" she asks him.

With you, I'd like anything, he thinks to himself. He motions toward her belly. "As long as that grumbling stomach of yours likes Italian, I'm down."

"This grumbling stomach of mine doesn't want to walk anymore, plus I'm a sucker for a street-side perch. Unless it's too hot for you?" She glances up and down at him and his long jeans and black tee.

"Sun's getting lower, I think I can handle it."

"Good," she nods, and they turn toward the restaurant.

A DELICATE EXCHANGE OF QUESTIONS and answers and a bottle of wine later at the iron table of the shaded street-side cafe, and X has learned three things about Reggie:

One—She is sexy without flaunting it. She moves with the grace of a dancer, though he's learned it was gymnastics that was her sport and in fact part of her motivation to go into physical therapy.

Two—She can eat pasta and bread in brazen quantities. While cooking is not her thing, she can appreciate good food and makes no attempt to feel guilt over it.

Three (and this is the most important point of all)—

Reggie is most definitely not madly in love with Joey.

And this revelation is going to torture his desiring soul even more than it already has been. Mainly because X is pretty sure she is feeling something for him, just as he's falling for her.

chapter eight

. . .

reggie

I SIT IN the bathtub and inhale the eucalyptus essential oil. Let it caaallmm me. Let it bring me peace.

Let it stop me from my horrific draw to X.

The water is too hot, or maybe it's the lingering wine, and I'm sweating even as I sit mostly soaked in here. Maybe August isn't the best time for a hot bath. But I have to get my mind cleared out and this seems like the easiest way. I need to get to bed, as it's close to midnight and I have work tomorrow, but my mind is racing.

All because dinner with X was…

I'm not even sure how to describe it, but "buzzing" feels like the most appropriate word. Buzzing with an electric energy that was confusing and exhilarating all at once.

It started innocently enough. A meal to share. Some basic "fill me in on the past several years" lines of conversation.

Me, trying to ignore his sexiness. That t-shirt stretched over his biceps. His black tribal tattoo peeking through and my curiosity to lift the sleeve and reveal the rest.

Me, wishing I could have been his therapist so I could touch him. Feel his skin.

Me, trying to focus on my food.

Me trying not to flirt or be sexy. Trying to remember my lovely Joey.

Me loving the sound of X's gravelly baritone voice.

Me wanting to jump out of my skin and then looking at my watch, hoping Joey would make an appearance and cure me from my evil sins.

Me, me, me, me, me losing it.

It was his question. That's what did me in. His question about the Thing. We. Don't. Talk. About.

The death of my twin brother and my dad.

You see, while I know that losing them is a devastating but interesting conversation piece (people just love a good sob story, I suppose), it's really not something I ever discuss. I mean, it was years and years ago, I barely even remember them aside from a few random photos we have. It's always been more about the concept of the loss, not actually feeling anything about it. It's all I've ever really known, the aftermath of the accident, so it's not something I feel a major connection to, right? There was no great Before Car Crash and After Car Crash for me. Just the after. Just the new story built by my mom. It's more her that had to deal with tragedy. Not me.

And my mom got lucky, really. She met Richard, my stepfather, and got her second chance at love. Boom, done. Life moves on. She was happy with Richard. We lived in his big and beautiful house in the neighborhood of McMansions where I met Lucy and Joey, and that's that. Happy ending. Even after Richard died, my mom eventually with time seemed superhuman in her ability to once again, bounce back and live and feel all her usual enthusiasm for the world.

Which is what it's all about, right? Finding the new path

toward your happiness? We make the lemonade out of lemons. Move on and move up.

Or so, that's what I was busy explaining to X before he asked me the question.

He tricked me into it. He'd said he wanted to talk to me to once again, apologize if he had made me uncomfortable a few weeks back after the Moon Lounge, when he first returned to town. I assured him I'm the epitome of resilience and strength and all that. I thought I sounded very convincing. Went into my whole spiel about the lemonade and whatnot. No need to worry about me, I'm a rock. No suffering here.

And that's when the bastard called me out.

"That's just it, Reggie," he said, looking at me over the table's candlelight. We had somehow shifted from daylight to the far too romantic twinkle of evening. Even now, I'm getting goosebumps just thinking about it, despite my surrounding hot water.

The streetlights had begun their soft glow, the patio string lights offering an enveloping canopy above us. I was beginning to curse myself for choosing such a romantic location, especially since Joey wasn't going to be able to join us after all.

"What's 'it'?" I asked, aware that the air around us was heavy with something I couldn't quite describe. A little breeze blew, and the candle flickered in a spiritual spell that magnified the surrounding energy. Enchanting—that's the word. It all felt enchanting.

His bicep flexed, or maybe it was my imagination. "You're strong. Resilient," he said. "I can see that." His voice held that low and sexy rumble of his.

I scanned his face, the full lips, strong jaw. "Oh, thank God," I joked. I perched my elbow on the table to rest my chin in my hand. "I sense a 'but' about to be dropped."

The corner of his mouth lifted, the tiniest of twitches. "No 'but,'" he countered. "Just an observation." I could see the rise and fall of his chest with his steady breaths.

"Go on," I prompted, hating how eager I felt to hear what he had to say. He scanned my face and I licked my lips, waiting for his response. I saw his gaze drop briefly to my mouth, and a blush crept up my neck.

He returned his focus to my eyes and I sucked in a breath. He held my gaze and softly said his next words.

"You mask your feelings with humor, Reggie."

Oh, my. I mean, here's this man, this real and grown-up *man*, making a simple observation about me, but he could cut right to it, couldn't he? His tone was soft, his countenance kind. I swear, he looked into my heart in that moment. I had this desire to reach across the table and grab his hand. I didn't, of course.

I huffed out a laugh, hell-bent on wanting to appear unaffected. "I gotta say, this is one hell of an apology," I blurted out, realizing too late that my joke just proved his point.

X just looked at me with this expression of debate. I could see the wheels turning in his mind, see the contemplation behind his eyes. It was like he had something to say but wasn't sure if he should say it. And I admit, a part of me wanted—no, *needed* him to say whatever it was he was thinking. I was quickly becoming addicted to hearing his insights on me and my apparent facade that, so far, no others had ever noticed.

And then he did share more, with the question. "Your poem— it was about the accident and the loss of your dad and brother, wasn't it?" I looked at him and saw the searching in his eyes.

Well, there it was. His question cut right through me.

There it was.

He sees me, right through me, I realized. It was if he was paying attention when no one else was. Not even my amazing Lucy had presented that connection. X sees my hurt.

I looked down at my hand that was laying on the table, noting how dangerously close our fingertips were to one another. God, I wanted to grab his hand and interlock fingers with his as he talked to me like this, opened up wounds I didn't even acknowledge were ever there.

I took a deep breath in and held it, his ocean and salt scent of masculinity filling my nose. I wanted to wrap myself in it, and I slowly nodded in confirmation and exhaled. "Mmm hmm," was all I could muster in response.

I too have felt that hole in my heart
In a babe's untimely passing.

My words rolled their way across my mind.

...too much oxygen
When there should be none.

Too much, when there should be none. The guilt of the surviving.

So we sat there for a moment in silence. A frozen vacuum in space and time. A truth unveiled but raw and fresh and untouchable in its fragile, infant state.

My pain, my loss, somewhere deep under the surface, though I didn't dare outwardly speak of it. Didn't dare open the wound, until that poem, I guess. And somehow X could see it all, it seemed.

I could feel the tear threatening to release if I so much as blinked. My emotion surprised me. My mind screamed for one of us to say something. Anything! Anything to break this spell that was threatening to unlock something buried deep within. "How did you know?" I eventually whispered, unsure if he could even hear me. And then the blink inevitably happened, and the tear rolled its way down.

Down, down, down it went, a betrayal of my pseudo-nonchalance. A raging tattle-tale of the hurt aching inside me. My mind flashed to an image of my twin brother. A quick blur of little JJ laughing with me after having found me in a round of hide-and-seek. JJ's smile and his chubby cheeks, and my chest squeezed with how much I still miss him and feel his absence.

But just as quickly as it came, the image was gone. Memory blank again.

I wiped my tear and X grabbed my hand that was resting on the table, rubbing his thumb over the back of it in gentle comfort. I closed my eyes and allowed the touch to do just that.

"Because I listened, Reggie," X finally said. "I wanted to hear what the incredible Raina Blake had to say."

He listened.

I opened my eyes and looked at him, and I could see a flicker of something in his gaze as he watched me. A chill swept through me with that simple look.

I let his words hang there, let the tear hang there too. I think I was barely breathing in that moment. It seemed dangerous to breathe or to do anything but sit frozen in that chair, on that brick sidewalk, under those twinkling lights, in my safe little town, across from this man that somehow had cut straight through to me. How, oh how, was he unraveling things like this? How was this happening? It was unfamiliar to be feeling these things.

So I just sat there. I closed my eyes again and focused on the feel of his thumb on my skin, injecting comfort.

He spoke quietly. "Pain is what's real. It's the current of what gives us life. It's the way we know what it means to love." He paused. The motion of his thumb on my hand paused too. "Our pain and grief mean that we've had the fortune of something to feel loss of."

I opened my eyes and focused my gaze on the flickering candle. Eventually, I looked back up at X, willing him to go on. I nodded ever so slightly.

He continued. "I know it hurts and know what it's like to want to push it all away and pretend it's not there and move on. But it seeps around the edges anyway, Reggie."

I huffed out a sigh. "That it does." With reluctance, I pulled my hand back and ran it through my hair, trying to step out of this bubble and break this spell. I looked up beyond the string lights and to the stars. "It was so long ago," I noted, as if that fact could keep me from continuing down this emotional path.

"It was," he agreed. "Doesn't make it any easier." His encouragement gave me a little boost of power, and I allowed my mind to explore.

I let out a heavy sigh. "It just seems unfair, you know?"

"Sure. What exactly feels unfair about it?" His voice was so soft, or at least, as soft as the natural roughness of it would allow. So gentle as he provided me this space of emotional exploration.

I decided to run with it. "Unfair that I can sit here and move on with my life, that my mom could find love again, when half of us are gone." I shook my head. "Yanked away like that. It just doesn't make sense." I returned my gaze to him, feeling more bold. "And I always felt like I was missing something. Not even just the loss of them, but something else. Like a discontent. Even now, it's like I'm missing this piece of me that's supposed to feel completely happy. I feel like I can't quite get there, and I don't know why." I sighed as I reflected on my own words. "My mom could get there. She could move on and just live and *be*, so why can't I?"

"Maybe she's not as happy as she lets on," he offered.

I huffed in disbelief. "Doubtful. She's like a fairy, fluttering around from one adventure to the next." I crossed my arms over my chest. "I can't even count the number of men she's dated since Richard died. And I mean, I'm happy for her, she deserves to have fun, that's not what bugs me."

"So what bugs you?" he asked, taking a sip of his water.

I shrugged. "I don't even know. I guess just seeing her live so easily, when I'm stuck with this thing missing in me, a purpose or something. It's dumb, my loss is not even as great as hers."

"You did lose your twin," he noted. "And there's no sense in attempting to create a hierarchy of someone's grief in comparison to another's." I flushed with guilt as I remembered back to his story of the Air Force and Army guys on the plane. His point on honoring the different experiences.

X leaned forward, resting his forearms on the table. "What makes you feel like you're stuck?"

I grabbed my wine. Took a sip and let the bite of the liquid pinch awake my thoughts. "It's hard to describe," I said, placing the wine glass back down and running my finger along the sleek stem. "I mean, on paper, I'm exactly where I've wanted to be in life. Checked all the boxes. And that feels good, I feel accomplished."

He nodded in understanding. "But you feel that something's missing," he said, bringing me back to my original revelation. "Maybe the courage and strength to see it isn't quite there yet. There's purpose to be found, and that can be tough." He said it like he knew exactly the feeling.

I looked at him, at the sprinkle of gray hair, the beard growing in, longer now than it was the last time I saw him. "Exactly," I said, amazed at his ability to succinctly put to words these feelings that I had locked beyond the surface.

And then I thought to myself about how that's what's kept me from moving forward with Joey, my sweet and lovely Joey. This missing purpose thing. I didn't dare say that out loud, though. But I realized in that moment just how true it was.

X took another sip of his water, seeming to collect his thoughts before speaking again. "If there's one thing I've learned over the years, something I can share, it's that Robert Frost was right."

I smiled at the reference, as it pulled on the strings of my wannabe-poet heart. And I couldn't help it, I had to joke, "Good fences make good neighbors?"

He smiled in return. "There she is, my jokester Reggie," he said with a laugh. My heart skipped a little beat at the use of his word 'my' when referring to me.

"That's me. Guilty."

His eyes tore into mine, searching for something, maybe. "God, I love it...I love talking to you, I mean," he said, shaking his head slightly like he didn't quite understand why. "Just something about you."

I know what you mean.

It was a bold statement though, and I felt the need to rush in and rescue him in case he heard it and regretted it. "I must admit," I said, "I've really been loving talking to you too." I aimed for casual and carefree with my tone.

He cleared his throat and continued with his original intention, his quote from Frost himself. "Funny as you are, though, the 'high fences' quote is not the one."

"So which one is it, then?" I asked.

"A better one, I like to think. *'And miles to go before I sleep.'*" His words felt like a spell, settling and calming me, though I wasn't sure what to make of them.

He let the line hang there. Said nothing else. I spun the words around in my mind for a minute before simply repeating them. "*'Miles to go before I sleep.'*"

And that was that.

So I sit here now, overheated and slightly nauseous in this tub, and I think about those words. What did they mean? We never did discuss the line further, as the waitress cut our moment with a look of "It's way late and you should probably be wrapping it up," and I really don't like pissing off my fellow local business owners or their employees.

But the words linger in my mind.

And I realize I have some figuring shit out to do.

september

. . .

Garnering all we can, come now and think
Reflect to nourish the shift
Consider
Dare to dream
After the play, we work
After the work
we understand that what's been poured out
Can't be forced back in

~Raina G. Blake

chapter nine

. . .

Twelve Years Ago

lori

THE PHOTO COULD have been taken yesterday. It feels fresh in so many ways, yet in reality it was a lifetime ago. Lori held the photo in its frame close to her chest and looked up towards the steel beams of the basement ceiling. Closed her eyes. She could almost feel it all again, that moment, years ago, when she and James were crowned Junior Prom King and Queen. Everyone's favorite high school sweethearts. The applause, the loving yells of adoration and admiration. The envy of all the school, Lori and her darling James. She allowed her mind for just a moment to drink it all in again. Absorb the blissful perfection of that night.

She popped open her eyes though, remembering that she's not down here in the musty basement looking for photos, she's looking for something else. Something better.

Something Reggie would never go for, Lori was sure, but she was going to try anyways. Her gown from that prom. Lori hoped Reggie would wear it to her upcoming homecoming dance.

Like mother like daughter, Reggie and Joey were rumored to be crowned Homecoming King and Queen. Without a doubt, they would win. Lori could barely contain her excitement. Just too perfect, those two!

She reflects on the style of the 90s and considers it to be adaptable for today's standards. Her hope is that Reggie would love such a treasure as her mother's dress.

If Lori could just remember where the hell she put it.

She hadn't been down in the storage part of the basement much since Richard died two years prior—she had his things boxed up and sent down there as soon as the motivation came to her. Lori had been afraid to get rid of anything in case one of his children came back later to retrieve it. The basement had since become a tomb in and of itself, and the morbidity of it stretched around her like the growing vines of a weed. Lori felt a chill as she looked over toward the section to her left where Richard's belongings were stacked high. A mountain of presence. Two smaller boxes sat centered on top, and Lori had the sense that they were a pair of eyes. Watching.

Figures. Even after his heart attack, he held the power and dominance. It had been that very power that had saved Lori from her heartbreak. Richard was the only thing strong enough to pull her out of her depression. She had needed his force then, she can admit. Craved it, became addicted to it. And here it was, even two years post-death, that force still lurking in the depths of this house.

In a staredown that lasted less than a minute, Lori decided she had enough. She rose from her crouched position by her cedar trunk, framed prom photo held firmly in her hand. She walked over to the towering mountain, quickening her steps until she was eventually stomping. She heard herself scream at the top of her lungs, yelling at the imposing eyes. She hurled herself at them as she slammed the photo over and over again into the boxes, stabbing the eyes with slash marks in a reckless pattern of rupture.

Stab.

Stab.

Stab, stab, stab, stab, cut, bleed, stab, scream. She stabbed away in a whirlwind of pain and emotion in a wanderlust hope to…

"Lori?" her mom Kathryn called from the top of the stairs, breaking Lori's volcanic tirade. She quickly snapped back to reality, looked down at her bleeding finger, the smashed glass of the photo frame. She looked around in panic for a towel.

"Be right there! Just looking for something!" Her voice was citrusy bright, too bright, even to Lori's own ears.

Lori could hear Kathryn rushing down the stairs, a threatening drum roll of exposure with each step her mother took. An old blanket revealed itself in a dusty corner, and Lori snatched it to wrap and hide her hand. She quickly spun the eye-boxes around to hide the wounds of their hideous attack at her hand.

"What was that noise, was that you?" Kathryn rounded the corner to where Lori stood. Smiling.

"Hi! Nothing, yes! Oh gosh," she rolled her eyes. "I just got lost in my head and I've been down here looking for my old prom dress, do you have any idea where it could be? You know, the fitted pale purple one with the skinny straps? And anyways I saw a, a spider and, and… just lost my damn mind that thing scared me so much!" Lori put a hand to her chest as nervous laughter chaotically spilled out of her. "I freakin' hate spiders, I just feel jumpy down here, you know? So yes, I was smashing it with this," she lifted the blanket to reveal the marred photo, "and still haven't even found the dress."

"Oh my, honey, we need to get that cleaned up, get you a Band-Aid." Kathryn interrupted her daughter's maniacal monologue and stepped closer to examine her hand and its weapon. "And that photo, oh no. I'm sure I have another copy of this at my house somewhere."

"But the dress, Mom!"

"What?" Kathryn's pale eyes stared at her daughter, confusion in concern etched on her face.

"The dress! My pale purple prom dress! I want to find it for Reggie."

"Yes! We'll find it too, but this needs to be looked at, Lori. This cut looks deep."

"It's fine," Lori said, snatching her hand back. "It's nothing."

"It's bleeding…"

"It's nothing!" Eyes ablaze, Lori dared her mom to say another word.

Kathryn

NOW, KATHRYN KNEW HER DAUGHTER well enough to know when to stop. She'd learned that the hard way. She'd learned that when Lori insisted on wearing butterfly wings on the first day of school, despite a backpack proving most difficult with said wings on. She'd learned that when Lori grabbed Kathryn's car keys at fifteen, demanding to take it for a spin to "help by picking up the groceries." When Kathryn refused, Lori later took the car out anyway, only to be pulled over by a local police officer who was concerned with the "very young-looking driver swerving on the road."

Kathryn had learned to stop when the more she tried to contain her free-spirited daughter, the more Lori proved impossible to contain.

Until James came into Lori's world.

Kathryn was leery of him at first. James came from…well, a different part of town, let's just say, and from whispers around, his family was not exactly one to be proud of. Alcoholic father, broken and zombie-like mother. Kathryn learned that James was the oldest of three boys and had his hands full. She was determined to keep this bad boy as far away as possible from her impressionable daughter.

But he proved Kathryn wrong, that's for sure. James was bright. Determined. He did well in school and apparently had a mission to move on and move up.

And he was smitten for Lori, and Lori was smitten right back. So much so that James tamed her—well, as much as Lori would allow to be tamed. And other than getting her daughter unexpectedly pregnant (with twins, nonetheless) at the young age of nineteen, Kathryn had to admit that James was good for Lori. Not that she'd ever let Lori know of her changing opinion, for Kathryn feared the rebellious spirit in her daughter would suddenly decide to drop James and move on to the next wild thing simply to upset her mother.

Which never happened, thankfully. No—sadly the only thing that proved strong enough to separate Lori and James was something else.

Bad fate and a patch of ice.

So Kathryn stood there now in the basement with her daughter's bleeding hand, clearly *not* from an encounter with a spider, and said, "Let's find that dress then."

Lori

"AAAANND, TA-DA!!!!" LORI SPUN AROUND to face her daughter, the garment bag held high in her hand above her head, as far as she could reach to keep it from touching the floor.

Reggie sat in defeat on her bed and covered her face with her hands. "Mom, you're not listening to me!"

"Don't you want to know what this even is? What's in here?" Lori shimmied the bag in a mini-dance.

"Your mom has been so excited to show this to you, sweetie," Kathryn chimed in, stepping closer to Lori.

Reggie flopped back down on her bed, the floral blooms of her Laura Ashley comforter exploding around her in a garden of feminine energy. Lori looked at her daughter in a mix of love and frantic grasping.

"I don't. Want. To go. To homecoming," Reggie's muffled voice said through the pillow she had covering her face.

Flinging the garment bag towards Kathryn, Lori rushed over to sit next to her daughter. She stroked Reggie's hair, the blondish-reddish tones sun-bleached still from the recent summer. "School dances were never your thing, I know."

"That's not even what this is about!" Reggie pushed the pillow aside and sat up. "Nana! Please, won't you reason with her?"

Kathryn retreated to Reggie's desk in the corner, taking a seat and curling the garment bag in her lap around her arm. She raised her free hand up. "I'm not getting in the middle of this."

Lori just needed to convince her daughter she was being stubborn. That she would be missing out on a once in a lifetime opportunity if she backed out of this. "Raina Georgia, you only get one senior homecoming."

"Except for college."

"Fine. Except for college. But who knows if you'll be voted Prom Queen then."

"You mean Homecoming Queen." Reggie gave the most irritating look of victory to Lori, and Lori wanted to smack that infuriating look clean off her daughter's face.

She let her have it. "You're impossible, Raina Georgia. And so selfish, you know I practically bled out down there in that basement scrounging up this dress for you, and you have zero gratitude. Absolutely none, you little..." she stopped herself just before spitting out the word she wanted. *Brat.* "It's unfucking believable!" Lori's fists clenched by her side, the anger rising with a quick and alarming red at the frustration of not being able to get through to Reggie. Why did this girl always have to be so damn *miserable?* Make everything harder than it had to be? Lori had the briefest moment of feeling like she actually hated her kid. Hated Reggie.

And just as quickly as the putrid thought emerged, Lori's guilt swept in and took over like a menacing bully. She fought the urge to burst into tears.

"Calm down, it's just a dance," Kathryn attempted, tucking gold and gray strands of hair behind her ear.

Lori shot her a glare. "I thought you were staying out of this, Mother."

"You guys," Reggie said, her voice low but firm. "It's fine. No need to get all worked up," she soothed. Lori knew what she was doing. Reggie was slipping into mediate mode, but Lori wasn't ready to relinquish just yet. Her emotions still sat hot in her chest, a surprise to her, yet also a welcomed vibrancy.

Reggie continued. "Just, give me a minute to explain." She stood up and made her way toward her bedroom window, staring out to the backyard beyond.

They obliged and Lori waited impatiently to hear the impossible explanation Reggie was going to attempt. A bird outside Reggie's window fluttered about, wings flapping in seamless union. Lori studied it, annoyed at its imposing presence. It paused on the window ledge, snapped its head to the side to stare at the three women beyond the glass. Unblinking. Its beady eye appeared to judge the fickle creatures in its view. It then pecked at something near its feet before flying off without a second thought.

Finally, Reggie broke the silence. "I'm breaking up with Joey."

"What?!" Both Lori and her mother exploded. Another flock of birds withdrew from a hidden nest down in the garden below and flew away with a frenzy. Reggie turned away from the window to face the two women.

"I'm not in love with him, and I don't want to lead him on."

Lori thought this was ridiculous. Completely absurd! All the hope in the world, this girl had, and she wanted to throw it all away.

Reggie turned and walked to her desk, still occupied by her grandmother, and started opening drawers, searching for some mysterious object. "He's talking to me about all these plans after we graduate, and I just know if I don't do this now then I never will, and it's wrong to keep going on like this."

Lori's eyebrows furrowed in confusion. Honestly, this child could be such a moron. "I don't understand. Did he do something? Or did you?" Lori narrowed her eyes. "Is it another guy?" Now *that* got Reggie's attention.

"Jesus, Mom. No!"

"I think what your mother means is, why now?" Kathryn offered.

"Yes, exactly. Why now?" Lori sighed and attempted to regain control. "Child of mine, you're overthinking this whole thing. It's no big deal, just a dance." Lori could feel tears welling up in her eyes. She attempted to find some inkling of understanding for what was going through her daughter's head. Joey was a good kid. Handsome and well liked. Fun and charming, perfect to balance Reggie's sensibility. "Is it because your dad can't be there to walk you out onto the football field before the game?" Lori remembered her own father doing it for her when she was seventeen, reluctant as he was. She couldn't blame Reggie if that's what upset her, but it was still no reason to not participate. They'd figure out another solution. Hell, Lori herself could walk her daughter out, now wouldn't that be something unforgettable?

Reggie seemed to soften. "No, Mom. I mean yes, that's crossed my mind, but that's not why."

"Okay, so what then?"

"He's just," Reggie paused her desk search, a divot forming between her brows and she closed her eyes in concentration. "Joey's so sure that we'll end up together." She fidgeted with her bracelet for a moment before opening her eyes again and resuming her search.

"Isn't that the idea?" Lori remembered so well the feelings of obsessive love she had for James at that age. Like oxygen. She couldn't get enough of him, he couldn't get enough of her. Missed him when he was just a classroom over. Changed hallway routes in between classes just so they could bump into each other. They craved one another like a drug, and it was the happiest she'd ever—

She shook the thought away; she didn't want to think about that now.

No. Now she needed to focus on Reggie. On helping her daughter through her senior year. On helping her get out of her stubborn *mind*, for God's sake. Reggie never did have that sense of spirit to her, and Lori half wondered if it was her own fault. Had she failed to allow Reggie to take risks? Lori didn't think she had, but so much had turned their world upside down in the past years. It was hard to say where she had gone wrong.

"Look at this," Reggie said, closing her desk drawer and handing a piece of paper to Kathryn. "Read it."

"Okay," Kathryn tentatively opened the folded notebook paper. "Oh, Raina honey, I don't have my glasses, I can't read this."

"Fine." Reggie snatched the paper back. "I'll read it. It's a note from Joey. A *poem*."

Lori exchanged a look of question with her mom before they both returned their gaze to Reggie.

"'Roses are red, and I can't get you out of my head.
Violets are blue, and my love for you is more than true.
You've been my best friend since forever.
I won't let go of you ever.
We finally had our first kiss at sixteen.
You were upset because your friends were being mean.
And I promised you then
to me you'd always be a ten.
Reggie
I promise to always keep things edgy!
Like with this poem.
Cuz it's a token.
Of my love for my queen.
Please will you go with me to homecoming?'" Reggie finished the poem and dropped the note to her side.

Lori spoke first. "Well, that's the sweetest thing I've ever heard." She fondly remembered her own poems James would write her, though she had to admit, James had more natural writing talent than Joey.

"He is a sweet boy, isn't he?" Kathryn added.

Reggie waved the paper in the air. "He asked me to homecoming."

"And?" Lori asked with confusion.

"My boyfriend of a year? I think it's pretty much assumed we'd be going together."

Kathryn reached up, running a comforting hand along Reggie's arm. "Well, not necessarily. You *were* just talking about breaking up with him," she shrugged. "Maybe he's picking up on that a little."

"So wait," Lori started. "I'm confused. Is it this poem that set you off?" She rubbed her temples. "I mean, I know it's not exactly Shakespeare, but you don't have to be such a *snob* about it." *Ungrateful brat.*

"Ouch, Mom. That's not the issue. The poem was sweet, yes. It's not just the poem, you guys. It's... it's..." Reggie sat down on her bed. Flopped herself backwards. "I don't know," she said, staring up at the ceiling. "I can't explain it. Maybe I'm just being stupid and overthinking."

Lori looked down at her daughter. She was such a beautiful girl with so much ahead of her to look forward to. Lori could go back in her mind to all those times she had crawled in bed with Reggie over the years, seeking comfort under the guise of her own motherly agenda. She'd sneak in with her, and Reggie's sweet little body would instinctively turn towards her mother. Her hand would rub Lori's cheek as if she knew that was exactly what her mom needed in the wee hours of the night. Just Lori and Reggie and the black stillness.

Lori still to this day would crawl in bed with her daughter every now and then, and Reggie still turned to hold and comfort her mother. The instinct was automatic, even in the dead of Reggie's sleep.

Lori looked at Reggie now in the daylight of her bed and laid down next to her daughter. She grabbed Reggie's hand as they both looked up to stare at the ceiling fan. It swirled around and around, a dizzying cycle. She could feel that now was the time to say something good. Something profound. Something that would help her daughter see all that she had in front of her.

"Reggie, sweetie. You've always been someone that's on a mission." Lori contemplated how to explain her thought with clarity. "You like to set a goal, and you like to make it happen."

"It sounds familiar," Reggie said, a smile in her voice. Kathryn cleared her throat somewhere in the background.

Lori continued. "And sometimes love doesn't really fit neatly into that kind of thinking. You can't just find some solution for love. It's not logical, it just *is*. And you definitely shouldn't be afraid of it." She turned her body to face Reggie. "Joey is a good kid. We've known him and his family for years, and they're good people. That's not always easy to find."

Kathryn rose from the desk chair and placed the garment bag over the back of it. She walked to sit down near the girls on the bottom edge of the bed. "Your mom's right, honey. It's not easy to find." She squeezed Reggie's foot gently. "But if you just don't like Joey anymore, then that's okay."

Lori hoped and prayed that that wasn't the case. "Do you? Still like him?" she asked. *Please, please say yes. Please be smart for once, see all you have. And please bring some happiness into this home.*

"I like him, yes." Reggie shrugged in defeat. "I love him, even. What's not to love? He's the sweetest. He's been my best friend since forever. Other than Lucy, I mean. But yeah, Joey's my best friend.

"And maybe that's just it, that he's my friend more than anything. And I guess what I'm afraid of is that he feels more strongly about me than I do about him." She dropped her voice so low that Lori barely even heard her last words. "I don't want to hurt him."

"You know, that's not a bad thing, maybe," Kathryn said to no one in particular. "That might be the key."

Reggie propped herself up on her elbows to look at her grandmother. "What's the key?"

Lori watched with nervous curiosity as Kathryn turned to look her granddaughter in the eye. "That a man should love the woman just a little more than she loves him." Kathryn glanced at Lori. "Rights the power imbalance."

Lori considered this. While she hated to admit it, she had to agree. "Then it's as simple as that." Lori rose off the bed and grabbed the garment bag. She could feel the sizzle of excitement as she unzipped and pulled out the simple lilac gown. "Your nana and I searched high and low for this, but here it is. Halle Berry wore something similar at the Academy Awards that year, and I just had to have something like it for my prom."

Reggie sat up right, the Laura Ashley blooms around her turning in interest as well. Curious to see this dress. "Wow, Mom."

Might that be actual excitement on my daughter's face? Lori thought. "What do you think, sweetie?"

Reggie stood up carefully, then bounded over and hugged her mom. "How the hell am I supposed to say no to that?"

"You like it?!" The sun appeared to fully emerge behind a cloud and Lori could feel the light returning to her daughter's bedroom.

"I do," Reggie said. "Believe it or not, I actually really do."

IN THE END REGGIE DIDN'T win Homecoming Queen after all, but Joey in all his charm and popularity won King. And Reggie's best friend Lucy won Queen, so all was well.

Lori knew Reggie would have hated the role anyhow. She may never completely understand her daughter, but this small win felt like a big victory in the long run of things. Lori put the photo of

Reggie and Joey in a double photo frame, right beside the newly restored photo of Lori and James from their prom. Matching lilac dresses, matching youthful love.

chapter ten

· · ·

Two years ago

reggie

DO YOU EVER have those funny little ideas pop into your head where you just want to do something ridiculous and dangerous? Like in a crowded theater on the mezzanine, as the lights go down, show about to start and you think to yourself, "What if I just jumped off this balcony right now, screamed at the top of my lungs and jumped?" And suddenly you're worried that you might *actually* do that, might actually scream and cause irrevocable damage to both yourself as well as the people in the way of a mass panic? But then you turn it around and think what if I screamed, and everyone just stared at the lunatic screaming, quietly assessing before turning back their attention to the stage, and you're left wondering when the vacuum around you appeared?

Well, *I* have these thoughts anyway, and apparently there's a name for it.

"The call of the void," my therapist informs me. She jots something down in her notebook before returning her gaze to me.

"The call of the void," I repeat. I look at her skeptically.

Caroline speaks calmly, without judgment, a skill I guess she's a natural at. Would have to be in her profession. I'd long ago gotten used to her frustratingly perfect poker-face, long ago stopped trying to figure out what she was thinking. I suppose I have her to thank for that freedom from desperately wanting to know her reactions. She's tried to free me of that need to know when it comes to other people as well, but apparently, it's a hard skill to master.

"Yes, *l'appel du vide*, the call of the void. Coined by the French. Usually it's associated with a dangerous impulse, like the urge to jump off a high building. Or a vicious curiosity of sorts to put your hand on a flame. Extreme momentary thoughts of danger despite not having any actual suicidal ideation."

"Well that's encouraging," I say flatly.

"There are some theories that suggest it's actually an indicator of a strong will to live, ironically. It's like a moment of..." Caroline pauses, collecting her words. I always like when she does that. It makes her feel more human to me.

She continues, "...like the briefest moment of recognition of the preciousness of life, and the upset you would actually feel if a demonic impulse took over your body and threatened you."

I ponder on this. A strong will to live. Scared of a demonic impulse. It resonates somehow.

"Maybe something's going on in your life that has sparked a recognition in you of the value of living?" she asks. God, she's good.

"I mean, I think I generally have always valued living," I counter.

She smiles warmly. "Good, I should hope so."

We sit in silence for a beat or two. It's like a game of chicken, these silences. Caroline had early on in our work together explained to me the value of silence in the therapy room. How it differs from regular conversation. It used to bother me, the discomfort of it, but by now I had experienced time and again the way that silence allowed me to push past my usual social rhythms of talking. Gets me to places in my subconscious I might not otherwise reach.

I break the silence, giving victory to Caroline yet again. "I do all around feel a little more...something," I say tentatively.

"Something. Something...?" I know she's trying not to put words in my mouth.

I furrow my brows. "Something good. I think."

She sets down her pen and studies my face. "You think it's something good, yet your two eyebrows just became one."

"Are you telling me I need a wax appointment?"

"The lighting is not good enough in here to know for sure." We both lightly laugh at her joke. I look around and take note of the comforting dim glow of this miniature living room.

"No, that's fair," I finally say. "I guess I'm just confused because there *has* been something, or some*one* rather, on my mind."

"Okay." She says this like she knows something. It's not "okay" like in a "Okay, sounds good," type tone. More of an "Ohhh, oh okayyy." Like she understands there's something stirring.

"It's a guy that's come back into town. A man."

She nods gently. "And the difference between a guy and a man?"

I fidget with the hairband around my wrist. "He's older than me. Thirty-nine. But he doesn't seem it," I quickly add. I don't know why, it's not like Caroline cares about his age or is going to judge.

"And what's brought him to the forefront of your mind?"

I love that she doesn't ask how I know him or who he is or any of that typical kind of thing. She gets right down to how it's affecting me. "I wouldn't say he's at the forefront per say," I say carefully. "But he's back in town, he used to live all over the place—a military man. He just moved back here, it's where he's from origi-nally. I recently saw him for the first time in years. Have seen him a few times since." I think about the small exchanges we've had when he's come in for his PT. They feel strained, brusque, even. There's an energy that is always there when I'm around him, but I think both of us have been trying to keep things as kosher as possible.

"How many years?" Caroline asks.

I scrunch up my nose. "Like, I was probably in braces and pimple-faced. Ten years. Eleven actually," I add, remembering with amusement X's correction of my timeframe that first night at the Moon Lounge.

"Eleven years. A long time for sure."

"Yes."

"You changed a lot in those eleven years."

"Uh-huh."

More quiet. Finally she elaborates, "I say that because you didn't just answer me with 'eleven years,' but you offered up the description of the awkward girl you would have been that many years ago."

"So?"

She shrugs slightly. "So maybe nothing, maybe that's just what popped up in your mind. But it makes me wonder what exactly made that braces and pimples reference pop into your head. What made that significant, why not the thoughts of how *he* was different eleven years ago?"

"You think it's my ego talking?" Ego and its frustrating ability to get in one's way come up a lot in my sessions with Caroline.

"I think you are focused on how you have changed in eleven years." God, she can be frustrating.

"Isn't that natural?"

"Well yes, of course. But remember, this conversation started with the question of what's been going on in your world that has led to some call of the void moments. Something that is sparking a feeling of loving being alive. Feeling a renewed sense of value in living."

"And I love being alive and no longer having pimples and braces."

"In this man's presence, perhaps?" she questions me gently, one eyebrow raised.

"Ughhh," I throw my hands over my face. "Yes! Yes. It's embarrassing. I shudder to remember how he last saw me," I dramatically emphasize the word "shudder" with a shoulder shake, "but truth be told, I don't even think he cares about that at all. Though I am *definitely* thankful to be the far more lovely woman that I am today." I look up at the ceiling tiles and sigh. "And I cannot. Stop. THINKING about him. There. I said it." I return my gaze back to her.

She doesn't say anything, bless her heart. Doesn't mention Joey or doesn't tell me my focus is all messed up or any of the things my own restless mind is saying. She just sits with her notebook and her pen and waits for me to continue. Smiles slightly.

But eventually Caroline again shows that she's human too, and she caves, breaking our silence. "Did you have a crush on him when you were a kid? When you last saw him?" She dropped it. Dropped the bomb of a question that I know I need to be asked.

I consider this. "I mean, I guess. I guess, yeah." I shrug. "A silly little nothing crush that I probably never even admitted to myself. He was quiet. Dashing, if you will. He had an air of mystery and wisdom. He was getting ready to deploy for his second tour. Everyone was long over the war at that point I think, but he was still going, still prepping to head to this great beyond that I was sort of fascinated by. And I remember talking to him, asking him about it. Asking if he...if he felt like the war was still worthwhile, or did he feel like we didn't need to be there at all." I once again cover my face with my hands. "I didn't even know what I was talking about, and I was afraid he'd see right through that."

"Well, I didn't know you back then, but knowing you now, I imagine even as a teenager you had the same moral conviction," Caroline suggests.

I drop my hands and think about this. "I like the idea of that, it sounds nice. But really, I think I just wanted to talk to him for some reason. Was as simple as me trying to find an excuse to." I sit with that recognition for a minute. Caroline scribbles something down in her notebook.

"And now? What do you feel around him now?"

I close my eyes. Force myself to focus, figure out this feeling. This pull I'm having. I take a few breaths in. Breaths out. I think back to the dinner we had. The patio. The subtle smell of that cologne of his, the feel of his hand on mine. Focus on the feeling in me from that night. My reaction to his words. "I feel like…I feel like he sees me. Like he sees a side of me that no one else can." Yes, that's it, I realize. I feel seen when I'm around X. And it's both thrilling and terrifying.

"Not even Joey?" she asks, her tone gentle.

Ahh, so she does bring up Joey. Well, I suppose the elephant in the room had to be invited in at some point. Welcome to the therapy room, step on up and join us in getting naked.

"No." I open my eyes and look at her. "Especially not Joey."

"Hmm," she nods. "And what's the difference? Between this man and Joey?"

It's a good question, one I need to figure out. "I'm not sure. I don't know if it's just that it's new, and that's the thrill of it, or if it's something else."

Caroline looks down at her notes. Reads back to me, "You said a moment ago that even when you were sixteen, this other man had an air of mystery and wisdom. That you found you wanted to talk to him." She looks back up at me. "Back then, you and Joey would have been brand new, right?"

I'm caught off guard by her take here. "Are you suggesting my feeling now isn't about the new-ness of it?"

"I'm pointing out that you had a pull back then, and you feel it now as well. Whatever it may be. Maybe it's just a girlhood crush resurfacing for shits and giggles."

I giggle reflexively. For some reason I find it funny when Caroline curses.

"Or maybe he evokes something in you that is missing from Joey, and while this all may have nothing to do with the character of this other man, it may be forcing you to face some hard truths on your relationship with Joey. One of the initial reasons you started coming here in the first place, right?"

Well shit, Caroline. Way to call me out and throw me to the wolves. She's good.

I stare at a canvas painting on her wall. A mess of colors in a circular pattern, the outer part of the circle red and scattered, brush strokes vivid. The center part of the circle clear and calm, yellow. Warm. I hold my gaze at that center as I answer her. "Yes," I reply carefully. "For someone that has never had a problem pulling the trigger, I've never felt ready to pull it with Joey. And I have absolutely no concrete reason why." I peel my eyes away from the warm yellow center of the painting. "But I think I'm getting it. I think it's me."

"How so?" She looks at me expectantly.

I start nodding my head as something dawns on me. "I need to start talking to Joey about things I actually care about. Be more honest. Vulnerable."

"Mmm hmm," she nods with encouragement.

"Allow him in more."

"A good start."

"And give him the chance to be the everything to me that everyone else believes he already is."

WE WRAP UP THE SESSION and I walk out to my car. I open the door and hop in. We've had a heat wave recently, hopefully our last of the season, and my car is an oven after baking in the sun for the past hour. The temperature engulfs me in molten suffocation. I open the windows for a desperate break. Sit for a moment. What did she say that thing was, call of the void? It speaks to me. I feel it sometimes not just in the concept of a theater balcony, but also on this bridge I frequently drive over. Like I might just turn off it without thinking, and then I try to quickly right the wrong in my mind and think, "Go straight ahead, go straight, keep driving straight ahead," until I'm off the bridge and safely on solid ground again.

Joey is solid ground. He's safe. It's me that's being the idiot ruining things with my thoughts of X. X is the bridge and the abyss down below, and I've got to get ahold of myself.

I pull out of my spot and drive off, all the while thinking, "Just go straight ahead."

chapter eleven

. . .

reggie

YOU KNOW, NOW that I think about it, I didn't have braces at all back when I was sixteen. Pimples, maybe, but no braces. I already had them removed by then. I know because I distinctly remember the time when my stepfather Richard had looked at me—I was fresh out of the car and walking into the house post-removal—and he teased that maybe there's hope for my face after all. And he died when I was fifteen.

So no, I didn't have braces back at that sendoff party for X.

But I did have a bracelet.

I've just finished my evening run (not nearly as hot as the past few days have been, much to my relief), and I'm putting my tracker watch back in my jewelry drawer when I notice it. The bracelet I mean, the one from way back when.

Joey gave it to me shortly after we had gotten together. I thought it random but sweet, and I used to wear it religiously. Don't give me too much credit now for being sentimental or anything, I just genuinely liked the thing. It's simple silver, a delicate rope with one tiny charm—a snowflake with a purple gem in the middle because my birthday is in February. There was a matching ring with it too, but I haven't a clue where that is now.

I wore that bracelet the evening when I had last seen X, before his deployment. We were at the buffet table and we both reached for the...well for the something, I can't really remember what it was, exactly. Salad or fruit or whatever bowl of nourishment is commonly offered during a summer party. I remember accidentally touching hands and feeling the electrical shock of that nanosecond connection zing right on up my arm and to my chest, right down to butterflies in my belly. I think X said something like, "Ladies first, after you," and it was then that I had the urge to talk to him about something, anything.

I had muttered a meek, "Thanks," and resumed my reach, and that's when he commented on my bracelet, complimenting it. Yes, it's all coming back to me now. He said something like, "Nice bracelet, I like the snowflake," and I explained that Joey had given it to me, and he nodded, and that's when I did my brazen inquiry about his thoughts on U.S. troops still being in the Middle East.

Embarrassing as that is to remember now, I do recall that he was kind to me. Indulged me in my thoughts and gave some explanation of service to country and a philosophy of how do we ever really know the right or wrong of anything. He told me about how for his first deployment he was excited in an almost cocky kind of way. I remember eating up all he had to say, thrilled that he was talking to little old me.

His hair was cut short back then, face clean-shaven, but it was his amber eyes that drew me in as he spoke. "I'd go around telling people that my profession is combat, and I'm a trained badass," he had said. I loved his little self-deprecating humor. I had laughed along with him.

"Is it hard to leave home? Anyone in particular you're going to miss?" I had asked.

He nodded, dropped the smile and I could see the pain in his eyes. I immediately wanted to take it away, yet I couldn't help but feel thrilled by this moment with him. With the inaccessible X. We had never talked like this before; hell, never even had an actual one-on-one conversation, probably.

I wanted to know more. "You said you felt cocky about it before your first deployment. What about now?" And he went on to explain the loss of innocence after that first tour. The loss of safety and security. How having your life at risk for long periods of time changes you. How it feels nearly impossible to reclaim the sense of security that civilians take for granted in their everyday lives, and I think it was right then and there that I fell in love just a little, because his words felt hauntingly familiar.

I think about that now as I peel the sweaty fabric of my running gear off my body. He had said so many things that stuck with me. The loss of security—in many ways I feel like I've never truly had that. I've always had a feeling like I have to stand on my own two feet, lean on no one. Sure, I didn't grow up in an active combat zone. But the loss of half my family has been a tragedy that has been woven deep into the fabric of my existence. It's impossible to feel too secure when tragedy is a narrative you've carried around with you.

I head into the bathroom and turn on the shower. My favorite part of running is probably this part—the post-run steaming hot reward for all my efforts. As I wait for the tell-tale steam to inform me the water temperature is ready, I think about the other point X had made all those years ago. The point about how we do ever really know the right and wrong of something. The decisions and choices we have and the moral compass we use to make them. How do we know what's right? Military missions, customs and traditions, societal expectations.

Or more pertinent in my mind currently, how do we gauge the right or wrong of a relationship?

MY RUN HAS REJUVENATED ME, though, and I'm starting fresh, I have decided. It's Friday night, and Joey, by some miracle, has off work. He, Lucy, and Justin are over now, and Joey has agreed to pizza takeout. Also a miracle. Though naturally he was adamant about the place. I usually order anywhere *but* the spot he likes, since the kids working there are more than likely high and half the time mess up the order, but what can you do. See Joey has a soft spot in his heart for those kids, and I must admit, it's the best pizza in town. Thin crust without being too crunchy, a light flavor to the sauce that still retains its freshness due to the sauce not being overly cooked. The perfect blend and quantity of cheeses.

Yes, Joey is the one to have pointed out all those checked boxes. I just knew I liked the stuff.

But as I sit and sip on my wine, (I seem to reach more for cabernet than lager these days), and listen to the hum-drum of conversation about the football season back in full swing, I contemplate the small topics of life and love and relationships and memories. You know, nothing big. Just trying to solve my world's problems one sip and maniacal thought process at a time. I'm wearing the bracelet for some idiotic reason and I'm twisting and turning that snowflake to the point of eroding the poor thing.

It's been dawning on me though, the whole right and wrong concept. How do you know when someone is The One? There's so much that is right with my relationship with Joey, and really nothing that is wrong. We're both funny, hardworking, we have so much history together, his family has welcomed me in always. Hell, welcomed my mom and Nana too. Is that it then? He's crowned the almighty The One?

"Your snowflake bracelet, is that..." Lucy looks at me with question on her face as she sits down on the counter stool beside to me. We're sitting at my kitchen island, overlooking the living room. She runs a hand through her dark hair as she waits for my explanation.

"It is, yup. I stumbled across it randomly. Was feeling sentimental I guess." I glance over at Joey and Justin, sitting over on the couch watching some sports discussion show. "You bored with the Eagles recap or what?"

She laughs, "A little, plus I was hoping to talk dresses with you." She has a twinkle in her eye as she starts up the wedding conversation.

Lucy is a great bride. Particular on some things, go with the flow on others. She's chosen a December wedding so that "we have something to look forward to after Thanksgiving and before Christmas." The girl has always loved the magic of the holiday season. She opens up her phone and starts scrolling through various black gowns.

"Oh, not what I was expecting," I say. "You're wearing a black dress?"

"So funny," she scolds. "My hope is that *you* will wear a black dress."

I'm thankful that she thinks I was kidding because that is literally where my mind went. I see now how off and out of it I am. Especially because her mom—a fashion designer—is making her dress, and it's most definitely *not* black—I've seen the sketch for it. Am I a love scrooge? I grab the phone and scroll through her screenshots. "These are all gorgeous."

"You can't go wrong with black, it's elegant and perfect for a December wedding."

I nod in agreement. "You pick the one, I'll wear it."

"Well, you're no fun. Don't you have any interest in something specific? Cut-outs, one shoulder, strapless, lace, deep V..." she looks at me expectantly, brown eyes wide and waiting.

"What's Lila wearing, did she pick yet?"

"Something simple, my mom's making her dress too. It's this whole vision she has of her girls in the dresses of her creation, which is funny considering my mom actually bought hers from a fellow designer. Gotta play the industry game, I guess."

"It's sweet though." I look back at the options and look for one that speaks to me. Scroll in search of something dazzling, yet practical. "I think I like something like this." I point to a slim, lacy fitted gown with two lace cutouts in the middle. "Keep the boobs in but still a little sexy."

She smirks, caramel hair cascading around her face. "For all the dancing you'll refuse to do?"

"I dance with enough champagne in me."

Lucy laughs at this. "That is true, I do recall the last wedding we attended."

It was a friend of Joey and Justin's, and Lucy and I had a grand old time drinking far too much champagne and carrying on like we owned the place. There's something completely fantastic about going to a wedding where one, you aren't actually in it and two, you don't know anyone there all that well. No pressure, no photo taking so you get to fully enjoy the cocktail hour. In fact, no one at all really cares where you are or what you're doing, and Lucy and I sure had fun with that to the best of our abilities. I highly recommend it. I think I now understand wedding crashing.

"Say, question for you my, Lovely Lucy," I say.

"Yeeesss???" She frowns at me. Narrows her eyes. "Why do I feel like I don't want to know this question?"

"I don't know, because you're planning a wedding and you've had to hear a million people's suggestions and demands and it's getting old and here we are talking about your wedding and I'm asking you a question?" I take a dramatic breath. Smile and turn back to my wine.

"Actually I think it was the 'Lovely Lucy' that did it." She motions her hand toward me. "Carry on."

I glance back at the guys, enthralled with their show. Return my gaze back to Lucy. "How did you know Justin was the one?"

"Oh boy."

"What 'oh boy?'"

"Oh boy, I didn't see that coming." Lucy tilts her head to the side in contemplation. "Or maybe I did, actually."

"You did?" Now I'm the one surprised.

"Well, yeah. You and Joey have been together for a thousand years, I think we all thought you guys would be first to get married." She takes a sip of her wine. "Or at the very least move in together. I mean, yeah. I get the whole he works in the city, you wanted your practice here, bit. But still, where there's a will, there's a way."

"Ouch." I suddenly feel horrifically exposed. "You think that's a thing? Like people talk about that?"

"Maybe."

"Maybe? That's it? That's all you have to offer me right now, Lovely Lucy?"

"I'm not sure what to say here."

"Try for profound or encouraging." I look at her in hopes to get something else out of her.

She bites her lip in concentration. I can see she's thinking of something, there's something on that mind of hers. "You know better than to think about what people say," she says tentatively.

"Uh-huh."

"And I mean, I've seen you guys since the start of it all, so I have a different take." Lucy looks at me as if to gauge my reaction so far. I'm breathless to hear where she's going with this.

"True. I could see that."

She grabs my hand with the bracelet, lifts the snowflake charm up onto her fingertips. "What made you put this on?"

"Lucy!" I say a little too loudly. Another glance at the boys and I realize they're lost in the TV anyhow.

"Fine." She drops the snowflake and my hand. "I think you and Joey are adorable, but that you see him more as yet another person you take care of."

"What?" I say. I'm completely thrown off, she's never once before said anything like this to me.

"Like the way you take care of your mom." Her eyes search mine, and I can tell she's checking in to read my face, see my reaction to that little bomb.

I sit with this for a moment. "Okay," I say. Lucy knows me so well. Knows that when it comes to my mom, there's always been little room for my needs or problems, because it's always all about her. And I'm fine with that, I've come to grips with it. It works for us and benefits me by allowing for my coveted privacy.

I nod my head. "I can maybe see what you mean." I cross my legs under the counter and lean forward, resting my face in my hand. "I suppose I do feel like the adult to both of them a bit." But as I say the words out loud, I wonder, is that even a bad thing? I really don't know, it comes so naturally to me. I guess I've just always thought I was one of those people, the type that takes care of things. Leads. Takes charge.

I think back to a point in time when we did a school trip to New York. It was in high school, senior year, I think. Despite not living too far from the city, most of the kids hadn't really been to New York, or at the very least, they knew nothing about navigating the subway. We had divided off into a little group of five or six— me, Lucy, Joey, Joey's best friend at the time, one or two others. And I was somehow the one to lead the way, figure out the plan, the lines, the stations, etc. Not that I really knew what I was doing either, but I wasn't just going to awkwardly stand around waiting for something, stuck in the overcrowded Times Square because we were too dumb and afraid to navigate beyond that.

And I have to tell you, nervous as I was to get something wrong, we ended up having an absolutely splendid time that day. Found great little shops and ate lunch at some place *other* than the Hard Rock Cafe. Other kids had been all bent out of shape wishing they had joined in on our group. I had swelled with pride that day. The Conqueror of New York City. Alright, maybe it wasn't all that special, but we had fun, let's just say that.

Did I mention I was voted "Leader of the Pack" in our high school yearbook? That's right.

Joey was voted "Best Smile." Those damn dimples of his.

Lucy and I continue to sit there for a moment. I break the

silence. "So with you and Justin, aren't one of you the caretaker? I mean maybe that's just how relationships work."

She nods and shrugs. "Sure, sometimes, I suppose." She smirks. "And yes, I'm most definitely the caretaker in the relationship, without a doubt. But you already knew that, don't lie."

I smile sheepishly, "Fine, yes I knew that."

"But you, Reggie. You act like you love to lead and command and all that, but you know what I remember?"

"Should I be scared?"

Lucy ignores me. "I remember in college when you met this random author or podcast host or something, and she was a guest speaker in your class."

"She was a guest to the campus doing a speaking event, yes," I interrupt.

"Right. That. And you went and stood in line to meet with her afterwards, and you were gushing, talking about the genius of this woman for like a solid month and I thought, boy Reggie is a nerd."

"Hey," I nudge her leg with mine under the counter.

"Whatever, you know you are."

"Your point?" I wait, having a feeling I know where this is going.

Lucy sighs. "My point is that when you stumble across someone you admire, who shares a passion with you, you come *alive*. It's a rare but beautiful side of you that comes out. And while Joey might be the sweetest and most fun guy anyone knows," she looks over to him, "he's not exactly neck and neck with you in passion on solving the world's problems. He's more a 'yolo' kind of guy, content to live in the moment." She looks back at me. "And maybe, just maybe, you feel a little of that disconnect with him."

"Uh-huh." I give her a look of "go on," because I can tell she's not finished, but she's a bit hesitant.

"For some there's good balance in that. I mean Joey definitely helps bring out the silly side in you."

"How kind of you to say I need help in that."

"Stop it, you know what I mean."

I drop the facade, "Fine, I know what you mean, yes. Continue."

"And I think you and Joey could live a long and happy life together. Happily ever after, no problem. I really do. I'm not sure I believe in one soulmate. I think we choose someone worthwhile and fight to make it work."

I nod, because I think she's making a lot of sense.

She continues. "In fact, I think you're the kind of person that could make just about anything work because you have that mindset somehow. You're not dramatic, you're sensible and pragmatic..."

"Like a wristwatch."

"Yeah, like a...wait, what? Oh my Lord, Reggie," She looks at me with faux annoyance. Rolls her eyes.

"And you say I need Joey to bring out my silly side," I tease.

"I did not, you're twisting my words around, woman. Do you want to hear what I have to say or not? Remember that you asked." She crosses her long, bronzed arms over her chest and waits for my response.

"Fine. Yes, I do. I really do. I need to hear this because everyone always seems to tell me I'm so lucky to have the perfect man—"

"No one is perfect," Lucy interjects.

"—even my therapist refuses to give me her opinion."

"I think that's on purpose."

"But I give you full permission." I nod in Lucy's direction. "Please. Go on. Tell me what you think."

She looks at me, really looks at me deep in the eyes. I can even see her eyes darting back and forth between mine, wondering how far to go. She takes a big ole breath in. Like, real big. And I brace myself for impact because I know my girl and I know she's about to say something solid, and hot-dog, oh man, I am on the edge of my seat wondering if she's about to spit some truth at me that no one around me has had the guts to share.

"Alright, you asked." She looks at me carefully. "Reggie, my fiery Reggie."

"Will you marry—"

"Don't interrupt with a joke right now." She puts her hand up to stop me. Glances back at the boys again. Leans forward towards me and says, "I think if you ever planned on moving forward with Joey, you would have done it by now." She leans back, crosses her arms again. "And it's why you're sitting here asking me how I know that my man is 'The One.'" Lucy nods in triumph, and I see maybe the tiniest bit of reflective worry in her eye.

Well, there you have it, ladies and gentleman. Words of wisdom from the one and only Lucy Ray, soon to be Lucy Harris. And my mind goes back to X, my brief conversations with him, the moments of intensity with him. How I know we've only just scratched the surface and I have this complete and total pull to wanting to hear more of what he thinks about the world, all he's seen, what he thinks gives us meaning, what creates things like a cultural tradition or whatever else he can possibly teach me.

What that "*Miles to go before I sleep*," poem line means to him.

The doorbell rings with our pizza and I reluctantly rise to go get it. Lucy grabs my hand real quick with a, "Hey, you okay?"

I nod once. "I am. I think. I'm just stirring up some strange thoughts, that's all."

"Okay," she says with a look that tells me she's not at all convinced and that I'm definitely going to be getting lots of check-in texts from her in the next few days. I want to shout it to her that I *have* felt a connection recently, that something *has* been stirring within the presence of a certain someone, but I push the thoughts down, down, down.

I smile to her in reassurance before turning my attention to the front of my house. Walk towards the door. Open it. And just about fall over because there, holding our pizza boxes and a brown paper bag of grease and fries and all that is good in life is...

Well, by now you've surely guessed it.

X.

I hear what I presume to be Joey's footsteps trot on up behind me. My heart is beating, *pounding* in my chest so unexpectedly and I find that I've forgotten to breathe.

X smiles down at me, *God he's so tall and sexy,* and I feel Joey's hand on the small of my back.

"Hey," Joey says, all blissful warmth and ignorance and enthusiasm. Meanwhile I'm just sitting there like a goddamn deer in headlights and poor X is looking at us like the last thing he signed up for was to be the pizza delivery boy, but here he is.

I step aside and look with what I hope is obvious question in my eyes to Joey.

"Right," Joey says, all smiles and dimples as he realizes he forgot to tell me about our added guest. "Did I not mention I invited Uncle Xavier to join us?"

Yes, my dear ones, you heard correctly.

Our mystery man X, my worldly crush, military hero and all that...

He's my beloved Joey's uncle.

chapter twelve

. . .

X

"**R**EALLY THE ONLY thing I can say is, I thought I might be better off dead for a little while there. In the months after returning stateside," X says. Four sets of eyes stare back at him, riveted by this revelation.

"Jesus, Uncle Xavier. I never knew that," Joey says, astonishment clear on his face.

The gang has made their way out back onto Reggie's deck. It's quiet. There's a rustling of trees and the perfect breeze. After so long in the desert, X realizes he's never appreciated the sound of rustling leaves more. Even when he returned back from overseas, he ended up stationed in the deserts of Arizona most recently.

X returns his attention to Joey and shrugs. "It's not exactly the type of thing you share with pride, wishing your life would end." Lucy's fiancé had brought up X's deployment again in hopes to hear some stories.

X was deflecting. Rehashing it wasn't something he liked to do all that much, even if he did have good stories that people wanted to hear. For him, the stories had a happy ending, but others weren't so lucky. It felt like a dishonor to go on about it when he knew there were families out there somewhere with a far less happy tale to tell. Families that would forever hold an ache and absence in their heart to loved ones lost. Lost in a distant desert in a land they'd never lay eyes on in their lifetime. That haunts him.

"I'd say we need to speak up about it though," Reggie responds to his last statement. She's sitting directly across from X. He turns to face her and waits for her to continue. "Right? I mean isn't that the big thing, veterans and PTSD and trying to destigmatize mental health and offer quality care for those that need it most, yet seek it out the least?" She leans back in her seat. He takes note of the passion in her eyes. It's dim out here, but there's just enough of an evening glow left to see how she lights up when she's talking. She scans around to the rest of them, Lucy and the fiancé and Joey. He wonders if she's looking for agreement on their part or challenging anyone to speak up and offer a solution. Then she looks back at him. "So what did you do?"

X shrugs. "I got help. Counseling."

"You did?" Joey asks, surprise in his voice.

"And?" Reggie presses. Her eyes dart back and forth between his. Searching with concern.

"I'm here now, right?" he says. He's not about to dive into the details of it. While going to therapy was definitely one of his smarter moves in life, there's still some things that deserve to remain private.

Thankfully, Reggie seems to quietly understand his need for privacy on that front. She smiles with a knowing look, and he melts at the warmth in her face. He loves when she smiles at him like that. There's a comfort to it. "Good. I'm glad you did," she says with soft encouragement.

Lucy speaks up. "We've come a long way with counseling and mental health, hopefully. Hell, Reggie and I both have therapists. We love our sessions."

The fiancé, Justin, nods in agreement. He'd been surprisingly quiet since X mentioned his raw thoughts, clearly uncomfortable with the conversation. "Yeah, definitely," Justin says. "Even at my work we have random speakers coming in to talk about meditation and shit. It's all the rage right now."

"All the rage and shit. How romantic, Justin," Reggie chides in a sing-song voice. X laughs to himself.

Justin throws his hands up in defeat. "Look, I admit it's not my most comfortable subject, alright? Can you blame me? Just being honest."

Reggie cocks her head to the side with a look on her face that says, "Really?" But then something in her softens and she lets out a sigh. "You're right," she says as she nods. "And I think you men especially," she waves her wine glass around to X, Justin, and Joey, "have the hardest time of anyone asking for help."

"Says my miss independent princess," Joey says before rising to give Reggie a kiss on the forehead.

X watches as his nephew maneuvers around the wicker coffee table and heads to the sliding door. "I'm grabbing some more fries, anyone want anything?" Joey asks.

"I'll follow you," Justin jumps up and joins Joey as he's heading inside. X can't help but feel amused and satisfied at having successfully shut him up.

X looks back to Reggie and Lucy. "Guess that got to be too much for them."

Reggie laughs. "That, and I'm pretty sure Joey's about to grab a leftover slice of pizza, stuff it with fries, sit on my couch to devour it and pass out."

Lucy adds, "You forgot to mention while holding a beer."

"Yes! Yes, of course. Poor guy works late all the time, but then struggles to stay up past nine on his nights off." She puts down her wine and fidgets with her bracelet. "You know, fries do sound kinda good right now."

"Want me to get you some before Joey makes them disappear?" X offers. He immediately wonders if he rushed that offer and has now given her the impression he, too, wants off this deck. In reality he finds that he loves sitting here with this woman. She captivates him. He wants to hear more of what she has to say. His attraction to her feels like a kind of sick torture, and he's starting to think he needs to find a way to steer clear of her given the danger of who she is— his favorite nephew's girlfriend.

Then again, if he was ready to do that, he wouldn't have chosen her practice for his physical therapy care.

He was fucked.

Reggie releases her bracelet and waves at him in dismissal. "No no, healthy eating and all that. It'll just sit like a brick in my belly all night. And that, I tell you what, is no fun at all." She shakes her head.

Lucy nods in agreement. "We're running tomorrow morning, right?"

"That's right," Reggie nods.

"Good."

They sit in comfortable silence for a bit, each of them looking peaceful and relaxed while enjoying the hum of the evening. Soft music accompanies their space. Reggie murmurs, "I love this song," at some point. It's a song he's not familiar with, a country/blues tune of sorts. The singer croons on about letting go and warm nights or something like that. She hums along and looks so beautiful in the glow of the citronella candle. She closes her eyes, and he watches as she allows herself to get lost in the melody. He wants to ask her what she's thinking, what's going through her mind as she is so clearly captivated by these notes. He has a feeling it's something beautiful, and hell if he doesn't have an ache in his heart to be in it with her. Touching her. Dancing with her, holding her soft body as she loses herself to the melody.

When the song finishes Reggie opens her eyes as if an idea has come to her. "You know, X," she starts. He's never heard her refer to him by that. Joey and the other nieces and nephews might do the occasional "Uncle X," but that's about it. He likes it.

She continues, "I'm beginning to worry we're never going to hear any more of these war stories of yours." She leans forward and puts her elbows on her knees. Cocks her head to the side and looks straight at him. He notices she does that sometimes, these little head tilts. "It's like you don't actually want to share at all. Isn't that right, hun?"

He mindlessly reaches his hand up to rub on his bearded cheek, the hair finally growing in after way too many years of daily shaving, a requirement to fit military regulations. He missed this beard. "You know, Reggie, I'm not sure I like that little smirk on your face. Hun."

"Sure you do." She smiles and holds his gaze. Starts to nod while now full-fledged grinning. He wonders with amusement how much she's had to drink. She seems like a bit of a light weight. "And I'll tell you why you like it. Like this smirk right here." She points to her face for reference.

"Alright, come on now, let's hear it," he says.

"You like it because it means," she pauses for emphasis. "That you," another pause. "Can get away with avoiding your dreaded big hero stories altogether." She sits back in triumph.

Lucy clears her throat. He and Reggie turn to face her. "Am I right?" Reggie asks her.

Lucy looks back and forth between them. She grabs her water glass and says, "What I think is that it's getting late and I gotta take Justin home, but you two carry on." She collects her phone and an empty wine bottle, her empty wine glass, and steps behind X to move around to the sliding door. X jumps up to help her with it, opens the door for her and gives a nod of "Goodbye."

"Wait, I'll walk you out," Reggie stands and follows them to the slider.

"It's fine." Lucy leans down and kisses the slightly shorter Reggie's cheek. "Love you, babe. Stay and entertain."

"You sure?"

"Yes! Bye Xavier." Lucy turns away and walks in the house.

Reggie leans in, saying, "See ya, Justin," before returning to face X as he closes the door again. "That felt awkward, did that feel awkward to you?" she asks him.

"I'm thinking maybe you should have some water," he says, smiling at her.

"Me? Oh me?" She reaches up to touch her cheeks. "I am a little rosy, aren't I? Damn it fair skin, always giving me away, even out here in the dark." She saunters back toward the wicker loveseat and coffee table where her water glass sits next to her abandoned wine. He watches as she takes a big swig of her water, then nods with satisfaction before setting it down and walking past X, over to the deck railing. She leans her forearms on it and stares out to the trees and the night.

He settles next to her and rests one elbow, shifting his weight to one side while facing her. He notices her playing with the bracelet again. "You alright?" he asks.

Reggie nods. "Yeah, I think so." She raises an eyebrow at him in a quick glance and says, "I was in fact thirsty," before returning her gaze straight ahead.

He wants to rub her back, wants to give a gesture of comfort. Run his fingers through her hair, push the mass of strawberry blonde to the side and expose her neck, those three freckles. He wants to ask her what's on her mind. *Fuck, life is unfair sometimes,* he thinks to himself. While he can't exactly pinpoint what conveys that Reggie's not in love with his nephew, he sure as hell can see that Joey is head over heels for her.

Joey. His sweet nephew that he's always had a soft spot for. What are the odds? Joey's dad worked long hours as a surgeon, and with only sisters, Joey's mom Isabella, X's half-sister, would have X step in as much as possible to be that male figure for Joey. He had a feeling Isabella knew how much it meant to X to be a part of their family. Isabella and X had the same dad, different moms. Your classic secretary-affair situation, though Isabella's mom was a saint and took her husband back after the affair was revealed.

Which left X and his mom, and she wasn't exactly your baking cookies and building traditions type.

But Isabella ensured X felt a role within the family, especially when she started her own. X was at every Little League game possible for Joey. Football game and whatever else. X taught Joey how to pump up his bike tires. How to do the math that Isabella hated, would take him fishing, shop for the sneakers Joey actually wanted.

The worst part about leaving for the military was leaving behind Joey.

That all seems like a lifetime ago, though, now. That's the funny thing about the military. You leave and travel and live all these different places, but in your mind the world back home stays the same. Just as you left it. Every tree and plant the same size, every person the same age.

Except that it doesn't stay the same. Not at all. The people in that world back home don't stay seven years old. They age, they turn eight and then nine and then years go by and they're teenagers. Then grown men with an unfolding career and a woman to love.

And you've changed too, like it or not. You've seen more than you wanted, and the youthful spirit and innocence is long gone and there's something darker in its wake. And all the while, all the running away you had been doing in the first place, it all proves that the tough stuff imprinted in your mind, those demons are only faster and stronger and the force of it all catches up. Or maybe it never needed to catch up, because it was never gone in the first place. You just pretended not to see it.

Pretended you had it all under control.

But you didn't.

He shakes away his thoughts and turns to rest both forearms on the railing, side by side with Reggie.

She breaks through their silence. "You know, I remember really well the last time I saw you. At your going away party before your deployment." He waits for her to continue. "I asked you your thoughts about leaving."

"I remember," he says. "My 'purpose there' you said." He links his fingers together and forms a steeple with his thumbs under his chin.

She huffs out a laugh. "It was a pointless thing to ask a man with no choice but to leave."

"It was a breath of fresh air, Reggie."

She turns her face toward him. "It was?"

He drops his hands to meet her gaze. "It was. Yes. *You* were a breath of fresh air." He watches as she twists the chain on her wrist again, the snowflake bracelet and matching ring X had helped Joey pick out for her years ago.

He hopes he hasn't made her uncomfortable. He tries to explain further. "See, when you deploy, you get one of two reactions from people: you get the heightened sadness of missing loved ones, though for a single man with no kids to leave behind I considered myself lucky on that front. But you know, you get the tears and 'be careful out there' well wishes."

"And the other reaction?"

He shrugs. "Just logistics. Do you need socks and underwear or when can we expect to hear from you, that kind of thing.

"But no one ever talks about how you feel about it. Not really. Maybe they ask if you're worried, but all you can answer to that is 'I'll be fine' because what more is there? But that's not you, Reggie. No—you instead asked my thoughts on the mission as a whole. Right at the very hour of the plunge into it."

"Right. Pointless."

"Not pointless, no. It was...well like I said, a breath of fresh air. It was honest. And I admired that. I almost needed that in some ways."

"How so?" she asks.

"Because it was validating. What is war, really? Any of them? It's the acts of decisions made by people all fighting for what they believe to be true, necessary. That's it. It's as simple as that, yet so detrimental to so many. Human lives whittled down to pieces of a puzzle.

"And I think before my first deployment I would have had a different take on that. Back then I felt this incredible opportunity to serve my country, and I still do feel that, don't get me wrong. But that first deployment felt like I was accomplishing something good. Being of service gives people purpose in and of itself, and you're high on that in a first deployment."

"So what changes? In the subsequent ones?"

"I guess it's the very fact that you have to return. The job's not done, and you start to wonder what the job was in the first place. You think about the way things were in the first round, and how they compare now, and suddenly it's this chance to zoom out, see a bigger picture." He watches as she licks her lips, and he wonders if she's going to say something, be she remains quiet, merely listening.

He continues. "I think a part of me even had a feeling that this next deployment was going to be different, and it was. Yes, everyone loves the hero that survived story, but I just got lucky. Got lucky when others didn't. Survived when others didn't, and that sits heavy. The actions I took are the same ones they would have taken for me. I just got to go home afterwards. I'm no different."

Reggie nods at this. An understanding. "The lucky survive."

"Yes. The lucky survive."

The words they both know too well settle between them in the evening air, in the rustle in the leaves, settle in the pocket that has formed around them, the pocket that threatens to implode in a destruction of the lies we tell ourselves to make ourselves feel better. Or worse, to avoid the pain all together. He can feel it, sense it's thick breath, and the hardest thing is that he knows there's no way out of this.

Reggie is a survivor, just like he is. And with surviving comes guilt. Nothing you can do about it. You just accept it for what it is and hope you can make some sense and meaning of it all.

But survivor's guilt is a cross to bear that no one understands except those that have been in it too. Those that have been the "lucky" ones to bear it. And it leaves a mark on your soul and makes it that much harder to go on and exist and worry about the mundane details of daily living. It's hard to worry about having the right type of car or house or pretend to care about the bullshit so and so said because you know that it's all just life, and it's fast. No guarantees.

At least, that's the way he'd been functioning for a while there. Seeing the world through a darker and darker lens, until one day he realized it just wasn't working for him. It's when he wondered what his purpose here on earth was.

It's when he thought he'd be better off dead. Because to live in this bullshit existence seemed like a pointless pain he could no longer endure.

Until he remembered. And clarity came to him, slowly unfolding around him little by little. He remembered that box that he had, the hexagon box containing the ornaments. The snowflakes. He had an awakening of sorts then, and had rummaged and scrounged and found the box, buried deep in one of his gorilla trunks. He had opened it and thought about the original owners of those crystal snowflakes. What they must have been feeling when they purchased them, the hope and excitement for the future they had. All held and symbolized in those prism ornaments.

That box and those ornaments reminded him of a greater purpose here in this life, something beyond him that kept making him live when others around him had died. And he saw then that to go on living wasn't a curse or punishment, it was a gift and responsibility more treasured than anything else.

Miles to go before I sleep.

"Xavier," Reggie says.

"Yes, Raina?" He holds his breath in anticipation. But it

happens, he can't help it, he takes his hand and rubs her back, just slightly. The warmth of her skin seeping through the barrier of the fabric of her shirt. A jarring mix of welcomed heat and the torture of the forbidden.

And then he freezes as she speaks her next words.

"I think I have to stay away from you." It's barely audible, but he hears her.

His chest squeezes, twists, pulls and he removes his hand from her back. Clenches and unclenches his fists reflexively. He takes a deep breath to collect himself. He already knows the answer, but he asks anyway. "Why's that?"

She rises to a full stand and turns to face him. She puts her hand on his chest and brings her luminous green eyes up to meet his. The touch quickens his pulse. He waits for her to say the words, say something out loud, say right here and now that there's something between them and it's undeniable and wrong. She has to say it, because he can't. And she doesn't even know the half of it.

"I think," she nods slowly, "I think you might just be my breath of fresh air too." She squeezes his shirt ever so slightly. Looks back out toward the trees, then returns to meet his gaze again.

He can't help it. He puts a hand over hers on his chest, and with the other he caresses her cheek, and then brushes a stray strand of hair behind her ear. He knows he shouldn't do this, but his movements are involuntary.

And then he continues the caress slowly down her cheek and places his fingers under her chin, gliding his thumb along her bottom lip. She parts her lips and inhales, a tiny gasp of...something, he's not sure what. Delight maybe, and intrigue. Intrigue and emotion and connection and longing and fear. At least, that's what he's feeling. He tells himself that this is okay. This is not crossing a line. Crossing a line would be to give in and lean down and kiss her, and he won't do that. He won't. So this gentle caress can't be crossing a line. It's only comfort.

He squeezes her hand, the one that's still on his chest. Raises it to his lips and kisses it with a tenderness and refrain that makes every cell in his body scream in reaction. He returns her hand to his chest, then looks at her and says, "Does that have to be wrong?"

THE FLORESCENT LIGHT IN THE hallway outside his apartment buzzes with annoyance and judgment. He unlocks his door and steps into the emptiness of his home. It's temporary, just a six-month lease until he can find a house to buy, a neighborhood where he can settle. There's something anticlimactic about retiring from the military. Twenty-plus years of service, of momentum and acclimating to new areas, and yet here he is. Back in his hometown of Garden Springs, PA, suburb of Philly.

Turns out there really is no place like home.

He had other options. He owns two homes already from previous places he had been stationed. One in Georgia, one in Florida, as he always imagined that he'd retire on the East Coast, and likely down south where winter brings sunshine and mild temperatures. And yet? A pull brought him here. Back home. Back to the place he had been running from ever since he was eighteen and joined the Army.

The beauty of buying a house near a base is that you have no problem bringing in consistent renters. Two-year lease standard, and often more thanks to the military families needing a home. He'd had offers in the past from some of his renters to purchase the homes, but with the mortgages covered plus a little extra, it seemed like a no-brainer to continue paying down his loans.

That patience has payed off, because at this point, after several years of chiseling away at those mortgages, he knows he will make enough money when he sells to buy a house with a cash offer. So that's the plan.

He pours himself a glass of water before retiring himself to his room. He's exhausted but not sure how he'll sleep after tonight.

His connection with Reggie is nothing new, not on his end, anyway, but tonight she confirmed that she feels it as well. *"You're my breath of fresh air too."*

Over the years he would get updates from Joey about her, Reggie's plans for physical therapy, the practice she was opening, their general life together. Never once did X ask Joey if he planned to propose or take things to the next level, because Joey always seemed content with how things were. He was proud and supportive and spoke like he understood that Reggie was an independent woman with a mission of her own. X admired how his nephew gave his girlfriend the space to chase her dreams, without influence or pressure from him on catering to what he wanted. Reggie was a star in her own right, and Joey was happy to help her shine.

Yet, there had always been the protective pull X had for Reggie. He found over the years that he'd celebrate the victories of hers that Joey would share, or in later years, post about online. As Joey and X's conversations and check-ins became fewer and far between with Joey's own personal growth and independence, X found himself pulling up his nephew's social media. Looking for signs of Reggie's latest accomplishments, her updates. It was hard to describe, this draw. But it had always been there.

What he hadn't expected was for her to feel it too. Was it his fault? Did he somehow put something out there, unintentionally? He didn't think so. He wouldn't describe himself as much of a Casanova. X's charms had always been more of the subtle variety. The women he had been with over the years were usually the ones to make a first move, then after a short time would become frustrated with him and his inability to open up or truly connect. Nothing long term ever manifested itself, and his constant geographical changes didn't help matters. No, X historically had been a rogue warrior, content to avoid any substantial attachments.

Until now.

But there was no attachment to be had here, no solution to

this, no matter how visceral the bond he felt with Reggie. He was a man of honor, first and foremost. And Joey meant more to him than he could possibly describe. So no matter how hard it would be, how painful, he was going to need to do what Reggie said, and steer clear.

He falls into bed with this in his mind. And hell if he doesn't fight back tears at the thought.

chapter thirteen

. . .

reggie

SLIPPER WEATHER. I wake up and peel away my blanket and plop my feet on the floor. My body is on the edge of the bed, and I feel it, a cold draft on my feet. My toes are small victims to an iciness. A welcome one, I should clarify, as I realize that for the first time in what feels like eons, this late September air means I will need some slippers.

There's a comfort in those soft little pockets of fuzz, isn't there? I must admit I have a bit of a habit of collecting slippers. Some in the form of a sock-bootie hybrid, some in the style of fluffy ballet flats, some that are lined moccasins that I've been known to wear out to the store for a pinch of milk a time or two.

My mother has always loved slippers as well, and maybe she's the one that has instilled the appreciation for them. We'd venture out at the start of each fall season to shop for a new pair. Hers were always feminine and sweet, a slip-on with lipstick and heart shapes decorating the tops, or those little fluff ball pompoms perfect to accompany her long, silk robes. I can picture her now, floating into my room with excitement and saying not the expected "sweater weather" but instead, with pizzazz, "Raina my love, it's slipper weather!"

And that's just the thing about her. Lori Meyers can embrace most anything with such enthusiasm, it's contagious. You can't help but join her in her excitement. (And as I'm sharing this out loud now, I recognize a deep similarity with Joey, so that explains that. We lean toward the familiar, don't we?)

But I've always admired that about her—that spirit. I'd call it tenacity but that doesn't quite seem to fit, not really. See, to me, tenacity implies a strategic force in clinging to some goal to over-come, but for Mom, I think it's more natural than that. She can shed away the useless pieces of the past and find new purpose in the here and now. I saw it in her love for Richard, in her commitment to his role in our lives, unexpected or unplanned as it was. No, he wasn't my father, and truth be told, I never really formed much of a bond with the man as he already had grown children of his own. I think he more politely accepted my presence as a parallel to my mother. I came with the territory.

But she loved him, and she embraced their time together with a passion that radiated from her. She'd buy clothing for herself in colors he liked and then try them on, looking in the mirror saying, "Raina Georgia, remember this. When your loved one feels your beauty, it becomes an image in his eyes, and forms a reflection so that when you look into them, you can see your beauty too. You can see and feel it just as he does. And that beauty is just the dress worn on love." My little girl brain would file away these tidbits of information like golden nuggets of knowledge. I wanted to be just like her, feel love like that too, especially in the wake of tragedy. *How incredible she is*, my child mind would think as I looked at her with wonder and awe.

As I rummage through my closet now, looking for the stashed away slipper pile lost in the heap of winter sweaters and scarves, I realize my relationship with Joey *has* proven I'm like her. Because I get it. I see the love for me in his eyes, reflecting right on back to me.

And it *does* feed and nourish me, I know it does. It's the anchor I need to remind myself of as I've been lost in this ridiculous crush on the forbidden fruit of X. Xavier Derian, uncle to my boyfriend, for God's sake.

I cover my face with my hands in a knee-jerk reaction to the memory of last night. Telling him he was my breath of fresh air, what was I thinking? Too much wine. I'm disgusted with myself and am determined to march myself downstairs, (slippers on, of course), greet my darling Joey and the cup of coffee he inevitably has waiting for me and fall in love with him all over again. Lucy is right, he does bring out the silly side of me. He *is* my perfect balance and I know I can love him just like my mom could love Richard. With a fierce passion and heart that allows you to take life exactly as it is. Accept its gifts as they are and feel...feel...the word escapes me.

Happy.

Yes, I think that's just it. Or maybe it's happy and content. Satisfied. Yes, all of those things. All of those things that my own stubborn mind has held just out of reach as I've been clinging to some stupid element of something missing. Nothing is missing, nothing at all.

And I'm sure as hell going to stop this stupid trauma bonding nightmare or whatever it is I've evoked with X.

I give up on my search for slippers as I am cutting it close to my run time with Lucy. I dress quickly, warm my cold little feet with good old-fashioned socks and sneakers, and head down to the kitchen where Joey awaits.

"There's my girl," he says as I round the corner. He hands me my coffee (always better when made by someone else, don't you think?) and kisses my cheek.

I sip the coffee, nodding approvingly as the warm liquid slips down my throat. Then I look at Joey and say, "Let me look into your eyes."

Right away Joey sets down his coffee, stands in front of me

square, separates his feet out wide to allow his body to drop down a few inches to better meet me eye to eye. I laugh at how seriously he takes my request. No questions asked, he just responds. "Have at it, gorgeous." His eyes are wide and those curly lashes that I love give the impression of a curtain valance, draping and enhancing.

I study them, Joey's eyes, very serious in my focus. "Yes, I see it now," I say as if a scientific discovery is taking place.

"Can I ask what you see?"

I nod. "Why all the love, of course." I kiss him on the lips and tell him he's free to go now and to carry on.

Joey smiles and says, "I hope you didn't think it wasn't there, right? The love?" He looks at me in earnest.

I shake my head and laugh. "Of course not. Just remembering something my mother used to say, that's all."

He seems satisfied with this and nods. "Good." He watches me as I head to the pantry to grab a granola bar. I'm not much of a breakfast person, much to Joey's dismay. "Hey listen. I'm sorry I forgot to tell you Uncle Xavier was coming over last night. You didn't seem too happy about it at first."

My stomach drops and I'm thankful for the barrier of the pantry cabinet door as I'm pretty sure a flush on my skin would reveal more than I'd like. I pretend to search a little longer for some other piece of nourishment, close my eyes and take a breath in. "Oh. No, it's fine. I just didn't expect to see him at the door instead of one of the stoner delivery boys, that's all. It's a pity too. I do enjoy when they come in with our food, realize they locked themselves out of their car and then join us for dinner while they wait for their parent to bring the spare key."

Joey laughs at my recount of the memory. "Good, okay. I just know he's been away for so long that he's out of touch with old friends. I promised Mom I'd take care of him, make sure he's entertained while he figures out his next steps."

I come out of my hiding and close the cabinet door. Peel down the wrapper of my granola bar and realize my hands have a slight tremble to them. *I just need to eat something*, I tell myself. "I'm all for it, he's welcome any time."

"I knew you would be. Thank you." He sips his coffee. "You know he likes you, by the way."

"Yeah?" *Oh fuck.* I'm all ears and gnawing interest and can't wait to hear what he says next, and this is exactly what I'm not supposed to be feeling.

"Yeah, he said you've got soul or something like that. I think it was after he heard your poetry reading. And I told him I know, I try not to hold it against her." Dimples flash as he laughs at his own joke. I roll my eyes at him. "I'm kidding, I'm kidding," he adds.

"Oh, you take my breath away with that humor, Joey," I say with a smile.

We continue enjoying our coffee and eventually kiss and part ways—him back to his apartment before work, me to my run with Lucy. My next mission is to clear things up with her. Hopefully it was just the wine talking last night and she doesn't actually believe I'm not willing to move forward with Joey. No matter what, though, I'm in need of some good one-on-one time with her, and this early fall air has an essence of cleansing to it that I'm eager to embrace.

If only I knew that Lucy was about to throw that plan out the window.

chapter fourteen

. . .

reggie

"YOU AND XAVIER," Lucy says. Well, she cuts right to it, I'll give her that. We run along side-by-side on our trail. A hill is approaching and I'm already dreading the burn on my thighs.

"Me and Xavier what?" I say, determined to squash this thing. No, not even a thing, it doesn't even deserve that much.

"Reggie, look. It's me, okay? You don't have to have it all together with me, just be honest."

"I am being honest, me and X what?" I lean my body forward slightly as we work our way up this hill. We're both huffing and puffing at this point, and she takes a minute to respond. It's small but steep, and I try and remind myself of all the great muscles I'm building in the effort.

"X?" she pushes out, and I realize I've referred to him by my internal nickname for him. *Dammit.*

We run a few more steps and make it to the top, then trot for a few more seconds on flat ground before I can manage the breath to reply, "Xavier, yes. What about him?"

"Something between you," she throws out there, and I about

die. This is a difficult conversation to be having and I'm increasingly frustrated with our struggle to converse in full sentences right now. Our breathing hasn't quite caught up to the newer, flatter terrain.

"How so?" is all I can muster.

"Chemistry," she breathes out.

"Bullshit," I say.

"Stop, you know it too." She takes a couple more breaths and manages to blurt, "Don't lie."

"Fuck." I stop and move to the side, place my hands on my knees to catch my breath. Lucy realizes she's now running alone, stops and turns around. She notices me keeled over and jogs back to my side.

"You alright?"

I nod. "I'm fine, just need to catch my breath." I inhale deeply, exhale. Repeat once more. She waits patiently, running in place as she waits. Finally, I stand upright again. "Okay, I'm good, let's go," and we continue.

We run for another minute or two, a little slower now. She broaches the subject again. "I don't mean to push, I really don't. It's just something I noticed last night. A definite chemistry between you two. And maybe it was the conversation we had earlier about knowing if someone's the one, and maybe it just got me seeing things, who knows. But I know you, Reggie, and you're feeling something. Maybe it's not Xavier-specific, but something's up."

I gesture to the right when we get to a fork in the trail and look to her for confirmation. It's a rockier option, but it runs along a small creek and is beautiful. She nods and we veer off down the winding path.

"Look," I say. "I fucking hate myself for what I'm about to say here, but yes."

"Yes what?"

"Yes there's a chemistry there." My foot slips a little on a loose stone, and I stumble. Lucy reaches out and catches my arm at the elbow to help steady me. I stabilize and we continue our cadence. "But it's nothing. It has to be nothing, right? I mean, I barely even know the guy..."

"I wouldn't say that. You've known him in some ways the majority of your life, haven't you? Didn't he live with Joey and his family for a bit when we were in like second or third grade?"

How the hell did she remember that? And that's the thing about your best friends from childhood that remain your best friends today. That loyalty is priceless, but you can't get away with shit because They. Know. All. They know everything because they were right there with you, living and growing and experiencing it too.

I'm paying for that now because Lucy's right, X had lived at Joey's house. Briefly after X's mom died when he was a teen, then again for a summer when he had an extended leave or something. Maybe even another time or two. "I mean, yeah," I pant. "For like a minute years ago, but I wouldn't say that makes us old buddies. We were kids then. Xavier was in his late teens, early twenties."

"He's always been hot, though," she says with a sly little smile, and I find that I'm instantly jealous and possessive, stupid as that is. "So cute. And you're not a little girl anymore, Raina Blake, and the age difference doesn't feel different at all now, really."

"I can't believe we're having this conversation." I wipe away the sweat pouring out of my forehead. Lucy, lucky girl, has barely a glisten. "Cute and chemistry do not equate to throwing my life with Joey down the drain and running into Xavier's arms."

That shuts her up. For the moment at least. We continue along on our trail for another half a mile or so, allowing our own thoughts to carry away, mine reminiscing on my friendship with Lucy.

She truly is the sister I never had. Growing up, I practically lived at her house, it was always the more fun one. My house was quiet with it being just me there. Richard had kids but they were all grown up, for the most part, and didn't seem to have a great relationship with him. And sometimes I just needed a little escape from my mom.

That escape came in the form of the Ray household with Lucy and her baby sister Lila. I'd spend every waking moment possible there—playdates after school, sleepovers on the weekends with face masks and makeovers and movies and all the fun. As kids we'd maybe go to my house to swim in our pool, but as we got older the appeal of Lucy's hot tub became more in line with our ever-so-sophisticated hearts.

So, yes. Lucy knows me better than anyone, and while I want to squash away the X thing, I can't help but find it interesting that she's not immediately scolding me.

We continue along a little further before coming out to a clearing near the parking lot. We slow down to a walk as we head up to the park pavilion and stretch, leaning on each other for balance as we work out our quads.

"I just want to clarify that I'm not suggesting you throw caution to the wind and go have some hot affair with him, okay?" Lucy says.

"Okay," I say cautiously. I'm a little scared of what she's about to say next because I know she's not done.

We release from each other, and she pulls her dark hair out of her ponytail to shake it out. "I'm here, though, and I want you to be honest with me. You're like a freakin' vault sometimes, always worrying about everyone else but never about yourself. But you don't have to always do that, you know. If something's on your mind, I'm here. Judgment free, alright?"

"I know that," I say.

"I know you do, I just think you need to be reminded sometimes. And you're stirring up something, I can tell. Whatever it is, just do me one favor."

"Should I be writing this down?"

Always a master at sidestepping my quips, Lucy continues.

"Focus on you. Your needs, no one else's. Not Joey's, not your mom's, just yours."

"I focus on my needs."

"Logistically, sure. When you have a solid goal in mind. Some tangible thing to accomplish. But on matters of the heart?"

"Yeah?"

"Well, *hun*," she looks at me with narrowed eyes. "Oh yeah, I caught that little flirtation last night." I grab and flick and fidget with the tail strap of my running watch, refusing to even respond, guilt and shame flushing my cheeks. She continues. "In matters of the heart, it's a little like you pretend you don't have one that needs anything at all."

Oof. That hits. It feels scarily accurate.

And with that, my faithful friends, the stronger than thou Raina Georgia Blake—well...

...I burst into tears.

chapter fifteen

. . .

lori

I T'S BEEN CONSISTENTLY busy with patient after patient, and the day has flown by. Business appears to be good, and for that, Lori's both happy and relieved for Reggie. It was a risk to start this business, one Lori herself isn't sure she would have taken. But Reggie has always been stubborn, especially once she sets her mind to something. And Lori can certainly see it's proven to be worthwhile.

She looks to her left to the bouquet of pens popping out of their holder and picks one up to read the clinic slogan printed on the side. *"Finding strength in our adaptive flexibility."* Lori feels she's been especially good at this in life, and wonders if Reggie chose the phrase out of inspiration from her mother. She smiles to herself and decides, yes. Yes, she did.

Scribbling down a few to-do list notes to revisit tomorrow, she glances to her right down the corridor toward Reggie's office. The door is open just a bit, and Lori can see the tiniest sliver of her daughter sitting at her desk. Reggie's hands are on her forehead, a look of worry on her face. Momentary panic crosses Lori's mind—did she forget to do something Reggie asked? Lori scuttles around her desk, lifting piles of paper and shifting notepads around, looking for some hidden clue as to something she might have missed. And then she relaxes, realizing she's probably over thinking and jumping to conclusions. She does that sometimes.

Deciding she'll go and check on her daughter, Lori rises from her seat. She walks the few steps towards Reggie's office and pops her head in. "Hey sweetie, you alright?"

"Hmm?" Reggie looks up before dropping back in her seat. "Yes, fine. Just tired, maybe." She rubs the heels of her hands in her eyes.

Lori studies her daughter, unsure of what to say next. She opts for helpful. "You work too hard, you know. You need to know when to take a break."

Reggie shakes her head with a slight smile. "No such thing. Work is what keeps me going." She looks up towards the ceiling and lets out a sigh. "Some things are just beyond fixing, I think. That's all."

Lori leans in the doorway and crosses one ankle over the other. She can see something's up with her daughter, she just can't quite figure out what. There's a recent quietness to her, a little less energy. Reggie's always been like that—she retreats and quiets when she's upset. It's a stark contrast to Lori's own roars that come out when she's upset, though she prides herself on not letting it happen often. She can find the good in just about anything! But occasionally, anger ripples out like an inky black poison. An oil spill barely containable.

Not often, though.

But she's determined to figure out what's going on with her daughter now. "Talk to me, sweetie. What's on your mind?" Lori knows opening up has never been Reggie's thing.

She looks up at her mother, a look of debate on her face.

"Apparently, I'm all kinds of transparent these days. Alright, fine. Come on in, have a seat."

Giddy with the opportunity to hear what's been running through her daughter's mysterious mind, Lori happily enters. She takes a seat in the small sofa that's perpendicular to Reggie's desk. The soft glow of Reggie's desk lamp casts an umbrella of yellow warmth. "What's up, you can tell me." Lori leans forward in hopes that she's in an open stance. She heard somewhere to do that—to not cross your arms over your chest or anything like that when you want to give someone the impression that you're open to hearing them.

Reggie clears her throat. "I'm going to say something right now, and I just want you to listen, alright? Not jump in and relate it to your life somehow, or offer solutions, just listen. Got it?"

Irritation flickers in Lori's mind. That's a mother's job, right? Jump in and solve? She racks her brain to remember some instance of solving being a bad thing, but all she can think is that she always means to be helpful. She tries to ignore her brief annoyance and concentrate on what Reggie's about to share. "Okay, I'm listening."

Reggie rolls her chair back and crosses her legs. "I'm at this crossroads with Joey," she explains, "and I'm struggling to figure out where to go next." She pauses and looks to Lori for a reaction, but Lori tries her best to remain quiet and only listen. Reggie continues. "I know he would love to propose, move in together, all that. And we've always fallen back on the excuse of keeping things separate while I opened the business and got that under way and profitable." She gestures her hands around the space. "And I have, business is great. Better than I could have asked for."

Lori nods and says, "I was just thinking the same thing not a moment ago."

"Right," Reggie agrees. "So the logical thing to do now would be to move forward with him, right? I know he's waiting for me to start that conversation, give him the green light. We've got Lucy and Justin's wedding in a couple months, other friends getting married, and I can feel that he's hoping we're soon in that lineup."

Lori furrows her brows, unsure of where this is going. Reggie is saying things Lori wants to hear, but her tone and body language are stoic. "Sure," is all she offers.

"I just…" Reggie pauses.

Here it is, Lori thinks. *My stubborn Reggie at it again.* "You just what?"

Reggie fidgets with a small pad of paper on her desk, running her thumb along the edges of the pages and letting them cascade down. "It's like there's this brick wall and I can't seem to push past it for some God-awful reason. And I keep having these random flashbacks of JJ lately, I don't even know if they're real because for the longest time my mind was completely blank on that front. No memories at all. And I just feel like I'm losing my mind or something and the brick wall keeps popping up and redirecting me, but when I try and turn, I have no idea where I'm going and there's this…blackness. A nothingness." She closes her eyes and shakes her head. "And I hate it."

Lori sighs, moving right past Reggie's mention of JJ since that's a place Lori refuses to let her mind go. She tries to collect her daughter's random thoughts. Reggie has always spoken in her own language and Lori at times feels like a foreigner to it. "Am I *allowed* to talk now?" she asks, sure her annoyance is obvious. On the other hand, she can't be bothered with trying to please Reggie when that always proves nearly impossible to do.

Reggie nods. "Yes, Mom. It's your turn, permission granted." She motions with a dramatic wave of her hand.

"Let me see if I'm getting this. You want to take the next steps with Joey, but are feeling like something's stopping you?" She studies Reggie's face for some kind of confirmation.

"Yes, yes. I think that's it."

Lori swells with a bit of pride in her ability to understand. She smiles, her annoyance from a moment ago melting away just as quickly as it came. She reaches forward to grab Reggie's hands. It's a bit of a stretch and she has to teeter on the edge of the small couch. "Reggie, sweetie. It's nerves! It's nerves and excitement and all completely normal. It's hard to take the plunge!"

"You never struggled with that. You married Richard within months of meeting him."

"True, but you know, part of that was because we had to move fast into his house to get you in the good school district. And it all just happened in a blur, and it seemed like getting married was the perfect next step. Not very romantic, I know!" Lori lets out a nervous laugh. "But sometimes you have to push aside those feelings of doubt because if you let your mind run wild with that kind of thing, then you'll never figure out how to make anything work. Nothing's perfect, right? You can look at a situation and see all that's not working, but it doesn't get you very far. Sometimes you just need to push to see what's going right. Focus on that, okay? That's the important thing. See all the good, all the pros and then it's not so scary." She smiles, satisfied that she's made a great point to help her daughter.

"See all the good. Focus on that," Reggie nods.

"Yes."

"Just a little taking-the-plunge jitters, maybe."

"Exactly," Lori gives one firm nod. "And you know, being as you are such the take-charge kinda girl, it wouldn't be a terrible idea if maybe you tried to propose to him? Wouldn't that be something sweet? Might even be just the right kind of Reggie move—you don't wait for a guy to propose to you, maybe that's what this is all about! You've always liked to do things your way, so it might be something to consider." Lori could see it now, polar opposite to her own style as it was. The younger kids are doing things like that, though, and Lori could get on board with it and help.

Reggie laughs and pulls her hands back from Lori's grasp. "Alright, I can see your glittery wheels turning with ideas here. Slow down." She rests her elbow on the desk and places her chin in her hand. "I hate to admit that does actually seem like something I would do. With Joey, at least." She shrugs a shoulder.

Lori rises and heads toward Reggie's door. "Well, if you decide to do that, you have my full support and help in any way. You just let me know."

Reggie gives a mock salute. "Will do."

chapter sixteen

. . .

reggie

THE SECOND DINNER roll was probably a mistake, I think as I sit here in the Tuscan kitchen of my mom's house, listening to her and Nana drone on about so and so and their new lawn fountain or some scandalous thing like that. Nana moved in with Mom a few years ago, and I swear these two are like little overgrown gossiping schoolgirls together.

"Does it have to be so big?" Mom says.

"And in the center of the lawn is just not tasteful, it really isn't," Nana adds.

My dinner roll and the steak and mashed potatoes are starting a war in my belly, and I realize I absolutely have to get up and move around. I rise and start clearing the table, Nana and Mom nearly unaware of my movements as they are lost in their trash fest of all the judgments on everyone else but themselves. I sound annoyed, I know, but really, I find it heartwarming. I'm glad they have one another. They need it. When my grandfather was still alive, he apparently had more interest in other women than the ones in his own home, and we know the tragedy my mom's faced. The two of them need the camaraderie, and heaven knows I'm happy to not be the sole source of comfort anymore.

I bring the plates to the sink but decide to procrastinate for a bit on the dishes, because I have another idea in mind. I'm going to find that matching ring to the snowflake bracelet Joey gave me. Noodle around with my mom's idea, initiating some next steps with Joey. Not a proposal, but maybe starting the talks of having him move in with me. I wonder if we just don't spend enough time together, given his hectic schedule and the distance between our places.

And I absolutely cannot keep up this crush thing with X. There's no answer there, no end point other than a hard stop. He's Joey's freaking *uncle* for God's sake—what the hell could possibly come of it? So that's that. I've been working really hard to put him out of my mind, hard as that is. And maybe part of the issue here is that I'd been using X as a distraction.

I've read that when our relationships are at all flawed, sometimes we find it's easier to look outside. We start innocently bonding with other people, maybe even discussing the issues that we'd been having with people outside of our relationship. But that's the exact recipe for disaster, and really, it's more an indicator of a bigger problem within our relationship. Something we're not facing head on. And the person to talk to, the *only* person to help solve your problem with your partner is the partner themselves.

Given that Joey and I don't even have any actual tangible problem, I'm figuring that the only issue is simply my own avoidant attachment style. I check all the boxes. I don't like being emotionally vulnerable with Joey, I fear losing my independence, I struggle with the idea of relying on him, I push down negative feelings, the list goes on and rings a blaring, high pitch of *"ding-ding-ding!"* in my head.

So it's time to take charge, push past my fears. And talk about having him move in.

My place would be a bit of a hike for him for getting into work, but I know Joey couldn't care less about that. So my plan is to give him a key with the ring that matches my snowflake bracelet as a little key chain attachment on there. I could do that, right? It wouldn't be so bad to wake up to Joey day in and day out. Fresh coffee and his dimples greeting me before I head out the door. I can grow out of my only child syndrome and share a space with him. My mind instantly goes to the briefest feeling of suffocation, but I push that thought away.

I head upstairs and briefly rummage around in my old room, but aside from the purple flowers of my Laura Ashley comforter, the majority of my things have already been removed from there. Packed away in my own house. The hall bath proves just as empty too, other than a stack of towels and spare bedsheets. Nana's room is likely pointless, the office is a mess I don't dare to even attempt. *This house is too big for these two,* I think to myself. The neighborhood is small, only twenty homes or so, and all of them luxurious and grand. It's how Lucy and Joey and I got so close. We were the only ones in the neighborhood to attend public school as opposed to the high-end private schools of choice for our neighbors.

I sigh and head back down the stairs, giving up. When I reach the bottom I look to my left, at the closed door of my mom's first floor master bedroom. Maybe her jewelry box? It's possible, I could see the ring having been set down somewhere and my mom finding it. Putting it in with her stash of things. I open the door to her room and ignore the little chill. Richard had a very masculine presence to him that still remains in the space today. There's this cross pattern of large, dark wood beams on the ceiling and I tell you what, I feel like they are downright oppressive. They give the sense that they're not fixed to the ceiling at all, but instead dangling with danger and ready to drop. If I could redecorate the first thing I'd do is paint those bad boys a crisp and clean white. Now, that would be beautiful in here. Why my mom never redecorated I'll never know, because I doubt it's her style either.

The bathroom is all dark woods as well, though spacious and

luxurious with black granite countertops, 2 separate sinks and vanities, high end faucets and light fixtures. There's a gorgeous chandelier to match, a timeless crystal piece that design-wise still works in the space even though it's likely original to the house. The bathroom is a mini room in and of itself. Paint those cabinets white as well, and this could be a stellar black and white bathroom of luxury.

I scan the room and see the red leather of my mom's jewelry box. It sits prominently on the right side of the room, on the vanity that she uses. Richard's side remains bare and abandoned, likely unused in years.

I open the jewelry box and allow its inner shelves to unhinge and stretch out before me, inviting me to poke and prod. I lift an amber necklace, smile at a memory of playing dress up and staring in the mirror at my adorned reflection. I shove aside a few other pieces, lift a couple smaller jewelry cases here and there to see if anything's underneath. Frustration bites at me like a gnawing insect and I realize this was probably a futile search.

Something out of place catches my eye, though. It's an envelope, I think. It's peeking out from under a tray, just a small sliver of a rectangle of it in view. I pull on the edge and shimmy the rest of the envelope out, freeing it from the weight of gems and stones and silver and gold. No writing or markings on it. It's unsealed so I open it up and pull out the three-fold sheet of paper.

And gasp.

It's a PFA application form, partially filled out by none other than Lori Meyers. Name of Accused: Richard Meyers. Type of Abuse: blank. Place of Occurrence: at home. I look and see that my mom has June listed as the time of abuse, and it's from the year of his death. Richard's heart attack was in July, so she had to have filled this out just briefly beforehand.

My stomach works against me, and I suddenly feel ill. My mom was going to file a PFA against Richard? It just doesn't add up, what could have happened? I think back to my memories of him—he had a temper, sure. But nothing earth shattering as far as I remember. No epic fights that I can recall, nothing beyond what you might expect. And where was I that June? I lean against the vanity counter and search the wells of my memory. I was more than most likely at the beach with Lucy's family at the time.

A wave of confusion and revulsion consume me, and I realize I need answers. All this time I had been thinking that my mom was some incredible romantic, able to find love in the darkest of shadows. That I'm the one that's stuck focusing on the wrong things, in denial of all the good I have right in front of me. Has it really been that all this time, she's been the one in denial?

I march out of the room, down the hall, paper in hand. I round the corner to the mustard-colored walls of the Tuscan kitchen and stand over the table where my mom and Nana still remain sitting and chatting.

"Hi, sweetie, where'd you run off to?" my mom asks.

"What's this?" I say, holding the paper in front of me. I hand it to her. Study her face as it dawns on her what exactly I'm showing her.

"Oh my God, where in the world did you find this?"

"Was Richard hurting you? Were you going to file this?" Nana sits there quietly, lips sealed. "Did you know anything about Mom filing a PFA?" I ask her. I see Nana's eyes dart back to my mom.

"This was nothing, really sweetie," my mom says.

"It was a long time ago," Nana adds. So she *did* know about it.

"I hardly find a PFA to be nothing. How did I not know about this, what happened?" I have a mix of emotions. A protectiveness over my mother and whatever pain she might have endured, a fury towards Richard who I'm now wondering if I ever really knew at all, and an unexpected feeling of betrayal that I had been kept in the dark all these years.

A familiar nervous laugh erupts from my mom. "It was nothing! So silly, really. I was being dramatic in this, if I'm being honest.

I never even filed it obviously. Why I kept it, I really don't know." She shakes her head. "Stupid, really."

My emotions are rising, and a frustration is taking over me. It's an odd feeling. Emotions seem to be popping up left and right for me lately and I'm frantic with the urge to understand and take back control. "Mom, stop it. Something obviously had to have happened for you to make the effort to fill this out in the first place. What was it?" I'm pacing back and forth now. "I can't believe it, all this time I've thought you guys had this amazing second chance at love story. Thought how incredible that was."

"We *did* have love, this stupid piece of paper doesn't mean anything, okay?"

"Lori," Nana interjects. "She's a grown woman now, come on."

Mom glares at her. "Come on what?! I'm being honest," she insists, her voice getting increasingly more shrill. "Was it perfect? No. But we had passion, and he gave me everything I needed. *Us* everything we needed." She gestures around her. "Look at this house! Could I have afforded this on my own? A single mother with a broken heart, a college dropout? No."

"So what, you just dealt with a little abuse now and then, thanks for the Viking stove and pool house though?" I bite back, my words clipped.

And that's when my mom rises out of her seat and slaps me. Clear across the face. I raise my hand to my cheek and look at her in horror. Nana just sits there, wide-eyed and frozen.

"You little brat, how dare you mock me. How *dare* you!" She's in hysterics now, and I think she goes to slap me again, but she stops herself. Her shrill voice has reached a maniacal yell and I retreat because I know I've woken something up in her that maybe never was supposed to come out. Tentacles of fury and rage are growing out of her, fast and strong. "You have no idea all that I've been through! The sacrifices I have made in order to make this all work. To provide for you and keep you living a beautiful life of wanting for nothing. I made that happen," she screams, slamming a finger into her chest. "I did that. For you, for us! And it damn near killed me at times, but did I stop? Of course not, how could I? There was no stopping. No point, what good would that do?

"So I focused on the good. I never stopped remembering the good, the big picture. The times where Richard's love came back full force. And I knew I could help him. He saved me when I didn't have an ounce of strength in the world, and I could save him too. I *loved* being the one to save him." She stops now, takes a quick breath as if that can erase it all. She tucks a loose strand of hair behind her ear, fluffs at the back of her head with a quickness, willing volume and life into her hair as if that's all she needs to move on and be strong. I watch as she bustles around the kitchen in a blur of frantic movement. Turns on the faucet, starts scrubbing away at dishes as if rubbing away their dirt will magically clean up the messiness of her life.

I want to ask a hundred questions. I want to ask how bad it was, was it just the one time or were there more? I know enough to know that with these things it definitely wasn't a onetime event, and in fact there were likely years of it building and growing, a cancerous tumor from which my mom believed there was no cure. I want to ask why she didn't leave, was she scared, where was I in all of it, did Nana know at the time, all these thoughts running and polluting my brain.

Instead, all I muster is, "How bad was it, Mom?"

She snaps her head back at me and I will myself to meet her stare with courage. "You want to know how bad it was?"

"Yes," I say.

Nana rises from her seat to stand closer to us. She attempts to terminate the conversation. "Alright now, there's no point in rehashing the past."

My mom laughs with that maniacal, splitting sound again. "Now she wants to know all about it. Miss Know It All wants to know the dirty details."

I take one step closer to her, willing her to see the concern in my eyes. "You deserve to free yourself from it, Mom. Get it off your chest. He's gone now, has been for years. You don't have to pretend it was something that it wasn't."

She slams the scrubber brush in her hand down on the counter. "*Enough*," she yells. The rooms freezes momentarily, the only sign of life is the steaming water rushing out from the faucet. I instinctively hold my breath. A wave of nausea washes over me, and my heart is pounding. I can feel the hot flush of my cheeks.

After a moment my mom shakes her head with sadness and looks out the back window to the darkness beyond. "You don't get it, do you." She spins around in a half turn to face me. "You think you find one piece of paper and suddenly you know everything? You have this whole idea formed now, 'Richard the Monster, Lori the Victim,' right? True love doesn't exist after all, just like you thought." Tears are rolling down her cheeks and she raises a soapy hand to wipe them away. "I had it good, okay? Richard treated me well. Showered me with not just jewels and cars and a beautiful home and security, but he *loved* me too. Don't you for one second think that just because he lost his temper now and then that he didn't love me. And I could handle it. I was the one thing that could get him out of his head, the dark spaces. Me. *I* was his angel. He saved me when I was lost, and I saved him too, okay?"

I nod, unsure what else to do. Nana steps towards my mom and puts her arms around her. My mom just stands there, locked in Nana's embrace.

"There was a lot to be happy about, Reggie. And the night that made me fill out that stupid form was not the norm, okay? I was standing by the stairs when we were arguing. I was hitting him, and he pushed me off of him. Yes, I fell down some stairs, but he did not mean to push me like that. It was a fight that just got a little out of control. Led to a—to an accident and he never meant to take it that far."

Every cell in my body wants to scream at how wrong that is, this delusional lie she is telling herself.

But I don't.

Instead I look at the two figures jumbled together before me, my mom and Nana. I think about all that I haven't seen, the burdens they've carried beyond my knowledge. Burdens that I'll likely never truly understand. And maybe I don't have to, maybe that's not the point. I've always felt my mom's burdens were my responsibility, but they're not.

Maybe Lucy's right. Maybe it's time I stop focusing all my energy on everyone else, because all I'm effectively doing is avoiding my own heart. And in sitting here presuming I know everything, I'm missing out on major red flags anyways.

I feel lost. Like I don't know a goddamn thing at all. Just that a crack in the glass has started. And I'm at a loss for how to stop it. Yet I feel an odd and unexpected freedom in not even wanting to try.

So I step forward, slowly and carefully, and join in their embrace. I inhale the scent of soap bubbles and Nana's perfume and Mom's broken heart. And I let it be.

I just let it be.

And in that silent embrace, I realize I know exactly what I have to do next.

october

. . .

Change inevitable
Fiery hot, blazing embers
Falling to the ground
At the mercy of transformation
Our wisdom knows it to be inevitable

~Raina G. Blake

chapter seventeen

. . .

X

HE ENDS THE call with Joey, shocked by what he just heard. He places the phone down on the Formica kitchen countertop and rubs his hand along his beard, absorbing Joey's words. The weight of his nephew's news.

"Reggie broke up with me."

X's emotions feel at odds with themselves. The pain he feels for his nephew is a sharp stab. He could hear muffled tears on the other end of the line during Joey's recount of what happened.

But then there's the stir of hope. Followed by a wave of shame and guilt. And a draw to want to reach out to Reggie.

Is it because of me?

At his past few physical therapy appointments, he'd either not seen Reggie at all, or only in quick passing with little more than a "Hello," and brief exchange of words. Lori, on the other hand, continued her flirtatious attempts, which he worked to successfully sidestep.

X cursed himself for starting treatment there. It was a selfish thing to do. He was a cat, and curiosity was going to kill him. The feelings he and Reggie were developing for one another had no hope of ever being able to amount to anything. On the one hand, this angered him.

On the other, he knew that it's just the unfair nature of life.

This new development though, Reggie breaking up with Joey, he wonders how he's supposed to react. It's an impossible situation. He needs to be supportive for his nephew, yet if he's honest with himself, there's a glimmer of false hope.

It's a hope that needs to be squashed.

He grabs his keys as he tries to push aside the infiltrating thoughts of Reggie. Of how she's doing. Of why she made this move, whether or not it has anything to do with him.

He tries his best to sidestep them all. Because for now, he needs to go see his nephew.

AFTER A QUICK KNOCK, X enters Joey's apartment. The blinds are closed, and his nephew is lying on the couch in a cocoon of blankets. The overhead fan whirs on high, the breeze of it waving the corners of discarded tissues like little white flags begging for peace in a war. It feels like depression in here. It wraps around X, coils around his feet and up his legs. It's a familiar and paralyzing feeling. For a moment X stands glued to the floor, unable to move himself forward.

"That you, Xavier?" Joey calls from his couch coffin. X feels unexpected relief that Joey didn't include "uncle" in his tired greeting. He's undeserving of the title.

X steps forward into the living room and lifts the contents in his right hand. "Yeah, it's me. With gifts." He places the six pack on the coffee table in front of Joey. Takes one out, opens it and hands it to him before grabbing one for himself.

Joey props himself up on the couch and raises his bottle to his uncle. "To misery."

They clink. "To misery," X repeats. How perfect.

X sips the beer and takes a seat in the lounger next to Joey, rocking back and forth in it. He waits for Joey to speak first because he knows better than anyone, sometimes words aren't what's needed at any given time. Just company. The whirr of the fan above is their only accompaniment. An occasional clinking of the nearby fridge's ice maker the only thing to break the silence.

Joey does speak eventually, his voice hoarse with the remnants of his agony. "I should have seen it coming." He puts his beer down, hangs his head low and rubs his hands through his dark hair. X can barely watch him. The waves of pain his nephew is feeling emanate off him with a force threatening to suck X in and under. "I should have known." Joey looks up and rests his chin between his thumb and forefinger. "She's always been a touch out of reach somehow, you know? Like there but I could never really grasp her. Never get a solid hold."

X says nothing, just listens. Listens and wills his own mind to stay present in this moment with Joey. Stay here where he's needed.

Joey continues. "We've been together for so long it's like I just took it for granted. Didn't even consider that we would ever be apart. Even through college and culinary school, she was this piece of me that I didn't even think about. It was what it was supposed to be, me and her. That was it. Easy." He shakes his head. Rubs his eyes. "I don't know, it just doesn't make any sense to me. I go back and forth between feeling like a fucking moron for not seeing it coming, then feeling so confused like how this is even possible. I just don't get it." He looks up at his uncle. Says words X does not want to hear. "Any ideas here? You've gotten to know her these past couple months, any idea what could be running through her mind?"

X winces and realizes with a disturbance that his nephew doesn't even ask if he thinks there's someone else. Not that X could really consider himself a "someone else" in Reggie's world, but the thought of that doesn't even register for Joey.

He tries his best to answer anyways. "She seems like a pretty independent woman. And her mom seems like a hopeless romantic, maybe she's afraid of falling into that trap."

"Trap?" Joey looks genuinely wounded by the word.

X quickly tries to retract. "Not trap, but something else. Open to the risk, maybe. The risk of getting crushed." He closes his eyes, hating his words because they don't fit. They're not right, it's all off.

Joey nods his head. "The risk of getting crushed, yeah." He reaches for his beer again and takes another sip. X is vaguely aware that he's inadvertently planted some idea in Joey's mind that is likely in no way any actual help to him. "I bet that's it. She doesn't realize it but she has this fear of fully opening up and loving when her mom has lost both of her husbands." He continues to nod. "That's gotta be it."

X curses to himself. This isn't what he's supposed to be doing, sitting here trying to comfort a young man's broken heart when he himself might be a contributing factor to it. Or was he delusional to think he had anything to do with Reggie's decision? How the hell could he even flatter himself to think he knows what's going on for Reggie? They had both danced around one another these past weeks and months, a bullfighter and a bull, staring one another down in a cabaret of tension and spark that they refused to fully engage in.

They came close, it's true. Too close.

But they jolted back apart just as quickly, too smart to jump off a bottomless cliff.

X tries to redirect. "What exactly did she say?"

Joey sets his beer down and drops his head in his hands again. "I don't even know. That we needed to end things, see what it's like to be apart or some shit like that, it didn't make any sense.

"When I tried to ask her what the hell she was talking about, she said something like how she's been struggling for a while with moving forward and she has to figure out why. And I tried to tell her that that's stupid, that I'm not expecting anything from her."

"Is that true? Is that how you really feel?"

"What, that I don't expect anything? I mean yeah, I guess. Sure, I wish we lived together. Being apart as often as we are gets hard. But I know her, she's gotta do things at her own pace, and I don't have any complaints. It's one of the things I've always loved about her." And X grimaces as he watches his nephew choke on those last words. He's not the man for this job. Joey should have someone else here, someone to slap him on his back, take him to a damn strip club or something. X feels like a complete failure.

"You know Joey, I'm probably not the best expert on these things. Never even had any serious relationships of my own worth mentioning."

Joey wipes his face and shakes his head. "No, that's just because you moved around so much, that's all. I bet it's a lot harder to make something last when that's your life."

X admires Joey's optimism, even in his darkest hour of heart-break. A true romantic. He doesn't reply though, just rocks in his chair and sips his beer.

"Seriously, Uncle X. You've always been the expert to me. Taught me everything I know and then some." X is physically aching hearing his nephew's words. They sting and burn at him, the atmosphere around his body transforming the kindness into acid left to burn and corrode his undeserving heart.

X is unworthy. Not just because of his mistaken feelings for Reggie, but for other sins too.

But Joey doesn't see it. He continues. "You were my hero long before you ever had an actual war story, you know."

And the words continue to sting on him, to rain down with an intensity fit for torture. He wants to hurl his words back at Joey. Tell him how wrong he is, how blind he is to the demons his beloved uncle possesses. X can't accept these words of love. He has no tolerance for them. He wants to physically crawl out of his skin with each and every one of them.

Joey stands, reaches his arms up and stretches. Furrows his brows in concentration. He speaks slowly. "I've been spinning around something though. I think I have an idea."

Thankful for a change in subject, X looks up and asks, "Oh yeah, what's that?"

"I think I just need to win her back. I told her I'd give her space, and I will. But in the meantime, I gotta come up with something. Show her love is a risk worth taking, and that I'm not ready to give up on her." He puts his hands in his pockets. "I've been too complacent. I took her for granted and the spark fizzled out, and now she forgets all that we have that makes us *us*. That makes us the couple that can survive anything."

X hates where this is going, yet he has no choice but to ask. "How are you going to do that?"

Joey starts nodding, and X watches as the hope in his face and his eyes come alive. "I gotta start at the beginning."

chapter eighteen

. . .

reggie

IT'S COMPLETELY UNBELIEVABLE to me the amount of tears I have streaming down my face right now. I hope Caroline is well stocked in tissues because I'm clearing out the current box. It seems like with every word I try to utter to her, with every truth I speak into this space, a hard and fast black wave of emotion rushes out and I'm left clinging to some semblance of composure that seems impossible to obtain.

I blow my nose yet again, drop the tissue in the nearby trash bin, and pump out my key chain hand sanitizer in an effort to refresh. I'm desperate to continue to explore and process my decision to end it with Joey, and to have her use her magic and guide me in the lingering aftershocks of grief I'm feeling.

I pick at my sweater and stretch out the holes in the knit of the gray fabric. The result is drab. It's fitting to my mood. I use the holes of the fabric as a distraction as I continue.

"The worst part of it was he just seemed so caught off guard and shocked," I tell her, my voice shaky. "I get it, I shocked myself too, so I can't really expect anything less than that from him." I shake my head, look up at the ceiling and will myself to stop crying so I can continue. "I hate hurting him so much. I hate it. I feel like a monster, but I think it was the right thing to do. I probably should have done it a long time ago."

"What stopped you from ending it before?" I look back down to see Caroline's face etched with the lines of concern. I can see it all over.

I smooth away some invisible particle from my sweater and sigh deeply. "The things we've talked about. That there was nothing actually *wrong* that I could pinpoint precisely, just a general feeling like he's my best friend or something, not the love of my life. And how do you know if that's okay or not?"

"And now? How do you know now that it's not okay?"

"I'm not entirely sure I do, frankly, but I know I can't keep forcing it. It's not fair to him."

"Or you," she says. Bless her, still kind to this heart-breaking monster that I am.

"It's like I've been scared of the risk all this time, the risk that I end things only to find that I'm an idiot. That there is no such thing as a visceral feeling of *knowing* someone is the one for you, and I did it all for nothing. I kept pushing aside all these feelings of doubt. But they were there anyways.

"Joey would do something random or silly, something very Classic Joey, and I'd look at him and wish he were just my friend so that I could actually laugh and appreciate him better, instead of feel..." I can see Caroline shift in her seat as she waits for me to find the words. "...feel. Gosh, why is it so hard to pinpoint this?"

"Is it hard or are you scared to say what you're thinking out loud?"

I shoot a glance in her direction. She's got me again. I bravely continue in my attempts to be brutally honest. "Feel disgusted and turned off by him."

There. There it is, my ugly truth. That at some point I had started to feel downright turned off by Joey. I hate myself and the words even as I say them. But they feel right. Saying them offers me some honesty and clarity. "Yes. That's what it is. I'd feel those awful things and it's like I knew they were misplaced, and he didn't deserve them, but I couldn't help it."

"We can't help our feelings, but we can try and understand their root cause. What's underneath them," she says. Caroline is all about that. Don't punish yourself for your gut reactions and feelings, but work with them and try and understand what they're telling you.

"I've always viewed Joey as someone that I love, but not in the way I imagine I'd want to love a husband."

"So what's the difference? In the love for Joey versus the hypothetical husband?"

I spin around this idea of a love for a husband in my mind. And I can't help it, my mind goes to how I feel when I'm with X. I try and verbalize it. "Like there's an urgency. Yes, an internal urgency of sorts like I can't get enough, and I need more. And a challenge, too. It's supposed to feel like I can learn from the other person too, that I'm challenged *by* them. In the best way possible. There's a thrill in the feeling that I can learn and grow. And it feels like a..." I furrow my brows in concentration, "...a beautiful transparency in the way I'm seen, fully and completely."

Caroline writes something in her notebook and I can assume it's those words I just spoke. She looks back up to me. "That's definitive. How do you know that now, your identified feelings of what the love for a husband is supposed to feel like? And did you ever feel that with Joey?"

I contemplate this. Shake my head no. "With Joey it's always been a friendly, fun kind of love. At least on my end, anyhow."

"And the urgency feeling and," she looks down at her notes, "and challenge, learning, growing and being fully seen?" She looks back up at me. "What's made you aware that that's the kind of love you want to feel now?"

I take a deep breath. It's now or never, time to reveal all. "Because it's how I feel with the guy I mentioned before." She nods with understanding. "His name is Xavier, and he's Joey's uncle."

Even the usual poker-faced Caroline shows a genuine reaction to this, her eyebrows raised. "I see, no wonder you've been struggling then." I study her face for traces of judgment on my black soul, but there's none. If she wants to throw stones at me, she sure hides it well. "So what made you pull the trigger finally with Joey? Now and not before when you first recognized these feelings with Xavier?"

It feels good to hear her say his name out loud. It feels like it's more real somehow, as opposed to this cloud of a concept that I grasp at only for it to disappear. It feels good to be able to finally face it head on.

I think about her question though, the why now, and try and figure out how to explain it. "I've always blamed myself for being too analytical with things, for driving myself nuts sometimes with the investigative look at everything I do or have going on in my life. And don't get me wrong, thanks to you I've come a long way in valuing that side of myself and seeing all the positives it does for me."

"The work in that has been yours, not mine, but go on." Of course Caroline will refuse credit to any of my personal growth.

"But all these years of me questioning my relationship with Joey, I've pushed and blamed overthinking as the issue. Yet you can't deny your feelings, can you? You can't try and remold them into something they're not.

"And I've looked to my mom for this inspiration, thinking that if she's able to fall in love as fiercely as she has, even after losing her husband and son, then I should be able to as well. I thought something was just wrong with me. Thought maybe I was allowing myself to get hung up on what's not right and that I wasn't allowing myself to see and feel all the good. I had actually admired her as a model of glass-half-full." I squeeze my eyes shut in regret for how much I hadn't realized.

"And now?"

I open my eyes and stare down at the fuzzy carpet. "Well, now I see it was all bullshit."

"What was?" I can see I've confused Caroline, and I try to explain.

"My mom didn't have this great second chance at love relationship. Richard was apparently abusive towards her, and a lot has been resurfacing for me since I realized that."

"Abusive?" Caroline confirms.

"Yes. I found a PFA application my mom had started to fill out years ago. It was apparently prompted by a fight they had just a few weeks before he died. Of a heart attack," I quickly clarify, trying to steer clear of Caroline accidentally thinking things were about to take an even darker turn. "I mean, I doubt you consider a PFA just for the hell of it, and the more I think about it the more I remember Richard and his lack of patience and general temper, the way he would talk to my mom sometimes, undermine her and things all under the guise of playful flirting, and yeah. It tracks. I've had this whole thing right before my eyes and never even realized it."

"How old were you during their marriage?"

"Five to fifteen."

She nods. "Young then. Too young to be looking with a critical eye on your mother's relationship. How about you, were you close with Richard?"

I shake my head. "No, not really. He rarely came on family vacations with us or did any activities for that matter. It feels strangely obvious to me now, the dysfunction there. My mom was this accessory to him in a way. I do have these memories of them fighting but I would stay in my room and turn on music and tune it out. As much as I hated it, I figured all parents fight."

Caroline drapes her elbow on the armrest of her chair. "True, it can be hard for a child to know what's normal or healthy and what's not, because it's all they know. How about as you got a bit older?"

"I've been thinking about that. When I look back, I realize he was around a lot less those last couple years. I can remember at one point my mom and him fighting. She was accusing him of having an affair." I try and concentrate as the memory of this surprises me.

"How old were you then do you think?" Caroline asks.

"I'm not entirely sure, I had completely forgotten about that." I'm genuinely amazed at this strange new memory resurfacing. "Maybe twelve or thirteen? I remember my mom crawling into my bed that night and I held her and wondered what she was going to do, if we would move out or what." The tears start up again to my surprise. Roll down my face and my hands feel a tingling sensation with this memory.

Caroline coaches me through. "What's coming up for you now as you think about it?"

I'm quiet and close my eyes while I focus on that night. My room, the warmth of my bed, my mother's slim body next to mine. "I feel a squeeze in my chest," I finally say. "Sadness for her. Definitely sadness, I hated seeing her so hurt and suffering. Seeing my hero so hurt and weak." The tears continue and I'm powerless in stopping them. "Like I had this sense that she was weak, and I was strong, and I felt this role in being able to take care of her. A purpose in my ability to comfort her and be strong for her when she so clearly wasn't. I remember thinking how frail she felt and feeling sorry for her inability to be strong for herself. Like I understood she just wasn't capable." I grab yet another tissue as my revelations continue.

"And also, something else is there, it's hard to describe." I squeeze my hands tightly, trying to hold onto and pinpoint this feeling. "I guess it's...I think it's that I felt empowered in my superhuman strength and the opportunity to be there for her." I look back at Caroline. "Yes, that's what it felt like, empowered by the opportunity."

"Empowered yet I can see your emotion. What's behind the emotion you're feeling now?" Caroline's voice is soft as she tries to keep my current trance intact. "If you have the superhuman strength as your mother's caretaker, what does that mean for you?"

I close my eyes again. Work through the dark bits of my mind to find the right words to describe the feeling. "It's that I have control. And that I don't need anyone to take care of me." The words slap me hard and painful as I say them, but I continue. "And I need that because there was no one *able* to take care of me." I can barely get the words out through my sobbing, they hurt so much. But there they are, heavy and so false and debilitating to hear them said out loud, it crushes my heart.

"Is that true, you don't need anyone to take care of you?" Caroline asks, voice as gentle as silk.

"No," I shake my head through my tears.

"What is true then?" she asks.

The words are bubbling out of me, quickly now. "I want to be loved and cared for too."

"Good. Say it again, Reggie."

"I want to be loved and cared for too," I whisper. My belly squeezes with the recognition of this. It hits right, a phrase generally so foreign to me. But it's true. I've had an underlying feeling of a lack of safety, just like X and I talked about. And all I want is to feel safe and cared for too.

I open my eyes slowly. Blink and adjust to the soft lighting, which feels absurdly bright in this moment. "I want to be loved and cared for too," I say one last time, as loudly as I can.

My mouth is a desert I realize, and I turn towards the table to my right to take a desperate sip of my water. The coolness of it aids in simmering down the burning of my body and its dredged-up emotions, ones I've done too well hiding and pushing down. So well, in fact, that I didn't even know they were there.

Our subconscious really is the iceberg hidden beneath the surface of the water. And that shit's cold and dark.

That memory of my mom and Richard's fight and his possible affair—I had completely forgotten about it. I locked it deep in a closet in hopes to never be seen again. Why? What was I hiding from? Since finding the PFA I've found myself angry at my mom for pretending her relationship was this great gift after tragedy, but apparently I'm no better. I was buying into it too for some reason. Maybe I was just too young to make any sense of it at the time. I do remember soon after that fight that they had made up, and it was as if nothing had even happened. I can see now the cycle of buying back forgiveness that Richard would do. He'd be around for dinners for a few days after their fights, charm and smiles in full force. He'd maybe buy me a random toy or gadget or something, bring home a bouquet of flowers or something nice for my mom.

But at what point did I temporarily erase the darker times from my memory? I'm mad at myself for it, mad that I chose to pretend it didn't exist, whether consciously or not.

It feels like my own mind betrayed me.

But I'm hopeful now, especially given the resurfacing that just happened, and maybe the catalyst of this change is the very act of finally following my gut. Hard as it was to break up with Joey, I felt an immense amount of relief afterwards.

"That was good work, Reggie. I'm proud of you." Caroline says. "I know that was tough, and I thank you for sticking with me through that." I nod silently in acknowledgement. "How are you feeling now?" she asks.

I'm oddly still and at peace. I look at the red and yellow swirl painting on her wall and feel the yellow center dominating it. "I feel lighter. More awake and aware. Though exhausted at the same time," I say with a small smile. "But lighter. And relieved. Because I know I did the right thing with Joey. I don't know what the future holds for me or any relationships, but I know I can't keep trying to make something be what it's not. I don't want to keep lying to myself and denying what's missing." I mindlessly reach in my bag for some ChapStick and apply it before continuing. "And finding the PFA just started the wave of opening that all up for me, I guess. Because yes, I care for others and it's my natural instinct, and I do it with Joey too. But I don't always like it; I started to resent him for it."

"Resentment is a byproduct of envy. What did you envy when it came to him?"

I consider this. It's resonating with me. I shrug. "That he gets to be cared for. It made me feel used at some point I think, though I know that was never his intention. But...it's so strange and foreign to say this, but it's that revelation. That I want, no that I *need* to be loved and cared for too, I guess." I squeeze my eyes shut and nod slowly to myself as I try on this new concept. "And while Joey tries, I just don't feel the complete and total sense of security with him somehow."

I open my eyes and stare at the red outer circle of the swirl painting. "That's it, that's the piece that's always been missing."

"What's the 'piece,' try and put even more words to it. Go a little deeper," Caroline prompts.

It's tough to, but I know we're right there at the space we need to be. I close my eyes to focus once again. I feel so much calmer now. And I can see and feel it, the piece missing. I try and assemble the right words. "It's the 'catch me if I fall' absolute strength, the security net," I say. "Because if I'm always the one taking care of him, then I never get to fall if I need to." I open my eyes. "I think now I finally have the courage to allow myself."

"To fall?" she confirms.

There it is. The final layer I was failing to see. I thought being vulnerable meant opening up to Joey, but it didn't.

To be vulnerable means something else entirely. It's the trust exercise of falling backwards in someone else's arms. Relinquishing control and leaning into your fears with blind faith that a safe and understanding embrace awaits.

So I answer Caroline. "Yes. To fall. And to have the courage and faith to allow someone else to catch me."

And the truth is, that feeling of courage never sat right when I tried to place it on Joey.

But it does with X.

chapter nineteen

. . .

X

THE ICE ON his shoulder burns with a sting so intense he winces. He always hates this part of physical therapy, the exercises followed by the ice, so cold that it makes a switch and begins to feel lava hot. He closes his eyes and uses the sensation as a distraction from his mind.

Reggie.

Reggie. Here in this building with him. He swears he caught a whiff of her vanilla scent when he walked past her office. He refrained from the urge to peek inside, but his peripheral vision confirmed she was in there. A shadow of a figure.

He wants to talk to her and check to see if she's okay. He knows she must be hurting too, even if she was the one to end the relationship with Joey. That couldn't have been easy to do. Even when we know something is the right thing to do, there's no shielding ourselves from the pain of it.

He realizes with dread that he still needs to tell her the truth. It scares him to do more than anything, because he knows she will never be able to look at him the same. But it's the only way.

Mary pops in to check on him and see if he needs anything else. She tells him he's free to dress and go whenever he's ready, but there's no rush. Usually he would pop up and leave at that point, but he's hoping if he stays a little longer he'll catch Reggie without the distraction of Mary. So X waits a little longer and listens to the muffled sound of Mary's voice as she says her goodbyes and explains her last patient is still in room three, then he hears Reggie give her permission to head home anyways.

He's hoping that means Reggie wants to see him too.

Lying there X stares at the ceiling tiles, pebbles of blackness peppering each one. A small abyss of escape. His adult life so far has been just that—escape. It was the force that had him joining the Army as soon as he graduated high school. It was the propeller moving him forward during every basic training drill. Escape was the side-kick accompanying him on his tours to the desert, and it was the protective blanket fooling his mind he was safe when every other cell in his body knew he was not.

Escape was his drug.

Is Reggie an escape for him too? The thought terrifies him, and he's not a man easily shaken up. Then again, only the terrified feel the need to escape in the first place.

No, he decides. Reggie is not an escape at all, not in the same way any of those other decisions he's made in his life had been. In fact, Reggie is just the opposite. She's homecoming. The velvet of her skin, the warmth of her reddish hair, the pillow of her lips. His mind is right back in the dream-like state on the elevated platform of her deck, touching her and sharing a space with her in a way that he knows he's never truly shared a space with anyone else before that moment. Never before has he been so fully present.

He's been a master at disassociation in the past. PTSD will do that to you. It will make you think someone else has taken over your body. Suddenly you're in the middle of a conversation with someone and you have no clue what you're talking about or who the hell they even are. Or you'll be driving somewhere and realize you have no idea where you are, how you got there. It feels as if someone else took over the driver's seat. And that's terror right there. It's the autopilot that happens when your lizard brain gets turned on, amygdala running at full force and screaming that something is after you, fight or flight, and the rest of your brain shuts down because all that's necessary is survival. Plain and simple.

Except you're not at war at that moment. You're not in trouble. You're not at the scene of an accident watching a mother and small child bleed and scream and the nearby car is twisted on its side and up in flames.

Yet your brain doesn't know that, it only feels something familiar that sends the alarms back into panic mode, and you disassociate. Trauma therapy taught him that. It helped him understand what his brain had been doing and how to rewire it. And now, thanks to Reggie, he's able to feel an experience of truly present in the moment that he hasn't felt in many years.

X blinks away the spiral of his thoughts and peels his eyes away from the tiny pebbles of the ceiling tiles. He sits up and removes the now room temperature pack of ice. With gentle movements he raises his shoulder and feels with satisfaction the improvement. Today was his last appointment.

His ears perk to footsteps around the corner. His nose picks up on the vanilla cloud before it's in his doorway. Reggie knocks, and he gives her the clear to enter. She opens the door and leans on the frame, her expression blank. They stare at one another for a moment before she finally breaks the tension.

"Come on, get dressed. I'm driving," is all Reggie says, before walking right back out again.

THEIR CAR RIDE HAD BEEN mostly silent. She had an intensity in her eyes, and he had the sense that to shut up and simply tag along was his best and only option. So he did. Right here to the place where he first saw her when he initially returned to town. To the bar, Moon Lounge. They pull in, walk up, and he looks up at the crooked sign above the entryway, greeting them in a lure of forbidden promises. A good dive bar offers its own kind of escape.

Reggie is all business as she marches not to the small hostess stand, but right past and directly to the bar. It's a Thursday night and football floods the screens, various shades of green surrounding them. She finds a spot, a singular bar stool as the place is packed given that the Eagles are playing. He watches as she flashes a smile at the portly patron next to the empty seat. She climbs up and situates herself next to the jersey-clad guy. He looks at her like his night is just about to get a whole lot better, then looks up at X with sheer disappointment. The guy gives X a nod that he's not sure is respect or the will to kill, but the man turns away so X backs down his reflexive guard.

The bartender tornadoes her way around the corner to greet them in a rush.

"Sarah, my darling, sweet Sarah, I know you're terribly busy, so I'll make this quick." Reggie points up to X. "Please make him something wickedly strong and delightful. Your choice, I trust you." Sarah simply smiles and shakes her head in amusement. "And I'll have a club soda."

"That it?" Sarah confirms.

"Yes, that should do the trick."

Sarah pours Reggie the sparkling water first and hands it to her. "Whiskey?" she asks X.

"Perfect," Reggie answers for him. "Your pick." X nods his approval, though he's pretty sure Sarah wasn't looking for it. Reggie has a commanding presence about her in that way.

"Nothing for you?" he asks her.

"No, X. Nothing for me. I need to keep my wits about me around you." She locks eyes with him and sips her drink.

"What makes you think I don't need to keep my wits about me around you?"

A closed-lipped smile slowly fills her face. "That's the idea."

That look she's giving him goes straight to his dick, he can't help it. He studies her, unsure of what game she's playing or what part he's got in it. "You should know I don't take kindly to duress."

She continues to stare at him with that smile. "Good," she says. Then she breaks the eye contact and turns to face a screen just as a rumble of a cheer fills the place. A touchdown.

They continue like this for a while, minimal talk as the place is operating at a cacophony too loud for any real conversation. She sips her water; he relishes in the burn of his drink. They watch the game, they cheer with the successes, groan with disappointment at the misses. She orders him a second drink when he finishes the first. He watches the surrounding men steal sideways glances at the radiating Reggie. Then back to him again, standing next to her, not quite with her, and he sees the question in their eyes. The "Is he her man?" and he can't help but feel that while he wishes he were, he's just the outside fixture. The man with no seat of his own, watching but not quite belonging.

And he has no idea where this night is going.

chapter twenty

. . .

reggie

AFTER A BAR food dinner, an Eagles victory and a third and final whiskey for X, I decide it's time to go. I'm not sure what exactly my plan is here but I don't really want him sloppy, now do I? Besides, the noise level is starting to make my skin crawl. I signal to Sarah to close out our tab and X swiftly throws his card down. I don't even bother trying to stop him or offer to pay half. Seems trivial to at this point.

We walk out and he places his hand on the small of my back. I let him do that too because it feels right, and I want his hand anywhere I can get it. In an act of lopsided chivalry, he opens my driver's side door for me to let me in before moving over to his passenger door and letting himself in. And we drive, once again in relative silence. I can feel that he's along for this ride for me and waiting for me to reveal my agenda, whatever that may be.

The truth is I don't really have one. For the past two hours since my mom and Mary left the office, I've just been acting on impulse.

Things with my mom have been civil. Tense but civil. I

mentioned that I ended things with Joey, and for once in her care-free and "live and let live" fantasy life, she didn't have a damn thing to say about it. It was nice, but the reality is we're in a strange new territory right now and neither of us is sure how to act. Our usual dynamics don't seem to fit anymore. I imagine it'll just take some time, but even the rest of the staff have been scurrying around us these past few weeks in awkward hesitation, not sure who did what or what's going on. Only that they are content to stay out of it.

Joey, my too good for me Joey, he's respected my request to give me space and has been surprisingly radio silent. Lucy thinks he's probably just hoping I'll ride out this phase and come to my senses, which of course breaks my heart even more because I know there's no returning. There will come a time when I'll need to confront him again, make it clear, trade belongings that we have at one another's homes. But I'm not quite ready for that yet.

That's the thing about a breakup with someone you've been with for so long. It's not like it can be done and complete just the one time. The breakup happens again and again and again with each logistical encounter, each tiny detail you forgot that still remains to keep a thread of connection between the two of you. Maybe that's why we stay in relationships when we know we shouldn't. We dread the multiplicity of it. But prolonging the inevitable only makes it worse.

Strange as it sounds, my head feels clearer now than it has in a long time. I wouldn't exactly say that I'm happy just yet, but I can feel that I'm living with more authenticity, and that's a start. My mind does wander to Joey though, and I know I have to ask the resource currently here with me about him.

I go for robotic, not willing to let my emotions surrounding Joey flood and drown us in this car, so I simply ask if he's okay. X confirms that he's doing better, he's been busy with work and taking extra shifts but doing okay. Lucy via Justin has said much of the same thing to me, and I allow a small amount of relief to wash over me. *I'll always care for him,* I realize. A nurturing instinct always in full effect when it comes to Joey.

My headlights light up the back parking lot behind my office as I pull in. I slip into my usual spot, turn off the car and say, "Coming in?"

X, I can tell, knows he has no choice. We're inexplicably connected to one another, and the invisible tether has been building in strength with every passing minute of this evening.

I unlock the office door. We walk in and I lock it again behind me. We walk down the corridor straight to my office, guided only by the minuscule nightlights plugged in the walls. The late fall darkness makes it feel like midnight, but in reality, it's not even ten yet. My eyes adjust to the inky blackness as X follows me into my personal office. I can feel his silent presence behind me like a protective force, a soft and low hum of energy that emits a feeling of safety I'm not sure I've ever experienced.

I flick on the small desk lamp and turn around, perch on the edge of my desk, legs crossed. I look up at him, a looming shadow in the muted light provided by the lamp. I can smell the whiskey on his breath, and the bite of his cologne. My eyes can just barely make out the amber of his in this low light. His tall frame fills the small space. Broad shoulders standing over me, quietly obeying in their presence here with me.

He takes a step closer. Reaches a hand to me to do that move he did before on my deck, the caress of my cheek and the brush of my hair behind my ear. But this time he keeps his hand there a moment, then slides it down and I can feel his thumb on my neck. He takes my hair in his hands and pushes it behind my shoulder, down my back. A chill accompanies the move and I reflexively uncross my legs and sit up taller. I'm like a sunflower begging to turn and reach its life source.

I reach forward with one hand and hook my fingers behind his belt and jeans. Pull him forward so his legs are between mine. Already I'm feeling the tiniest drop of relief in just this simple act.

Of having him here, my legs on either side of him. Yes, this right here is what I need.

My other hand finds its way under his shirt, the texture of the cotton blanketing my wrist, my forearm, inch by inch as my hand moves up, my fingertips just barely grazing his stomach, all firm and warm beneath my touch. I continue my search with a patience I never knew I had. I'm exploring with quiet curiosity his skin, his chest, the sprinkle of chest hair that my fingertips find as I make my way up and up.

His hand moves in a reverse mirror to mine, further down my back. An embrace that feels like a comforting source of power and courage. I need it too, because I've only ever known one other body aside from my own, and this new territory here in front of me feels as foreign and complicated to me as any untouched virgin might feel.

I increase the pressure from fingertips to my full palm on his skin and work my caress and exploration to around his back. I press and the warmth beneath me radiates its way down my arm, to my body. I feel it deep in my belly and between my legs. I feel his hand reach up and grab a fistful of my hair, and I lean forward into his chest, breathing in with a desperate gasp to inhale every bit of him I possibly can. It's cotton and ocean and masculine and I can't get enough of it, of him. I take my other hand to meet in the middle of his back, and he does the same on mine. The hardness in his pants presses against my belly as we hold this embrace. I want to melt into his skin and relinquish myself to him fully, I feel such a wanton hunger in this I can barely stand it. My skin, my whole body is on fire with need.

"X," I whisper into his shirt. And then I look up at him, my eyes begging him to kiss me. To cross this line once and for all and do this, to connect with me. I have to, there's no stopping this and for once I don't give a damn whether or not it's wrong. I only know my own need is a force beyond any control I could possibly have.

There's a conflicting agitation in my need to be kissed, because his height means he'll have to back away from me slightly to lean down for his lips to meet mine; we'll have to sacrifice some of the tightness of our embrace. Yet my legs can't possibly stand to meet him either, the idea of me raising myself up right now seems impossible. My legs are nothing, useless limbs on a body that has spent all its energy elsewhere.

He seems to know how to solve this though and swoops a hand around to my jaw, thumb on my bottom lip, only now he pushes it into my mouth. And it works, it feeds my greedy mouth's hunger. I close my eyes, bite gently, then suck, roll my tongue on the pad of his thumb, the taste of salt and X a momentary relief. It's nearly enough, at least for right now.

He groans and I reflexively react with a slight dig of my nails into the skin of his back. I want to consume him, want to possess him, this rock of a man in front of me. I don't know how I've gone as long as I have without him. Don't know how I've lived with this missing from my life. But it's here now and there's no turning back from what we both so obviously feel.

Eventually he removes his thumb from my mouth. Pulls back in an instant of utter emptiness that leaves me feeling small and deserted. I'm amazed at how quickly I feel starved and desperate all over again by his body's absence from mine. I dare to meet his eyes again and I can see the matching hunger in them too, a look of visceral intensity that tells me he's not nearly done, and relief cascades down from his eyes into my body and soul.

He leans down again, pushes his forearm under my thigh and ass as he lifts me up off the desk to straddle him with a thunderous force. I match it with the squeeze of my legs around his hips. We're nearly eye level now, and I lean down to his mouth with my own. Our lips meet, my mouth to his mouth, finally. Finally.

He holds the contact of the kiss and adjusts me in his arms, and we crush teeth and explore each other's mouths with reckless speed and power. It's sucking and biting and pulling and it's messy and sexy. I know my lips will be swollen from it all and that only makes me take more and more. I want to take all of him I can. My hands are in his hair grabbing and twisting between my fingers. I pull my mouth back from his, wanting to explore more of him. I slide my lips along his temple, inhaling all I can while his mouth finds the space between my neck and shoulder and sucks with intensity I know will leave a mark. And still, I only want more.

He walks us over to the small sofa along the wall. I delight in imagining him trying to fit his whole body on it, knowing he'll just barely manage, and it means our bodies will be as close to one as possible as he'll consume me. With a gentleness in stark contrast to our previous intensity, he lays me down on my back, and his eyes meet mine as he towers over me. The soft light illuminates only half his face, the other remains in shadow. I place my hand on that blackness to touch and explore, my hands becoming my eyes for me. His beard under my palm feels both soft yet rough in an exhilarating contrast I can't make sense of, I can only experience it right here and now.

"Reggie, baby," he whispers. Hearing him call me baby brings me to yet another level I never knew I needed. He leans down for one gentle kiss on my lips. But I can see he's hesitating, doubt and guilt and turmoil in his honorable eyes as he's not sure about this. Not sure if he should cross this line. I'm clawing at him trying to get him to see that this has to happen. There is no way I can go on and live otherwise. I have to have him, he has to know that. Whatever this thing is between us can no longer go untouched.

"Reggie," he whispers again as he closes his eyes and I'm screaming in my mind for him to please, please, call me baby again and please turn off that doubt and be here with me in this moment.

"X, please. Please don't stop, I need you," I say, my feeble voice no match to the raging roar of need inside me. I close my eyes, afraid I might burst into tears if I dare look into his and see the concern and doubt again. I feel his face in my hair as he leans down towards me. He breathes me in, says my name again. Whispers something, then slowly kisses his way back to my jawline, my cheek, my closed eye, my temple. And then he pauses.

"Please, X," I say again, louder this time, needing him to keep going.

"We can't," is all he says. They're words I refuse to hear. I refuse to accept.

"Yes, we can. We can," I say, grabbing at his shirt and refusing to let go. I can feel his arousal on me, I know he needs this just as badly as I do. He has to know that I have to have him, I don't care. There is nothing else in this world, just me and him.

He moves his head from my hair, down lower to my chest and I feel his defeat as he drops the weight of his head and chest onto me. I cradle him and kiss his hair, run my fingers through it, then move to his face, his beard. There is anguish, actual pain in the idea of him leaving this space tonight without taking me. Without filling me and completing this connection we both so clearly have felt for longer than we can admit.

And like a dam threatening to collapse, streams of what I'm feeling pour out of me into the air between us, and I whisper, "I love you," much to my own surprise. I breathe it into the soft waves of his hair, and as soon as the words are out, I know they are true. I don't even know if he heard them.

But he must have because with this he rises, balancing himself back over top of me. Maybe, just maybe I've unlocked him. His eyes meet mine and I see the traces of hesitation nearly gone, down to a flicker. "Are you sure," he whispers, and I reach up to kiss him again, tell him yes, I'm sure, and in that moment, I've never been so glad to be sober because something tells me he wouldn't have continued if I had so much as a drop of alcohol in me. But I don't and so he knows he can trust my word as there is absolutely no poison clouding my judgment.

I can feel it too, that he knows my certainty to be clear, and he finally, finally allows his hand to meet my skin on my longing body. His hand runs up under my shirt, *God I've needed this touch*, and he grazes over the lacy bra on my breasts and I nearly finish right then and there under his touch, such an answer to my needs. I lift my hips in response and his growl in return only further awakens my senses.

As if in wonder and amazement, his hand lightly lingers on the edge of the lace where my bra meets my skin. My hips raise even higher, moving against his and I feel him between my legs. I feel him there and I cry out with anticipation and ache.

He answers me finally and lowers his hand from over my breast, slowly. Down along my ribs, my belly. Every centimeter of his fingertips on my skin sends ripples of chills radiating beyond his points of contact. And then he goes where I'm begging him to go, he slips into my pants, and I twist and turn my hips to allow him better access. He unbuttons, unzips my pants and I arch and throw my head back and tighten my leg over his. *Yes, please touch me.* I'm blind with the thoughts, starbursts behind my closed eyes.

But he doesn't touch there. He hovers over and hesitates. I feel the slightest caress on my inner thigh and for a moment I wonder if he's trying to stop again. I open my eyes and look back into his, questioning him and his hesitation. He's already looking at me, an intensity in his gaze like he's studying me. I reach up to hold his face, say again, "X, please," but he only shakes his head slowly with a smile.

"I will," he says. He leans down, kisses just under my eye, says again, "I will." I'm confused by his delay; I don't understand what's happening and the ache in my body is threatening to be my undoing. I'm not sure I can stand it. I feel it everywhere—in my back, my hips, a tingle in my toes threatening to completely knock me out. "Slow down, baby," his voice purrs to me. "Slow down," and he kisses my temple, my cheek once again. I'm helpless beneath him and his infuriating pace, slow to the point of torture.

Now that I know his intention, his attack, I'm putty beneath him and I allow my body to go slack and succumb to his complete and total control and will. I'm his to do with all he plans. I'm his.

"That's right," he says and his hand moves from my pants back up under my shirt, to my bra again. He grazes over my nipple and I whimper in helpless torment.

"Fuck," I whisper, and a wave floods between my legs and I realize I'm close to the edge. So close and he hasn't even touched me where I want him to.

"Yes, baby, just breathe," his gravelly voice is so hoarse I can barely make out his words. "Breathe and feel it," he prompts me. "What do you feel?" His voice is a whisper, an echo in the back of my mind.

I focus on my breathing and the buzzing all over every inch of my skin.

"Tell me what you feel," he prompts again, light kisses on my lips and my neck.

"I feel..." but I can't string together words. I can only squeeze the cotton of his shirt, a life raft in an ocean of undulating intensity.

"You feel..." he says yet again, relentless in freeing me from this exquisite torture of forcing my mind and my body to connect with one another as fully as possible. "Tell me," he says.

"I feel you," is all I can manage. I lift my hips again, riding him as I squeeze my legs around him and relinquish the control.

"Reggie," he says with the slightest flick of his thumb over my nipple. *Finally.* Once, twice, and with the third stroke of my nipple I come undone. So unexpectedly, just like that. My orgasm is intense and surreal, despite no actual direct parts to part contact or touch. My body arches and swerves and my voice releases a high pitched moan into the air around us as I tremble beneath him, helpless and fluid as my orgasm possesses every corner of my body.

"Yes, baby," he says with a groan that only intensifies my experience. He's holding me tight and I'm thankful for the embrace as I've now lost complete and total control over my own ability to engage any muscles. I'm a rag doll beneath him, all soft bone and flesh. Completely beyond understanding to what just happened to my body.

I release my grip on his shirt, the last bit of strength I had left in me, and I fall back onto the couch, sinking myself in my own abyss. Everything feels alive suddenly, the texture of the sofa a feverish extreme, the roughness of his jeans on my ankle a piece I never before had noticed. My senses are completely intertwined, I can hear the color blue of his jeans, I can taste the sounds of our bodies against one another. It's a high like I've never felt before.

X leans down and kisses me on my lips with a gentle caress of his tongue along my flesh. I start to awaken again and I reach for his face and look into his eyes. Smile. I await what's next from him, my trust and submission completely his.

And with that, he yanks down my pants, my panties, down my legs and off to the floor along with my shoes and socks. I feel the chill on my naked skin, and I'm lit up all over again. He readjusts my legs back around his hips and reaches to his own pants, unbuttoning them, but he leaves them on. He reaches behind him to pull his shirt up over his head to be discarded onto the floor. He's above me now, all skin and torso, and I get full access to see the black tribal tattoo snaking its way on his shoulder and bicep.

There's such a command in his presence that's exhilarating and novel to me. I see the slightest hint of a smile in the half of his face that's illuminated, and I close my eyes unable to take in the view any more without reaching up to touch him. My one hand can feel his jeans over his thigh, and I focus on the texture and work to steady my breathing. I'm spread before him, lower half naked and exposed, and I'm completely at his mercy.

"Keep your eyes closed," he says, and I nod. I hear the hum of the silence around us, the firmness of his thick and muscular legs beneath mine. "Now tell me what you feel," he says, and I furrow my eyebrows in a mix of anxious exposure and concentration and pleasure. I start to shake my head in protest, but he urges me on, tells me to get out of my head and into my body, to feel all I can feel. The whiskey smell on his breath is a biting sweetness, and I concentrate. That senses intertwining experience starts to happen again as I oblige to his commands. I hear colors, now red and purple, all melting together.

I flinch at the sudden feel of warmth on either side of my torso, both of his hands now there. Still though, "I feel you," is all I can manage to say, though I'm desperate to get it right, to be his good little student and drop into myself even further. I bite my lip and try again. "I feel your hands."

He responds with a gravelly "mmm hmm" and starts tracing small circles on my belly with his fingers, little spirals moving their way up and up my skin, my ribs. I don't dare open my eyes but I'm dying to see his face and read what he's feeling or thinking or something. Anything.

As if he can hear my thoughts, he answers me. "You're exquisite, Reggie. Completely exquisite and I'm powerless to you." The circles stop and he lifts my shirt up over my breasts, placing his mouth just above the lace of one mound, and he breathes out hot and slowly. The impact hits me straight between my legs. I'm flooded with warmth, and I know I must be soaked. I can't help it though, I raise my hips and grind against the bulge in his jeans once again.

I can feel the cool metal of his dangling belt buckle on my lower belly, and I bravely tell him so. "There you go," he says, and he rewards me with his tongue on my nipple. I cry out in response, and this seems to be his weakness because he finally lifts my shirt completely up and off. He deftly removes my bra so I'm finally fully naked beneath him.

It's torture waiting for him, and I'm amazed at the ache deep in my hips, the hot wave that roams beyond any parts I've ever thought of as sexual. Waves of heat behind my hip bones, at the tops of my thighs. My body has never felt so completely alive.

And still, still, he hasn't even touched me *there*.

chapter twenty-one

. . .

x

HE LOOKS DOWN at her, this divine goddess beneath him, his Raina Blake. To see her fully naked, blooming in her arousal beneath him is almost more than he can handle.

Almost.

But he's a man of patience, and he knows he'll only get this one chance at the first time with her. And he'll be damned if he rushes it.

Her eyes begin to flutter open, and he gently places a hand over top, saying, "Not yet, baby." He runs a finger down her lips, her chin, caresses small circles down her throat and her collar bone, but he stops there. He wants to hear her ask for it, ask to be touched. He can see from her moments of confusion that she's not used to this kind of lovemaking, and she needs to learn it for herself.

He can be patient.

"Please," she whimpers and a smile tugs at his lips with pride at his beautiful Reggie learning and exploring.

"Please what," he encourages her to continue. Her hips wiggle beneath him, and he can't help it, he has to give her something, so he moves his hand over her breast. Not touching, just letting the heat of his hand radiate down. Her nipple further hardens in response to the heat. He caresses a fingertip along the soft roll of her breast, and her hips move more. He gently places his other hand on her hip to still the movement, limit her ability to stir, and she moans in heavy frustration.

"Please touch me, X," she says and it's the most beautiful music to his ears. With one swift motion he moves the hand from her breast down to the slickness between her legs. She tries to buck in response and his other hand steadies her hip with greater force, stilling her. She's so wet for him, so beautifully wet. He rewards her hard work and patience with steady motion, sliding in and out and up and down until her body is trembling beneath him once again, and she's crying out more loudly now, and he knows the torture of her climax is nearly too much for her to bear. Too much yet not nearly enough because his hands are not enough. She wants him, filling her completely, and no amount of pleasure will be enough until that happens.

He can barely wait himself. And she's been so good.

X rises to stand and instructs her to open her eyes. She does and he watches as she reorients herself and finds him in the dark room. He smiles down at her, his beautiful goddess, golden, strawberry hair draped over the curves of the couch, milky skin glowing. He pushes down and steps out of his jeans and boxers. Exhales at the relief of his cock finally able to spring free. For a moment he contemplates the need for a condom, though he suspects she's using some kind of birth control. It kills him to cut into her spell that he's worked her into, but he knows he needs to ask.

"Do I need..." his question hangs in the air as he stands above her. She looks at him confused. He takes her hand and kneels on one knee next to her hip on the couch. Places her hand on his cock, *God that feels good*, and he asks again. "Do I need protection, baby?" He strokes her cheek softly, eager to show his concern for her. He would do anything to make sure she's okay, that she feels safe and cared for. She needs to understand this. Even now in this moment, her needs are all that matters.

Understanding meets her eyes and she blinks. "Oh. Oh um, no. I mean, I'm on birth control." She hesitates and he knows where she's going next though they both realize it's likely not necessary. He assumes given her history there's only one other man she's had, though he refuses to allow his mind to complete that thought. "And...clean," she says tentatively.

He nods. "I am too." He resumes his position on top of her, between her legs. She closes her eyes, and he tells her to open them. As much as he can't stand to, he asks one last time. "Are you sure?" Because the logistics of safety have in fact put a crack on their spell, and he needs to make sure she's still okay with this, though his stomach knots at the thought that she might have changed her mind.

To his relief she nods, reaches up a hand to his cheek and says, "Make love to me, X," and he nearly slams into her right then and there, but he holds firm. He nods his head.

"Okay. Keep your eyes open," he says. He takes one last look at her in this form, before he goes to that place from which he knows he will never be able to return. Because he knows once he does this, once he has her completely, there will never be any going back. She will forever be his and only his.

And then slowly and gently, he pushes himself into her.

chapter twenty-two

. . .

Fourteen years ago

lori

S HE HAD BECOME a rock. No, a boulder, that's the word. Yes. A boulder is heavy and unmovable and that's how she felt. A boulder somehow pinned to this bed, staring up at the suffocating wooden beams above. Was there any feeling? She couldn't really tell. She couldn't even comprehend what feeling was. The only thing she knew was that she was stuck, and that her bed was absent of any life aside from her own.

Her eyes moved to the right, to the comforter and pillows still plush and full even after the hours of the night, no markings or signs of human life having been there. No warmth trapped in from a recent form's residence.

There wouldn't be ever again.

And yet somehow, despite the freedom in Richard's absence, his untimely passing, Lori could barely move. A current still existed above her, oppressive and containing.

Her mind flashed back to her dream.

Him on top of her, pinning her down as her squirming body yells at him to get off her, her wrists engulfed in his constrictive grip. His maniacal laugh a thunder as he watches her suffer beneath him. His hand moving to her neck in a grip so tight she is left gasping for air while he whispers and quiets her screams, "I could squeeze as hard as I want, you know, squeeze until you can't breathe," though she can't even hear the words through the noise in her mind. Silent screams that fill her skull. It doesn't matter, because his eyes tell her exactly what he's saying. Ice blue, daggers staring back down to her that tell her everything. She realizes looking up at those daggers that she doesn't even feel fear, just the state of existing. She exists here beneath Richard's authority, a recipient to his mercurial temperament, to his reverent love strangled by his own hatred.

It will pass, he'll snap out of it. He always does. I think.

My poor Richard...

Lori shot up in the bed with a gasp, the boulder suddenly gone and, in its place, the eroded shell of her body. She shook the vision out of her mind and willed herself to be centered as she screamed into the space, a roar of anguish blasting through the silence. The scream twisted and wound through the air, shaking and trembling the furniture, like the aftershocks of an earthquake. She screamed until there was no air left in her lungs to release.

She grabbed her wrist, still throbbing though no actual force was there. Hadn't been for three months. She instinctively grabbed at her neck as well. No hands there either. Freedom existed, only to her it seemed like a cruel joke being played.

A joke and a curious cocktail of grief and agony. How can you miss someone so dangerous? She moved her trembling hand to her chest. There's an emptiness inside, a cave of shadows and mystery. She looked around the hollow room, too quiet and limitless. A chaotic, incomplete map of winding paths and roads and no direction at all. No compass with which to orient herself, no key to help her decipher. It was terrifying, this new freedom in the wake of the era of Richard. His bed, his room, his house—hers for the past ten years, but never really. All hers now, and it repulsed her.

How could he have left her here alone like this?

A rumble of footsteps came down the hall, and Reggie burst through the door yelling, "Mom!" Her daughter rushed over to her in the bed. "Mom, it's okay, I'm here. I'm here," Reggie soothed, grabbing her mother and rocking her. Back and forth, back and forth. Lori was numb as she sat lifeless in Reggie's arms. Her eyes glazed over, staring ahead, staring at a reflection in the mirror. A reflection that was half blank.

"Mom, are you okay?" Reggie pulled away to look Lori in the eyes. "You're scaring me, say something."

With a blink Lori willed herself to speak, to open her mouth, to say something, anything at all to her fifteen-year-old daughter. "A dream," was all she could muster.

Reggie fell back into the embrace with her mother. "Oh Mom, I'm so sorry." She rubbed her mother's back with a gentle rocking. "It's okay, Mom. I'm here." Reggie continued to rock and console with repeated apologies and reassurances, and Lori stared again at the reflection on the wall, a vision of two ghosts and only one actual life in this room.

november

. . .

And now we pick up the pieces
Mother Earth has shed tears
Healing can begin
And with it, gratitude and grace

~Raina G. Blake

chapter twenty-three

. . .

Two years ago

reggie

"CHEERS TO YOU, Lovely Lucy. I think today proved that you will in fact have the most incredible wedding, with an even more incredible happily ever after." We clink our sloshing margaritas and congratulate ourselves on a productive day of final details. Her parents' house for the dress reveal—it's gorgeous ice white satin and silk, you should know. Few could pull it off, but our Lovely Lucy sure as hell can. We took one last look at the venue to finalize table placements and that kind of thing, did a little cake tasting just for fun. It had been a day of anticipation and glamour, which I've come to realize is half the fun of having a large wedding in the first place. Not exactly my style, but seeing the glow in Lucy's eyes makes me enthusiastic by proximity. And she promised me tacos and tequila to finish off the day, so naturally I'm on cloud nine.

Dare I say, a certain mystery man might have something to do with that as well.

But it's not all roses, not at this point, anyway. Unfortunately, things with my mom are still off. I'm giving it time, but I really can't recall another instance like this where we've skated side by side in silent apprehension for quite so long. I'm not sure if it's her or me or if we're just waiting for some judge's gavel to drop and tell us where to go next. But whatever it is we need, we haven't found it yet. I think my own stubbornness might be getting in the way. She's my mom and I'll always love her, but lately I'm just spent, *spent* I tell you, from being her savior. I can see how long I've done that for, albeit for different reasons than the ones I initially understood. But that's just it—she used me in her own avoidance, and I don't have it in me to continue being used anymore as a means to her denial.

On the other hand, I feel like I have this potential new anchor in my life. X feels like a strong and steadfast support, though it's foreign and rather delicate. I suppose that's most accurate. The support really is delicate and questionable due to the sensitive nature of it all. I mean while I'm in this incredible new state of experiencing something that I now know I had been lacking, I also know that there's no easy way through. None whatsoever.

X will always be Joey's uncle first and foremost. There are so many people to potentially hurt if we come out with our relation-ship, (if you can even call it that yet). Not just Joey, but Joey's entire family. I shudder to think what his mom would think. Even the magnanimous Isabella would surely have a fiery response to the indecency of it all.

And while for me it's something I know I could eventually move past, I'm not sure that X can. That's all the family he has.

I wish I could sit here and tell you that things have been all magical since that night in my office. I mean, yes... I have felt a floaty glow that I'm drinking in, but of course, nothing in life is that simple now, is it? X and I have kept apart physically. We're both dancing around the subject of when we can see one another again because it's not like he can just drop on by my house, cook me a meal and make love to me over and over again, right?

No, he can't. Because he'd look up and see a framed photo of me and his nephew, dressed to the nines at a black-tie event three years ago. Or maybe he'd stumble upon the spare toothbrush and deodorant Joey has kept at my house, or God forbid, X would cook me a meal and use the frying pan that his nephew surely can use more skillfully than X can. (I'm guessing. Truth be told I have no real idea what X's cooking skills are, and fuck if I don't even care.)

I'm learning a lot about myself these days, and the thing about self-reflection is that some things can never go back to the way they once were. Once you see your own truths, you can't unsee them. There's a tectonic shift that's happened. Our own changes cause a ripple effect that inevitably impacts those closest to us. And in our growth and rebirth caused by the shifts of it, there's also devastation. Casualties of your internal war.

Like it or not, intentional or not, Joey is that very casualty.

So for the time being, X and I have placed things on hold. We text, we talk on the phone. X is always diligent about checking in on me and making sure I'm okay and that usually turns into long conversations where I hang up feeling both fulfilled and starved for more. It's a hell of a cognitive dissonance and I wouldn't trade it for the world. Go ahead and judge me for it, I bet I would if I were on the outside looking in.

But ultimately, I'm just not sure there's any real great way out of this.

So for now, I'm focusing on Lucy, on the wedding, and on the not quite strong enough margarita being held in my hand.

"You're strangely quiet, what's been on your mind?" Lucy asks in between bites of rice.

Oh you know, just breaking hearts and giving up on responsibilities of being a daughter and all the while deciding that I'm free. Free and wish everyone else could just as easily accept and get on board with that.

"Well, we officially have one of those incredibly long and annoying waitlists for new patients at work, so that's pretty wonderful. I'm looking to hire another therapist. Business is good," I deflect.

She's on to me though. "Uh-huh. I mean yes, congratulations on that, but you know that's not what I'm after."

I'm radio silent as I stare at her. What could I really say? She's getting married in just over a month, and I'm not about to throw a wet blanket on that with my impossible dilemma.

She tilts her head to the side in annoyance. "Don't Bride-Shelter me."

"Don't what?" I'm actually pretty amused by that one. She's funny, our Lucy.

"Bride-Shelter. You know, like I can't talk about real things in life because I'm a bride and only a bride, so the rest of the world needs to not exist."

"I'm not Bride-Sheltering you," I say, but I'm smiling wickedly.

She tosses a tortilla at me, clearly the tequila has gotten to her, and says, "Bullshit. You may strut around like you actually give a shit about the floral displays and linens, but I know you're just being the good bridesmaid here. Talk to me, tell me what's been going on." I start to reply with something generic and she raises her hand to stop me. "Don't puff up and sit all tall in that chair there, Raina Georgia Blake, because that only gives you away."

I sit back in defeat. Slump my shoulders. "Fine." I contemplate throwing a chip back at her, but I refuse to stoop so low. "X and I fucked, is that what you want to hear?"

I don't know why I'm so blunt about it, we did not just fuck, we...I don't even know. In fact afterwards that's what I said to him, I said, "What on earth was that," because it was not anything I'd ever experienced before and I'll drive myself nuts if I think about how much more I want whatever his style of lovemaking is and who knows when I can get it again.

Lucy looks like she just found a treasure chest. "Yes, yes that's exactly what I want to hear."

I throw my hands on my face, "Ohhh you don't think I'm a horrible person?" I mumble through my palms.

She reaches her long arms across the table and pulls my hands away from my face. "Oh my God, Reggie. No, you're not a horrible person. There's so much more to this than just giving in to some desires with the forbidden uncle."

"There is?" I ask, a little stunned at her gentle candor.

"Absolutely."

"How so, what do you see? Because I'm spinning here with disbelief, but also the ease that I feel. It's hard to explain. I hate knowing that I broke Joey's heart. That's a fact, there's definite guilt there. But I also don't really feel shame about it, does that make sense?"

Lucy shrugs. "There's just something there between you and Xavier, that's all. I saw it that night at your house. And maybe even a little before that, at your poetry night."

"You did?"

"Mmm hmm. He was watching you up there like you were the most magnificent creature alive."

"No he was not."

She leans forward, resting her forearms on the table. "He was, I'm telling you. And look, Justin may be the love of my life, but I don't think he'd really go for me reading poetry. And Joey never really got that side of you either. Which is saying something. To the outside world you come off all business and crazy intelligence and a little scary even, but underneath there's a real softie inside."

"I'm scary?"

She waves me off. "It's just a front you like to hide behind."

"You're too kind."

She sips her margarita and licks a little sugar off of the the rim. "Listen to me. I would support you no matter what you ever chose, but a part of me always thought Joey was not exactly it for you, okay?" She sets down her glass. "There, I said it. Now forget it all if you and Joey end up back together again."

See, that's the risk of being the best friend. You can know the truth better than anyone, but you have the impossible decision of whether or not to share it. Do you say what you think in hopes to protect, and risk the friendship if it's not received well? Or do you keep your mouth shut and play along?

It's so painfully obvious to me now that Lucy has felt some kind of way about things for a long time. And while my initial reaction is to be livid at her lack of honesty about it, I know that anger is misplaced. Because what could she do? She was in an impossible situation, as best friends often are. You just hope in time that it all works out, and that the friendship can survive through the hiccups.

I reassure her. "There's no getting back together, Lucy. Not now or ever. Even if X decides to move away and run from this," I swallow as I realize it's been a fear of mine, "there's still no going back."

She grabs my hand and gives it a pat. "Good. Then in that case I'm proud of you." Her phone buzzes and she releases my hand to grab it. "Oh, it's Justin," she informs me. "Hey, what's up?" she says, holding the phone to her ear.

I hear a muffle of something from Justin, it sounds a little like "surprise outside," and something else. She glances up at me with a look that tells me something's wrong, then quickly drops her gaze from mine and turns around to look out the front door. "Yeah, we're almost finished. Give us like, ten minutes." She turns back around to face me as she turns off the phone.

"What?" I ask.

"Um, Joey and Justin are outside."

"Okaayyy..." My stomach does a little flip.

"Apparently they had been scheming up something. Something I had no idea about," she rushes to add.

"What?"

She finishes the last sip of her margarita and signals for me to do the same.

"Reggie, they're outside planning some grand double date night for us. On a school bus. For you, specifically."

I peek around Lucy's shoulder to the door and sure enough, I catch a glimpse of horrid yellow. "What the..."

"I guess Joey wants to recreate his famous kindergarten cheek-kiss and win you back."

Well, fuck.

chapter twenty-four

. . .

reggie

A PROFESSOR IN college once highlighted to us the importance of knowing your audience. As in, when writing a great paper, know who your audience is, what they're looking for, the general tone they would appreciate, facts to back it up, etc. Basically his way of saying, "Write for me, you assholes."

Let's just say it was a skill I had some trouble learning. I usually thought my way was the best and was convinced that I could convince anyone of my reasoning behind taking an assignment. I'd go a slight step out of line with it and redirect it in a way I thought was infinitely better. I mean, to me it was generally obvious.

I did at one point have a professor who indulged me and understood my passions and delights. But she was my fun-class instructor, art history or something like that, so I think she just let me get away with a little more. We had a mutual understanding, she and I, that creativity was a beautiful thing and that I had a voice to be heard and explored.

But right here and right now, I know that I have no such audience. My audience is like professor number one—clear and simple with the agenda, and my thoughts and opinions are not exactly the welcomed ones. Would Joey hear me out? Sure, because he's a good guy. But I know my audience, and turning down a grand gesture bus excursion that he is no doubt tickled pink by, right in front of his two closest friends—well, it's just not an option. I know my audience, and what my audience needs is a win.

So the question—give him what he needs and betray myself? Or be honest and crush his soul and spirit to an even further low?

I'm a coward, I tell ya, and so naturally I chose the former. Karma be damned, yet again. So here we are.

Thank God Joey's grand plan also included Lucy and Justin. Each of us are in our own seats because this is a full-sized bus, and I'll bet even Joey can admit it feels ridiculous having just the four of us and the bus driver on here like this. At least it's dark out and that offers a softer space where the empty seats are not quite so obvious. Lucy's sitting in the seat behind me, stretched forward and holding my hand as we smile and play along to this whole scheme. She gives a reassuring squeeze as the bus bumps along to some unknown location. I imagine it will be quintessential Joey, silly and playful and romantic to the point of my regurgitation of tacos and tequila. Which I'm having more of as we speak (the tequila, to be clear).

The speaker on the bus fills the shadowy, hollow space. "Our stop is coming up, so everyone brace yourselves for a little twist and turn as we make our way to the farm." The driver is Mr. Jay, retired teacher turned bus driver enthusiast and I guess yet another Big Fan of Joey's. How Joey keeps up with these people years later is beyond me, but here we are.

We pull in and I see it—a tractor, the attached wooden concoction with faux seats of straw. Justin and Joey rise to grab blankets and coolers and who knows what else. And I'm sick and for once in my life, at a loss for words.

Joey returns to the seat next to me. Lucy has dropped my hand by now, and Joey leans over and grabs both my hands in a delicate cradle. "Hey," he says, eyes so sincere I almost promise to marry him right then and there just because he looks so *deserving* of happiness. The only thing that might be stopping me is the wretched sinner he'd be attaching himself to, and he sure as hell doesn't deserve that.

"Hey," he says again, "Look at me." He grabs my knees and pulls them so that they're parked out in the aisle between us. I can just make out the flash of his dimples in the floor lights running along the aisle.

He begins. "Many years ago, a little reddish, blonde-haired girl sat down next to me on the school bus. She had just moved into our neighborhood, and the school year had already started. None of us knew her, but I could tell she was something special. She walked on like she owned the place, and she marched right on in and sat down as if being the new girl was no big deal."

I'm completely frozen just staring at him, willing myself to listen. His voice is sort of a distant echo, and my mind plays tricks on me like he's moving further and further away. I'm somewhat aware of our other companions sitting and listening as well, though politely turned so as to not be too direct of an audience.

If there was an "exit" button that could eject me from this moment and into another, *any* other moment in my life, I'd press it now. *Please, just fast forward this moment in my life,* the internal coward in me begs to deaf ears.

Joey continues. "They say when you know, you know, and I swear it, I knew right then and there that I was going to make you mine, Reggie." *No no no no no no no no no...*

"So after a couple weeks of bus rides and playground tag and getting to know you better, I did what any five-year-old boy would do." He leans forward to reenact the scene. "And I kissed you on the cheek." He kisses my cheek right then, and I'm right back to that moment of humiliation and shame and the big kids laughing, and Lord if that wasn't an indicator of the doom my journey with Joey would eventually lead to, I don't know what is. *Exit button, exit button now, dear God.*

I smile as brightly as I can. "No one can say you lack sentiment, that's for sure."

"Why thank you, m'lady." He takes a slight bow. "I don't know if you remember, but also in kindergarten we went pumpkin picking on a field trip. To this very farm right here."

I look around. "Isn't it a little dark for pumpkin picking?"

Joey laughs like I'm the most funny and clever woman he's ever known. It feels forced, and I wonder if even he is second guessing this whole thing. He carries on valiantly, though. "I thought you'd enjoy a bonfire instead, but I think you still get the idea."

I nod and keep my smile plastered on, unsure what else to do. I turn back to Lucy and Justin. Lucy's eyes say, *"Holy fuck,"* and I've never been more grateful in my life to have my best friend by my side.

So off we go, onto the tractor, on a hayride bumpier by a cause that goes far beyond any uneven terrain. Our guide sets us up with a bonfire and cider and cider doughnuts and a comedic little spiel that I'm sure he's said a million times about not falling in the fire and nature's bathroom and all that. It's everything I hate in life, and again I'm filled with shame for my lack of appreciation of America's Favorite Guy.

I MAKE OUT THE SHADOW of Lucy as she rounds the corner to the wooden picnic bench where I'm sitting alone. I don't know how she's doing, but I'm a little beyond buzzed at this point and deathly afraid I might spill out something that would be a major problem. So I'm hiding.

And texting X.

Lucy plops down next to me, her puffy jacket a tempting

pillow. I rest my head on her shoulder. "I'm texting Xavier, shhh don't tell."

She pats my cheek. "And?"

I hand her my phone so she can read our conversation. "He swears he didn't know Joey had this planned, just that he mentioned doing something for me."

Lucy scrolls up and beyond tonight's messages. She does a few quick swipes and I raise my head to see her reaction. I register her surprise on her face, illuminated by the glow of my phone. "Wow, you guys are like, *in* it."

"I guess so."

"Yet we're here." She glances around the other side of the bonfire to where Joey and Justin are sitting in their own private conversation. She turns back to me. "This feels like a middle school dance, doesn't it?"

"This boy-girl split?" I nod. "It does." I pick at the fingers of my gloves, pulling and snapping the soft fabric. "Think he feels like this was a bust?" I feel truly sick to my stomach at the thought, because as much as I'm trying to play along and have fun, it crushes me to think that I will yet again have to break Joey's heart.

"Maybe hiding in a corner over here is giving him some indication."

"But it doesn't feel good."

"Honesty in the face of unmet love rarely does."

I think about that for a moment. How unmet love has been the quiet theme of my relationship with Joey, I just never coined it as such. Maybe it's because I *do* love him, only not in the same way.

"I love Xavier," I say out loud softly to both our surprises.

This is why I love Lucy, because all she does is grab my hand. Two gloved hands held together in silence as we watch the glow of our beautiful bonfire. We watch the flames dance and sway and watch the two men behind them come in and out of our line of vision beyond the fire. And I think about how this night will end, how I'll politely say, "Thank you," to Joey and fight off any other advances and how maybe that's exactly what Joey needs to really and fully understand that this is over. How what was meant to be a sizzling, romantic gesture ended up being merely a casual and friendly evening.

And how casual and friendly doesn't actually feel all that different from what our nights together were always like anyways.

chapter twenty-five

· · ·

X

A THROBBING HEADACHE tells him it's time to turn off the computer. He's been slammed with emails from his realtor for one of his houses, as the tenants in there had expressed interest in purchasing the home. It was something he had encountered in the past, a tenant wanting to buy, but he always wanted to wait a little while longer and have that much more equity acquired. These tenants seemed eager to call the home their own before the holidays, and X no longer had any real reason to say no.

He signs off on the last of the e-docs before closing his laptop and rising from the desk. He should have felt better about what was sure to be a quick and easy sale, but a knot in his stomach and the pounding in his skull are keeping him from any celebratory response.

What he really wants is to see Reggie.

Saying it was hard to stay away from her was the understatement of the century. But it had to be done. He isn't sure where this could go, and he's holding on to more secrets at this point than he cares to admit. It seems like every way he turns, every choice he makes he's disappointing people and causing harm, even if they themselves don't even realize they're experiencing it. But just because they might be unaware doesn't make it okay. It only further poisons his sense of honor.

Joey is hurting and X has been doing everything in his power to stay away there too. Even X's sister Isabella, Joey's mom, had been aware of X's distance and had said as much in a recent call to him.

"I've had a lot going on," he had tried to explain to her.

"Like what? You're retired now. You take up bird watching or something?"

He tried his best to deflect. "Yes, that's it. I've got real avian flair."

She heaved out a sigh on the other end of the line. "I wish that were true." It was hard to hear the concern so clear in her voice. "Listen, Xavier...we miss you. And you need to stop shutting us out," she added in that scolding big-sister tone of hers.

"I'm not shutting you out."

"The hell you aren't. I know you, Xavier. You tell yourself you're a loner, but you need to be with family. It's not healthy to hide away. No more excuses now that you're finally home for good. Learn to reintegrate, have a good meal now and then."

Always the big sister to X, Isabella was yet again attempting to take charge and ensure he felt welcomed. She tried harder than any of his other half-sisters to let Xavier know he was one of them, and not the bastard child and mark of shame on the family that his own internal mind often told him he was.

He tried in earnest to explain his whereabouts to her. "I've been driving around different areas, trying to find a house or space that feels right. Looking into work options, that kind of thing."

This seemed to appease Isabella, as she muttered some encouraging words about his talents and being excited for his next chapter and whatnot. She reassured him she'd be there to help in any way she could to figure out his next steps. X was both warmed by her steadfast love and affection, yet sick with the thought of his betrayals.

Unfortunately, the conversation eventually went exactly where X feared it would. She said, "Have you talked to Joey? Do you know how he's doing?"

Shit. It was the kind of question he had been avoiding. He was lying by omission, and it went against every bone in his body. "Not much, he seems to be trying to keep busy."

Isabella let out a heavy sigh. "He's crushed, and I'm at a loss for what to say to him at this point."

No kidding. "They're young," X said in attempt to placate. "Plenty of years of love and heartbreak up ahead of them both." As soon as the words popped out of his mouth, he regretted them. He hadn't meant to refer to both Reggie and Joey. Bringing up Reggie was the last thing he wanted to do. This was already dangerous waters to be treading in, and that only increased the risk.

"He's always been my little romantic. Oh, Reggie's so good for him, too. There's gotta be more to the story that Joey's not telling me." She lowered her voice to nearly a whisper. "You know, I debated calling Lori to see if we can help these kids figure this out."

X heard the distant voice of Joe Senior, Joey's dad on the other end shout, "Stay out of it, Belle! Don't you dare!" X sighed for a little relief for Joe's input, as otherwise Isabella would have undoubtedly already meddled.

"I know, I will! It was just a thought," Isabella shouted back to her husband. "Aren't you supposed to be getting ready for work!" She turned her attention back to X. "Apparently I'm not *allowed* to call Lori, though," she said, her tone mocking.

X pressed his eyes shut and squeezed the bridge of his nose. He was trying to think of what a normal response would be. "Just let it be, Belle. Relationships end and people move on. Happens all the time. He'll be alright."

And then his sister said something X was not remotely prepared for or deserving of. She said, "You know, I always wondered what would have happened if you never joined the military. If you had a chance to stay in one spot for more time, settle and really get to know someone. I worried about you with not being able to do that."

"You did?" he asked, unable to hide the disbelief in his tone.

"Of course. You should have been able to meet a girl and fall in love and have some babies. You'd be a wonderful father." Once again, he received the compliments like a stinging spray of acid. "You would, I know it," Isabella pressed. "Look at you with Joey and the girls, you were always a natural with them. Maybe now that you're home, you'll get your head out of your ass and put a little effort in."

He needed to squash her line of thinking. She had no idea how badly he wanted just that, but with the wrong woman. "Jesus, Belle. You think you know what I need, huh?"

"I think your mother was selfish and never let you need anything, may she rest." He could almost hear her crossing her chest. "And Dad did the best he could with the little time she let him spend with you." Xavier winced at the reminder. His dad's household—with Isabella and their other sisters—was the closest thing to a normal family he had ever experienced. "But you need to think about yourself, now and then. Drop the loner act and open yourself up to dating, at the very least."

If she only knew.

"I'll take your advice into consideration," he said dryly. "It's one step at a time right now. Let me find a place to live before I start entertaining...anything else." What more could he say?

He had hung up the phone with a head full of questions. Did Isabella really pity him and his lack of relationships? How would she react if she knew that he had committed this cardinal sin, that the reason her only son's heart was breaking right now might very well have everything to do with him?

But he can't think like that. It does no good, and there was no doubt in his mind that Reggie had her reservations long before X had waltzed back into their lives.

Reggie.

He had to see her again. As much as it pained him to continue to cross this line, the fact of the matter was they'd never know what exactly this thing was between them if they continued to avoid one another. Right now, they're acting as if in a long distance relationship. He smirks. Hell, he knows all too well what long-distance relationships look like. For him, they never worked.

But Reggie isn't far away. No, she's right here in his town, and for once he wants to know what could be. She had told him she loved him. He heard it that night with her in her office. It broke him and his will to do the honorable thing, and he was completely at her mercy. Helpless to her. It was the first time a woman had said that she loved him where he actually believed it.

Still, he wonders if she could love him fully, all of him, if she knew his whole story.

There's only one way to find out.

chapter twenty-six

. . .

reggie

THE FLOWERS ARE gorgeous, I'll give him that. They sit on my porch as I'm walking into the house, and I don't even have to look at the card to know they're from Joey. With a sigh I grab them and take them inside.

I drop my keys and place the vase on the counter. I stare at the card—some innocuous piece of paper that to me, sends a siren signal of danger ahead. I sigh and open it.

Had a great time with you revisiting our beginning. Here whenever you're ready. XO-Joey

I'm at such a loss I don't even know which way is up, which is down, and I feel like I have zero good options. But something's gotta give. As much as I'm learning about myself and working to pay attention to my own needs, I must admit I'm a little dizzy in the mix of it. With my mom and I in our strange funk, and with my efforts to not engage with Joey, I'm recognizing a space of deprivation in me. It feels like without those two leaning on me, I'm no longer sure where I stand. What's my purpose and role anymore? I'm amazed at how much I've depended on those roles as a distraction for my own needs. As much as I've been feeling used as an escape for my mom, I can't help but admit that I'm guilty of that escape as well.

My mom and I have both used our relationship with one another as a hiding place from our own pain.

It's a startling realization, one that I wonder if I can approach with her. Would she be angry at the suggestion? Or has our time living and working quietly parallel to one another given her the space for similar reflection and insights?

As the dust has been settling around me, I realize how grounding it had been to fill those previous caretaker roles. I'm the go-to gal. I solve the problems, I make the tough decisions, I have the plan. It's who I've always been, but I guess I never realized how much I did those things within the framework of other people. Now that I've stepped out of those dynamics and have this new sense of freedom, I'm feeling an unsettling and unexpected amount of loss as well. A void that feels like it needs to be filled, though I question how healthy that is in the first place. Is it a void that is supposed to be filled, and just had previously been filled in the wrong ways? Or should the void not exist in the first place? I'm really not sure.

Maybe our tragedies and pain are simply a void that we must learn to contend with. No escaping it, no rushing past it. No attempts to fill the void with external distractions.

We can only accept the discomfort of our voids fully and with open curiosity.

My phone buzzes and I see a text from X.

X: I have an idea. Got a minute to talk?

Me: Sure, I can give you a call.

Me: Everything okay?

I anxiously await a response. What kind of idea could he

possibly have? God, I hope it's a solution to this whole mess we're in. I set my kettle to boil water for tea and run upstairs to change into sweats, feeling a little more hopeful with each passing moment. My phone buzzes again.

X: Think you can get away for a few days?

My heart starts thumping in my chest. Get away for a few days? I want to say yes and throw all caution to the wind, and I don't even know what he has in mind. But it feels like a light in an otherwise aimless space devoid of any direction. I quickly type back.

Me: I'll make it work.

chapter twenty-seven

. . .

reggie

SOMETHING I REALIZE I already adore about X—he's not into surprises. As much as I hate to do it, I can't help but compare him to Joey, and I'm riddled with guilt each and every time. But Joey is the only relationship I've ever known, so my mind tends to automatically wander in comparing things with him. Which then makes me wonder, is what I have with X right now even considered a relationship? Is he my boyfriend? Not exactly I suppose, but that's circumstantial.

Anyhow, I find myself comparing the two, and I think about how Joey would have tried to turn a mountain cabin getaway into a surprise, somehow. He'd tell me I can't know where we're going, he'd have me pack everything from summer dresses to winter boots even though he'd know half of it was unnecessary. It would all just be to build up the surprise and throw me off. It would drive me nuts and I'd force a happy face and remind myself how sweet Joey is, how most any girl would kill to be dazzled in this way.

But not X. His brand of romance is a little more subtle. Make no mistake, this cabin I'm walking into as we speak screams of romance—there's a fire already burning, there's snow lightly falling, there's champagne and chocolate covered strawberries and soft music playing.

But X had the courtesy to tell me to bring boots and that no sundresses would be necessary.

"How is all this set up?" I ask him as he puts our bags down in the foyer.

"Friends of mine own it and a few other cabins in the area. It's a service they do. I let them know when we'd be arriving."

I'm impressed and in love with the space. It's all warm wood walls of the perfect log cabin, yet sprinkled with luxurious touches. Modern chandeliers and dark granite counters in the kitchen to the back. Floor to ceiling stone fireplace surround and an open loft space above where I can see a peek of an exquisite king-sized bed. With the holiday season just around the corner, it's stirring up excitement for more to come. Cozy spirit and romance with someone I love, if we could just figure out how to come out with an "us."

"I'm in heaven," I tell him. I grab his hand and lean against his arm. "This was a good idea."

He turns to face me and leans down to kiss me, our first kiss since that night at my office. I release his hand and reach my arms up and around his neck and relish in how natural this feels. His arms wrap tight around me and I run my hands through his hair. His tongue explores my mouth with such careful curiosity, gentle as if I'm something delicate and priceless. It's different from any other kiss I've experienced. I feel treasured. Yes, that's it, treasured, like I'm the most valuable thing in the world and need to be treated with care. And I recognize that in the past, I've felt that used feeling, almost. A kiss could feel exhausting at times, but I'm determined not to let my mind wander there.

This right here is all about me and X. To be together and figure out what this even is, and fully explore without thinking about anything else. I know that had to be a tough decision for him to make, to take me here and try this. He has so much more at risk than I do.

He releases me and his honey eyes look down into mine. "I'm glad you're here," he says, and I can see there are a million other thoughts behind his eyes. I see the pain in them, and I want to reassure him that it's all going to be okay, that this is okay, and we have nothing to feel guilty for, but I know that's a lie.

So instead I say, "I have a feeling I'm never going to want to leave." Because that's the truth.

With this, he kisses my forehead. "I'll go take our things upstairs," he says. "You pour us some champagne."

"You need any help?"

He smiles at me. "Not a chance. Go relax."

I watch and admire as he effortlessly hauls our bags over his shoulders and up the stairs to the loft bedroom. I walk into the kitchen where the champagne sits in a bucket, two flutes beside it waiting to be filled. I open the champagne with a *Pop!* and pour some into each glass. I sip mine and moan in appreciation at the taste of the citrusy liquid.

I place my glass down and notice the cream-colored card folded in half next to the strawberry tray. I pick it up and open the handwritten note. It reads:

"Welcome to your romantic getaway! We've stocked the fridge and kitchen with your requested supplies, but if there's anything else you need, don't hesitate to ask. Here, the main goal is to relax and recover, to connect and discover. We hope you enjoy our cabins as much as we do."

I smile at the ironic simplicity of it. So easy! Just relax and connect! If only matters of love were that uncomplicated.

chapter twenty-eight

. . .

X

E ROUNDS THE corner to where Reggie stands in the kitchen, an enticing vision. She's biting into one of the strawberries and he's pretty sure she's trying to kill him slowly. He watches as she succeeds in taking her taste, chews and lets out a gratifying moan before returning the strawberry to the tray. She licks her fingers, her thumb, then grabs a napkin and dabs at her mouth. He can't help but smile at this opportunity to watch her. Seeing the way she can enjoy something only further enhances his own desire.

He wants to give her something more to enjoy.

"Mind if I join you?" he asks. Reggie jumps back, momentarily startled and places a hand to her chest.

"Jesus, you scared me." A flush rises up her neck and cheeks, but she's smiling. "Watching me make love to that thing, are you?" Her raised eyebrow and wicked glint in her eye are only doing even more things to him that make him want to ravage her.

But not yet.

He takes a few steps towards her and leans against the counter beside her. She watches him carefully and he notes that she's different here in this space. More vulnerable maybe, softer. He realizes she's out of her element, and the usual assured Reggie has taken a bit of a back seat.

She lifts her champagne glass in a toast to him, and he grabs a glass as well. "I'm not really sure what to do next, but this seems like a good place to start," she says.

He nods in agreement. "It does." He clinks his glass on hers. "Cheers, Reggie," and they both take a sip. The cool bubbles slide down his throat and he's relieved to find it's not too sweet. Champagne isn't really his drink of choice, but he wanted something special for her.

She steps closer to him and reaches up to run her fingers through his hair. There's lust in her green eyes and once again he has to remind himself to rein it in. He already knows they work well in that way. What he needs to know is whether or not she can love him if she knows all the darkness inside of him.

"Patience now, hun," he says. But he can't help himself, he takes her hand. Pushes up the sleeve of her sweater and dots the soft skin of her inner forearm with gentle kisses. "Plenty of time for that later."

She closes her eyes, disappointment on her face. "Why does this feel like torture?"

X smiles, amused by her once again. He takes her hand and continues his soft kisses on each of the small bumps of her knuckles. "Torture done well can be exquisite." At this she shoots her eyes open and stares back at him in startled amazement. He drops her hand and kisses her temple. "I'm kidding. Mostly." He takes her chin in his hands and lifts her face to look at him. "I would never hurt you, baby." He rubs his thumb along her jawline and to her mouth.

"I feel so at a loss right now," she says.

"What do you mean?" He hates the idea of seeing her unsettled.

She shrugs. "I don't know. Not really sure what it is exactly."

A cloud of concern overtakes him, and he studies her face for signs of pain or regret. "Are you second guessing coming here with me?" The last thing he wants to do is coerce her into something she's not ready for.

"No, no, not at all," Reggie reassures him. Her eyes are sincere, and a slight relief washes over him, but still, he's guarded. "X, I mean it. This right here, being here with you is the one thing I *do* know about. I think you were right, I want this time with you. We need to do this to...to see what this even is. That's not the problem."

"Okay," he nods. "Then what is, talk to me."

She sips her champagne and seems to contemplate his question. "Nothing. Everything." He's patient as he waits for her to continue. These little opportunities into her mind are exactly what he's hoping for here. It's for both his and her sake as well, as he knows she's going through so much more than she lets on. His hope is that here in this space, safely secluded from any unexpected surprises, they can both drop the last remaining layers of armor. The start of this whole thing has been crafted in a place of land mines, and they need to know what it could be without caution or barriers in their way.

She walks over to the window, wide above the sink with an unobstructed view of mountains. "I have always been the one in charge of things, you know?" He can relate, but he remains silent to allow her to continue. "For whatever reason, I'm the one who will do the things no one else wants to or are too scared to figure out on their own. Even when it comes to Nana, my mother's mom. She and my mom are like these two little girls that have their heads in the clouds, and I've gotta be the one to set them straight. Always moving and directing and ... *producing*. It's like I measure my own value in how much I've done on any given day." She turns back around to face him. "And I've been fucking exhausted and didn't even recognize it." She shakes her head and runs her hand over her face. "There has been something there that felt like it wasn't work-ing, and I could never quite figure out why."

"Not working how?" he asks, hoping to help her sort through.

She tilts her head to the side in contemplation. "It feels like I'm that hamster on the wheel, running and running, but not going anywhere."

"Where are you trying to go?"

With this Reggie looks up at him, and he can't quite read her face. She walks back toward him, steps right in front of him and he sees a little of the assurance pouring back into her. "You ask the best questions, you know that?" All he can do is smile at this. "Where am I trying to go, yes. That's it. Exactly, because when you're that hamster on the wheel working and running, there is no place to go. It's an exercise in futility. We humans do it all the time, but usually don't quite realize how hard we're working until we're completely spent and burnt out. And all the while we lost track of where we were running to in the first place. It's because the goal is always moving. You accomplish this thing you'd been chasing, and then there's the next goal. Then you reach it and it moves again. A new goal arises. No time to just sit and be and enjoy, and with each step you become more and more disconnected."

"Disconnected and on autopilot," X offers.

"Exactly. On autopilot. But running on fumes. And I guess I've found that at some point it switched from running towards my goals, to using running as a means of escape. My productivity and all the taking care of everyone else was really just an avoidance of anything I need."

She looks so beautiful standing here with him, her mind twisting and turning with an intriguing force. He reaches forward and grabs her hand in a gesture of support. "So what do you need?"

She smiles. "I think that's the problem, it's where I'm at a loss. I've avoided it for so long that I don't even know."

He tucks a strand of her strawberry blonde hair behind her ear. "Maybe it's simply to be still." X thinks about his words and realizes he himself has been doing so for the first time in his life, and while unsettling at first, it really has been the key to unraveling the constant tightness in his chest.

"I think you're right." Reggie raises both her shoulders in a deliberate shrug, then drops them both with an exhale. "I'm working to not worry so much about my mom right now, because it's been a harsh lesson to learn that I was putting so much energy into the wrong kind of worry for her. You can't care for someone properly if they're not being honest with you. And letting go of that has been the thing to start this wave of letting go elsewhere too. So now I'm still. Trying to be anyways. And it feels really good. Odd and a little wobbly, but good."

She steps closer to him and wraps her arms around his waist in a hug, then drops her head to his chest. She feels so small and delicate in his arms, and he kisses her hair, happy to see her physically letting go just as much as she has emotionally been trying to. He breathes in and smells the lavender and vanilla of her hair, wishing he could freeze this moment.

chapter twenty-nine

. . .

lori

THE LAST APPOINTMENTS of the day always seem to be the longest. With Reggie out of town and the office down to only two therapists, Lori expected an easy, breezy workday, but in the manner of Murphy's Law it's been busier than ever. She's fielded a million phone calls, tackled paperwork, smiled and greeted new patients, refreshed coffees and waters and supplies. And she swears the new, young physical therapist was giving her an attitude at one point. Over some goddamn mini tabletop fan that she claims is hers.

Lori makes tiny adjustments to her hair, a fluff here, a sweeping of a stray strand there. She then works to tidy up the desk. The office is empty now, patients and therapists finally gone and she's ready to call it on this Friday evening. The fish swim in luxurious tranquility, the hum of the tank filling the space. She looks at them with envy, not a care in the world they have. The office feels eerily empty, and the fish are her only company.

A knock on the front door startles her, and she looks with annoyance at who would be so rude as to try and barge in when they're clearly closed for the day. But her annoyance quickly vanishes as she looks to find that it's Joey, smiling back at her through the glass. She rushes over to unlock it for him and let him in.

"Well hello, sweet Joey, you nearly gave me a heart attack. But I'm so happy to see you!"

Joey drops the large paper bag he's carrying to the floor and opens his arms for an embrace. "I tell you what, I think I've missed you the most these past few weeks." Lori feels instantly warmer with the pat on her back Joey gives her. He releases her, extending his arms and holding her shoulders before giving her a wink. "Still just as gorgeous."

"And you, just as charming."

"Aw, now you flatter me," he says, releasing her.

"You deserve to be flattered, kid." Lori lovingly pats his cheek. "I hope you know that."

Joey appears to have an uncharacteristic nervousness, Lori notes. He places his hands in his pockets and shifts his weight to his toes a couple times in an energetic bounce. "I don't know about all that, but I try the best I can." His eyes scan around the waiting room. "Is she here? I was hoping to surprise her with her favorite pasta."

Lori notes the bag by his feet and realization dawns on her. "Oh, no sweetie, I'm so sorry, she's not here."

"Damn, I got here as fast as I could. Thought I could catch her. You know if she went straight home by any chance?"

Lori's heart squeezes as she knows she's about to disappoint him. "Actually, she wasn't here at all today. She took the day off."

"Reggie did?"

"Yes."

"Took the day off? She okay?" The surprise on Joey's face mimics the surprise Lori herself felt when Reggie told her she wouldn't be coming in. She made Lori cancel her patients and everything. Lori nods to convey that yes, her daughter is in fact okay despite this strange behavior.

"That's a first," he says. He seems to absorb this information momentarily before nodding. "Good for her, she should."

"I suppose," Lori shrugs. She glances back at the bag Joey brought and smells it's creamy, garlicky contents. "But she's not home either, I should warn you."

"Oh. With Lucy maybe?"

"I don't think so. She's actually out of town, in the Poconos. A 'mental health getaway' she said, whatever that means." Lori waves a hand and tries with all her might to pour all the sympathy in the world onto her face to be poured back to Joey. She wants so badly to show him how wonderful he is, even if her daughter is losing her mind right now and can't see it.

"Huh. Okay. Again, good for her."

Sweet Joey, so committed to supporting Reggie. *That girl doesn't even know how good she has it*, Lori thinks to herself.

But an idea sparks in Lori's mind. "You know what? Why don't you go and surprise her there?"

He pulls his head back. "What? No, no. If she's trying to decompress and get space, I don't think that's a good idea," he says with a frown.

"Why not? It's a great idea, yes! That's what you're trying to do now, right? Surprise her? What better grand gesture than to surprise her in the mountains!" He seems to contemplate this, and hope blooms in Lori's chest.

"You know where she is?" he tentatively asks.

"I know she's in some cabin up there, and I can probably track down her location. Let me go get my phone." The buzzing energy Lori feels now is maybe the happiest she's felt all day. What a wonderful idea! Lori's mind is spinning, she thinks how Joey can surprise Reggie in the mountains and they can sort this whole thing out. Reconcile and things can move out of this strange place once and for all. Lori's thrilled with the perfection of it, and all right before Lucy's wedding. And an even better thought floats into Lori's mind—Joey could propose to Reggie there at the wedding! Yes, things were looking up. She finds her phone, brings up the location finder app, and sure enough—she sees Reggie's spot.

"Here it is! I was worried service might be an issue there, but I think that's pretty clear." She practically throws the phone over to Joey.

He lifts his brows as he takes in the blinking dot on the map. "Yup, there she is," he says before handing the phone back to Lori. "I don't know. I'm not sure barging in on her escape is the best idea."

"Of course it is! What girl wouldn't be swept off her feet by a grand gesture like that?"

"Reggie, probably. That's what girl." His tone is matter-of-fact.

Lori waves him off. "Stop it. She doesn't know what she wants. Don't let that prickly exterior of hers fool you. A girl wants to be *fought* for, Joey. A girl wants to be proved to how loved she is. I think all this madness with her has been a little burst of cold feet. Lucy's wedding right around the corner and all, Reggie never has been one of those people to know how to have a little faith if there weren't some hard-core facts for her to research. So go and be her fact. Show her the good fight so she knows exactly how committed you truly are."

Joey looks at Lori with skepticism in his brown eyes. "I want to believe that's true, but I don't know anymore." He gestures down at the bag. "Actually, I was hoping to have more of a peace offering talk with her tonight. You know, assure her we could in time be friends, if that's what she really wants. No more attempts to win her back. We got Justin and Lucy's wedding in a couple weeks, and I want to make sure she's comfortable since we're both in it."

Lori's excitement comes to a screeching halt. She can't believe what she's hearing. "Joey, that's exactly the way to lose her forever."

He grabs the back of his neck and blows out a heavy sigh.

"What if," he says, dropping his hand and placing it in his pocket. "What if I already have lost her forever?"

"I hope that's not the case."

"Lori, it's been several weeks now, she barely acknowledged the flowers I just sent her. Only sent a 'thanks' text. I'm starting to believe that ending things was not just some impulsive decision on her part."

Lori crosses her arms over her chest. Tries her hardest to stand tall and look Joey square in the eyes. "Joey, do you still love her?"

"I'll always love her," he says without hesitation.

"Then what do you have to lose?"

"Lose?"

"Yes, what do you have to lose in trying one last grand gesture?"

"Another chance with her," he says flatly.

Lori reaches up and pats his cheek one more time. "Joey. If the girl isn't swept off her feet at this, then there was no chance with her again anyway."

chapter thirty

. . .

reggie

LOOKING UP AND soaking in the misty freshness of the limbs and pines around us, I feel more at ease than I thought possible. I inhale deeply and squint at the starbursts of sunlight poking through the greenery above me. It's cold with a dampness in the air, yet I feel nothing but warmth. A liquid maple syrup in my chest that is sweet and delicious. There's a feeling of tranquility and freedom in this space around us, and I think about X's poem reference from that night on my deck. *Miles to go before I sleep.* I'm still not sure what his meaning was there, and I suppose now's a good time to ask and maybe eventually I will. But for right now I just want to continue our side-by-side silence.

A part of me feels like this is a test. As if X is setting up a scene in which we simply coexist with one another, no agenda or goal or task in sight. And in that, there's a force I must contend with to break out of any usual comfort zones. Which is genius, really. When we are plaguing our minds and spirits with the busyness of life, we can lose vital bits of ignored information along the way. The bits become lost in the far more obvious factors of whatever our daily achievements had previously been deemed to be.

But like floating particles of fairy dust, our ignored and lost pieces must land at some point, and that dust builds up gradually. There's an uncanny heaviness that sneaks in. At some point we have to face it and clear it all out.

For me the things ignored that have been weighing heavy have been not just a layer of fallen dust, but a dungeon of cobwebs. And I'm not only talking about Joey, either. I've come to recognize that he was a gatekeeper for me more than anything else. Joey wasn't the ignored contents of the dungeon; he was the handsome bodyguard meant to distract me and keep my mind from even remembering there was a dungeon at all. I used him in that way I suppose.

With the bodyguard now gone, I'm forced to look beyond those blocked doors and see what's beneath. And it's been surprising.

For one, more and more flashbacks of JJ have appeared. My father remains a bit of a blur in my mind, but images of my twin brother have presented themselves out of the shadows. His grin, most notably. Little playtime scenarios that I can't even be entirely sure are real or imagined, but there they are.

Caroline says my memory networks are lighting up and assures me it's a good thing, but it still catches me off guard. Waves of emotions accompany each flash of an image, and they're such a jarring mix that feel so tempting to run away from, run right back out of the dungeon and into the faux safety of ignorance and denial. But I'm hell-bent on facing and trying to make sense of the emotions instead.

X looks at me now and asks what's on my mind. He has this way of giving a smoldering look that feels both intimidating yet protective. I'd fear for anyone not on his good side, and I'm love drunk at the thought of his greatest mission of protection being me.

I attempt to neatly gather all these thoughts on my mind to

share out loud with him. I note a surprising flutter in my chest as I string together for X my images of JJ and my returning memories. He listens without interruption, something else I'm not quite used to. With Joey (*damn my comparisons*) there was always more of a back-and-forth cadence in our talks. Was that due to his inability to sit with silence, or was it my own inability to share anything that required the space of silence in that way? I likely never even gave Joey that chance.

But X simply listens and allows my mind to wander, providing gentle words of encouragement or acknowledgment every so often that he hears me. When my throat catches on a lump of emotion as I share my most dreaded thought—*what would JJ be like if he were here today?*—X grabs my hand and kisses the back of it. No attempt to squash the painful thought, no solutions offered on how to make amends with the reality of JJ's absence, just silent comfort. Validation. And with it I feel as though my thoughts can float out and up to be released beyond the pines of our surroundings.

When we return to our cabin oasis, I'm even more intrigued by my need to be physically near X. I watch as he slips off his jacket, revealing his broad shoulders and sculpted biceps beneath a fitted navy-blue henley shirt. He turns to face me and he helps me balance as I remove my boots.

His nearness to me sends me aching with need to continue to be touched by him. I'm hyper aware of our surroundings, the sudden consuming heat of the cabin in contrast to our blistery walk. I register the smell of his cologne, the masculine freshness of it. I watch as X gathers our things and arranges them neatly on the small entryway bench before turning back to face me. My breath catches at the sight of him towering above me. His amber eyes darken as he takes in the sight of me in my leggings and fitted sweater. I'm aware of the slightest bit of sweat on my neck and chest as my body acclimates to its new surroundings.

I step forward and begin to wrap my arms around his neck.

But he stops me.

X grabs my forearms, holds them in place in front of his chest in a locked position. Access denied, no further movement allowed. I frown in confusion. I search his eyes for some indication of why he won't let me touch him, but there's none. Only a dark cloud that I can't see beyond, and I instantly feel the horrific sting of hurt.

"Reggie," he says, my name falling softly out of his mouth in a whisper.

My stomach squeezes in rejection. I pull my arms out of his grasp and back down, stepping away. He drops his head and runs his hand down his face. I feel suddenly so unsure now, confused by the once again inaccessible X. A singular curl of hair wraps around at his temple and I want to brush it aside and kiss him, but it feels like I've lost all rights to.

His pulse throbs under the stubble on his neck, a torturous ticking that stills the air between us. I can't stand it anymore, so I turn around and walk away from him, out of the entryway and into the kitchen. I'm completely parched all of the sudden and reach in the fridge for a bottle of water.

I hear his footsteps as he slowly walks in behind me. "I'm sorry," he says.

I turn around to see him as he leans his forearm and elbow against the frame of the doorway, his forehead resting on his arm as he squeezes his eyes shut. I imagine he's clenching his jaw under that beard. There's such pain on his face and all I want to do is run over to him and comfort him, but I'm afraid to only push him further away.

So instead, I sip my water, the cold liquid a sharp bite in my mouth. I place the bottle down, unsure what to say. Finally, I land on, "What's wrong?" but I instantly regret it. Because I know what's wrong.

What's wrong is he's tormented by the idea of stealing away his nephew's girl, of being with me and thereby risking the favor of his entire family. Am I worth it? The thought cuts on my mind like the stabbing fall of an icicle. I twist the rubber band around my wrist and shake my head. "That's not what I meant; I know what's wrong."

X glances my way, smiles with a little sadness. He drops his raised arm and takes his hand to run it contemplatively along his beard. "It's not that, nothing's wrong."

Nothing's wrong? At this I'm annoyed. It's one thing to be unsure about things, but another to flat out deny it, especially when he's shutting down like he is. We have enough hard truths to potentially face without having to add to it by avoiding honesty with one another. "You could have fooled me," I say, my tone revealing my irritation.

"Not sure there's any fooling you, Reggie."

"That might be giving me too much credit."

"How so? I don't think there is such a thing as too much credit when it comes to you." His voice is husky, seductive even, and it only stirs more uncertainty and annoyance in me. He's all mixed messages, and I'm not one to sit well with that kind of thing.

So I huff in disbelief and roll my eyes. "You sure do make for quite the enigma, you know that?"

At this he crosses his arms over his broad chest and smirks. I try to avoid looking at the swell of his biceps. "How so?" he says.

I can feel the damning blush creep up my neck now. "How so? Maybe it's the whole hot and cold thing, I don't know. One minute you look at me with admiration like I have all the answers in the world, the next you're grabbing my arms to keep them from touching you. It's a little..." Damn, I can't find the words. I don't want to say "rejecting," because it feels too big and exposed.

"A little what?" He's looking completely amused right now and it's infuriating.

I throw my hands up. "This whole thing was your idea, remember? Taking me here? Up until four seconds ago it's been an incredible day, and now it's right back to the distant Xavier, cold wall of stone, inaccessible." I start to walk towards him to exit the kitchen, but he steps aside to block me, arms still crossed over his chest like a statue. He's massive and I'm tempted to try and physically push him just to test his hold in this position. I look up into his eyes, burning amber and mischief.

"Where are you going," he asks, but it's more of a statement than a question.

I motion toward the foyer behind him. "Based on my intended direction I think it's obvious."

"Leaving another room again?" I try and read his face, but it remains impassive.

"As delightfully welcoming as you are, I'm not sure I want to share a space with you right now."

He smirks and it's felt right down into my core. He slowly shakes his head in a scold. "No running out when things get a little uncomfortable, Reggie."

I huff in disbelief. "Oh, I'm perfectly comfortable. You're the one that seems to mentally exit a room while keeping a cold physical presence behind left to chill me to the bones." My face is hot, and I go for it, I try and give him a good shove to push him out of the way. In one swift move he unwinds his arms and snatches mine, pinning them to my side. Panther reflexes, and my mind floats back to when I first saw him crossing the room at the Moon Lounge. A hunter. My breath catches at the sheer power of him, and I look up to see the intensity in his eyes. We're at a standstill now, and I'm both physically and emotionally frozen in place under his grip, his hands firmly wrapped around my arms.

His grip on my arms softens just a little, and his eyes drop down to my mouth, then back to my eyes again. "I need you to have patience with me, Reggie." He releases me completely. Raises his hand and runs his thumb along my lower lip. "You have no idea how hard it is for me to love you with so much at stake. There're things I still need you to understand."

I'm on a twisting and turning ride, my mind in a million

different dizzying places. But I have to say it, have to confirm what I heard. "Love me?"

And with that, he leans down to me and meets my mouth with his. His kiss is all hunger and desire and I'm helpless to find my former fight or disregard. All I want is for his mouth to stay right here on mine, his tongue to give in to all that I know he's feeling but has been trying to fight. I feel his arms wrap tightly around me and I steady myself with my hands on his biceps, then up around his neck. He deepens our kiss and I'm swaying beneath his grasp, his hold.

He lifts me up and carries me upstairs to the loft bedroom, the blue of twilight seeping in through the windows. He lays me down on the bed and kisses me once again, soft and delicate this time. I'm not ready to forgive him so easily though, and so I roll to force him on his back as I straddle him. X looks up at me amused. "Yes?" he questions.

I look down at him, trying not to get swept up in the hunger in his eyes. Hunger for me. I'm trying to hold strong, but the words just don't seem to come.

He removes his hands from my thighs and interlocks them behind his head, looking casual and nonchalant like he has all the time in the world. "You seem to have something on your mind, hun. So what is it?" His smug smile is going to be the death of me.

I give his chest another shove. "You. It's you."

"Me what?"

"You can't shut off on me like that. It's like you go to this distant place in your mind and I'm left behind in the dust, no clue what I even did."

Concern fills his face, and he unclasps his arms behind his head. He sits up to face me eye to eye. "I know. It's not you, baby." He leans forward with a kiss so tender, so warm that I'm all melted liquid inside. I squeeze his shirt and allow myself to give into him. I can't help it. He pauses our kiss and rests his forehead on mine. "I love you, Reggie," he says softly. "I've known I've loved you for a while." He says it like it's a confession, which I guess it is. He pulls back and looks me in the eye. "But there's things I need to say to you and I'm not sure where to start."

I'm terrified he's going to tell me he can't do this, that he can't break Joey's heart and that in this impossible moral dilemma he's going to choose his family over me. Over this, us. And maybe that's where this has to end up, who knows. But I'm not ready to hear that yet. Not right now. Right now, all I want is to be lost in this cocoon of ours and to pretend nothing else exists.

"Not now," I say, and I pull off my sweater and drop it beside the bed. I reach behind and unhook my bra too, dropping it. Sitting there on him topless and exposed I somehow feel more powerful and secure than I have all day.

He groans and grabs my face for a kiss so deep I'm crazy with the feeling of being devoured and consumed. I want more and more of it, of him.

X rolls me over back onto my back and removes my leggings and panties. I see him smile down at my fuzzy cream socks, and he strips me of those as well. I'm completely naked now, in stark contrast to him still fully dressed in the navy shirt and black jeans. A chill sweeps over me and he takes note of my nipples hardening. I watch him walk over to grab the remote for the overhead fan, turning it off.

"Close your eyes," he says and I do, wondering what he's doing, where he's going. I hear him walk alongside the bed closer to where my head lies on the pillow. I feel his quick kiss on my lips, then a gust of air heavy with his cologne as he steps away again. I don't dare open my eyes, just lay there naked and waiting. Waiting for whatever it is he has planned. I know from last time he's slow and methodical, and I'm filled with anticipation to see what's coming.

After a few moments I hear him return to the room, by the bed. I'm so tempted to open my eyes and sneak a peek, so I squeeze them further shut to counter the urge. He must be watching because he says, "So ready, aren't you?" I nod my head and can't help but smile, then move both my arms over my face to hide my revealing grin.

"You drive me crazy," I whisper through my grin, beneath my arm. I don't know what exactly I'm in for here, but I'm mad with the excitement of it. I'm not used to this, to lovemaking as anything more than a quick and urgent means to an end.

"Good," he says. "Because I've wanted to drive you crazy for some time now." He removes my arms from my face, grabs them and gently pulls them both above my head. "But we can't have this, I need to see your face, baby." I pop my eyes open without thinking, but he only looks down at me and smiles. I feel a silky fabric of some sort wrap around my wrists. "I'll keep this loose, okay? Just as a little reminder of restraint, but you're free to slip out of it if you need to."

I want to tell him not to be gentle with me, to go for it because I'm thrilled at this idea, but I remain silent. I can't help but fall in love with his tender care of me, desperate as I am to allow him to take me wherever the depths of his mind wants to go. So I simply nod and close my eyes again. I feel another piece of fabric cover my eyes, and he gently lifts my head to tie that as well.

"You okay?" he asks, and I nod and tell him more than okay. At this he groans, and I'm all flushed at the way I can please him so easily. "My God, you're so exquisitely beautiful, baby," he says, and I can't help but smile again. "You've put one hell of a spell on me."

The bed sinks with the weight of him next to me. He kisses my neck, the space just below my breasts, his beard tickling and scratching as he drags his face between spots on my torso. He reaches for something on the night table next to us, and then I feel something on my nipples, like a mini heating pad. It's warm and unexpected and I raise my hips and feel the heat mirrored between my legs. "So responsive," he says, and he keeps the heated object on my left nipple. His mouth covers the right, a contrasting combination of senses my mind is wild with trying to focus on. I groan and writhe, my lower body aching with need in its absence of attention.

I feel vacant and hungry. My hands are still above my head, and I grip at the pillow.

He works his mouth down my belly, to my inner thighs, the heating device trailing along behind each of his kisses. It's tantalizing and I'm pretty sure I'm never going to want to leave this bed. In slow movements his mouth eventually finds its way between my legs. He tortures me with slow kisses on my inner thighs. I giggle at the tickle of his beard on my sensitive skin. After what seems like hours, he eventually maneuvers his tongue exactly where I want him to. He's methodical with it. I feel little bites and firm pressure, his tongue working up and down in a tortuous rhythm. The buildup is so slow and intense that I shudder beneath him with an orgasm that rips through my entire body.

But still, I only want more.

This time I know to ask. "Please be inside me," I say. I have no more patience to wait. "Please, X. I need you now." I feel his kiss on my lips before he turns me over onto my stomach. More kisses trail along my back, the rough skin of his hand warm and exploring my body. I feel the weight of him on the backs of my thighs as he straddles me. I hear him take off his shirt. Then feel his brief absence as he moves off me. I hear what I assume is his removal of his jeans.

I lay there, face down alone on the bed, listening with intensity for signs that he's coming back to me.

And then I feel the welcome sink of the mattress as X returns to the bed. I feel the skin of his thighs back against mine as he straddles above me again, naked now. I feel the hardness of his cock between my legs, teasing me. I wiggle my ass up towards him and beg him again, "Please be inside me."

He's fast with it now and enters me with a roughness so unexpected and delicious I cry out, bite down on his arm next to mine, his hands firmly holding mine, fingers interlocking. His thrusts are hard and fast, and my breasts rub against the texture of embroidery on the blanket beneath me, sensation everywhere. My blindfold still on and wrists still tied, I'm hyper aware of every nerve in my body. And I'm filled by him in such an extreme way I can hardly stand it, his body moving on top of mine with force that only further revs up my desire. We build and climb together. I'm at the mercy of his movements, and it's a ride I never want to end. My body is on fire as another orgasm explodes through me.

With one final thrust I feel him finish too, and I suck and bite on his arm here next to me, his hands still locked with mine.

"Fuck," he says as he drops his weight beside me, and we lay there and steady our breath for a moment. Eventually with tenderness he releases my ties and blindfold, but I keep my eyes closed, still lost in a delicious trance.

He kisses my shoulder and says, "Baby, you are my undoing. I'm powerless to you."

I smile in his grasp and moan, because all I can think is that I know exactly what he means.

I'VE DECIDED THAT I'M NEVER leaving this cabin. The past several hours have been nothing but heaven. It's dark now, I'm hardly even aware of what time it is as we've spent the evening naked in bed, switching from consuming one another, indulging in the snack plate X brings up, sipping wine, tearing each other up yet again. I look at my phone and see unread text messages and emails, and I don't even care. I check the time and with surprise see that it's eleven o'clock. Usually I'd be tired, but I feel wide awake in a sea of sheets and X.

I prop my head up on my elbow and look to my side at the profile of his face. Once again, I see the turmoil in the furrow of his brow. I run my free hand along his chest, down along his torso, back up again. I want to know what he's thinking, what's behind those troubled eyes, but I'm afraid I already know.

He breaks the silence and reaches to grab my hand, mid-caress on his collar bone. His next words are so unexpected, I'm not even sure I hear them correctly.

"What do you remember about your car accident, Reggie?" He closes his eyes and kisses my fingertips.

"My car accident?" I'm caught off guard because this is not exactly the post-lovemaking conversation I would expect to be having. "I mean, not much, if anything at all. More just what's been told to me. It was cold, it was December." I have a pit in my stomach as I talk. I'm not liking this, and I have no idea why he's bringing this up. "Why do you ask?"

He releases my hand. I watch as he rises out of the bed, searches through his bag to pull on boxer briefs. I feel insanely deserted on the bed now, and I rise to grab my robe from my things. I tie it tightly around my waist and look out the window to the pitch black of the sky, cloudy and starless in the night. Swirls of fat snowflakes dance in their slow descent, illuminated by an outdoor light.

X walks to my side and grabs my hand, then pulls me to sit on the edge of the bed. He kneels down on the floor in front of me and grabs both my hands within his. My head has a million alarm bells going off now as I'm once again left feeling in the dark with the mystery of his thoughts. I look down at him, wondering what he's thinking, why he's asking me about this. "Call me crazy but I'm not really interested in talking about my car accident right now, Xavier," I say.

He winces and closes his eyes. I search his face for signs of what's on his mind, but find none.

Finally, he opens his eyes, looks directly up at me and says, "I have for many, many years felt a need to protect you, Reggie. I can't explain it, but I've watched from afar as you've grown up. I've had a draw within me to make sure you were okay."

His words dance recklessly in the air between as I try to make sense of them. "I don't understand, you mean because of Joey?"

Had X been worried about me? Surely he knows Joey was nothing if not a perfect gentleman. This isn't making any sense.

X shakes his head and sighs. "No, not because of Joey. If anything, when I realized you guys became friends as kids, I felt better."

"Better? Better how, better than what?" He's implying an impossible comparison. A before and after. But before what? I have this uncomfortable feeling like I had been watched or something. "You didn't even know me before I was Joey's friend." The pit in my stomach is growing as I have the strangest inkling of where this might be going, and it's too horrifying to even explore.

"I didn't know you, it's true," he says, and for a moment I'm temporarily relieved. He looks me deep in the eyes now and softens the embrace on my hands. "But I was there the day of your car accident."

A wave of nausea consumes me and I try to pull my hands back, but X keeps a firm hold. "Please, Reggie, just listen." My head is shouting now to get out of here. Nothing good can come of this confession, this can only end in disaster. I can't even let my mind wander to the terrors of where I fear this is going.

No one else was involved in the accident, and he would have been too young to be a paramedic or cop on the scene at the time.

"I don't understand, what do you mean you were there?" I ask.

He keeps his eyes held on mine, his tone steady. "I was a pissed off teenager, and I had run out of my house and was wandering around on the road."

I look at him with confusion. "Like on a walk?"

He nods. "Yes, on a walk. My mother and I were living in an apartment by the mall. We had some fight, and I was cooling off. I was being stupid, walking too close to the road. The sun was low in the sky behind me and probably blinding in between the trees to any cars that might come along. I realize that now. But I didn't think about that at the time. I was just angry and careless.

"It was a wooded back road and there wasn't much traffic, until this one car came along. Your car, I would later learn. And the driver saw me and went to swerve out of the way a bit to give me more space." He inhales sharply and I can feel him tremble beneath me. I watch the throb of his pulse on his neck, just barely in sight beneath his beard. The beard that only moments ago I had been relishing feeling all over my skin, my body. His pulse is quick, a thunderous beat too fast for the stillness of the rest of his body.

"And it was icy and he—"

"My dad, you mean."

He nods carefully. "Your dad. He lost control of the car, and it swerved and spun and swerved again before slipping down an embankment onto its side."

I watch with eerie calm as tears pour down Xavier's face. His hands are still clasped around mine, smoldering hot and suffocating.

There's a flip in my stomach. A familiar flip like the ones driving down the hills of the back roads. The previously buried memory hits me like a roller coaster drop. I remember the roads, the little flutters as my dad would drop down a hill, and JJ and I would laugh at the tickles in our tummies. *Faster, Daddy! Again!*

I remember that last drive, tummy flips and tickles on the drops downhill.

But I try to focus on Xavier's words. I have to know more. Never before have I heard any of these details or had these flashes of memories, and I have to know. It's a wreck I can't turn my eyes away from, in every sense of the phrase.

"What did you do?" I ask, my voice all scratches and tone deadpan.

"I ran over to the car. It was a little down below me wedged between the hill and some trees, and I managed to open your mom's door." He releases one of his hands and wipes the tears from his face. I'm numb and impatient as I wait for him to continue. "I was terrified at what I would find, but she was there in her seat belt, half conscious. I unbuckled her. I put my back against the door to keep it held open and I pulled her out.

"And then I remember her whispering 'the babies.' I'll never in a thousand years forget that."

His tears are streaming down faster, and I'm numb yet utterly irritated by his emotion. As if he has any right to it. *I'm* the one who should be crying, not him. *I'm* the one who lost half my family that day because of some stupid teenage kid with a death wish.

But all I can do is sit here, frozen and annoyed.

"It's all a bit of a blur, but I remember setting your mom aside, worried she'd be too close if another oncoming car came. I knew I had to act fast. The car was smoking. I went for the back seat but couldn't get that door open. I had to smash the glass with something, I think I found a branch maybe, I can't be sure.

"But there you were. You were in a car seat, and I panicked because I was fifteen and had no idea how to get you out of it. I grabbed my pocketknife, scared to even use it, I was scared I was going to cut you by accident, but I managed to cut the straps. I pulled you out and ran you over to your mom. She was still on the pavement where I left her, propped up by a guard rail. I don't even know if she was fully conscious at that point, but I put you in her arms and went back to the car. But..."

He stops and I wait as he chokes on his own quiet sobs. I'm not sure I've ever seen a grown man fully cry like this, and I'm stunned and stoic in the presence of his emotion.

Because I know the rest. I know the answer here, that he went back to the car to find that my dad and JJ were already dead. That's what the reports said, anyway. That their death was quick because by the time paramedics reached them, they were dead already. The car was engulfed in flames at some point, but dad and JJ were dead already.

Because of a patch of ice.

Because my dad was trying to give some kid a little space on the road.

They thought it was a deer, my mom never did quite remember why my dad swerved in the first place. She couldn't be sure, she couldn't remember clearly.

But it was X.

Xavier Derian.

I throw his hands back to him and rise up off the bed to a stand.

"So then what?" I say, cold as ice. "They were dead already, I know that. So then what?" I cross my arms over my chest and look back to him, waiting for his response.

He wipes his face again and rises to stand as well. "I was frozen. I saw your dad and your brother and...and I knew they were probably gone and that I couldn't get to them anyway, and I froze. The car was smoking, I knew flames were coming soon. I didn't know what to do. But then I saw a car coming from the other direction, and I bolted. I ran off into the woods and hid.

"I got sick at some point, I think. This part's still a blur in my memory, just bits and pieces that I can pull. But I remember watching from a distance as the other driver got to you and your mom, and the car...the car, it was fully on fire by then. I waited for the sound of sirens, and then I ran like hell. I stayed out in those woods for I'm not even sure how long. Time stopped existing for me. At some point I registered feeling cold, real cold. I worried I'd freeze to death and knew I needed to get inside somewhere."

"And then?"

He shakes his head, his eyes blank and staring at nothing. "Made my way back home. Holed myself away in my room and never told a soul about what happened."

An image of flames breaks its way into my head, and I squeeze my eyes shut as hard as I can to shut it out. I feel physically sick to my stomach, and I run to the bathroom just in time. I watch as the contents of wine and grapes and cheese make their way back up, a mangled mess so far removed from their original form. I feel X's hand rubbing on my back while the other holds my hair and I can't even find the strength to push him off me, but I want to.

Eventually I finish. I sit on the floor and he hands me a bottle of water. I mindlessly grab it, take a sip and spit it back out into the toilet. I take another sip, swallow it this time as I flush. X kneels down next to me and strokes my cheek with the back of his fingers. I'm numb and motionless. Time seems to slow to an absolute halt and the only real sensation I can register is the cool tiles beneath me, under my hands, under my bare feet.

At some point my eyes flash up to Xavier, and irritation boils my blood. "Can you please go put some fucking jeans on or some-thing?" I snap, surprising both of us. Suddenly his barely clothed body is an irritation beyond which I can handle. I hate his body. I hate the mass of it, the muscles, his stupid black tribal tattoo on his shoulder like he has any link to ancient traditions. I hate his masculinity, his humanity, his flaws, and his protective attempts that did nothing for my family.

I hate that I'm here with him right now. Stuck in a mountain cabin.

And the rage boils sickeningly inside me as I rise to follow him back out to the bedroom where he's slipping on his black jeans. Fitting for his black soul.

"Did you fucking bring me here to trap me?" I scream. My voice is shrill and unrecognizable, even to myself. I don't yell, that's not me. Something else has taken over my body.

I shove him hard for the third time tonight, only this time he keeps his reflexes in check and lets me. It infuriates me even further.

"Answer me, you lying, fucking *sonofabitch*!" The tears are streaming down my face now, hot and sharp, pocketknife blades down my cheeks.

X tries to grab my arms, and I push him again. "You brought me here to *trap* me! So you could safely share your secret and I have nowhere to go! *Nowhere*!" I'm screaming and sobbing now, manic with emotion and rage.

"I've wanted to tell you for so long, Reggie. I never expected you to come into my life..."

I snap my head at this. "What did you say?? Huh? Well, Xavier, so sorry to incon-*venience* you with my *SURVIVAL*!" I scream that last word at the top of my lungs before racing down the stairs, my limbs acting as wings as I fly down the flight of grainy wood steps, and I crash-land into the sitting area below the loft. I steady my limbs with a determined force, look up to the loft, see X leaning over the railing, disgustingly exasperated and covering his face.

My body is like a motor, ready to burst with an energy I have no outlet for. I want to break something, anything. I see the empty champagne bottle in the kitchen, and I rush over to it. Slam it on the granite, over and over and over again.

With that destitute champagne bottle, I slam with the force of years of hurt and loss that I couldn't ever express. It's years of anguish and confusion that have been side-stepped time and time again. It's the anguish of a twin brother lost, my other half, over-shadowed by my mom's agony of losing a child, so that I couldn't allow my own pain to ever take any real shape in my own mind.

Permission of feelings denied.

It's my mind feeling like it's not been allowed to exist.

My mind's denial and repression.

My mind's torment and suffering, always dismissed.

"You're fine, you don't even remember anything."

"You're lucky it's nothing to you."

But I remember.

I remember.

It hurts. I can't breathe, my chest tight.

But I *remember*.

It's not nothing.

I drop the bottle, hunch over the counter and sob into my forearms. I attempt one last weak hit onto the counter, but my energy is suddenly zapped.

I feel X come up behind me in a tight hold. "You're bleeding, Reggie, please." His voice sounds panicked.

In a burst of eerie calm I rise to a stand. "You've seen my blood before," I say flatly. "It shouldn't bother you. It's how we met." My words are sharp and clipped.

The force of his body behind me takes over, and he half pushes, half carries me to the sink. He turns on the faucet and runs my hand under. I watch as the blood and water mix like two joining rivers, swirling together down the drain. I'm mesmerized by it. Captivated by it. It's the most beautiful sight I've ever seen. Like the red swirls of the painting in Caroline's office. I wonder if the painter saw this scene once too. So, so beautiful, crimson red fluid swirling around and down. I reluctantly peel my eyes away as nausea rises once again, the pain in my hand searing.

"What the—" I hear X say as he steps back and stares out through the entryway to the kitchen, looking toward the front of the cabin. "Who the fuck?" he whispers, but I'm too numb to see what he's looking at. I can only see my distorted reflection in the window in front of me. It's a ghost, the face of beautiful agony, masked in an absent stare.

And then X's words snap through to me, though I'm powerless to move or respond.

"Someone's here," he says. "I think it's Joey."

chapter thirty-one

. . .

X

THE HEADLIGHTS TURN off on his nephew's truck, and everything in his mind goes dark. Autopilot takes over as X prepares for what's to come.

First, he needs to get Reggie's bare feet out of the kitchen with the remnants of the glass threatening all around. He tells Reggie not to move, walks to the front door and slips his own bare feet into his boots. He steps over to where Reggie remains standing motionless by the kitchen sink. He lifts her over his shoulder, a near lifeless rag doll that seems to have lost all the fight in her. He grabs a kitchen towel on his way out. Walks to the living room and sets Reggie down on the couch by the front door.

The sound of Joey's steps on the gravel driveway is amplified in the silence. By now Joey would have seen X's car, he realizes. X pops the front door ajar before returning to kneel in front of Reggie to wrap her hand. His heart is pounding in his chest, knowing what's about to happen.

He hears Joey's footsteps on the front porch. Out of the corner of his eye he registers Joey's hesitant face peer through the open door, barely illuminated by the porch light. "Hello?" Joey says tentatively as he slowly pushes the door open. "Uncle Xavier?"

X continues his work on Reggie's hand, worried that she may still have glass in her skin. His mind slows down, his training takes over as he mentally assesses the multiple dangers currently in his space. The glass still on the kitchen floor, in Reggie's hand, his own nephew walking into the scene, X's bare chest as he's wearing only jeans, Reggie's catatonic state on the couch, wearing nothing but a robe, loose and now hanging off her shoulders after the commotion. Her breasts are nearly exposed, and X lifts the fabric back over top to cover her.

"What in the hell?" Joey looks at them both, confusion consuming his face. "The *fuck*?"

"She's bleeding, I need to make sure the glass is all out."

Joey rushes over next to X and grabs Reggie's unharmed hand. "Baby, what happened? Holy fuck, what happened? Baby, look at me!" Joey's voice is filled with torment as he grabs Reggie's face and directs it towards him. "Reggie! Say something, what the fuck is going on here!" Joey looks up at his uncle in panic. "What's wrong with her?"

"She's in a stress response state. Cut herself. She came up here with me. We came together," X adds, his voice calm and mission-like.

"For what?" Joey asks, incredulous. "Why the fuck would she do that?"

"We've been seeing each other. After you broke up," X attempts to clarify, though he knows it does nothing to soften the blow.

Joey barks out a humorless laugh. "This some sick joke?"

X grabs a piece of glass wedged into Reggie's skin. Drops it on the coffee table behind him. Reggie is still motionless in front of him, her face drained of color. He's worried she'll pass out.

"Reggie, are you okay?" X asks her, ignoring Joey for the moment.

Reggie ever so slightly shakes her head no. Whispers, "I don't feel well."

X darts his eyes over to Joey. "Get her a bucket and some water. There's a trash can under the sink, use that."

Joey looks back and forth between X and Reggie, then down to Reggie's injured hand. X watches as the color drains from Joey's face as well. *Fucking great, now I'll have two people passed out.* "Joey, go! Into the kitchen!" He's hoping to get his nephew focused on a task to distract him.

Joey rises and X hears him as he takes in the kitchen chaos, the broken bottle and glass. X hears him mutter something he can't quite make out.

Satisfied that the glass is all out, X wraps Reggie's hand again. "How you doing, baby? We got it all out, I think you're good now. I need you to breathe, you hear me? Just breathe." X grabs her face and runs his thumb over her cheek. Her green eyes are nearly black, they're so dilated. Beads of sweat dot her forehead. He places his face next to hers, scratches his beard alongside her cheek. "Breathe with me. Stay with me, you're okay, Reggie." Her body sucks in a deep breath and he closes his eyes in relief. "That's it, there you go."

Joey appears by his side with the trash can and water.

"Grab the water, Reggie," X says, pulling his head back to face her. Joey starts to put the open bottle to her lips and X shakes his head. "Have her do it. Put the water in her hand." Joey does as his uncle says and gives Reggie the water in her good hand. "Hold the water, baby," X says. Joey's eyes shoot to X as he remains focused on getting Reggie back in the here and now. He gently assists her as Reggie raises the bottle to her lips. She takes a sip and closes her eyes. Then another sip.

She nods her head slightly and whispers, "That's good. I'm so thirsty." X breathes a sigh of relief.

"That a girl, just keep drinking."

They sit like that for a while, twenty seconds, maybe more. Her face is still pale, but X notes more steadied breathing. He checks her pulse and relaxes when he finds it resuming a more normal pace.

After a while she nods her head slowly. She whispers with force, "I'm okay. I'm good."

X props up some pillows and swings her legs up to lay her down slightly. He points to a blanket and tells Joey to cover her up. Joey follows orders without question.

"Keep an eye on her," X says, and he rises and walks to the kitchen to clean the glass.

He leans against the entryway to the kitchen, the same frame he stood in just hours earlier with Reggie standing before him. When she had been wondering where X's mind had gone. She thought it was because of Joey. But it wasn't.

He had known then that there was going to be no easy way through this. Knew the darkness of his secrets needed to be revealed.

But he was weak with his need to both have Reggie and protect her from himself.

With a sigh X gets to work and finds a dustpan under the sink. He picks up the larger pieces of glass, sweeps up the smaller ones. He rises and winces as he takes in the sight of Reggie's blood. Her words stinging his memory, her reminder that he's seen her blood before.

He never forgot.

It's an impossible puzzle to him, the bloody three-year-old girl he grabbed from a wreck, and the bloody woman laying mere feet away from him now. Why have their worlds led them both here like this? Why have their paths traveled alongside one another, intersecting at all the wrong times? He can't understand it, can't make any sense of it, yet here they are.

And Joey. In the million scenarios X imagined telling Joey about Reggie, none of them were like this. X sees it, sees the damage he causes no matter where he goes. He's the broken glass he's sweeping up now. He's dangerous and risky and shattered and pointless. A mess to be avoided. More harm than it's worth.

With the last of the glass cleaned up and disposed of, X wipes down the counters and splatters of Reggie's blood. They're everywhere it seems, on the floor, the cabinets, splatters of red a menacing sign of all that is reckless and problematic about him. The bastard child that should have never been.

And then he turns around just in time to see Joey's fist meet his face.

chapter thirty-two

· · ·

reggie

I BLINK AWAY the last of the blotches and attempt to get my bearings. I've been hearing everything around me. I've registered the arrival of Joey, the confusion in his voice. I've felt the stings of the glass as X tended to my hand. I've watched it all as if from afar, as if someone else was in my body and I was floating just off to the side.

But I'm back in it now, and I register the intent of Joey's walk into the kitchen. I watch as he pulls his arm back and lurches forward with all his might in a punch square to X's face. Then another. "Stop it," I try to say but my throat is dry and my voice is weak.

And another punch. X just stumbles back, no fight in him.

I summon all the strength in my body to rise, my legs twisting in the blanket in a frustrating obstacle fit for a nightmare. I finally free myself and stumble to my feet. Shout again, "Stop it!" My voice is louder this time, but not loud enough.

I watch as X grabs Joey's arm, slams him against the wall. I'm dizzy, but I force myself over to them. Joey attempts to break free of

X's grasp, and I see X back off. Joey lunges forward, his shoulder slamming into X, sending him backwards and into the fridge and I shout again with all I can, "For the love of Christ, stop it!" I lean against the doorframe, dizziness consuming me as I try to breathe my way through it. I raise my hand to my forehead, close my eyes and attempt to steady myself.

Joey's back is to me, but X sees me, and concern fills his eyes. "Reggie," he says just as Joey gets one more punch into the side of X's abdomen. X lurches forward, caught off guard, thanks to me, and I can't help but stumble forward to him. My reaction is instantaneous, all instinct and pull to help X.

Joey steps back and bumps into me, sending me tumbling backwards onto the floor.

"Jesus," someone says and both X and Joey rush to my aid as I struggle to keep my robe closed and rise to my feet as quickly as I can.

I need to get control of this situation, *now*. And I know I'm the only one who can do it. I feel them both try and grab me to help me, and I throw my hand up in a gesture to stop them. "Both of you get the fuck off me. And if you want to help me, get the fuck off each other or I'm *walking* out that door barefoot in the snow and freezing cold in a goddamn robe, got it?"

"I just—" Joey says, attempting a step forward and I press my hand up further.

"Leave it!" I shout.

I rub my forehead and attempt to gather my thoughts. "I swear to you both right now I *will* walk out that front door if you don't do what I say. Do you hear me?" Two sets of eyes stare blankly back at me, but they're standing still. Both men remain rigid with clenched fists and chests rising in heavy breaths.

I take in a deep breath. "Let's go sit down. I need to sit down." I turn around and walk to the sitting area, fighting dizziness. I perch on the armrest of the couch. X and Joey remain frozen in the kitchen. I start talking anyway.

"Joey, I imagine you want some kind of explanation here, and I wish I had a better one. But I don't. This is it," I say, fighting to find the right words and blinking away blotches polluting my vision. "Yes, I came here with Xavier. Yes, we've been seeing each other. Sort of. Talking, more than anything. Figuring out what was between us." I look up and see Joey's rage return as he looks back at X.

"What the fuck did you do to her?" Joey shouts.

I try to stop him. "He didn't do anything. This isn't on him, it's on me. And it's shitty and awful, I know. Nothing happened while you and I were still together, though, I assure you." My words seem ridiculous even to me, but I have to say them.

"And since?" Joey asks, looking back at me with horror on his face.

"Please step out of the kitchen and come here, Joey," I say. I don't want them cramped in that space together, because what's coming out of my mouth is in no way going to feel good.

Joey does as I say and steps forward. I direct him to sit on the coffee table adjacent to me, and he does. He leans his elbows on his knees, drops his head and runs his hands through his hair. I wait for him to absorb what I've said so far, but he repeats his question.

"And since? Has something happened since we broke up, Reggie?" His eyes roam over the sight of me, my robe. He glances back toward the kitchen where X remains standing, arms crossed over his bare chest. Joey returns to look at me again, and the pain in his eyes is nearly unbearable to look at, but I hold his gaze. He deserves that much, at least. "Please tell me you didn't, Reggie. You didn't sleep with him, right?" He's shaking his head and tears stream down his face. "You're mine, you always have been. I'm yours. That was it. Just us. There's no way you broke that."

The lump in my throat is threatening to choke me, but I nod. "I did," I say.

Joey rises to his feet, and I'm worried he's going back to the kitchen. I grab his hand to stop him, and he looks down at me, wide-eyed. "We need to go home right now," he says to me. "I'm taking you home. I don't know what he did to you but I'm taking you home." He looks down at my wrapped-up hand.

I shake my head. "This I did to myself," I say, raising my cut hand. "And it's nearly midnight, Joey. No one's going anywhere. Not like this."

His eyes stay wide as he looks down at me with disbelief. "We can't fucking stay in this cabin."

"Yes, we can, and we will. It's snowing, and I've lost enough to car wrecks in my life. I don't need more. No one is in a condition to drive, so we will stay put right here. It might be the longest goddamn night of anyone's lives, but we're staying here."

"She's right," I hear X's gravelly voice chime in from the kitchen. He uncrosses his arms and leans back against the counter.

I'm relieved to hear X agree but know Joey will need more convincing. I aim for distraction.

"Does Joey know you were at the car accident?" I ask X. He shakes his head, and I return to look at Joey. My heart breaks for all that's being thrown at him, but he might as well know. I take in a deep breath. "Before you walked in here, Xavier disclosed to me that he had been there the day of my car accident. When I lost my dad and brother." I suck in my breath as the newness of these words find their way out of my voice. I need to soften the words, the story, both for me and for Joey's sake so he doesn't feel the need to attempt to be the hero and pummel X yet again. "Xavier pulled my mom and me from the wreck, apparently. Brought us to safety before running away from the scene."

Joey scoffs, and I hear just how absurd the words sound. "Is that what he told you to get you into bed?" he says with a bitterness so unlike him.

X steps forward toward Joey, fists clenched and enraged, and I rise and rush toward him, placing a hand on his chest. "No, no. Don't." I drop my hand. "For fuck's sake. It's enough!" I yell.

I rub my temples and try to think. But I'm spent.

My next words I speak as slowly and calmly as I possibly can. "I'm going upstairs to bed, gentleman. I think we've all had enough for one night. But please for the love of God, because by some twist of fate I love you both so much, please promise me you will stay put here, and not kill each other. Okay?" I look at them both, but their expressions are unreadable.

With desperation and pleading in my eyes I speak again. "Listen to me now." I look again, and register the slightest gesture of a nod from X. I go with it.

"My life has known tragedy. Horrendous tragedy and heartache, and it's unfair. Life is unfair, plain and simple.

"But we have choices we can make, right? We have to choose how to handle it. If we're going to ignore it and pretend our focus is needed elsewhere, or do we face it head on and work through. Face our demons." I look up and see Joey sigh. He crosses his arms. I take it as a good sign that he's listening.

I continue. "I'm sick and tired of not facing mine, or of being told they are something they are not. And for whatever reason, life has brought us here to this cabin right now, all three of us. I don't know why, but it has. So we're going to be fucking adults about it, and face it. Got it?" My eyes dart back and forth to them both. "And for right now, I need you both to find some separate corners somewhere and attempt some sleep. You are family first, and I need you both safe and alive. So you will do as I say."

"Your hand," X says.

"It's fine. It's feeling better," I lie. I know I may need stitches, but that's the least of my concerns. I turn to walk towards the stairs but stop just before stepping up. I turn around to face these two men in my life one last time. "Just promise me you will stay put here tonight, okay? Leave first thing in the morning if you want. I'll have Lucy come get me." I see Joey's eyes dart toward X, who simply nods once back to him. Joey looks back up to me again.

"Please don't drive like this. Not angry down a snowy mountain in the middle of the night. Don't put me through that. Please," I plead.

With that I walk back up the stairs, to the room, to our wrecked bed oozing with sex and passion and heartache. I gather X's things and place them in his bag at the top of the stairs. Shower and crawl into bed.

Sleep must have miraculously found me at some point, because in the morning I wake to X's car keys on the nightstand next to me. There's a note instructing me to take his car home when I'm ready.

And I go downstairs to find a completely empty cabin.

chapter thirty-three

. . .

X

THERE WAS A moment in the plane heading to Afghanistan where X had truly thought he might die from the over-whelming feeling of dread. Up until that point he had been caught up in the hype, in the mission of serving his country. The energy on the flight was loud with the uniformed bodies all around him, chanting and singing as a distraction from the plummet they were about to make. A sea of metal and grays and greens surrounded them in the industrial cacophony of the fuselage. The soldiers and airmen blended into the background like a mass blur of monotone, shapeless and distant.

Something happened for X, though, that displaced him from the fired-up energy. The roar of the engines suddenly took on a deafening degree of burn in his ears, and a pit of dread filled his belly. He sat there on top of his body armor, strapped into the jump seat, and the trance of excitement halted. Instead he became fully connected to that exact moment, hyper-aware of where he was and what he was about to do, the uncertainty lying just minutes away. His excitement and spirit were then replaced with unease.

It's the same feeling he's experiencing now as he stares at the glittering wreath on his sister's front door and prepares to enter her home.

Isabella was adamant he come today, of course, despite her being made aware of the egregious offense X committed. News travels like a missile in this family—good, bad or otherwise. It's fast, precise, explosive.

But a holiday where he was actually in town was not to be missed, and Isabella would allow no rift to threaten her beloved family.

She made it clear that he had no choice in the matter. Xavier was to arrive, with his assigned contribution, bottom line.

So here he was, showing up with the obligatory pumpkin pie and beers.

As soon as he steps through the door he braces himself for the mayhem. It's voices of all ages, kids running and screaming, mid playful chase. It's kisses and hugs. Comments on his growing beard, a mock at his black eye. He cringes at the reminder of it, his very own scarlet A at the hands of Joey.

He inhales the warm smells of a turkey cooking. Someone takes the pie and beer from his hands, only to replace them with a slob-ber-mouthed infant. X holds the baby curiously, having no clue which cousin or niece or nephew of his this particular one belongs to. There's too many now to keep it straight when he's been away for so long.

The black wool coat he's in feels like a torturous heater in the tropics. The temperature in the house here with everyone feels about eight thousand degrees warmer than outside, and the baby in his arms is not helping matters. His mind wanders to Reggie, and he realizes with crippling sadness that he wishes she were here by his side. He imagines she'd be far more natural in this setting; she's probably been at these holiday gatherings for years accompanied by Joey.

A sting on his cheek shakes his dejected thoughts away, and he looks down in shock at Isabella. "Did you just slap me when I have a baby in my arms?" X asks her.

She shakes her dark hair out of her eyes, raising an eyebrow. "That's for stealing my baby boy's girl," she says, but he sees the warmth in her eyes, the love still there for her baby brother.

X huffs out a dry laugh. "And to think I was worried I wouldn't be welcome here."

Isabella grabs the baby from his arms and kisses his stinging cheek. "You're family. You're always welcome." She smiles and starts to walk away, but then turns to add, "You still deserved a slap though. Couldn't let that slide." She signals to the coat closet. "Now go take your coat off and help peel potatoes."

"She's not my girl either, you know," X calls after his sister.

To his surprise she turns around and shouts, "Oh, she will be. In fact, she better be."

The fuck is that supposed to mean? he thinks.

BELLIES FULL AND HEARTS WARM in a post-dinner haze, the family disperses for various cleanup duties. For the most part the evening has proved to be smooth sailing. The wonderful thing about a big family is that there's always another story to tell. More drama and updates and new jobs and pregnancy announcements. Dance recital mishaps and game winning goals that make yesterday's news old with a relieving quickness. When his mom was around, X always felt like his household was set under a microscope. It was just the two of them, and nothing was ever lost in the chaos. Each and every mistake was front and center, in plain view.

But not here. Isabella's house has always been the main meeting point for any family that remained in the area, which was most of them. X appreciated more than anything the safety in numbers here. It cast a much wider spotlight. Still though, he knows he needs to find Joey, as they'd not spoken a word all evening. Their car ride home from the mountains had been mostly silent as well, with the occasional slam of a steering wheel from Joey when X assumes a particularly painful thought would pop into his mind. But it was all entirely too fresh to even attempt to address at that point. So they had driven in silence.

X walks out back to where he figures he'll find a few cigar smokers. The burst of cold air hits him with welcome relief, the waft of sweet smoke a familiar and comforting sensation. He scans the deck, the moonlight allowing just enough of a glow to make out the figures. Sure enough, he finds Joey out here along with a few others. Joey's dad points X to the cigars and he reaches for one, glad to have something to do with his hands.

Joe Sr. puts out his own cigar before patting X on the back and calling out to the rest of the gang to let Xavier and Joey have a moment. A few mumbled "Good luck," and "Oh shit," comments are met with a slap upside the head, compliments of Joe Sr. X looks over to Joey and sees the slightest smile, and for the millionth time tonight, X is reminded of the Herculean strength of character of this family, and in particular, his favorite nephew.

"Mind if I join you?" X asks Joey. With the deck now cleared of anyone else, X feels like his voice is on a loudspeaker.

Joey pushes a tray toward X, a mini outdoor tabletop-bar setup of whiskey and glasses. "Only if you join me in some medicinal refreshments as well." Joey pours the amber liquid into a glass and hands it to his uncle. X takes it, and Joey holds up his own glass in a salute.

Joey leans back in the small sofa. "I'm tempted to say a dirty toast to temptresses and their wicked ways, but that seems too easy."

"How about to the shitstorm that can be life sometimes?" X offers. He puffs on his cigar and rolls the smoke in his mouth before exhaling.

Joey shakes his head. "Nah. Life's not a shitstorm. It's people and their choices that cause the problems. Blaming it on life is a cop out."

X nods and sips his drink. "That's fair." It's unfamiliar territory for X. He's used to being the one with attempted words of wisdom for his nephew, not the other way around. Not that X ever felt he had anything of particular worth to share, but he always tried the best he could for Joey.

Joey finally meets eyes with X. "I thought I'd have more questions for you, but sitting here I realize I only have one," he says. X waits for him to continue, glad to hear Joey is willing to talk. "How long have you been in love with her?"

The question shouldn't surprise X, but somehow it does. "How do you know I'm in love with her?"

"Because you wouldn't do this to me if you weren't. So you fucking better be."

X realizes he's damned either way, so he reaches for simple honesty. "Yes. I am in love with her," he says.

Joey's clenches his jaw. "Right. So how long?"

X considers this. It's a question he himself has wondered but has had little luck in understanding. His connection with Reggie started years ago, with that first incredible dilemma of not being able to get to her in the car. The door not in a position to open. Then the threat of the broken window glass, the car seat straps, all with smoke and impending fire. For him, the connection started right then and there, an incredible responsibility to save her, protect her. As a teenager lost and aimless, she presented the first real sense of purpose that he had ever had, other than Joey. Life or death based on his actions and decisions in those critical seconds.

And after that wreck, he kept up with news stories about it, found out their names. He wandered back to the scene of the accident countless times afterwards, placing flowers on the roadside memorial someone had constructed.

At some point, he found the ornaments. The box with the crystal snowflakes, strewn from the car and abandoned in the woods. He knew they were theirs, the kids', as each one was engraved with the twins' nicknames. "Reggie" and "JJ," and their matching February birthdate. That box and snowflakes were like a beacon to him. A glimmer of hope and direction where previously he'd had none.

He thought about figuring out how to give them back or where he could leave the ornaments without having to reveal himself. But over time he grew more and more attached to the crystal snowflakes. When his own mother died unexpectedly just a year and a half later, he abandoned the idea of ever returning them. They became a security blanket to him. His own secret source of comfort in a life that seemed to be scarce of it.

But for now, his nephew deserves an explanation, and X wants to try his best to give him one.

He takes another puff of his cigar and attempts to find the right words. "It's hard to say for sure when exactly I started to really fall for her, but I can tell you that I loved her in some way for a long time." X looks to see how Joey's taking this, but Joey's eyes remain focused on the table in front of him.

X continues. "I was always curious about her, even through the distance. My interactions with her throughout the years would stick in my mind and offer an unexpected anchor point of sorts. It's something I never really understood." X again looks at Joey, his face still giving nothing away.

He continues. "I know you weren't around for this, but life was different for me at my mom's house growing up. Not like your mom's childhood home. Your grandfather, my father, he was older by the time I came along. I know the circumstances of my birth didn't make things any easier for anyone."

Joey nods. "I know a little about it, from what my mom and aunts have said."

X thinks about this, hating the thought of being the subject of family talk. "I wish I could say post-deployments was the first time I questioned the value of my life, but it's not. Your grandparents, your mom and aunts all did their best to make me feel welcomed as much as possible, but I always felt like an imposter. I was the outsider trying to fit my way in. Pretending that I belonged in this family too, in the big and beautiful house. It always seemed so picturesque to me, and I wanted in.

"But then I'd go back to my mom's, and it would crash down on me all over again." X winces at the memories of every time he'd walk back into his own shitty apartment after time spent at his father's house. It was always hard for X to imagine his mom as the mistress that temporarily stole his dad's heart. The two worlds of the households were such opposites. Sunshine and warmth in contrast to his home's cool darkness.

The only mom that X knew was the mom of after the affair. She was bitter with rejection when X's dad returned to his wife. He knows his mom had been hopeful his dad would leave. X was always torn at the idea of breaking up what he thought to be a picture-perfect family.

Of course, he himself knew better than anyone that the Derian family had their skeletons too. X's very existence was their biggest one. And his mom never let X forget who he was, and who he was not. Despite sharing the family name with his father and half-sisters, Xavier Derian knew he could never fully be one of them.

He sighs and attempts to shove those thoughts aside as he continues to explain himself to Joey. "When that car wreck happened and I first saw Reggie," he continues, "I think my mind went to you. I was twelve when you were born, and your mom had me over as much as possible to help out. Maybe because you were new into the family, someone finally younger than me. It helped me find my own role. It was easier for me to just focus on you. I was able to watch you grow right along with me." He rubs his hand along his beard as he thinks about this, the accuracy of it providing him some clarity.

"So at the accident, I could tell this little girl was about the same age as you, and it stirred something in me that I always felt with you. A need to protect. Maybe because of the way your mom made me feel like I had a real role in your life, her first boy. She'd tell me you needed a good male role model that wasn't just a parental figure." X smiles at this. "Your mom's good like that. I can look back and see how she was working that for all she could. She saw an opportunity for me to feel connected and she ran with it." He shrugs at the memory. "It worked."

He looks over to check on how Joey's taking all this, gauging his reaction before continuing on. X notes with relief that Joey's face has softened some. "So there I was, pulling a little three-year-old out of a car, and it felt familiar. My first wave of needing to be her protector hit me then. And then when I saw Reggie playing at your house a couple years later, I thought I'd die from the shock of the coincidence. It was like the universe had brought this girl into my life again for a reason, and I was just happy to have the opportunity to see her again and see how she was doing. This kid that had lost so much, missing so much just like I was.

"It's hard to explain, but I always felt a fascination toward her. Not just because I'm the one that pulled her from that wreck, but because she was also living life with the background of her tragedies. I wasn't the only one who was tasked with doing the same. She had lost half her family, and by then, I had lost part of mine too. And here she was, just hanging out with you and your little sisters. In my sister's house. She was trying to find happiness in that household just like I always had."

Joey shakes his head and sips his drink. "Fucking wild, what a small world it is. But why didn't you ever say anything?"

X shakes his head with a deep sigh. "Part denial, part fear. I started to feel like I had made it all up, being there at the accident. I would question my own memory. I had pushed it down so much. And then when I did think about telling someone, I could never find the words. Your mom is likely who I would have told, but I was afraid of how she'd react. And when my mom died, I guess I went into survival mode. I knew I'd be joining the military, and figured I'd start over. Build a new life away from here and the messy memories and secrets."

They both sit for a few minutes and finish their cigars, the smoke swirling around them in a warm haze. X finishes the last of his drink and sets it down. "I always thought when I retired, I'd end up somewhere other than here. Having lived in so many places though, you come to realize there's no perfect spot. It's the people you're with that make a location, nothing else. It's not the climate or the tourist attractions or proximity to a certain city, it's just the people. And after years of running away from any possibility of roots, I finally felt ready to stop. Wanted to try and make meaningful connections. I had to, because retiring from the military meant hanging up the main source of identity that I had clung to for so long. Without it, I needed to figure out who I was all over again."

A divot forms between Joey's dark eyebrows. "You have no idea how strange it is to hear you say that, like you didn't have your bearings. I've never seen you in that way," he says.

X shrugs. "I've always been more the keep to myself type." He smiles at his nephew. "You usually call me out on it."

The corner of Joey's mouth lifts. "What can I say, you're an easy target."

"Glad you think so."

Joey drops his smile, face serious once again. "So then what? Have you figured out your identity outside of the military? Because as much as I love you as my uncle, I'm having a hard time reconciling that with how Reggie and you...became a thing." Joey grimaces on his words. "And I gotta tell you, the only reason I'm even sitting here right now is because Mom made it clear that I needed to hear your side of the story. Apparently, executing your murder wasn't an option."

"I'm relieved you listened."

"You kidding? As if I had a choice. She can be terrifying when she wants to be." He's not smiling, but X is thankful for a glimmer of Joey's humor.

"Your mom's always been a force to be reckoned with," X says.

Joey tilts his head to the side, eyebrows raised. "She is, and she seems to think there's something here that I'm not getting. But I'm struggling, Xavier. I really am.

"My whole fucking world blew apart. All the things that I thought I knew now feel like lies. And I'm struggling to trust my own instincts anymore, so no pressure here," Joey says, his voice raising, "but I really, really, really am hoping that you have some key to all this that helps make any fucking sense." He sits back and crosses his arms, his face stern.

"I hear that," X says gently. "I guess I'm also trying to figure it out, because it sure as hell wasn't planned. Coming back home threw me for a loop. Seeing Reggie was something I knew would inevitably happen, but I wasn't prepared for my gut reaction.

"She read a poem that first night I saw her. It was about her car accident. And it was like a plummeting force came crashing down onto me. It woke up memories I hadn't looked at for a very long time. Here she was, both of us adults now, both still grappling and processing this thing from our past."

Joey runs his hands through his hair, then rubs them down his face. "Look, I can appreciate that there's some history there that I'll never quite understand or get. Fine. I can accept that. What I struggle with is why did it have to turn romantic?" He spits that last word out and turns to look at his uncle with such pain in his eyes, Xavier nearly looks away. "Why, Xavier? Why couldn't it just be this strange coincidence that you eventually shared, and we all have a good laugh and cry or some shit like that, then move on?" X sees the tear stream down Joey's face and watches as he wipes it away just as quickly as it came. "Why'd you have to take her from me?

"You were always my hero, Xavier. I looked up to you. I wanted to be like you. You may have felt like you were lost, but to me you felt like my greatest source of guidance. My incredible Uncle

Xavier, war hero out there doing things in the world, answering the call of action. Doing all that's right in the face of what's wrong." Joey's voice is elevated, and X sits braced at the impact of seeing his favorite nephew's raw emotion. All because of his own actions.

Joey continues, his voice pleading. "So why? Please, I need to understand. What the fuck possessed either one of you to make it more than that?" Joey wipes another tear away, sniffs to clear his nose before leaning back in his seat. He crosses his arms and waits for X's response.

But for this, X knows he'll never have a good enough answer. Because what are the laws of attraction? Attraction lies in the similarities that tie us. It's a physical essence that we can't deny our draw towards.

It's opportunity and proximity, which in the wrong circumstances can be dangerous.

But ultimately, with attraction comes a choice to either act or not to. And X chose to act when he came to town. When he chose Reggie's clinic for his therapy, when he took her out for dinner and each and every time he consistently said "Yes" when he should have said "No."

Joey's right—their connection might have existed, but did it have to grow to anything more? Would X have made the choices he did to lean into his feelings if Reggie hadn't met him halfway? Probably not. But they both did. Connections and attractions between people will happen, and it's a choice we're faced with on how we'll proceed.

Which is why X has made the choice now to walk away. He may never be able to undo the damage done, but there's no way he can let his own damaged soul continue to wreak havoc on those loved ones around him.

He's broken glass.

And so he says to his nephew, "You're absolutely right. It didn't have to go further than that, and it never should have. And for that I'm not sure you can ever forgive me, but know just how sorry I am, Joey. And that I love you more than life itself, and I'll do all in my power to make it right, if that's even possible."

X takes in a deep breath as he prepares to say his next words. "Including leaving town and walking away from her."

At this Joey, looks up at him. "You what?"

X nods. "Yes. I've not talked to her since the cabin, and I don't plan to. I'll leave town, leave you be to figure things out. It's best for everyone. I've done enough harm. I don't need to cause anymore."

A female voice clears her throat, and X looks up to see that Isabella has joined them. "I better not have heard that correctly, Xavier Derian," she says, folding her arms across her chest as she marches toward them. She lifts her chin and narrows her eyes. "Because if you think walking away is what makes this right, *especially* after all you've done, then maybe you need another slap to wake you up so you can see clearly."

december

. . .

...start anew and face with courage
The cold can feel harsh
But we adapt in quick time
Allow December to reveal to us
Things we likely already knew
Only then are we awake

~Raina G. Blake

chapter thirty-four

. . .

lori

THE REFLECTION IN the gilded mirror is older, she notes with sadness, but still lovely. Lori looks to her left and her right, her mother and daughter on either side of her. All three of them stand in the glow of the black marble bathroom, adjusting their last looks before heading back into the party.

The Ray household of Lucy's childhood is by far the grandest in the neighborhood, the perfect place for a rehearsal dinner. The marble tiled floors of the entryway are similar to Lori's own home, but that's where the resemblance ends. Whereas Lori's house has one sweeping staircase greeting the entryway, the Ray house has two. Instead of a small patio, pool and guest cottage out back, the Ray household was built to entertain. There's a kitchen fit for royalty, multiple layered decks, slate stone terrace and sitting wall overlooking acres of a wooded oasis. A tennis court and a hot tub the size of a small pool complete this entertainment paradise.

Really they should have had the actual wedding here, Lori thinks to herself. What a shame.

She fluffs and plumps her hair one last time, then smiles. "Shall we, ladies?" and her mom and Reggie nod in return. They make their way back out to the terrace, now covered with a custom tent and dotted with heaters. It's a perfect December evening, much needed after their quiet and depressing Thanksgiving. In years past the ladies would spend Thanksgiving with Joey's family, but Lori supposes those days are over.

Their Thanksgiving did prove, however, to be the opportunity to clear the air with one another. It was an emotional evening. Reggie apologized for her harsh words after finding the PFA, and Lori thought she'd faint to hear her dominating, stubborn daughter admit any wrongdoing.

But ultimately, Lori had been thankful. Because there was so much unsaid, a decade's worth of pain within her marriage to Richard that she herself hadn't wanted to face. She could admit that, hard as it was. And while Reggie may never fully understand the dynamics of Lori's relationship with Richard, at least the holiday dinner had provided the opportunity to get some truths out on the table.

Lori attempted to make Reggie see the reasons Lori stayed. The strength and fight that she lacked to leave at the time, the belief and love for him she still so firmly held, and the surprise at Richard's death right in the moment of a crossroads.

See, Lori had chosen to rewrite the narrative. We have to do that sometimes. It was the only way she could survive in the aftermath of her second husband's passing. To admit that to herself, and to her daughter and her mom has been painful, but it feels good to find words for the cryptic emotions and strategies Lori has lived by for so long. For years Lori had rewritten the narrative from a place of avoidance, side-stepping the bits that were far too traumatizing to face. Now she finds that there's strength to be had in being able to verbalize it all out loud.

Little by little she's braving integrating the shadowy parts and discussing with more honesty. She's learning to look back and see the whole picture. Yes, there was love in her relationship with Richard. But there was abuse as well, and Richard's love could only go so far. To say "abuse" still doesn't quite feel right for Lori, she's not sure it ever will, but she knows deep down that it's true. She hates to label it as such, hates to diminish the relationship to a category of statistics. But Lori has been working to cautiously face and admit all that she endured.

With a deep breath and renewed energy, Lori returns her attention to the gorgeous party and their surroundings. So much to be happy for, past tragedies be damned.

Maybe the magic of tonight can bring about a new spark of love for Reggie, she hopes. Or hell, even Lori. She adjusts her bra, hoping her breasts aren't so pressed together as to form tell-tale wrinkles on her chest. At the very least she's dying to get an update from Reggie. She had been radio silent regarding any relationship news. But based on Reggie and Joey's stiff rehearsal walk back down the aisle as groomsman and bridesmaid, Lori knows for certain they're done. She never did find out if Joey took her up on her idea to surprise Reggie in the mountains. She assumes he did not.

The ladies return to their table and drop their clutches and beaded bags onto the white linen tablecloth. Lori's mom Kathryn nods over by the bar. "There's Renata and Hank over there, I haven't seen them in ages! Let me go say hi." She leans over conspiratorially. "He always did have a thing for me, you know."

With this, Reggie laughs with a sparkle that meets her eyes and Lori can't help but feel warmed to see her daughter in reasonably good spirits once again. She tells her as much, and Reggie grabs Lori's hand.

"I'm coming around," Reggie says. Lori admires her daughter in this moment. The fierceness in her, the courage to act on things that must be difficult. While Lori will never quite get what exactly happened with Joey, she knows in her heart Reggie must have had her reasons.

She grins at her daughter. "I'm glad I forced you in that dress. You look positively ravishing in it."

Reggie looks down at the emerald green sequined strapless dress, and Lori notes how her daughter has the curves and long legs to pull off the fitted dress perfectly.

"It feels a little show-off like for a mere bridesmaid," Reggie muses, but she flashes a smile at her mother. "Luckily, Lucy is all about that and loved it too."

Lori laughs and pats her daughter's hand. She takes a sip of wine before braving her next confrontation. "Are you going to fill me in on the latest?"

"Latest what? There's nothing to share, the breakup still stands and always will." Reggie says.

Lori rolls her eyes. "First off, who exactly are you looking for? I keep seeing your eyes scan the room as if you're hoping to find someone. Shopping already, or is there someone specific?"

Reggie gives a half smile. "I'm scanning for someone who will in no way show up here tonight, so not sure why I keep doing it. It makes no sense to." She shakes her head and spins around one of the bangles on her wrist.

"So there *is* someone," Lori says, raising an eyebrow and smiling.

Reggie's eyes widen as she realizes her reveal, then she slumps back in her seat.

"Aw come on, if you can't talk to me then who can you talk to about it?" Lori presses.

"Talk about what?" Lucy asks as she waltzes over in a gauzy ivory gown adorned with black sequined florals. She plops down on the other side of Reggie with a kiss to Reggie's cheek. "Spill the tea, I need a break from pleasantries talk." Lucy pulls her dark hair to the side and steals a sip of Reggie's wine.

Lori reaches over and swoops a strand of hair behind Reggie's shoulder. "Just wondering about the man Reggie keeps looking for when she thinks no one's paying attention. Though apparently he won't be showing up here tonight."

"Oh, so you've shared about our Mr. X, have you?" Lucy grins.

Reggie glares at the bride-to-be. "I have not, but I suppose now's as good a time as any, thanks to you." She gives Lucy a mock shove.

Lucy waves her arms around. "The night is beautiful, the champagne is flowing, and love is in the air. Lighten up and tell your mom all you told me. I want her take on it. I think you need it."

Lori is really intrigued now, eager to know what these girls clearly have been holding back on.

Reggie sighs. She spills out in a furious flurry an array of words Lori struggles to keep up with. "Ever since Xavier Derian returned to town I've had a strange flirtation with him, and had been feeling all mixed up and confused, but at the very least knew that having feelings for someone else was a big problem. So I broke things off with Joey. Not just because of X, but that was part of it."

"X?" Lori asks.

"Xavier, yes."

"Okay. So you have something going on with Xavier Derian?"

"This is where it gets good," Lucy chimes in.

Reggie shoots Lucy a look with daggers in her eyes, then returns her attention back to Lori. "Lucy and I differ on this next part slightly." Reggie uncrosses her legs, then recrosses them, switching sides. "So Xavier and I started talking more. It was clear that he was feeling the same things I was. It was him I went up to the mountains with."

"Oh my God," Lori puts her hand to her mouth. "I sent Joey up there to surprise you when he came to the office."

At this Reggie rolls her eyes. "I figured as much."

"He didn't, did he?" Lori's eyes are wide with the terror of sending poor Joey up to have his heart trampled on unbeknownst to either one of them.

"You know how they say rip off the Band-Aid?" Reggie asks. "Well we just amputated the whole fucking arm." But she chuckles softly, rubs her forehead. She leans her chin in her hands. "That's not even the worst part, Mom."

"It's not? What the hell else more could there be?"

Lori watches as Reggie glances over to Lucy who appears to give a sympathetic nod. "Go on, she deserves to know," Lucy says.

Reggie tilts her head to the side and lays her cheek in her palm while facing Lori. "While in the mountains, Xavier shared with me that he was there the day of our accident. Walking along the road. He's the one that pulled you and me out of the car."

Lori furrows her eyebrows. "I know."

"You what?" both Reggie and Lucy cry in unison.

Lori shrugs. "I know. I mean I didn't know at the time of course; I could barely remember anything. But when I met him years ago at Joey's parents' house at one time or another, well…"

Reggie's jaw drops, a look of sheer horror on her face. "Well, what?"

"I recognized him."

Reggie grabs her wine and downs the rest of it. Drops the glass and wipes her mouth. "Holy fuck, you what?"

Lori can't help but shrug again. "I pieced it together over time. Xavier looked so familiar the first time I met him. I vaguely remembered him somehow. I thought about the day of the accident, all I could recollect. Your dad was driving a little fast, he used to love making you and JJ laugh on the hills, you know." Lori smiles sadly at the memory. "There was a kid and I think I yelled out something for your dad to slow down, and then the agony of feeling the car out of control, waiting for what felt like a lifetime for the car to come to a stop. My memory goes black at some point. But then I have this image. For years I could always recall someone handing you to me, but their face was always sort of blank in my mind. A blur.

"Until I saw Xavier, and it clicked. Based on the look in his eye, his reaction to me, I figured it had to be him. So there it was. It was Xavier's face coming through in my vision as he handed you into my arms." Lori squeezes Reggie's hand.

"I just...I," Reggie stammers, eyes wide and staring ahead. She returns her gaze to Lori. "You've known all this time?" Reggie says.

Lori can see how this pains Reggie. She leans forward to grab her daughter's hands. "I suppose I never really knew for certain, just had a gut feeling about it. But I guess this confirms it, doesn't it? Xavier was in fact our rescuer." Lori smiles at the bittersweet confirmation of this fact.

"See? Your rescuer," Lucy says, all warmth and smiles. "It's incredible."

Reggie is shaking her head in disbelief. "But it was his fault. He was walking too close to the road, he said so. He's the reason we're just two instead of four." She looks up at her mom, anger and hurt on her lovely face. "Why didn't you ever say anything if you remembered? I thought you didn't remember anything?"

Lori sighs. "Reggie, first of all it wasn't Xavier's fault. Your dad was speeding on an icy road. We were young, still relatively inexperienced drivers. Not even old enough to rent a car on our own.

"And I figured if Xavier didn't want to say anything, if I was even right about it in the first place, then that boy had been traumatized enough to let it be." Lori tucks a stray strand of hair away from Reggie's eyes. "My Raina Georgia. You can be quick to judge, you know. But think about it. Xavier was just a kid himself then. Can you imagine what that must have been like for him? How terrifying?" She drops her hand back down to squeeze Reggie's. "We weren't the only ones that were scarred that day," she says softly. "And I figured if he had in fact saved us and wanted to keep quiet about it, then the least I could do to show my gratitude was honor that."

Lori looks at her daughter, so innocent suddenly when usually Reggie seems more confident and assured than anyone in the room. Lori sees the confusion and sadness in her eyes, and she thinks of all the years Reggie has taken care of her. All the protective nature that's oozed out of her daughter's old soul. Lori sees the shell Reggie has worn over herself, the vulnerability beneath it seeping through now. The fight Reggie has always had and the energy it must have zapped out of her to keep up that fight. Lori sees all that she has asked of her daughter, without once thinking about the long-term repercussions of what it might do to her. The toll it might have taken on Reggie.

And Lori vows to change it starting now.

She cups Reggie's face. Grabs Reggie's hand. "My sweet baby girl. This world brings darkness sometimes and often we don't get the gift of knowing the reason why. We simply have to have faith that there *is* a reason for everything.

"And maybe, just maybe, you and Xavier have the answer."

chapter thirty-five

. . .

x

HE HANGS UP the phone and presses it to his forehead. It's crazy, a completely absurd idea, but it might just work. It hinges on assuming that everything Lucy just said is true. But if so, then this might be the key.

Maybe it's the way out of this mess, and through to the other side.

He walks into his bedroom and scours through his closet to find the nicest thing he owns. A simple black suit. A crisp white shirt. A slim black tie.

Perfect for attending a wedding.

chapter thirty-six

. . .

reggie

THE ENERGY OF the guests is palpable as I link my arm into Joey's and we descend the aisle of the majestic hall. Aware that we are in full view of everyone, I plaster on my smile and can practically feel Joey doing the same. His suit jacket feels tight and rough beneath the bare skin of my arm, and my stomach is doing a little flip. Our practice walk during last night's rehearsal was so polar opposite from any of our usual interactions that I've been nervous to be repeating it for the real thing. Thankfully, Joey seems more at ease today.

We make our way toward the end and to the clearing in the back. Joey leans over and says, "You look gorgeous, by the way." It's unexpected and kind and the exact icebreaker we need.

"You're looking fetching as always yourself," I say.

"Fetching? That's your take?" His voice is warm and I begin to relax.

"What would you prefer I say?"

"How bout 'devilishly handsome,' too good for the likes of

you, that's for sure." I glance up at him unsure how to take that, but he's all smiles. All sweet and funny Joey.

"Touché," I say, and I'm a thousand times lighter as he gives me an extra quick squeeze in his arm before releasing me altogether. We part ways, him to Justin and Justin's brother, me to Lucy and Lila.

As a group we make our way out back into the sprawling gardens, then around the corner for photos. The cold December air is biting, but a welcome reprieve from the heat of the luxurious hall of the historic hotel. Lucy and Justin are absolutely beaming, and she turns to me and Lila. "It feels good out here. I'm sweating something fierce, I was so nervous in there," she says.

Lila beams. "I was just trying not to cry. The whole thing was beautiful."

I give the very tall Lila a little side hug around her waist, then poke Lucy's shoulder. "I'm calling your bluff, Mrs. Harris. Bullshit because you don't sweat."

"Ah! You're the first one to call me 'Mrs. Harris,' it feels surreal! Too grown up or something." Her grin is barely contained on her face. "But I'm so glad that's over and the fun can begin. Come on, group photos real quick so we can get this over with and get to the cocktail hour."

Lucy saunters off toward the photographer and I look around and take in the scene. I do love a good wedding, I must admit. Smiles everywhere, everyone looking their best all polished and poised. The winter grounds of the hotel offer an enchanting backdrop with the early evening setting sun cascading an amber blanket over the lush greens of gardens in hibernation.

The photographer shouts some directions to us, warning of losing the light, and we assemble around the bride and groom. Joey returns to my side and reaches out his arm for me to link in again. "Ready for cocktail hour?" he says.

"What do you think?" I reply.

"Ten bucks says you even brave the dance floor tonight. I'll be sure to have my phone ready."

I glance up at him, eyes narrowed. "I'm a terrific dancer."

"With enough champagne," he counters.

"You, on the other hand, need none at all."

He looks down at me, flashing his dimples. "It's called confidence, kid."

We look toward the camera as the photographer starts snapping away. Last night Joey and I only exchanged an awkward word or two with one another, the bare minimum as if strangers thrown together in a wedding. I'm so relieved that he's softened up and talking to me like this today. So thankful to have the wedding as the perfect opportunity to attempt some semblance of friendship. With our best friends being married, there's truly no avoiding one another. Joey's always been an easy-going guy, but after the disaster at the cabin, I really had no idea if he'd ever want to speak to me again.

I break my pose and turn to face him. "I don't know if there are the right words for this, but I'm so sorry, Joey. I need you to know that. I really am, the last thing I ever wanted to do was to hurt you." There's a lump in my throat as I speak, and I'm surprised at the emotion in my voice.

He pats my hand that's still holding his arm. "I know. I know you well enough to know the struggle you must have been feeling. And I'm not gonna lie, the past two months have had some pretty dark moments."

I'm crushed hearing this, but he deserves to speak his truth.

"Followed by the worst car ride of my life from that cabin." He catches his words and looks down at me with concern. "Sorry, poor choice of words."

I give him a little side smile. "It's okay, it's a fair statement, I imagine. How are you and Xavier doing?"

He nods but holds a frown. The photographer moves us over a bit and then returns to her position. "We're okay," he says. "I don't think I'll ever be able to call him 'uncle' again, but we're okay. Not gonna let some bimbo get between us."

My heart beat quickens momentarily, but I offer a small smile. "I guess I deserve that."

"Reggie, you know I'm kidding. But I gotta say," he continues, "I wouldn't worry too much about me." I turn to face him and see a mischievous glint in his eye.

"Oh no?"

The photographer instructs us to look back at her as she yells another count down.

"Definitely not."

"*Definitely* not? Oh, do tell, Joey."

We hold our smiles for a few more clicks.

"You sure you want to hear this?" he asks. I nod for him to continue, my curiosity growing, mixed in with a little hope. "I don't know how your bachelorette party weekend was, but the bachelor party was a blast."

"I'm listening," I say, encouraging him to go on. I don't tell him how I was probably the worst bridesmaid ever at poor Lucy's bachelorette party. Each moment of fun felt like a forced effort, despite Lucy's incredible attempts at distracting me from my depression.

Joey clears his throat as he says, "Let's just say, girls apparently really love these dimples." He gestures to them with a shit-eating grin on his face.

"Do they now? Girls? Plural?"

He nods. "Girls. Yeah. Suckers for the dimples and more."

And I can't help myself, I have to ask. "As in, girls simultaneously?"

At this Joey releases his pose and looks down at me, all mock seriousness. "Redge, baby doll..." He pats my hand quickly, then turns away to face the photographer once again. "I plead the fifth," he says, breaking out into a smile with a side wink thrown at me.

I throw my head back in the deepest belly laugh I've had in a long time, right as the photographer starts snapping away again.

Lucy would later tell me it's one of her favorite photos from the day.

chapter thirty-seven

. . .

reggie

LUCY HAS ALWAYS been a unique combination of elegance and spunk, and her wedding is no different. The Ray family spared no expense, and it shows. I've been approached every five seconds by a tuxedo-clad waiter and silver tray, delicate delights to eat and drink. Reverberating off the walls are the music notes of the band. For our cocktail hour we're treated to soothing tones of upbeat favorite songs dialed down to just instruments. The perfect backdrop for conversation, the light buildup before the blast of reception party magic really begins.

The wedding party is lined up outside the ballroom, waiting to be introduced. I'm once again hooked into Joey's arm, but thrilled to say it feels natural and friendly. I think that's always been our issue, we were always so *friendly* with one another. No tension, no real spark, just convenient familiarity. I wonder if he is recognizing that as well. I hope so for his sake.

The buildup of the music begins, and the band starts the introductions of the parents of the bride and groom. Joey and I will be first to be introduced in the wedding party, and I suck in a deep breath as the anticipation builds.

"You ready, kid?" Joey and his apparently famous dimples say to me. We have a fun little spin and dip thing planned (his idea, naturally) and we all know I'm not the bravest on the dance floor, so we'll see how this goes.

"Just promise me this isn't one last revenge thing and you end up dropping me," I say, leaning into his arm.

He shoots a finger gun at me. "Damn, that is a good idea."

"I'll kill you."

"Might be hard to do with a broken back."

With that, we hear our names—

Raina Georgia Blake, escorted by Joseph Conti Junior!

I flash on my most dazzling smile possible and do a silent prayer to not trip on the hem of my lacy black dress, putting all my confidence in Joey that he can help pull off this thing. The guests all roar with applause. The photographers flash away in starbursts of blinding lights. I feel Joey's hand on my hip as he pushes me into my spin, then pulls me back against him again and throws me back effortlessly for our dip.

It's an absolute blast and it makes me realize how much fun I always used to have with Joey, and how that fun seemed to stop for me the closer we got to expectations of further commitment. I should have been more honest with myself right then and there. Should have realized that something was keeping me from feeling that same level of joy with him that I always had in our earlier days. I suppose I did realize it on some level, but I was hiding behind fear and second-guessing things.

We take our place to stand alongside the dance floor as the Maid of Honor and Best Man are introduced, Lucy's sister and Justin's brother. They do a sweet little curtsey and bow combo before joining Joey and me by our sides.

Tears begin to prick at my eyes as the moment we've all been waiting for arrives. The new Mr. & Mrs., and the band announces them—

Mr. & Mrs. Lucy!

The whole room erupts into laughter as Lucy and Justin enter the grand ballroom. Justin mocks shock and contempt before dramatically nodding in a gesture of agreement. It's completely adorable. And then they get their real introduction—

Mr. & Mrs. Justin Harris!

—Justin drops down to the ground in a full-fledged deep bow to the floor. Lucy pops one royal blue heeled shoe on his back and gracefully does a small bow of her own. She releases him of her foot hold. He rises and grabs her for the sweetest kiss and embrace, teeth clashing as they laugh through their kiss.

The guests are all instructed to take seats as the bride and groom have their first dance. I walk over to the head table with the rest of our bridal party, toward the long rectangle at the back center of the ballroom. Joey pulls out my chair for me at the end of the table before walking to the groom's side of the table and taking his seat. I sit and try not to cry as I watch Lucy and Justin swaying away in front of me.

But something's off. As Lila takes her seat, I notice she is two seats over to my left, leaving one setting in between us. I catch eyes with her, and she points to the seat between us and says, "Sit at this one, Reggie."

I mindlessly rise and do what she says. I look down and see that my place setting and the one next to me do not have the place cards Lucy had chosen for the wedding—glass tiles that double as coasters.

Instead, mine and the one in the mysterious extra seat next to me are crystal snowflakes. Mine simply says "Reggie," along with my birth date.

My stomach drops as I see that the one on the end, my previously occupied seat, says my twin brother's nickname. *JJ.,* and his date of birth, the same as mine.

My mind swirls with confusion and hope. I inhale a deep breath and am rewarded with the most incredible and unexpected smell of his cologne behind me.

Ocean and salt.

X.

I feel him before I hear him, and a chill runs down my body. "Do you have any idea what it does to me when I see you in lace?" his low baritone voice whispers in my ear.

God, I love the gravelly rumble of his voice, and the slightest brush of his hand on my shoulder causes me to catch my breath.

I dart my eyes up to Lucy on the dance floor. She's staring at me, grinning and nodding. My eyes shoot to the left to Joey, who leans back so he's in my line of sight. He simply shrugs and smiles.

The band invites the rest of the guests to come join the happy couple on the dance floor, and X reaches out his hand to mine. I slip my hand into his and finally brave looking up to him, brave the sight of his face.

He's all smoky sexiness in a black suit, slim black tie, crisp white shirt. His beard is trimmed up, his hair curling around his temples and it's all I can do to not reach up and run my hand through it, but I'm too aware of just how on display we are.

Without releasing his hand, I reach my other hand to grab a gulp of champagne—I need the liquid courage—and then rise to a stand. His amber and honey eyes are so warm. "What's happening?" I ask. I point down to the crystal snowflakes and ask, "And do you know what these are, where they came from?"

He closes his eyes and I see momentary pain on his face. He nods and opens his eyes and says, "They're yours."

My mind races as I try and make sense of what's happening here, where I've seen those snowflakes before. I'm grasping at fragments of memories of seeing them in the past, at the fancy crystal store with my family. My whole family, all four of us. My dad, JJ, my mom. I remember green velvet lit up in glass display cases. Then a fragment of a memory that appears of hearing my mom talk about how we had bought these ornaments that day of the accident. How they were lost in the wreck, never to be seen again.

"You found them that day?" I ask X.

"Not that exact day, but later when I went back to the scene, yes." He leans down and kisses my cheek, then whispers in my ear, "But I fear if we don't give our audience what they want and head out to that dance floor, then this is going to look like it's going badly." He pulls back and meets my eyes, brushes my cheek with the back of his fingers. "And Reggie, I'm really hoping you want this to be a good thing, not bad."

I scan the room and sure enough, only a few people have joined Lucy and Justin on the dance floor. A large majority of the rest seem to have their eyes on me and X. I meet eyes with my mom and Nana, who appear just as confused as me, but are smiling. Then I lock eyes with Joey's mom, a woman I've been avoiding—X's sister Isabella. Even she is smiling and nodding to signal us toward the dance floor.

My breath catches in my throat at the kindness in her eyes. I'm beyond shocked at the support even after all the hurt X and I have caused. The guilt and shame I've been feeling seem to be unnecessarily self-punishing, as I feel nothing but warmth from everyone in this room. It's incredible to me. All this fear I've had of being the villain, none of it appears to have been warranted. Those that know what's going on seem to see our love just as much as we've been trying to understand it ourselves.

I return my gaze to X and smile nervously. "It's a fucking amazing thing," I breathe out, and hell if the tears don't stream down my face. I lean my face into his chest, embarrassed at my emotion, especially while so on display here at the head table, and the soft love song playing sure isn't helping.

X reaches his arm around me in an embrace. I hear a "Go dance with him!" from some unrecognized voice. I pull back and take a deep breath to collect myself, say okay and allow X to lead me out to the floor.

My heart is beating in my chest, butterflies in my stomach and I'm so thankful for the strong arms of X practically holding me upright. We reach the dance floor and X reaches his right arm around my waist, then pulls my right hand up with his left as he begins leading us in a slow dance.

I'm floating, absolutely floating on cloud nine as I take in everything happening in this moment. X here with me, *God I've missed him these past couple weeks*, the freedom to be out in the open like this. The unsolvable dilemma proving to be not so terrifying after all.

But mostly it's the support that I can't believe. How is everyone so okay with this?

As if reading my mind, X interrupts my thoughts. "I think you've missed a few critical conversations that took place recently."

I laugh at this. "To have been a fly on the wall for those."

He kisses my head and says, "Better you weren't. It got worse before it got better."

"Then I appreciate you doing the heavy lifting for me."

He looks down at me, all seriousness in his amber eyes. "I'll always do the heavy lifting for you, Raina. Because I love you with such an intensity, there's no force in the world that could stop it." He leans down and kisses me, soft and slow and warm, and then pulls back far too soon because we are in front of a whole damn ballroom of people.

"I love you too," I say, smiling sheepishly as tears are threatening to cascade. But the words feel more full and meaningful than I think they've ever felt before in my life. Countless times I've uttered those words, *I love you.* Countless times I've felt various weights of them, but never before like this. Never with every cell in my body lit up like a Christmas tree as I say them. And it's all X, all because of him. Saying *I love you* to him feels like this new, untapped level I didn't even know existed. I can barely even contain it, and I release his hand, breaking out of the traditional slow dance pose so that I can reach up and fully wrap my arms around his neck. I bury my face in his chest, wanting to hide away in his body, and tell him I love him so much it hurts. I feel his kisses on top of my head as he holds me. He holds me here, on full display surrounded by people we've loved, some we've betrayed. All apparently rooting for us no matter what and thrilled to see us embrace like this.

And I've never felt safer.

IT'S THE END OF THE dinner service now, and the music plays softly as the guests mingle and chatter, the last of their dinner plates being cleared from their tables. I lean back in my seat and pick at the black lace of my dress. The wedding dinner was naturally fit for royalty, but my stomach has been a ball of nerves all evening. I feel X's warm hand as he grabs mine to stop my fidgeting. "Hey," he says, turning my chin toward him. "What's wrong?"

I look up at him and smile. "I love that you immediately know something's on my mind," I say, shaking my head. "I mean, it's a little terrifying, but I love it."

His golden brown eyes look back at me with concern. He grabs my hand and raises it to his lips, kissing the back of it. "What's on that beautiful mind of yours, Raina Georgia?"

I reflexively dart my eyes over to Isabella's table. X turns to follow my gaze, then looks back at me, realization clear on his face. "I see." He strokes the back of my hand with his thumb in soothing circles. "You don't need to worry about her," he assures me.

I exhale a long, slow breath. "Logically I know that, but I'm still nervous to face her."

"What are you nervous about exactly," he asks. It's another one of his thought-provoking questions he's so good at. Forcing me to think through and sort my emotions. Most anyone else would go for pseudo-soothing, tell me there's nothing to be nervous about.

But not X. No, instead he urges me to explore further. It's the exact kind of thing that made me fall for him in the first place.

I sigh and try and find the right words. "X, I've known that woman the majority of my life. And for the past decade plus, she's known me as her son's girlfriend, and has treated me damn near like another daughter. In many ways I've connected with Isabella moreso than my own mother; we're more alike somehow."

He looks at me intently and I wonder what he's thinking. Before tonight, before the nightmare at the cabin and the arrival of Joey, I had been focused on X, knowing he was the one that had the most at risk with our potential relationship being exposed.

I didn't think about myself, what revealing ourselves would mean for my relationship with Isabella. How that would change.

"She loves you, you know," he says. "She's a pretty significant part of the reason we're able to sit here together right now."

"She is?" I ask, though it doesn't surprise me.

X nods and kisses my cheek. "Go talk to her. See for yourself."

"You're going to send me to the lioness' den all alone?" I ask with a mocking pout.

He smiles and shakes his head. "It's a moment for just you two," and I know he's right. I wouldn't want him there for this conversation anyhow, I don't need a bodyguard.

He releases my hand. "I'm right here, baby. You got this."

I take a deep breath and rise to head towards Isabella's table. She's casually chatting with an older woman I don't know, and I quickly try and think of how to cut in on the conversation. Because I have to do this now, there's no sense in waiting. The dance music will be playing soon, and I'm determined to put myself in party-mode for my Lovely Lucy.

I approach the table and Isabella looks up at me with a beaming smile. "Well, if it isn't our little closet romantic, Reggie Blake," she says, and my eyes go wide.

"That's...generous," I say tentatively.

She rises to a stand and grabs my hand. She's the picture of stunning elegance in a long, black skirt and sleeveless sequined top. She turns to the woman she was talking to and says, "Gloria, do you know Reggie? This is my brother Xavier's—" she turns to me, "girlfriend, I do believe?" The title dings in my mind like one of those little triangle instruments from grade school. Light and floating adrift in its own key, but pretty and charming, nonetheless.

"That's right," I say as confidently as I can, and I reach out to shake Gloria's hand. "Hi," I say, and Gloria murmurs that it's nice to meet me, what a beauty I am, to enjoy it while I can, and how Xavier is lucky to have me.

Isabella interjects. "Gloria used to work with Joe Sr. years ago, before any of us even had kids. We hadn't seen each other in ages, and then low and behold, here she is at Lucy's wedding! A second cousin to Lucy's mom, was it?"

"That's right. Troublemakers of Rehoboth Beach, we were, back in our day as kids. Smoking cigarettes and breaking any rule we could, I could share some stories, you know!"

I smile at the woman, the signs of a sun-loving, tobacco-smoking spitfire clear on her weathered, but beautiful face.

"Unbelievable what a small world it is, right?" Isabella looks at me and winks. "But if you'll excuse us, dear, my Reggie and I have some catching up of our own to do."

I tell Gloria it's nice to meet her and trail along with Isabella as she hooks her arm into mine. "Now, I remember her as a wild woman, and I guess some things never change," Isabella whispers to me, guiding us toward the bar. "On her fourth husband I think she said. One of them was apparently a movie star, though my guess is she was exaggerating his fame a little." She chuckles. "Sometimes we like to repaint a picture to make it look a little nicer in our memories. Helps us survive."

I nod, unsure of what to say here.

Isabella squeezes my arm with hers as we approach the bar. "Champagne, please. For her as well," she orders for me. Her brown eyes look back at me, and I note they are a similar warm honey to Xavier's. "You're not one to be quiet, Reggie. Don't start now," she scolds.

I reach for the champagne glass and toast Isabella's. "I apparently owe you a thank you. But I feel like an apology is in order as well." I sip my champagne and search for Isabella's reaction.

"Apologies are overrated. Especially when it comes to women, we apologize all too often, and for what? Apologize if you broke something, honey. Don't apologize for having feelings."

"But I'm afraid I did break something," I say, hoping she won't make me say it out loud.

"What, Joey's heart? Alright, I suppose you have a point," she says, and I wince. "But he's a lovable young man, Reggie. He'll be fine, that I'm sure of. Good men with hearts of gold are hard to come by. And he's young. It's only a matter of time before some girl snatches him up. Someone even better suited for him than you were, with any luck."

It's hard to hear her be so blunt, though it's always been one of the things I love about Isabella. I smile and nod my head. "Agreed. No doubt about that."

Her face is serious now as she looks at me. "Reggie, you and I have always understood one another. You have a wise spirit that reminds me of myself in many ways. But you're still young too, and when we're young we overestimate the need to make everyone around us happy." I furrow my brows at her. "Oh, don't give me that look. You'll see. Think about the last favor you did for someone. The last time you agreed to something when really you were tired and should have said no. Whether you're a people-pleaser or not, when you're in your twenties you do that kind of thing a hell of a lot more."

I nod and consider this. I can think of at least three recent things that fit the bill for what she's referring to.

She continues. "I used to fear getting older, but I tell you, being my age is far better than the struggles of my twenties. Though the youthful skin would be nice," Isabella reaches up her hand to touch her cheek, "but there's a self-assurance that takes its place, and that's priceless.

"And with self-assurance comes a greater ability to forgive, too. See, when we're young and more insecure, we make everything about ourselves. If someone's rude to us, we think, 'I didn't do anything to deserve that,' and we get defensive. But with self-assurance comes a lack of need to make everything about us, do you understand?"

I nod slowly. "I think so. Less likely to be as sensitive to things."

"Exactly. Because we no longer rely on other people's opinions to validate our own self-concept. It's a liberating place to be." Isabella sips her champagne. Drops the glass from her mouth and nods over towards Xavier. "That's my baby brother. I've always worked to see him happy." She looks back at me. "And you apparently make him happy."

"Were you mad when you found out?" I ask. I have to know.

"See? A people pleaser and you didn't even know it. What does it matter my reaction?"

I think on this for a moment. "Because I respect you, and I hate the idea of you thinking that I don't," I say carefully.

Isabella shakes her head. "The men you fall for and the respect you have from me are not the same thing, honey. I know you're a good egg. I know you wouldn't do anything malicious. And if I didn't know that or didn't see that, then that would be on me, not you. It's not your responsibility to make people like you. You need to have the courage to face that."

"I've never thought of myself as having a hard time with that, usually."

She lifts a manicured eyebrow. "Only because you weren't ever faced with the potential of really screwing up with someone you care about," she points out.

I nod my head, because she's right. "I didn't mean to hurt anyone," I say, my voice low.

"But you did. And it's okay, Reggie. Like I said, you can't live your life for everyone else all the time. It's just not possible. We're all different, we have different needs at different times, but the value of each and every human and their journey is the same. It's equal, no matter what.

"We must learn to see past people's mistakes or perceived offenses and ask ourselves the why behind their actions. And then think about what their worth is within our own lives. If we decide they aren't worthy to us? So be it. Move on, then. No sense in holding onto an anger for someone we recognize as holding no value in our lives anymore. But those that we recognize as holding value for us? Traits we appreciate even through their inevitable mistakes? Well, those are the people we treasure the most, and sometimes that requires digging a little deeper to reach understanding. And you my love, are worthy, and worthwhile of forgiveness and understanding for your actions."

Isabella looks at me with a tender smile, and I'm flooded with love from her. I reach forward for a hug, quickly and ungracefully and undoubtedly spilling both my champagne and hers. "Thank you," I say. "Thank you for saying that." I squeeze her sturdy frame tightly before letting go and pulling back, teary eyed.

"I'm happy Xavier has you, Reggie. I really am. Yes, I was livid at first. I'm human too, and my heart hurt for my son. I had a right to be. A little more honesty might have been the better way to go before sneaking off like you two did."

I nod my head, hating the lecture from someone I do in fact respect so dearly. "I understand."

"But after the initial reaction, I put myself in your shoes. And realized how hard that must have been for you as well. And ultimately, the thing I loved wasn't the idea of Joey having someone, it was that I loved you. So now I get both. I get you and I get to see my baby brother finally settled and happy. Though break Xavier's heart and I'm not sure I have any more chances left in me, I should warn you, Reggie."

I laugh nervously, but her eyes are dead serious, and I shudder a little at their intensity. I feel the urge to salute for some reason. Yes, ma'am, orders received.

Instead, I nod and simply say, "Noted. I won't be breaking his heart." And as I say the words, I feel just how deeply I know I can say them with confidence. It's a fucking fantastic feeling.

"Good," Isabella says, nodding once. "Because our family has a spot for hiding dead bodies, you know."

I'm ninety percent sure she's only kidding.

chapter thirty-eight

· · ·

Two years later

reggie

SO THERE YOU have it, darling friends, ladies and gentleman. I've exposed so much of myself here and can only hope that I've cleared my name and earned that original trust I had been seeking as I revealed my sins.

That the love of my life was not in fact my childhood one, but instead, his uncle. I know, I would hardly believe it myself if I hadn't been the one living it, believe you me. But here we are. Life's like that sometimes. We catch feelings we believe we aren't supposed to, but in my experience if we pay attention, there's something there that our minds are telling us. Some message of error that we might have been ignoring. Maybe it's to turn inward and fix pieces within our relationship that we've been too complacent to address. Or maybe it's face the fact that a relationship isn't right in the first place. Either way, when we can bravely face what our minds are telling us, we can learn a hell of a lot more about ourselves.

But I'm cold as I stand out here in front of our house, ready to give these gifts to their rightful owner. Remember that? The red brick looks downright majestic, and these flurries provide the perfect ambiance to what I hope to be a magical day. Because my gift to my mom is those crystal snowflake ornaments. I never did return them to her after Lucy's wedding. Just forgot to as I had been so consumed in the high of the unfathomable acceptance of my relationship with X.

And then when I thought about it again, I had an idea. A wickedly genius little idea.

See, I never thought much about having kids myself. Not until X. It just wasn't something that was high on my radar, likely because I had been trying to imagine it with the wrong guy. But when X and I got together, that all changed, and suddenly I couldn't wait to have his babies. Knew it would happen, and knew that when it did, I'd have the most perfect way to share the news with my mom.

I'd give her the snowflakes and include a third one in there as well. A third one for our baby on the way.

I reach for X's hand, and we walk up the winding sidewalk together. I wouldn't have in a million years guessed that I'd be able to afford to buy my childhood home from my mother. It's a grand home and likely one of the only great things left to us by Richard. But that home is starting a new chapter, with our growing family at the start. Apparently, X had a few cards up his sleeve in the way of real estate to unload. I like to tease him that I only married him for his money.

We step through the marbled foyer with our gifts in hand. I can already smell the aromas of roast and potatoes and homemade bread. Nana and Mom have been cooking all morning while X and I ran out to grab a few things.

X helps me out of my coat and my mom offers me a glass of wine.

"Red for you sweetie, I assume?" she asks, and I shake my head no.

She looks at me with suspicion and I nearly reach for the glass just to throw her off, but I'm too late. She knows and she throws her arms around me in an embrace that wobbles me unsteady. "You're pregnant, I knew it!" she practically shouts. Actually no, not practically, she *does* shout it. Over and over again she's screaming into the walls around us, "A baby! She's pregnant! I knew it, I knew, I told you, Mom. I knew it!" She looks over at a startled Nana and screams, "I told you so!"

X returns from the hall closet and repeats my stumble as my mom throws herself into his arms. "How did you know?" he asks her, and I shoot him a look because now her surprise is ruined. He pats me on my head. "I think she already figured it out, baby."

"You've had a glow, you've been tired, I knew I heard you getting sick the other day at work, what idiot wouldn't have figured it out?" I can't help but smile because my mom is just so incredibly happy, positively beaming and it's contagious.

I reach over to our small pile of gifts on the counter and hand her the box. "Might as well give it to her now," I say to X.

I watch nervously as my mom takes it with confusion. "No gifts yet, what's this?"

"Just open it," I say.

"You'll like it," X adds.

Nana has joined us by now and I squeeze her in a side hug. We all watch as my mom unwraps and reveals the small green hexagon box. Her breath catches and I watch as recognition takes over her face. "It can't be, did you..." she looks up at X and he smiles and nods his head.

Her fingers are trembling, and she pulls out the ornaments one by one, first mine, then JJ's, and then the third one. She looks up and says, "For the baby?" And I nod and wipe the tears from my face. I see her eyes well up as well, and then she pauses.

"Wait," she says, and she puts aside the ornaments on the counter while holding firm on the box. We all watch her with confusion as she starts to pick at something inside the empty box, a frantic determination in her eye. "Is it still in here?" she asks X.

"Is what still in there?" he says, confused.

I look quizzically at my mom, but she only replaces her frown with a bright smile. "Oh, never mind. Just confusing something," she says with a shake of her head.

I reach out for the snowflakes and hand them back to my mom. "Well, what do you think? Should we finally get these ornaments up on a tree?" I say.

She takes them from me with a gentleness that speaks to their delicacy. "They've waited long enough," she says. She walks out of the room, back to the marbled floors of the two-story entryway where our tree awaits. Massive and earthy, it's decorated with simple whites and silvers of ornaments, ribbons, and sparkling faux flower arrangements. She hands me my snowflake, hands X the one for the baby, and she holds on to JJ's.

I reach over to Nana and have her hang mine up, unsure of where to place it. The responsibility feels too incredible to handle. I think about the journey these crystals have been on. Did they have any idea the path they were about to take? The stray from the norm? These snowflakes were not meant to come out once a year, but instead have seen a thousand stories. They had been the audience of death and had witnessed the saving of lives. Like life, their journey has taken on unexpected twists and turns of fate. I watch as my loved ones each place their ornaments on a branch, and I think about the great purpose those ornaments have served.

Soon after we were officially together, X further explained to me his love of the line *"Miles to go before I sleep."* He said that for him, it challenged his humility in the face of questioning his need in this life. To recognize our importance and significance can feel like the tactics of ego, but it's not. It's about knowing our internal value, owning our purpose especially when we're faced with the haunting of our demons. Because those demons can threaten to trick us into believing we hold no worth.

But to deny our significance is to elude our responsibilities.

It's a lesson we've both learned. We're more than just lucky survivors.

We're worthy heroes with miles of stories ahead of us, waiting to make our mark.

chapter thirty-nine

. . .

lori

BACK IN THE safe confines of the guest cottage, Lori and Kathryn's new residence, Lori tucks herself into bed. She reaches over to the box and picks at the lining at the bottom. She lifts it up and exposes a hard cardboard edge. She peels away the rest of the lining, but only finds the exposed board.

She looks around the room for something to pry it open, praying she's not delusional in what she thinks might be underneath. She spots her reading glasses and tries to wedge the arm of them into the space between the inside edge of the box and the board, but the plastic arm is too thick.

With frustration she rises out of bed again and quietly creeps into the small kitchen. She looks over to the bedroom door on the other side of the bungalow and notes with relief that it's closed. No light shining beneath. Her mom must be asleep.

She rummages through the drawers and finds a butter knife. With her tool in hand, she returns to her bedroom, closes the door and climbs back into bed. She wedges the butter knife in, this time with success.

The cardboard bottom pops out and reveals a small cream square of folded paper. Her mind rolls back to James, the notebook he asked her for while they were at the restaurant with Reggie and JJ that day. After their shopping.

Their last meal together.

"What for?" she had asked.

"I want to write you something," James had said. She had smiled with delight, knowing he had something romantic up his sleeve.

Lori played along, though. Asked, *"Why?"* She had watched with curious excitement as he took the box with the ornaments, placed the snowflakes on the table before picking around the empty box until he found a way to separate the bottom board.

"So you have a surprise on Christmas morning," he had said.

Lori had looked over to little Reggie and JJ, yellow-rimmed mouths greedily consuming spoonfuls of mac n' cheese. She smiled and told them their daddy was the sweetest romantic. She reached in her purse, grabbed the notebook she always kept with her, and ripped out a page from inside. She handed it to her husband.

"No peeking," James had warned. She continued to eat her meal while her husband scribbled furiously away, pausing now and then to think. Smiling and pulling back when Lori would try and steal the paper.

When he had finally finished, James folded the paper up small and placed it in the box. He replaced the board, the velvet fabric lining, then checked to ensure it was secure. Lori watched his hands work as he carefully reassembled the box's contents with the precision of a sculptor. With a glisten in his eye, he handed the box back to her and said, *"Promise me you won't read it until Christmas."*

She had pouted in mock upset. *"Why do I have to wait?"* And he told her it was more special that way. That she deserved special.

Emotion rises in her now at the memory, tears threatening her vision. Lori's hands begin to tremble as she looks at the box and the folded letter. All these years tucked away in secret, never having been read. A time capsule, holding the last words James ever wrote.

Words to her, the love of his life.

With hesitant care, she opens the folds and turns the paper around to see the words upright. The slant of James's handwriting in black ink causes her breath to catch in her throat. She nearly bursts into sobs at the sight, at the life force of James that appears to float off the pages with the image of his handwriting. But she sucks in her breath, holds her tears to a mild, steady stream. She wipes at her wet cheeks with trembling hands.

Nothing will keep her from waiting for this moment a second longer.

So she breathes.

And scans the words—a poem. With the very first line, James's soothing voice fills her head, fresh as if he were sitting with her now.

To my queen
Before there was you
There was barely a me
My heart dark and damp, loneliness running deep
Respite only in midnight's sleep.
Before there was you
Sleep my closest friend, solitude and escape
No need to be awake
Death an inviting call of a friend.

Until one day, a spark of hope
In a pretty girl's joke
And when there was you, there became a me.
And with that, I awoke.

After there was you, when you found me too
You burned down my walls, left in their place ashes

With the power of your laugh, your touch, the curl
of your lashes.
And with that, I awoke.

Fifteen, already found my queen
Scared it was just a dream
Yet you appeared again and again
Made me a brave man
And with that, I awoke.

After there was you, there was me, there was us
And _two_ us became _four_ us
Your motherhood role
An exquisite bloom I'm blessed to watch grow
I dare not close my eyes
Yet again, I awoke.

You hold the power
You breathe life into everything, into me, into
us four
A gift you have, my queen
I'm an unworthy man
But because you uncovered me, created _we_
With that I know, I will remain awakened.
Yet again, I awoke.

Afraid to miss a thing, my eyes remain wide open
Eternally awakened with you by my side, forever
grateful
Because of a you, there became an us, and a we
So much to look forward to in the future of what's
to be

Memories to be made as our family grows
Kisses and victories to come
And I'll be there to wipe away any tears of woe

You took my midnight
Carried us to our December.
It was then, it is now
That I awoke
And will always remain
Awakened.
-forever yours, James

acknowledgments & thoughts

If you're reading this then I imagine you just finished those last words...breathe, loves, because if I did my job right then you're feeling all kinds of feels.

Let me tell you, those last words were the absolute hardest ones to write in this entire book. How do you take an opportunity like a long-lost love note and resurrect it with the magnitude it deserves? Many, many, MANY scraps of paper sacrificed their lives to get those words right. Ultimately, they came to me at about 3am when I woke with the revelation that it wasn't a letter at all, but a poem. Of course! And suddenly the perfect words finally came (written on the hard tiles of my bathroom floor so that I wouldn't wake up the whole house...fitting, because I don't know about you, but it's my favorite spot to shed tears).

Really though, I want to thank you for reading my work at all. It's been a lifelong dream of mine to write love stories, and because of you, I'm slowly finding my audience. You have no idea how honored and grateful I am that you are here, having faith in a therapist writing romance.

Let's talk about the three points-of-view thing—it's a stray from the more common dual POV romance setup, and it was really Lori that caused it. Originally I mapped out just the two—X and Reggie, but this pesky character Lori kept trying to take over the story. I finally gave in, and thanks to her the story became infinitely more rich and vibrant. Moms and early caregivers are a therapist's favorite subject for a reason—they are inevitably beautifully flawed humans just like anyone else, and understanding their struggles and how they may have impacted their parenting is such a valuable thing. All four books in the Dog Tags & Lace series follow the three POV format. You'll find grandmothers, sisters and more in the other three books to follow. May you love, hate, want to scream and cry at those characters with all the compassion and emotion that are so very valid and familiar.

Speaking of mothers—shout out to mine. Babs, aka Barbie, aka Queenie. She gave me my first romance as a fairly young teen. It was *Shades of Twilight,* by Linda Howard, and man did I drink it up. Read it. That's all I have to say.

My right-hand gal, Gwenna. Social media help, logo design, cover design, my sanity design, thank you, love!

Carrie Juanillo, my model for all my crazy ideas over the years.

Elisabeth Oliver, my Act One reviewer, your support allowed me to write Act Two and beyond with that much more grace and direction.

Nancy Horisk-Sherr, design consultant extraordinaire.

This book started with the scene of Reggie and her mom in the pool. I sent that chunk over to my friend Lauren Brown, who promptly responded "Tell this girl's story!" I listened, and so badly needed that initial boost to have the confidence to keep going.

My beta readers! Jacqui Muller for quality control in all the best details. And you know, you donate kidneys to strangers, is there no end to your kind heart? Kim Gomes, for all the best tweaks of character development. Emily Laughlin, you felt that pace issue I couldn't quite pinpoint and are the reason it smoothed out in the end. Jen Denver, for patience and also pointing out that men don't "dab with a tissue." I fear we may not have found X quite so sexy had you not!

Tawny Martin, you wily minx, you, (who ALSO donated a kidney!). I adore you.

Sarah C., one of my bravest, earliest readers. You saw the difference in voices of Reggie and Lori, and that was yet another badly needed boost to let me know I actually knew what I was doing.

Carly Pinato and Julia Pritchett—Team Joey gals. You

admitted your sadness for Joey, which was golden because it was the intention. Meg S. (Goldie!), Debby Risley, Marlena Lafferty, Sarah SK, Marina Ventresca—for all the best encouraging words to prove to me that someone might actually want to read this thing, and maybe even relate to these characters. Jen G., Jen L., Stacey E. Lattinville, Sara Haq, Dana Pusey-Conlin, Natalie P., Ashley K., thank you!

M. G.—EMDR mental rehearsal was everything in seeing this baby's birth. Keep killin' it with your therapy skills.

Catherine Skeans—my accidental editor. But really thanks are owed to Catherine for teaching me how to write the perfect best friend like Lucy. I'll cry if I say anymore, so let me leave that right there.

Willow Winters! This is ALL your fault, you know ;) Thank you for writing deliciously salacious romance, and somehow also being one of the sweetest people I know. Thank you for your help, and for the stunning cover!

Huge shout out to Lynda Hambright! The early parts of this book were surely my roughest, and Lynda took a chance on me and feathered through to help me achieve a far more smooth first few chapters. Boy what a difference, her vision is stellar. Thank you!!!

And finally to my husband and our babies, G, Rizzle, Radical, and V-Lo—I love you all.

about the author

A believer that life is all about the great stories we live to share, Vanessa Zian loves helping people find the heart and ah-ha moments in their own tales. Her two loves are romance novels and tapping into underlying emotions.

When she's not writing or reading romance, Vanessa works as a therapist, helping clients heal through the powers of introspection. She writes with the same goals in mind—to find value in the conflict and strength of character in beautiful stories, and to celebrate our happy endings.

Vanessa lives in Delaware with her childhood crush-turned-husband, their four kids, and their rescue pup Mikka.

And lots of high heels.

Readers—please consider leaving a rating or review! As someone brand new out here, it's not only so appreciated, but vital to helping me keep writing.

Were you Team Joey? Want to watch his love story unfold as he falls for singer-songwriter Ruby Francesca?
Check out the next Dog Tags & Lace book, *Ruby in July*, available on Amazon
Join my newsletter where I will randomly ask for character name ideas, offer therapeutic tidbits, share sneak peeks, etc! Visit
vanessazian.com
Email: Vanessa@vanessazian.com

(Photo from 2010, our family of 3 at the time, in our post-deployment reunion)

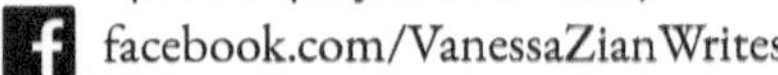 facebook.com/VanessaZianWrites

instagram.com/vanessa_zian

tiktok.com/@vanessazian